Finding Love in the Chaos of Time

Quo Vadis, My Love

NINA HANN

Brilliant Books Literary
137 Forest Park Lane Thomasville
North Carolina 27360 USA

Prologue

The sun was shining brightly, a lone, gleaming white hot star nestled against the sheer, sapphire skies, all alone, not a cloud in sight. It was hot that day, so hot and beautiful all one wants to do was to take the day off and head towards the nearest sandy beach…

Which is exactly what two best friends forever did, having packed their diving gear 4 hours earlier in the dawn of the day, safely tucked inside the back trunk of the green-brown Jeep Wrangler, its frame structure open all around, the better to enjoy the sharp breeze of the wind, the hot rays of the sun, and the utter pristine beauty of the mountainous district of the Anatalya Province.

After giving each other a hearty high five, the two best friends both scrambled into the Jeep Wrangler and settled down with their seatbelts on, anticipating the joys of their favorite shared passion, deep sea diving. The ignition was started and, with a roar and shouts of delight, the wheels of the Jeep Wrangler dashed forward to the end of the driveway beside the family summer home of the one best friend, circumnavigating the winding, gravel road towards the beach.

Two miles away from the beach on the rented charter boat, the two friends embarked on a diving journey into the indigo-colored depths of the ocean waters two miles from the shore. The water temperature slowly dropped significantly, the deeper they pushed themselves down, their flippers stroking mightily with the push of the hands in breastrokes, the bubbles of their breaths fading back towards the surface.

Soon, they both arrived at the depth of 100 feet, the wispy fog of murky, muddy waters became more widespread, making it a bit more difficult to see beyond the first few feet of their vision.

The two best friends, both of them long-time experienced divers, their devoted passion their whole lives, had met that one fateful day, one year ago, at a swim and dive convention expositing the latest technological diving apparatus, flippers, and bodysuits. Gordon, an American, and Ballesso, a Turkish national, were their names.

"So you live in Turkey, huh?" Gordon asked, fingering the strong, rubbery material of the latest design diving suit. He checked the price tag.

"The Anatalya Province, yes." Ballesso responded, moving the diving equipment around on the table to inspect its components. "Specifically, near the Beldibi Beach, not far from the Duorakara Valley. It's where I dive a lot. Beautiful diving spot. I personally recommend you go there. You won't regret it."

"Duorakara Valley? That famous valley of underground caves? Sounds good." Gordon smiled, picking up the brand, new flippers and turning them over, eyeing their quality. "What have you found so far yourself?"

"Hah, something exciting…" Ballesso remarked with a chuckle, his eyes gleaming, as if hiding a secret behind them. "Something no one knows, nor care about."

"Seriously?"

"Cross my heart and hope I die." Balleso gestured firmly at his chest. "You have no idea what I found…mucho explosive…care to join me? I could use a partner in this venture of mine. There could be mucho dinero in it." He rubbed two fingers.

"Are you kidding." Gordon grabbed Ballesso's hand, shaking it firmly. "I'm sold. Tell me what to do."

One year later, the two best friends and long-time divers found themselves deep inside the depths of the ocean waters, their eyes searching for that place, that special secret location.

"Are you sure it's around here?" Gordon asked earlier in the day, when they both outfitted themselves with the breathing tanks and regulators. "It's hard to fathom anything here."

"You got to trust me, Gordon." Ballesso urged, placing his mask in position. "I checked and doubled checked that ancient treasure map I found encrypted within the myriad of ancient writings inside the caves of the Duorakara Valley. Even the archaeologists missed that cryptic writing. It's has got to point to something significant. A treasure, perhaps."

"Boy, you talk like an archaeologist, yourself." Gordon joked. "Lead the way, Ballesso. Of course, I trust you. I have no choice. I'm now stuck here with you going into the depths of the ocean searching for what?"

"I have no idea myself, Gordon. I got to find out." Ballesso stepped up towards the edge of the charter boat. "Follow me."

"No problem. I'm in." The two men jumped over, splashing water all around.

Ten minutes later…

"Are you sure this is the place?" Gordon asked in diving signage, his eyes struggling to see through the shadowy fog of murky waters. "Boy, there is an awful lot of fishes swimming around there." He pointed beyond him.

"That's it, my friend!" Ballesso responded in diving signage. "That's it! Go where the fishes are! Come on!"

Both of them moving forcefully ahead towards the gathering of the fishes, their flippers pushing them on and on through the murky waters, their eyes focused on that one sweet spot that the ancient writings on the walls of the caves spoke to them. At least, as Ballesso was able to determine.

To go where the fishes are…

As they slowly approached the school of fishes swimming in circles all around them, their eyes finally adjusted to the shadowy fog of the waters, the two best friends found themselves silently searching around the fishes in the precise manner of an ardent archaeologist pushing away the dirt of the ground to reveal…

"There!" Ballesso waved triumphantly and pointed to a place, that, at first glance appeared to be a supposedly live carbonate coral, fully encrusted with seashells and polyps and sea anemones, but upon closer scrutiny…

"Oh, my god…" Gordon signed back. "Oh, my sweet Jesus. We found it. Right? We found it!"

Ballesso nodded excitedly, two thumbs up, his thumb and fingers making the motion of money. "Mucho, mucho dinero!! Come on!" He gestured at Gordon to follow him, to explore and inspect the secret they had finally found, unknown to the outside world, all in plain view. "There, see?"

Gordon moved closer to the massive triangular object sticking out of the depths of the heavily muddy sand, carefully scratching away the encrusted surface appendages with the knife he brought with him, just in case. As his hand moved along the perimeter, he could feel and see that it was in the shape of a bow…a bow of a ship, a massive ship of modern design, no question about it.

He looked back at Ballesso, who was also examining the bow at the other end, his hand also brushing the surface with his own knife, looking for something specific. His eyes once again examining the bow, Gordon shook his head with amazement at their discovery. If the ancient writings spoke the truth, then thousands of years ago, a massive modern ship, go figure, had apparently encountered terrible destruction at sea, its broken bow slowly sinking to finally hit the deep ocean floor, its steel and iron surface becoming corroded with rust over time, its broad area finally becoming home to the various tiny living sea creatures.

"And there it is…" Ballesso gestured with aplomb, urging Gordon to approach him. He pointed at a section of the bow he had cleared just below the deck line. Feeling the hairs of his back tingle with anticipation, Gordon focused on that section cleared by his friend. What he saw stunned him beyond belief. As his eyes followed the scratchy, almost invisible, blocky letters precisely imprinted on the barely exposed, corroded steel and iron surface, the bright light from his headband flashlight glowing on each exposed letter, he gasped at its implications, challenging him to rethink all that he had ever knew about reality, his own reality.

Gordon and Ballesso stood still for several seconds, treading water before the ship's bow, staring at the blocky letters in front of them, the entire tableau making the bow appear like a ghostly image from out of the forgotten history of the ancients, thousands of years ago.

The USS ARCANUS…

Chapter 1

January 20, 1962.

It was already midnight and still she couldn't sleep. Eyes wide open and staring at the stark, plain ceiling above her, Senefreya slowly removed the blood-red silk sheet from her tired, naked body, relishing the cool air settling on her. She lifted herself around to sit at the edge of the king-sized bed for a moment. Sighing dejectedly, she tossed her thick hair back and turned to look behind her. There he was on the other side of the bed. A lump of massive, whale blubber, snoring, no, not that, more like heaving, as he slept without a care in the world, his back away from her.

Finished with her.

Anger burning in her eyes, she took the risk and spat at him. She gave him the finger. She waited. He did not move, his body still heaving with every loud breath from his mouth.

Senefreya walked towards the master bath suite and turned on the faucet in the shower niche. After a moment, she tested the water gingerly. Just the right temperature. She entered into the rushing, heated water and breathed deeply, letting the endless flow of hotness and liquid cleanliness wash all over her body. Picking up a scented lavender soap, only the bogachi class can afford, she lathered the hand towel thickly with white foamy bubbles. The soap smelled sweet and calming. She rubbed her skin hard from top to bottom not daring to miss a single part of her body and even her luscious, long, raven-black hair. Turning around, she let the hot streaming water wash away the soap and every trace of misery and disgust that had enveloped her lithe, lissome body, the minute he was finished with her.

And still she could not feel clean. Senefreya sighed, as she dried herself with the thick Egyptian towel. It will pass in time. She had no choice.

She picked up her clothes and proceeded to dress herself.

Seconds later, Senefreya buttoned the black, woolen overcoat. She picked up the grey, faux-fur ushanka from the foyer table near the front door. She adjusted the ushanka around her head, making sure the soft, furry flaps covered her ears just right. She could not bear the cold. Berlin was in deep winter season and right now, watching through the window by the door, she could see the wind howling fiercely outside in the dark, adding misery to the already bone-chilling cold. She must hurry. It would not do to wake him up and she didn't want to be around if he did. He had a bad temper. She had done what she was supposed to do. She wanted to leave and never come back.

She only hoped he will hold up to his end of the bargain. Quid pro quo.

Senefreya held her coat tightly around her body, as she stepped outside the door and closed it behind her. Turning around, she found herself struggling against the powerfully harsh force of the winter wind, as she walked away from the house. The wind was violently pushing her back. She pushed ahead and walked in determined strides towards her home, several blocks away from the house behind her. A house of luxury and lavishness located in the bogachi class zone. The zone for the well-to-do and the well-connected. And from there she was heading to her home at the far other end, the proletariat zone comprised of the working class and humble peasants. It was a three-miles long walk in this awful weather. Senefreya continued to push herself against the feisty wind. Two miles later, she found herself carefully sidestepping the endlessly long infrastructure that struck terror in every poor citizen living in the city.

The Berlin Wall.

For a moment, Senefreya stood still in front of the Wall, still so new, only built several months ago in November 1961. She grasped the lapels of her coat, as she huddled and shivered against the mighty force of the cold, blustery wind. She shook her head sadly. Like many others in the city, that monstrous, fortified Wall had changed her life for the worse. She was always looking for a way out to no avail.

And yet, she was determined not to give up.

Senefreya lived in a humble small apartment with her parents. Her mother was a peasant who cleaned homes for the socialists and communists, who lived in the bogachi zone, including that idiot who had just ravaged her body. Her father did not work to bring home food and money, preferring to stay at the apartment in total isolation, mostly looking out the window at the busy streets in the city. He was always with a book in his hands and a gentle smile on his face. He never explained the reasons for his hesitancy to venture out and, at one point, Senefreya stopped asking him. All in all, there was never a want for food, water, clothes, and all the wants for a comfortable life in their little, cozy apartment.

Still staring at the Wall, Senefreya closed her eyes, her mind drifting to a time in 1961, when she and her mother were just a footstep away into the other side of Berlin. Into freedom. Almost. Her father had chosen to stay behind no matter how much she had protested that he join her and Mamoshka in their flight to freedom. It would seem that he had an awful dread to be outside for any reason whatsoever. Still she had given up asking a long time ago, kissing her Papa in both cheeks, and promising one day to come get him and bring him to the other side with her. Standing surreptiously by the curtains of the window, Papa had waved at them, a sad smile in his face, as Senefreya and Mamoshka hurriedly left the apartment to join several other people in their desperate quest to escape the Soviet-sponsored, weapon-wielding soldiers closing in Berlin. They were already arranging the large razor-wire chicken fencings along strategic positions of the city. The points where the daunted concrete enclosure of the Berlin Wall would later surface for miles along the route, permanently blocking their pursuit for freedom.

The small motley group had tried to help each other to enter the other side through the razor-wire fencings, painfully scratching their skins, their hearts beating fearfully, gasps of breaths pushing out from their throats.

"Hurry! They're coming!"

In an instant, they found they had soon found themselves blocked by the Soviet-sponsored Communist troops brutally pushing what's left of the group, including Senefreya and Mamoshka, back with the sharp sword tips of their dreaded bayonet rifles. All around them were loud, angry commands to turn back under the pain of death. And yet, some in the group had chosen death, preferring it to this harsh, lonely life in a city run by the almighty Soviets and their brutal campaigns. Several people were flaunting the commands of the soldiers, the bullets ripping into their bodies, as they tried to enter the razor-wire fences.

Horrified at the bloody scene, Senefreya and her mother pulled back instantly and hugged each other in silent terror. They knew they were not going to be able to go to the other side alive. Not like this. And there was Papa to consider. Crossing themselves, arm in arm, Senefreya and Mamoshka reluctantly turned around and walked away from the razor-wire fences, the pointed bayonet rifles of the soldiers pushing them on into the city.

They both had just missed freedom by a footstep. A footstep.

Soon, the past faded away in her mind like a gray mist disappearing into the air.

"So close. So damn close." Senefreya whispered to herself, shaking her head. She looked at her watch. It was now almost 2:00AM. Grasping the faux-fur lapels tightly, Senefreya turned and walked away from the Wall towards her apartment home in the shrieking, freezing night.

Chapter 2

"Missed me?" A sultry female voice whispered into his ears. Throwing all restraints to the wind, Gaston pushed her against the thick oaken wall of a large non-descript log cabin hidden in a forest and proceed to lock his mouth into hers, his tongue desperately searching for hers. Their bodies gyrating in passion and need, the couple rocked their lips as if there was no tomorrow.

A few seconds passed.

Gaston released his mouth from hers, causing her to hyperventilate, her hands spread back against the stone wall behind her. She was heavily aroused, blushing hotly, and her blue eyes were bright with passion. Gaston placed his hand on her blushing cheek and rubbed it softly with his thumb. He smiled slowly, revealing the distinct dimple in the chin of his rugged handsome face.

"Where the hell were you, Sharona? He whispered softly. "I waited for over an hour here after a seven hours drive, mind you. I was this close to leaving, you know." Not waiting for an answer, he kissed her swollen mouth briefly, then lifted his head again, his eyes glazed with passion.

"Explain." He urged, his hand now brushing her tousled, blonde hair.

Sharona protested vehemently, her hand reaching around his neck, bringing his lips to hers once again. "I had no choice, my darling. Back there on the road as I was driving through the Bolshoi Bluffs, I had hoped against hope that you would wait a little bit longer. You see, there had been a massive traffic holdup on the connecting road to the Pacific Coast Highway and there was really nothing I could do except follow the traffic slowly around the crash incident. And I finally saw it. A truck had been hit by a rock slide and veered out of control ending in a jackknife position. And multiple speeding cars behind crashed into it. They never had time to stop. It was a mess."

Gaston lifted his head. "Go on."

Sharona breathed in slowly, her chest heaving from the exertion of their lovemaking. "And all of a sudden, there was an explosion and fire and you know the rest. I was lucky to get out alive, my darling. And believe me, there was not even another way out for another mile."

"I'm sorry you had to go through that." Gaston's mouth reached down to kiss her neck. "I'm grateful you made it alive. I only wish there was a better way to communicate in an instant."

Sharona's hand gripped his thick, sandy hair, moaning at his ardent kisses. "Yes, my darling, and like you, I was definitely ready to turn back." She lifted his head, worries entering her mind. "Darling, us getting together like this, this is too high a risk for both of us. Too high. You could get into trouble with the brass, not to mention the both of us getting dishonorably discharged."

"Shhhhh.....shhhh....." Gaston put his finger on her mouth, silencing her flustered protests. "Really, I'm glad you kept going. I never left. How could I? I needed you. And look, we are here together now." He reached out for her hand and Sharona grasped it tightly. "Come on, darling. Let's go to that secret shed. I'll feel better in there."

Sharona nodded in agreement. "Lead on, my love."

The panoply of the giant redwood trees and the indigo night sky combined with the crescent moon nestled against a corner combined to create a spooky tableau where nothing seemed to begin or end. The only light came from a tiny military issued flashlight Gaston brought with him. Together they walked away from the log cabin cafe bypassing her parked white Ford Fairlane 500 car. The bright laser light guided the couple into the deep hollows of the Emerald Forest, the abode of the giants. Sharona looked back briefly and could see the tavern diminishing into the dark. She knew where they were going, but the dark never failed to make her heart stop at her throat, as she followed Gaston into the deepness of the enveloping giant trunks.

Gaston too looked back for moment. But he was not looking at the cabin. Instead, he was looking briefly at the tall, wooden sign embedded in the ground of the small asphalt parking lot adjacent to the log cabin café. Large, beautifully scripted, neon letters flashing in green, red, and gold invited weary tourists and night drivers from the Pacific Coast Highway to come inside and relax to a meal of a mega burger, fries, and German beer.

"The Ausbringen Tavern" it was called aka the "Drink It Up Tavern".

Suddenly time stood still as the memories of long ago flooded his mind. Memories that had led him to this marvelous, somewhat hidden place in the forest of the giants. A place where he could secretly rendezvous with the love of his life.

"The Ausbringen Tavern".

He had helped with the construction of the log cabin café to mimic the beloved tavern in Germany as a gift to a special lady he had brought here to the United States. That special lady was a German immigrant, who upon arriving in California, had fallen in love in with the giant Sierra redwood trees and, with his help, built her German styled log cabin café in a small opening surrounded by the gigantic brown trunks of the magnificent redwoods.

Tucked away among the giants, the tavern was a sanctuary and rest stop to many weary travelers, who have driven long hours on the Pacific Coast Highway and also the many visitors, who walked long hours admiring the beautiful environs of the beautiful Emerald Forest.

Outside the café, Adirondack chairs of copper, burnt sienna, and forest green peppered the vast, exterior front wooden deck allowing the visitors to relax with a glass of spirits, a flute of wine, a shot of whiskey, or a mug of the iconic German beer imported from Germany. The panoramic view the giant redwoods all around the deck filled the visitors with awe and wonder at its majestic beauty.

He knew the owner, that special lady. She called herself Frau Marijana Von Braun, a feisty German woman with a large bosom, a sunny smile and loud belly laughs. She was always wearing the traditional Bavarian dirndle dress with an apron tied around her waist and her thick, blonde hair twisted into a braided bun. She loved her country, Germany, and it showed in her dress, her smile, her laughter, her hands carrying goblets of beer to her customers.

He had met her, while on vacation in Germany, in the summer of his high school graduation, a present from his parents, now long dead. He had just graduated from San Aloysius Xavieros with a successful football career with the goal of applying to the U.S. Naval Academy when he arrived back in the United States. In a non-descript day of touring around the German village, he had stumbled into the iconic German tavern, where Frau von Braun worked and struck up a conversation with her, laughing at her stories. She had invited him to stay at her hostel in a village at the province of Hannover. Having lost her husband to a heart attack, she was suddenly all alone with no children to help her in her old age. A stranger in a strange land all by himself not knowing the language, he had felt instantly at home in Marijana's comfortable hostel, where she took great care of him and provided delicious meals of German potato salads, bratwursts, and sauerkraut washed down with German beer.

One day, while serving him a hearty breakfast of kartofellpuffer, fried eggs, and delicious sausages in the drawing room on the first floor, she had expressed to Gaston, her interest in going to America to live. He had asked where in America would you like to live? She had laughed aloud with her hands in the air and cried "the redwoods, of course!" She clapped her hands and closed them to her heart. "Such beautiful, beautiful trees! Here we do not have der gigant baums! I will never feel lonely among them, the trees!" Gaston nodded with a smile, as he sipped the hot, black German espresso.

Already he was making plans to make Marijana's dream come true.

After returning to the U.S. he had made arrangements for her to arrive in California, where the beautiful giant redwoods graced the Emerald Forest along the Pacific Coast Highway. And there among the ancient trees, near the Bolshoi Bluffs, they both had built her German styled tavern and dubbed it "The Ausbringen Tavern". "The Drink It Up Tavern". Yes, it seemed a fitting name. And, as he had promised her in Germany, he became her sponsor for citizenship and often visited her tavern for a quiet place to relax, to sit on one of the many colorful

Adirondack chairs on the sprawling, wooden deck of the tavern, slowly imbibing on shots of scotch and bourbon.

It was safe place where he could think and contemplate far, far away from the stress of an unhappy marriage and a challenging naval career.

One evening at The Ausbringen Tavern, Gaston had stood outside on the wooden deck with a shot glass of bourbon cradled in his hand. After slowly sipping the golden liquid that burned in his throat, he breathed in the air and looked around at the giant redwood trees surrounding the tavern, their rippled trunks the color of burnt sienna and golden mahogany. The trees being immensely tall and gigantic, he could only see the trunks in front of him and had to stretch his neck upwards to see the equally giant branches overhanging and spread outwards towards each other, each of them heavily nestled with red, gold, and brown leaves signaling the passage of the fall season.

Squinting his eyes through the small, poky openings of the branches, Gaston could see the minutiae tableau of sky enveloped in the wispy softness of the dark, velvety night. He could not see the stars or moon, both of them entirely covered by the dense leaves and branches of the redwoods. He knew they were out there in the night sky, just that he couldn't see them where he was standing. Listening attentively as he drank his shot of bourbon, he could hear the tiny click, click chatter of the crickets and the haunting hoot, hoot of the owl.

He smiled and downed the last drip of bourbon. In the dim distance, a sudden flash of white light burst out among the darkness of the giant trees and was gone in an instant. Gaston blinked his eyes.

What just happened?

He waited a bit longer, cradling his shot glass. Nothing.

And just like that, he decided he wanted to take a walk in the forest right now at this time of night, see what it was like in the unfamiliar darkness in front of him. Bolstered by the warm bourbon filling him with unexpected courage, Gaston had felt a curious sense of adventurous spirit overcome him with the need to explore the unfamiliar.

Why not?

Right now he was bored as hell. And he was not afraid of anything having been toughened by years of the Navy life, not to mention his unexpected marriage to the daughter of an old Navy family, their bloodline harking all the way back to Captain Douglas Nathan James, the founding father of the small, fledgling U.S. Navy created by Congress in 1812, that in 200 years, eventually grew into a large and powerful force to reckon with. The unrelenting pressure to rise in his naval career had been challenging at best and tiresome at worst, both daunting and yet comical, competing with that condescending fellow, encased in a 4 square feet of gold baroque frame, largely adorning the living room wall just above the fireplace.

Always staring at him. Always reminding him. Always pushing him to get up there with the very best. Placing the empty bourbon shot glass on the picnic table, Gaston took in a deep breath and held it for a moment, before expelling it. He was bored. He was tired. He desperately needed respite right now. Do something drastic.

So why not explore that dark unfamiliar forest?

Flipping on a small flashlight in his hand and waving it around the darkness, he had wound his way deep into the unfamiliar forest, dark, silent, and foreboding, save for the soft chitter-chatter of insects along the way. An owl hooted from a branch above him, startling him briefly. He smiled with relief. As he continued to wander in further, following the flashlight's path on the brown, mottled ground, he noted that the giant trees with their extended branches and leaves in the dark appeared to resemble the fabled monster trees of his childhood bedtime stories, the Ents of Fangorn Forest, his parents having read the dog-eared beloved book, "The Lord of the Rings-Two Towers", by J.R.R Tolkienn, night after night to its last page. In that story, lead by Treebeard, the troops of Ents had had their last march following Frodo in the war with the Orcs. Gaston closed his eyes and breathed softly.

Soon, he will likely have his last own march.

He walked on further and further into the darkness, flashing the bright cone of light here and there to guide him. Seconds passed. And all of a sudden, among the thickness of the giants a little further on, the light settled on non-descript gray walls not too far from where he was standing. The walls did not seem like stone, at first, and yet, he could not tell from his distance in the dark. He squinted his eyes and approached the mysterious set of walls. They were fully covered with ivy leaves and thorn-encrusted bushes all around its 10 square feet perimeter, perfectly blending with the dark and silent mysteriousness of the forest. He touched the leaves, still alive and soft in his hands. Pushing aside the hanging leaves and bushes, he eventually felt what seemed like rows of stones placed on top of each other, all of them smooth and solid to his touch. He could see no mortar in the lines adjoining these stones, lines so tiny it would seem impossible to put a razor blade in between.

How odd. Frau Von Braun never mentioned that stone structure near her tavern. He wondered if she ever knew about it. Curiosity consumed his soul. Exploring the enigmatic stone edifice some more, he saw that it was the size of a small cabin with only a heavy stone door and no windows. He was puzzled. How does one live in there and have no windows and why was it here in the middle of nowhere? Placing the flashlight in his mouth, he stubbornly tried to open the creaking door with all his might. Soon, the door relented with a groan. His flashlight back in his hand, he entered the building and disappeared inside.

Several minutes later he had come out dazed with shock and amazement. So that was why there were no windows. The obviously hidden stone cabin seemed to be a nuclear bunker, very old and obviously abandoned. Perhaps from the 1950s, when the Cold War started between the United States and the Soviet Union.

But who built that bunker?

He stared at the solid gray stone-topped walls for some time. Yes, it seemed old, very, very old, but the infrastructure apparently was still solid and usable, the foundation still strong. And it was so expertly hidden in the forest of the giants, that it seemed almost invisible. He felt certain that no one knew about that bunker, not even Frau Von Braun. He smiled softly. It was a perfect place to hide his tryst with Sharona.

Even now, a few years later, none was the wiser. He gripped Sharona's hand behind him. It was a cold October evening, but that did not deter the couple from their secret trysts inside the cabin in the woods.

Sharona willingly followed Gaston into the woods, as they both walked towards the secret bunker, her wary eyes glancing at the strange brightness of the massive moon now appearing to suspend much too close to them in the night sky. It almost seemed like a large, round flashlight pointed upon the devious couple in silent running, as if to remind them that someone, something, was watching them.

The couple approached the bunker and entered. Sharona gasped softly, breathing in the dust and cobwebs scattered all around the dark room with no windows. The only light was the moving ray of the flashlight in Gaston's expert hand. Letting go of Sharona's hand, Gaston reached down and lifted the planks of wood on the floor, revealing an opening with a ladder at the side. "Follow me." Gaston beckoned, as he entered the opening and walked down the ladder. Once inside the opening, Sharona adeptly placed the planked cover back on top.

Now it was utterly dark and silent as Sharona clambered down the ladder.

Her feet finally reaching the floor of the underground shelter enveloped in total blackness, Sharona breathed in softly to steady herself. Touching her shoulder, Gaston quickly seized her body towards him and held her in a passionate embrace, once again kissing her warm lips in the dark.

"God, you scared me". Sharona whispered. "Where are we?"

"Shhhh" Gaston replied placing his forefinger on her lips. "You'll see". He lifted her body and carried her towards a long, dark tunnel that stopped abruptly at the edge of a staircase that descended into an even darker abyss below. Sharona looked down at the abyss and then looked back at Gaston.

"Huh?" Her eyebrows lifted up. "Put me down. You're not taking me down on those steps like that. We could get hurt."

"No, we won't. I know this place. Every wooden plank of it. Every stone standing in it. Nothing to worry about."

"Hah." Sharona smiled removing herself from his grip, her feet landing on the ground. "Still not taking a chance, Gaston. Now where are we and why is it so dark in here. Why are there no windows?"

"It's apparently built that way, my darling. Perhaps, it's a bunker for a nuclear mishap, as you well know by now, although I have no idea why it is built so far from civilization. Look, Sharona, I found this place for us. It's the safest place to be for the rest of our lives. Come on, let's head down the stairs." He grasped her hand. Sharona did not protest, her feet carefully stepping down behind him.

After what had seemed like eternity, the couple finally reached the end of the descending staircase. A few feet ahead through one of the two forked tunnels, still in the darkness, Gaston stopped and grasped a rusty doorknob on his left. The door squeaked open.

"Scary." Sharona whispered as she entered the room. "Why does everything here have to be so dark?"

"I don't know. I don't even know who built it." Gaston responded. "Wait here, Sharona."

"Okay."

Letting go of her hand, Gaston walked into the darkness, leaving Sharona standing by herself in a frozen stance.

Seconds later, the room lighted up, a military issued lamp standing in the corner of the room run by batteries. Sharona sighed with relief. She looked around from where she was standing.

There in the corner of the earthen burrowed room was a modern-design, twin-sized bed, replete with a thick, warm blanket the color of blue and yellow intertwined in a mosaic of circular patterns. The bed looked so cozy and inviting. Sharona smiled at Gaston as he walked towards her. He had thought of everything. Gaston smiled, picked her up, and placed her body on the mattress, brushing her blonde hair into a halo around her face. How beautiful she was, he gazed into her eyes. Yes, he had met his match. A match that doesn't even have to be one with a royal bloodline. Just a beautiful, strong woman with a mind of her own. His type. And yet, Margaret was nothing like what he wanted, what he needed, but he had to marry her, pathetic as it was, he had to marry her. There was a reason for marrying Margaret, unfortunately.

Sharona stared at Gaston. He seemed to be far away. What was he thinking?

"Gaston?" She reached out to touch his cheek. "Where are you?"

Startled from his trance, Gaston looked down at Sharona, holding her hand upon his cheek. He shook his head, brushing away his thoughts. "Enough with Margaret." Gaston remonstrated to himself silently. "You're with Sharona now. Make the most of your limited time with her."

He smiled with love glowing in his eyes.

"I'm here, no worries, my love. Come here." Slowly, Gaston proceeded to remove her clothes one by one and threw them on the floor beside the bed. Then he slowly removed his clothes, all the while his burning eyes locked into hers. Sharona's chest heaved with each breath, her breasts begging to be touched. Gaston moaned and reached out for her and together their bodies locked into a passionate embrace. She moaned softly, delighting in the touch of his wet tongue traveling along her throat and breasts, as she reached out around him, pulling him tightly into her body, her legs wrapped around his waist, as he rocked against her softness, the both of them lost from here into eternity.

Outside, the night was quiet and dark save for the lone chirps of the crickets and the hoot-hoot of the owls.

Chapter 3

An hour later, away from the bogachi class zone, her mission accomplished, Senefreya continued her walk on the lone, narrow sidewalk running parallel to the hated Wall. She found herself sidestepping the numerous small, gravel cracks pockmarked here and there on the sidewalk. She looked ahead, squinting her eyes against the furious, cold wind. The sidewalk in front of her appeared endless in the dark night.

She must hurry. It would soon be dawn and it would not do to hover around the Wall among the numerous, sentry soldiers with their deadly submachine guns at the ready. She was already a suspect walking alone in the night.

Another mile covered in her walk, Senefreya lifted her head against the blustery wind and looked up, her eyes blinking from the freezing cold, her eyelashes and eyebrows already frosted. She was at a familiar place. Finally. The apartment building where she lived with her father and mother in the proletariat zone was not too far by now. She could almost see the towering, multi-colored, crumbling concrete-based building not too far from where she was standing. A very old building splashed in patches of fading cornflower blue and pale yellow, each color overlapping each other, a stark reminder of how poor they are, how desolate their lives, and that there was no hope for them in this community already in the grips of evil.

Suddenly, the wind down into stillness, leaving behind the shivering cold of the night. And suddenly, she felt surrounded by this awful sense of loneliness, a sense of foreboding growing in the pit of her stomach.

Senefreya felt compelled to look up. Yes, there it was. The sign she asked for from the universe, over and over in her long walk home. Her eyes rested on the beautiful, giant supermoon gently nestled in the velvety, starless night sky just above the rooftop of the apartment building where she lived, its soft sheen glowing in the dark, embracing the building all around. Senefreya smiled, her body becoming tingled with a sense of warmth. It was as if something out there was speaking to her through the power of the moonlight shining brightly in the dark night, giving her a sense of hope, of a future, somewhere out there in the vast universe.

She nodded, whispering into the air, the words coming out effortlessly.

"Wherever you are, my love, my true love, whoever you are out there in the dark night. I feel you are watching this beautiful moon with me just now, whether you are near or far. Until we meet one day, my love, as the Fates have ordained by the power of our interwoven braids of life."

Chapter 4

Gaston slowly opened his eyes and glanced at his watch. It was almost 3:00AM. In a couple of hours it would be dawn. He must hurry. He carefully removed his arm from around Sharona's torso and laid her back on the bed, her golden hair framing her head in the pillow. He kissed her forehead. God, she was beautiful. And smart. And strong. Coming into his life just like that after her graduation from Miramar Naval Aviation Academy. An excellent Navy fighter pilot. He was her assignment, her commander and with just one look at her standing tall and strong, saluting him in her freshly pressed, white Navy uniform, he could feel his heart beat faster and his body become white hot with heat. He quickly fell in love with her and it was not long before they came together in several secret trysts, always at that bunker behind the café, the place that no one knew existed.

He kissed her forehead, brushing her hair around once more, and touching her cheek with his hand. Sharona opened her eyes. She smiled at him, breathing softly. Their lovemaking had been exquisite, so full of passion, she had gone right into a deep sleep, feeling contented in his arms.

"I must go now, Sharona." Gaston whispered as he picked up his clothes from the floor and dressed himself. After buttoning his shirt, he brushed his hair with his hands one last time. He smiled warmly and held her hand.

"You know what to do."

Sharona nodded. "Yes, I do. Wait twenty minutes, get dressed, and head for breakfast at the café. No worries. Please be careful driving out there, Gaston, especially at Bolshoi Bluffs. That accident, you know." With a sigh, she stared at him pensively, almost worried.

"Your dress whites. They're a mess."

He kissed her forehead gently, stood up, and pushed down the hem of his dress white jacket. "Doesn't matter. It was necessary to keep the lie. Besides, I have more where those came from." He smiled and put on his white cover hat. "Goodbye, Sharona. We won't meet like this for a while, you understand?"

Sharona nodded. "I understand. Goodbye, Gaston." She blew him a kiss.

And hour later after leaving the bunker in the night, Captain Gaston Andrew Caine breathed a sigh of relief and contentment, as he drove the SUV on the empty lane of the Pacific Coast Highway, his thoughts drifting toward Sharona, their lovemaking, and her warm body against his in the short minutes of the aftermath, her arms draped against his chest.

It was a dark, hollow night, not a star to be seen against the sky, as he entered the olive-green Discover Land Rover, ignited the engine, and slowly entered the Pacific Coast Highway, cruising forward at a moderate speed towards his home in San Diego, the indistinct bunker diminishing far, far away behind him.

Driving on the lonely two lane highway all by himself, Gaston noted to his right, the breathtakingly beautiful panorama of the dark, blue ocean peppered by foamy white waves pounding endlessly against the layers of rocky outcrop just below the highway, the misty sprays filling the air. As his eyes traveled upwards, he saw above him to his right, the silky blackness of the night that was now framed by the brilliant sheen of the vividly bright supermoon, the biggest he had ever seen from his point of view in the Land Rover. It seemed as if it was bearing down upon him with a secret message enveloped in its patina. After a brief second of stunned immobility, his eyes fixated on the moon, he felt compelled to stop the Land Rover. He pulled over on the shoulder of the highway and turned off the ignition. He waited, his chest softly rising with every breath.

A tiny voice whispered in his mind. The voice was barely there, and yet, it was clear and succinct, with a melodious, soprano lilt.

The voice of a woman, whoever she was.

"Wherever you are, my love, my true love. I hope you are watching this beautiful moon with me just now, whether near or far. Until we meet again one day, my love, as the Fates have ordained by the power of our interwoven braids of life."

Gaston opened his eyes and shook his head briefly, pulling his eyes away from the moon. He listened again. But the voice was gone. Nevertheless, he knew what he had heard.

"My true love? Until we meet again? Fates? Our interwoven braids of life? What nonsense is this?" Gaston let out a loud breath, feeling irritated and tired by now. He rubbed his forehead and looked at the moon again, his voice rising. "Listen, I already met her, whatever nameless voice you are. I have met my true love. It's always been Sharona. What in hell are you trying to tell me? And where the hell is all this coming from? Show yourselves!" He demanded at the moon.

But the supermoon stood still in its place in the dark skies, still and quiet, its haunting light sheen still embracing the Discover Land Rover.

It was as if there was a stubbornness in it that wouldn't go away, a curse imposed by the moon towards him. The voice would soon not go away at all, following him like a relentless albatross in his mind, still repeating the words of nonsense in his head time and again, as the days passed into night henceforth.

Gaston waited a few more seconds in the Land Rover, listening with a grimace. Still no voice appeared in his mind. Soon dark, wispy clouds of twilight appeared out of nowhere in the sky and slowly enveloped the supermoon, wrapping the highway and the Discover Land Rover in its ominous shadow. Still no voice. But he remembered the words, some of them at least, and the second refrain of the words had only served to frustrate him some more. Soon all was quiet and still.

Gaston eyes widened. Was he going stark raving crazy?

"Damn it!" Gaston slapped the steering wheel with his hands, his voice becoming a self-imposed rant. "Damn it! Damn it! Damn it! There is no such thing as a disembodied voice telling me meaningless nonsense and gibberish! Get a grip and move on! Stop wasting time!" He chastised himself in exasperation as he started the ignition. The Land Rover purred back into life.

He closed his eyes once more and listened. Nothing. The air was quiet save for the distant roar of the ocean waves crashing on the rocky cliffs below.

So, it was all in his head. It was all in his head, he grunted softly. Angry at himself for feeling like a supreme idiot, Captain Gaston Andrew Caine, U.S. Navy, abruptly shifted the gears beside him and urged the Land Rover over the stone-graveled road shoulder, driving back on the Pacific Coat Highway towards his home.

Chapter 5

The twilight clouds soon covered the regal, dazzling supermoon having blessed her with a magic spell. The wind having returned, now howled relentlessly against her shivering body. Senefreya looked up from beneath the ice-encrusted fur of the ushanka. It was now at the twilight between dark and dawn, but still not so easy to discern any shape in this blustery snowstorm having returned after a moment of miraculous stillness interacting with the supermoon.

It had been so magical, so hopeful, so blessed. And now it was back to that awful reality.

Senefreya squinted her eyes and searched ahead of her, the snow burning her eyes. Yes, there it was. Her apartment home, where she lived with her father and mother. The old concrete building stood silent and foreboding in the backsplash of the snowstorm, its iconic multi-colored paint graffiti of blue and yellow splashed around the ugly grey exterior. Each floor of the building was punctuated row upon row with equally ugly windows and tiny balconies.

There it was, almost glaring out at her among the furious torrent of wind and snow. Senefreya smiled softly. How ironic. That she could see the path to her home in this blinding snow conditions, as if someone, something was lighting the way. For once, the ugliness, the drab colors, the tiny balconies did not matter. She was no longer lost.

She was almost home.

After several minutes, Senefreya approached the wrought-iron gateway leading into the property on which her apartment building was situated. She was so relieved to finally be inside that gateway and on her way home safe and sound. What she needed was a hot cup of tea. A hot bath would be nice too, even if it was too small, but still. God, just how much longer is this snowstorm going to thrash and batter this city? Already it had made impossible the only way she could get to university. On her bike. It would now be a terribly long walk in the snow for who knows how long.

A grinding noise startled her. Senefreya stood still, watching carefully ahead of her, listening attentively, not wanting to advertise her appearance.

An unmarked black van suddenly appeared in the foggy, grey twilight, its tires screeching loudly, spilling snow in the air, as it came to a stop at the curb of the apartment building, just in front of the main entrance door. The few standing early morning bystanders taking a smoke outside, suddenly broke into a frenzy, trying to escape the building in all directions.

Senefreya stood frozen in place, her eyes wide open, surveying the bizarre scene. She could see four dark figures in thick trench coats quickly jump out of the black van, each carrying bayonet rifles. One by one, they hurriedly ran into the main entrance door of the building, as if their lives depended on it. Lights blinked on inside the building at each floor through the windows.

What is going on?

Senefreya found herself becoming nervous and hesitant, an automatic reaction in the presence of evil, which consistently ruled this city no end.

Who are they now? What did they want?

Looking back at the van, she saw the nameless dark figure of a driver hunched over the steering wheel, waiting in the black van, which was purring its engine, at the ready to leave quickly. Slowly, his enigmatic face turned towards her, deep pools of black, evil eyes staring at her like daggers of knives.

Senefreya gasped. She felt her heart beating faster and faster.

STASI! AHHHHH! NOOOO!! Mamoshka! Papa! Please hide!! Please, please hide!! Oh no!! No!!

Crying amidst her loud screams, Senefreya exploded into a desperate run towards the apartment building.

Chapter 6

The garage door ahead of him opened slowly and silently, as Gaston deftly maneuvered the Land Rover through the driveway and into the carriage house/garage building situated several feet behind his house in Willowbrook Landing, an elite, gated community in San Diego, CA.

Although, he had preferred living in a nice, fairly large house within the naval base, his wife, Margaret, had vehemently opposed it, preferring a life of luxury denied her after years of transferring from one naval base to another with her parents and siblings. He had no choice. His father-in-law paid for the two-story, colonial mansion encompassed by a large, perfectly manicured, green yard all around that house. A lone, giant, oak tree stood at a corner providing shade in the hot, summer days, the dark-green Adirondack chairs nestled near its trunk.

And above the garage, through the corner stairway, was a suite of rooms they were hoping to rent out one day. Putting the Land Rover in park, Gaston shut down the ignition and sighed deeply, looking at his watch. It was nearly 5:00AM and he could see a small hint of the morning dawn behind him, as the garage door slowly worked its way down.

Perfect.

He opened the driver's door and instantly felt a rush of cold air causing him to gasp and tighten his uniform jacket. He could see the cloud of air from his mouth at each breath. So cold. It would be good to have some a glass of Johnny Walker bourbon and just sit in front of the fireplace and wind down. Hopefully, he would not run into Margaret. He was tired. He didn't feel like dealing with her adolescent angst.

He entered the back door inside the garage into the kitchen. It was dark and quiet. Looking ahead, he saw a small light inside his office through a half-opened door. Why was light on? Who was in there? Margaret should be in bed at this hour. He had expected it. He had told his wife of seven years not to wait up for him, as the years went by and his career moved up. The promotions all meant more responsibilities, more meetings, and less time for her. And often, he had told her, he had to leave for an important meeting at a conference hotel situated hours away from home. He may even spend the night there, if necessary. Sometimes, it was the truth. Other times, it was not the truth. His mouth in a tight grim, and irritated once again in having to face her problems, he placing the white naval cover hat on the kitchen table surrounded by wide bay windows. Straightening his white, naval jacket, he turned and steadfastly walked through the living room towards his office.

With a smirk on her face, he could see Margaret elegantly sitting cross-legged on his favorite, well-worn, brown, leather armchair, wearing her thick, velvet, indigo-colored robe, cradling a glass of whiskey in her hand. Gaston sighed wearily, pressing his hand against his forehead, willing himself to be patient. Not only was she sitting on his favorite armchair, the armchair no one was allowed to sit except him, and he had told her that repeatedly, but now she had her ass on the most important assignment ever given him. Her ass. As if she did not give a damn, if it was even half damaged. Not one damn like everything else in his life. Letting out a long breath, Gaston fervently hoped she would not spill the bourbon on the dark-blue, canvas satchel lying just under her ass.

Poignant justice, it would seem.

He waited patiently, his arms crossed, staring grimly at his wife, worried about that file folder under her ass.

"What are you doing in my office at this hour in the morning and why are you sitting in my chair?

Margaret slowly raised her eyelashes at him. She lifted her glass of whiskey in a toast, her smile still in a frozen smirk.

"Come, darling Gaston. Come. Have a drink with me."

"Absolutely not." Gaston walked to the chair and firmly grasped her arm, lifting her off the chair. "You should be in bed, Margaret. Let's get you there."

Margaret instantly pulled back her arm. "Will you just go away and leave me alone. Go away." She picked up the bottle of Johnny Walker whiskey from the side table and poured the amber liquid in her glass. With a shaky move of her hand, she proceeded to drink the liquid.

Gaston became livid.

"At least, get up out of my chair." Gaston tried again to clasp her arm, becoming worried about the file of documents in the canvas satchel under her ass. *God knows how many drinks she has had so far, tonight.* He could see his drunken wife was about to lose her grip in reality.

Keeping her eyes locked with his, Margaret smiled lazily and again wrestled her arm away from his. She slowly tried to raise herself.

"Oh, who cares about your stupid chair. I'm going to go…" In that instant, failing to balance herself, she stumbled, her glass falling out of her hand, the amber liquid spilling out on the floor. At that same instant, Gaston quickly grabbed the canvas satchel from the seat of his chair, thankful it was only splashed with a small amount of the liquid. He brushed away the droplets with his hand.

He threw the canvas satchel on the desk behind him. Disgusted, he gingerly stepped over the broken whiskey glass on the carpet next to the fallen body of his drunken wife, who was struggling to get up. With a heave of his breath, he picked up Margaret.

"Ah, Gaston, so strong, so loving." Margaret caressed her long fingernails over his muscled arms. He yanked his head away, feeling disgusted at her touch. Unruffled, she placed her head onto his shoulders, her breath heavy with rank aroma of whiskey. Steeling with all his might to restrain his temper, Gaston carried her upstairs to their bedroom, almost stumbling along the way. Entering their bedroom, he dumped his wife with disdain on the bed and quickly covered her with the down-feather blanket. Her hand pulling the blanket around herself tightly,

Margaret instantly fell asleep. He had not even bothered to remove the robe and slippers, desperate to get away from her.

After closing the bedroom door carefully, Gaston walked across the hall to another bedroom door that was slightly ajar. He carefully opened it and looked into the nursery room. The entire four walls were painted in a mural of Winnie the Pooh, Christopher Robin, Eeyore, Piglet, Kanga, Roo, and Tigger romping around in a light blue and green scenic background. Above, the ceiling was painted in soft black with a scattering of tiny, bright twinkling stars circling around in tandem with the ray emitting from the projector on the nightstand. The nursery room was filled with a warm ambience and so much love. Gaston smiled softly. Anything for his little girl.

Caroline.

Hearing a baby's soft coo, he walked inside and looked for her in the nursery crib. She was awake. Turning her head towards the ceiling, Caroline's eyes locked with his adoring eyes. Daddy. She quickly bunched her fists and flailed it in the air, while her restless body bounced on the mattress. So happy to see him, Caroline laughed and laughed, her giggles punctuated with the recognition in her big, blue eyes and a big smile from cheek to cheek.

Daddy.

Gaston smiled warmly and picked her up. He hugged Caroline, as he walked around the room and gave her kisses on her forehead. As he rocked her softly in his arms, hoping to get her to sleep, his mind wandered to the past few months of her life.

After their wedding and honeymoon was over, Margaret had become pregnant. In due time, their little bundle of joy, Caroline, was born and the happy couple settled down to life as a family.

In time, the more often Gaston was away at work, Margaret turned to whiskey and bourbon and whatever spirits was available to pour into the glass. Day by day unfailingly. Disappointed at first, Gaston eventually lost respect and whatever feelings of love or like he had mustered up for her just so he could survive this marriage. The drinking was the final straw.

And yet, at the same time, he could not blame Margaret for wanting to have that drink. The pregnancy had been hard on her small, lean frame, and she was often relegated to bed rest for days, even months.

When she reached her 8th month, things turned to worse.

"I'm sorry to have to tell you, but it does look like you have the risk of eclampsia. We need to perform the caesarian section and get the baby out. You cannot have a normal birth, I'm sorry." The doctor was adamant that the normal birth could kill her.

"And what about the baby?" Gaston asked.

"From the ultrasound, the baby looks healthy and should survive the early caesarian section process. As a preemie, she will go into NICU upstairs for some time, until she is ready to go home. It is your wife's health that concerns us. She could die and this is the only way to save them both."

Gaston nodded ruefully. He actually didn't care if his misbegotten wife died. It would be a blessing for him. To be rid of an unhappy marriage. But her family would give him hell. And his career would be shot down. He could not risk that.

"Go ahead." He signed the release papers.

"Oh, and one more thing." The doctor warned him. "It is my strong recommendation that she never give birth again. Her body cannot handle the stress of the pregnancy and the risk of another eclampsia. It is the nature of her body, she is built that way. I'm sorry. I'm truly sorry."

Gaston's eye narrowed, as he absorbed the news. At the moment, he wasn't sure if it was good or bad news. Only time will tell.

"I understand."

The doctor smile wanly. He put his hand on Gaston's shoulder. "Again, I'm very sorry. I must go attend to your wife right now."

Gaston watched the doctor walk away into the surgery room. It seemed that the world was getting smaller and smaller and darker and darker with each passing step down the hallway disappearing behind the surgical doors. At least he had his baby girl, soon to be taken up to NICU, and then to home.

Suddenly, Gaston saw himself inside Caroline's nursery room with its gentle, ambient light, the baby wrapped in her velvet-jersey onesie, still in his arms, breathing softly. He looked down at Caroline. She had finally fell asleep, her tiny chest raising with each tiny breath, her arms laying softly against her body revealing her tiny, open palms. Gaston kissed her tiny, puffed-up cheek and placed her carefully inside her crib.

Chapter 7

The morning sunrise was just peeking at the horizon, its pink, lavender, and gold streams painting the soft, gray sky. Senefreya could barely see its beauty through her tears, as she desperately ran towards the apartment building, skirted around the ominous, black van, and into the open door of the building. The building elevator was not working. Had not been working for a long time. Groaning with frustration, she bounded upstairs two steps at a time, her heart racing, her fear increasing, her tears spilling from her eyes. When she reached the third floor, she found herself stopping with a gasp, stunned at the face of an angry, disheveled man that appeared in the dark opening, his hand grasping the door. His malevolent, obsidian eyes locked into hers and an evil grin appeared in his dry, wrinkled face.

Senefreya stepped back, shocked at his revolting reaction towards her. Time seemed to stand still. And all of a sudden, her mind worked in synchronicity with the awful, awful feeling building in her stomach.

"Why?" Senefreya whispered, her wide sapphire-blue eyes brimming with tears, "We did nothing to you. Nothing. Why did you do this?"

The dark face at the open door did not move, his eyes still locked with Senefreya's terrified eyes. He smiled wickedly, the dark circles under his eyes twitching uncontrollably. There was a horrible cackle in his voice.

"I needed money. Money. My family is starving."

"Starving? Starving?" Senefreya was incredulous, her eyes widening ever more, as she backed away a little bit more. "But we have food every day. Every day. Our own garden. We share with everybody! All you had to do was ask! No, no, no, no, that is not why you called the STASI. No." She mustered her courage to approach her neighbor slowly, her anger building up fiercely in her heart and mind. "Oh, oh, yes, I know it was you." She pointed her finger at him. "You. It was you who called the STASI."

The old man, his shoulders hunched, said nothing, his eyes continuing to twitch relentlessly, staring at her, taunting her come closer.

Unafraid this time, Senefreya moved closer, her anger reflected in her eyes like a dagger waiting to strike.

She kicked the wall next to the old man with her leg. "Tell me the truth, old man. The truth, if you dare, goddamn it. Why did you call the STASI!" Standing back, shocked at her behavior, Senefreya realized she had left a gaping hole in the wall. And all of a sudden, she didn't care. Not this time.

She looked back at the shriveled old man, still holding the door, unaffected by the blow on the wall.

For several seconds, the old man did not say a word. His squinted his twitching eyes as if surveying her appearance, up and down her body, before settling on her face. He was enjoying himself, god. Senefreya felt oddly uncomfortable. She found herself backing away slowly, her eyes still locked to his constantly twitching obsidian eyes. It all felt creepy, even disgusting. But she had to know why.

She waited for him to speak, her back against the wall.

"Look at you." He whispered with a cackle of an evil gnome, his lips curled as he spoke. "Black hair and light-brown skin. Impossibly blue eyes. You are not of your parents. Hell, you are not even of the golden race of us in this town. You are truly unholy."

He spat at her, the sputum landing on one of her shoes.

Senefreya recoiled, walking back further away against the wall, still watching his evil eyes pierce into hers. He continued his tirade, pointing his skinny, arthritic finger at her. "Who, who…who the hell are you? We all here in the building, we all are afraid of you. It's time you be gone. Gone! You are not like us. You are the daughter of the devil with your hair and eyes walking among us. No. Time you are gone away. Now."

Senefreya was stunned. She gasped in surprise, the fear building up in the heart now landing in her throat, finding herself barely able to breathe. Before she could utter another word, the sound of running feet reverberated in the air.

The old man quickly looked up the stairs.

The soldiers were scrambling down the stairs in their haste to leave the building. The old man's lip curled evilly. He was satisfied. They have done their duty. Time for them to rid this unholy spawn of the devil in front of him.

The old man quickly slammed the door.

Sensing danger coming at her, Senefreya quickly turned around and leaned tightly against the wall near the door, as if trying to give whoever was coming down all the space they needed to run past her. She covered her face with her furry ushanka and scarf, praying with all her might that the soldiers could not see her face. That they would ignore her, as if she just happened to be there at the moment coming home to her apartment. So many thoughts were running around in her brain. She tried to sort them out. What if the what the old man had said about her was true? If so, then she truly was in danger. Mortal danger. Not only from the STASI, but from everyone else in this town. This town where she grew up, oblivious to the gossip and finger-pointing at her for being different. For standing out among them.

She knew that she was brown and they were white. She knew that she stood out like a sore thumb in a sea of golden haired, white-skinned people. With a small gasp, she realized that these white-skinned people were truly afraid of her. Had always been afraid of her all the years she was growing up in this town. Perhaps they always wondered where she came from out of the blue, too afraid to ask her or parents. Even she herself could see that she could not possibly be the daughter of her parents. Like the old man had said, she was dark. Dark-skinned, dark hair, and dark eyes. Her parents were golden. White-skinned, golden hair, and normal blue eyes like most of these people in the town.

Senefreya shook her head. Something was not right. Not right at all, but she could not put a finger on it.

And yet, all her life, her parents assured her over and over how much they loved her and that she was their blood daughter. There was nothing wrong with her. Nothing.

But how? How could they be so wrong? How could they even lie to her?

The footsteps became louder and louder, rhythmically booming against the surface of the floor. Stressed by anxieties, she leaned even more against the disintegrated wall, willing with all her might that in all the frenzy of their actions, they might not see her. She pressed her face against the wall, barely gasping against the smell of dust and grime from the fading, crackled wallpaper. She closed her eyes, her body tensed, a mantra appearing in her mind in her desperate attempt to be still and quiet.

That she might be invisible.

By the time the heaving thudding of the boots approached, her body was already fluttering in and out of nothingness. In and out. In and out, as Senefreya quietly uttered the words of a mantra with all the might of her willpower.

I am invisible. I am invisible. I am invisible.

In an instant, her body disappeared into nothingness. Without any fuss or noise. Just in time.

Frozen against the wall, barely gasping at the moldy dust entering her nose and mouth, even Senefreya herself was not aware that she had faded into nothingness. That she had actually became invisible. She felt nothing at all, as her body changed. Looking down, she could still see her clothes and shoes. She could still feel her weight. Seconds passed. The heavily armed STASI with their noisy, black boots instantly ran past her, one by one, not realizing she was there against the wall, completely invisible. All they saw in front of them was an empty, quiet hallway.

Then all was quiet. Deathly quiet.

Senefreya waited a few more seconds, her eyes peeking out from within her ushanka, carefully scanning the hallway and stairwells. She allowed herself to cough out dust and soot inhaled from the wall. She tensed for a moment, her ears perked up.

Soon, she heard the roar of a vehicle outside, leaving the building.

Relief flooded her body. She breathed in small gasps of air, as she turned away from the wall and rearranged her ushanka and scarf, not realizing she was still invisible, except now with the loss of control, her body was actually fluttering in and out of invisibility. The door opened slowly, the old man, with whom she had earlier argued with, stared at her with shock, his eyes wide with fear. He slammed the door.

Aghast at his behavior, Senefreya could hear the deadlock click. She shook her head, still not realizing she was still fluttering in and out of invisibility. Her focus was now on her parents upstairs. Were they still alive? She looked up the stairwell, her hand gripping the banister, her heart thudding with fear.

In an instant, Senefreya bounded up the stairs, two at a time, towards the next floor and then the next floor, and then the next floor, all the way to the ninth floor, where she lived with her parents. And there it was. Das Apartemente 901 at the end of the 9th floor hallway. She stopped and gasped loudly. The door was open. Wide open and dark inside. There was no sound coming from inside the apartment.

"Mamoshka! Papa!" Senefreya screamed in terror.

She quickly entered the open door and burst into the dark, living room, her eyes quickly scanning the four walls. "Where are you?" "Oh, please, please, please, where are you, Mamoshka? Papa?"

She looked around the living room desperately, waiting for her eyes to adjust to the darkness, still not aware of the fluttering of her body filled with fear and uncertainty.

The entire living room was in disarray, as if a mini tornado had gone through and uplifted each and every artifact, and furniture, and paper from their places and tossed them around the room like toys. It was total destruction everywhere. Every table and cabinets had drawers opened and thrown about, as if someone was desperately looking for something.

But what?

Eventually, her eyes settled upon a body not too far from her, lying beside the couch, the only thing not strewn about in the room. The body was lying face down on the floor. It was still and quiet, the arms and legs splayed out in a pool of blood. And blood was everywhere, on the walls and on the floor.

Horrified at the scene, Senefreya fell to her knees beside the body. "Oh, Mamoshka…oh, no, no, no…Mamoshka!" Tears fell from her eyes, as she lifted the limp body and hugged her dead mother, rocking back and forth, loudly bawling out in terror and grief, her tears spilling from her face. She looked up with blurred eyes, hoping an unnamed god of the heavens would hear her cries.

"Why? Oh, why did she have to die? What were the STASI looking for that they had to kill her mother?"

After several seconds, her tears spent, Senefreya breathed in deeply and gently laid her mother down back on the floor. There was nothing she could do. Her mother was gone. Sniffing softly, she closed the open eyelids and mouth on her mother's blood-spattered face and put her mother's arms in a cross over her heart. Closing her eyes, Senefreya prayed for her mother's safe journey into the heavens. "Rest in peace, Mamoshka. You are now free from this horrible world. One day I hope to see you when my time comes". She lifted herself from the floor and reached out for the heavy, woolen Zaalberg blanket from the couch and covered her mother's body.

Tears welled up against her eyes once more. She brushed away the mucus from her nose. Sniffing loudly, she looked around the living room, the light from the dawning sun streaming through the small window behind her.

"Where are you, Papa?" She called out softly. "Where are you? Are you alive?"

And then she heard a thump. She turned around.

Soon, she could hear a moan coming from the dark recesses of the hallway just beyond the living room, leading towards their bedrooms. Hope filled her heart. Could it be?

"Papa?" She called out. "Where are you, Papa?"

A strong, baritone voice boomed out, reverberating through the hallway. "Senefreya! Solnyushka! I'm here. Near the bedroom door. The hallway!"

Quickly, Senefreya opened the small drawer of a side table beside the couch and grabbed a flashlight. Flipping it on, she cautiously walked into the darkness of the hallway, away from the living room and her mother's body. Pointing the flashlight all around the darkness of the walls, she saw nothing at first.

"Papa? Where are you?" She called out. The walls seem to echo her words in the darkness. "Papa?"

Then at the far, right corner near the door of her parents' bedroom, she saw a figure struggling to emerge from the darkness. "Huh? What's happening?" She sound herself staring at the shimmering transparency of the human form appearing out of nothing. Pointing the flashlight at it, she watched with her eyes becoming wider, as the form became more and more opaque and darker than the blood-soaked wall behind it. Finally, a full body emerged slumped against the blood-soaked wall, the legs splayed upon the blood-soaked floor. It, he, was breathing heavily, its chest heaving with every breath. His face and body drenched in blood. So much blood. A trembling hand reached out to her.

"Papa!"

"Senefreya...." He gasped, blood crawling from the corner of his mouth. "Solnyushka....I have waited for you...." And then, he saw her body flutter in and out of invisibility, as Senefreya slowly approached his body. "Oh no...Solnyushka, not now. Damn it. Not now!"

Baffled at his remarks, Senefreya chose to ignore the words and bent down to cradle his head, placing the flashlight on the floor. "Oh, Papa, you're bleeding everywhere. Oh, let me get help!"

He grabbed her arm. "No! I have not long to live...I waited for you, because there is something you must know...about yourself." He coughed loudly, hanging on to her arm.

"Papa, what do you mean? Oh, Papa, I don't want you to die. Look!" She pointed at the living room, where her mother's body lay. "Mamoshka is gone. I will be all alone. I will have nobody. Just please let me go to get help for you. I have got to try."

"Senefreya, stop it!" His hand gripped her arm harder.

Senefreya flinched in pain. "Papa, you are hurting me."

"I'm so sorry." He let go of her arm and sighed. He looked straight into her eyes. "Solnyushka, look at me. Look at the truth."

"Truth? What are you talking about?" Senefreya whispered. "Oh, Papa, I don't care if I'm not your blood daughter. I don't care if I'm adopted. I love you and Mamoshka. Always have. I don't care what people say about me."

Papa shook his head.

"No, no, no, Solynushka. You are my blood daughter, more my bloodline than your mother's, but you are also your mother's blood daughter. People talk. People are scared. They don't understand the truth."

"I have no idea what you are talking about, Papa!"

"Look at me, Solnyushka. Look at me carefully. What do you see?"

Senefreya gasped.

Papa's body was changing. He was no longer her beloved Papa, as she always knew him growing up. In slow motion, she saw that his white skin, blue eyes, and long, golden hair with silver streaks were slowly morphing into a thick gel of tan-brown color moving like flowing molasses all over his body. Fear and horror gripped her heart. She sat frozen.

What was happening to Papa?

The undulating thick, brown gel soon transformed back into the solid mass of a live body, still breathing heavily, still pockmarked with the bullets from the STASI weapons, still bloody, but still alive and warm in her arms.

Except it was no longer her white-skinned, golden-haired Papa.

"Oh dear God…" Senefreya covered her mouth with her hand, reeling from the shock and terror, the body in her arms now changed into a complete stranger, not even a human being. "Who are you?"

The eyelids opened revealing dark pupils. Senefreya stared at his eyes. They were so big. They were shaped like cat eyes, almond-shaped and slightly slanted upwards with thick, dark eyelashes. And his head, oh my god, his head was now long and extending out behind his forehead, spilling his dark hair all around his shoulders.

"Who are you?" Senefreya repeated.

He smiled, reaching out for her hand and grasped it tightly.

Senefreya gasped softly. Brilliant, blue, obsidian eyes with vertical, slanted pupils looked at her not with the unfamiliarity of strangers with each other, but with the love and tenderness of a father and daughter reunited after a long respite. It was as if a whole world disappeared from around them and there was only the two of them looking at each other in wonder and awe.

"Look at me, Solynushka. I am just like you now." His voice was calm, no longer booming in a loud, baritone echo. "Look at me. I'm dark like you. I look like a cat, don't I?" He chuckled. Senefreya nodded with a smile. "Yes, you do."

Papa continued. "But yes, what you see now is my real form. The form I have been hiding from the world for a long, long time, including you."

Stunned at his words, Senefreya stared at his elongated head. The only thing they had in common now was their brown skin and light blue eyes, nothing more. She shook her head vehemently. "But, Papa, look at me. I don't have your head and eyes. How could I?"

"Here, hold my hand." He closed his large, sapphire, feline eyes, the thick lashes settling down. Sweat came out visibly on his forehead like drops of rain. At that moment, Senefreya could feel a tingling at the back of her head, becoming stronger and stronger. In an instant, she could feel the back of her head growing, her velvety, black hair becoming longer, spilling over her shoulders.

What was happening to her?

And then it was over. Papa looked at her lovingly. "Now you look like me, Solnyushka. Except you need to control your abilities. It is happening now unfortunately."

"Huh? Abilities? My head!" Senefreya stood up shakily, feeling the back of her head, her hands desperately ruffling through her long, silky dark hair. Feeling her skull seemed to go on and on to the top of her head. It felt disturbing. She looked down at Papa. "What abilities? Where is that mirror? Oh, what happened to my head?"

Papa grabbed her arm again. "No, you can't go to the mirror. Trust me, there is a problem. It is time to tell you."

"What problem, Papa?"

"For some reason, you seem to have unwittingly and intentionally made yourself fluttering in and out of invisibility. No one can see you except me. You are basically non-existent in the mirror."

"What?"

"Yes, you are invisible. Just now. But barely."

"Barely?"

"It is a growing power inside you. Just nascent. Only fluttering. You need to learn to control it. But it's true. No one can see you. Only I can see you."

"Not even the STASI?"

"That's right. Not even the STASI." He groaned softly. "I knew they were coming, but I chose death over my power of invisibility. I did not want to leave your mother."

"Oh, Papa…." Senefreya's eyes widened. "So that's why they passed me by so easily, the STASI. Why they somehow seemed to have ignored me, as they ran downstairs. They could not see me. How did I do that?"

"You willed yourself, Solnyushka. You are now at the age where you are starting to activate your dormant DNA containing the powerful abilities you have inherited."

"Inherited? How do you mean?"

"You come from a long line of royal women with powerful abilities, including your grandmother, my mother. It's in your DNA. You must learn how to control your abilities or harm will come to you and everyone else."

"Royal women? Papa, where are you from?"

Papa smiled. "I am from ancient Egypt of long ago. A beautiful land, nothing like we see nowadays. My parents were Pharoah Ra-Azeris and Queen Nerilka. I was flying towards a beautiful island on the great, wide, blue ocean. An accident happened. The island is gone now. My home? I don't know. I managed to escape the cataclysm, thousands of years ago."

"But how are you here now?"

Papa smiled. "In time, you will understand. It is a long, long story. In brief, your grandmother, my mother, assigned me to be an ambassador to that island. And then I was gone."

Senefreya stared at him with fascination.

Papa continued his story, coughing from time to time. "When I came to, your mother found me at sunset on her way home from hiking in the woods of the Swabian Jura. She was beautiful and kind, your mother, not afraid of me, my appearance. She took me in and cared for me. We fell in love with each other. You were born from our union. In time, I had to change myself to blend with this world."

Senefreya nodded.

Papa coughed again. Blood spurted from his mouth some more. "It's time, Senefreya."

"Oh, Papa, please don't go." Senefreya whimpered, gripping hard on his hand with both of hers. "Do something. You have abilities. I'll be all alone looking like this."

Papa shook his head. "Listen to me, carefully. You must learn how to control your abilities on your own."

"But how?"

Papa pointed his hand at the corner wall adjacent to him. "Over there is a loose floorboard against the wall. You must open it. Inside is a small black box holding the sacred crystal, a Merkabah, your birthright, when the time was right. Unfortunately, it has to be now. Keep the Merkabah close with you always. The STASI know about that crystal and you. You are in now danger."

Senefreya nodded. It all made sense, this stupid, money-grubbing neighbor downstairs. Somehow, he found out and called the STASI.

"Good. My Solnyushka. The first thing you need to do is control is your invisibility. It is now weak, you are fluttering in and out. Learn to control it with the Merkabah. And then find a way to leave Berlin. Go to the land of the free people. The ones who gave us food in 1949. Remember that story? Your mother's parents?"

Senefreya nodded. It had been a bedtime story when she was a little girl.

"Ah…..I see my Tehani behind you, her hand outstretched towards me."

Senefreya looked behind her seeing nothing. Papa coughed again. This time, he laid back his head against her hands, smiling up into her sapphire-blue, tear-filled eyes. "I must go to her now. Your mother and I, we will watch over you. Be brave, my Solnyushka."

"Goodbye, Papa". Tears spilling onto her cheeks, Senefreya gently held his head and rocked back and forth, watching with sadness, as her father's body faded away into the nothingness of air, his hand reaching out into the air behind her.

The flashlight shorted out.

Suddenly, the dark hallway seemed heavy with silence and grief. Wiping her blood-soaked hand over her bloodshot eyes, Senefreya glanced at the living room behind her.

Her mother's body had already faded away, leaving the colorful, woolen blanket spread out flat on the floor.

Chapter 8

Careful not to awaken his sleeping baby daughter in her crib, Gaston closed the nursery door behind him and headed for the stairway. He felt furious and helpless, his hand grasping the banister, as he walked down the stairs towards his private office adjacent to the living room.

It had been bad enough to explain to his wife that the doctor adamantly explained to him that her body could not handle another pregnancy. The news had left her devastated and yet, at the same time, elated. He knew that she had not been sure if she wanted another child and the news seemed to have solidified her resolve.

And yet, like Gaston himself, she had been wrangled into this arranged marriage by her Navy parents and conceived a child she apparently did not want. In time, he could see that the stress of her situation finally drove her to drink, if only to lessen the resentment and anger that had built up over time, since the marriage was sanctioned by a priest of the Roman Catholic Order.

She just didn't care anymore.

He had tried to get rid of the bottles of whiskey and bourbon that he stored in a mahogany side table in his office. But she always found a way to obtain the bottles on her own. And so, he never bothered to ask.

It just seemed to easier to let her drink and drink each day. He needed to get on with his life, his career was at stake.

And there was Caroline, whom he adored with all his heart. She was the shining light peeking through the dark clouds enveloping his life.

Entering his office through the French doors, he opened a bottle of cognac and poured it in a shot glass. He gulped the entire contents, the gold liquid warming his throat. He poured another shot of the cognac. It had been months, since the doctor had told the couple to watch for the changes in her, their baby daughter. Margaret had become inebriated daily by now and so it was left to him to watch his child for the changes. Would she become blind? Deaf? Brain-damaged? He gulped the second shot and placed the glass on the desk.

His mind went back to that day, when, Caroline, already 8 months old, had become sick. Extremely sick with a high fever. It had started with a supposed bite from whatever bit her in the backyard, when they took her outside for a bit. It had been in a hot, humid summer day, the kind that attracts mosquitos and flies. They had been careful to plaster her tiny arms with a creamy insect repellant, but somehow one found its way there. It was quick and then it was over and the baby yelped into cries.

In minutes, that random bite had formed a small red welt on her exposed upper arm. After massaging copious amounts of ointment to lessen the pain, the cries had ceased and little Caroline proceeded to take a nap in his arms. Her mother had been sitting on the lanai, imbibing on a glass of bourbon, not caring what had happened to the little babe in his arms. Gaston had glared at her furiously. Alarmed at her lack of interest in Caroline, he had to hire a nanny, who at the moment, was inside the house, while he enjoyed the summer air with the babe in his arms.

And then, two days later, little Caroline started to sniffle and cough and soon became listless, throwing fits here and there, wailing loudly. And try hard as he and the nanny could, they were not able to console her. Eventually, the fever was so high that she had to be transported to the hospital by ambulance. Gaston accompanied the feverish, screaming baby in the red and white striped vehicle, her mother not caring to join, only lifting her next glass of bourbon, as the ambulance proceeded to exit the driveway.

Hours later, the doctor had approached Gaston in the waiting room, his wife apparently having decided to join him, drunk or not.

"Captain Caine?"

Gaston nodded. He stood up from his chair and faced the doctor, lines of worry plastered on his face.

"I'm Dr. Stefano Ricci. I work in pediatrics. We just had consultations with an infectious disease expert and we also had to call for an immunologist as well." He smiled weakly. "The prognosis is not very good, I'm sorry."

"What is wrong with Caroline? Why all these expert examinations for her fever?"

"She has autoimmune encephalitis. Normally, we can treat it with corticosteroids and intravenous immunoglobulins, but it is apparent she has two strikes against her ability to recover. She is 8 months old, too young to handle the stress of the syndrome, and then there is the fact that it has nothing to do with the tick bite, as we initially thought based on your recount of her history."

Gaston felt uneasy, the worry lines on his face etching deeper. "What do you mean?"

"A traditional encephalitis is from a tick bite, for example, the West Nile virus. We thought she had that tick bite, as you had explained the bite that occurred a few weeks ago, on her arm, when you took her outside. But she did not respond to the treatments for traditional encephalitis. We had to bring in an immunologist, who diagnosed autoimmune encephalitis, a far worse condition, I'm afraid."

"Far worse? How so?" Gaston demanded. "And how did she get it, if not from that bite?"

The doctor placed his hand softly on Gaston's shoulder. "It's not a disease. It is a genetic disorder. We think it is inherited and that tick bite was just a coincidence, perhaps an environmental trigger causing the onset of the flaw in the body's autoimmune system."

Gaston sighed wearily. "So, which one of us gave it to her?"

The doctor carefully watched Margaret. "Both of you gave it to her. One gene from each parent, unfortunately. It is rare, but it happens."

Stunned by the news, Gaston held his head in his hands. It was hard to take in. He had no control over this and now Caroline was in a fight for her life, still a baby.

He looked up at the doctor once more. "And?"

The doctor continued. "The point was with this condition, she took too long to get here at the hospital and is already in a coma from the high fever. Her age renders it a high risk of not surviving the coma."

"How long?"

The doctor clasped in hands behind his back. "We don't know. We are watching her 24/7 in the NICU. Anything can happen. She just might wake up one day. But, I must warn you that should Caroline wake up, she likely will sustain repercussions of the genetic disorder."

Gaston was aghast. "Repercussions?"

"Could be blindness, deafness, brain damage. We don't know."

"What can we do?"

"Go home. There is nothing you can do now. We will alert you if Caroline shows signs of waking up. You must go home, now. We are watching her."

Suddenly feeling tired through his bones, Gaston lowered his head into his hands once again. Tears flowed from his eyes. His beautiful baby daughter, so close to death. He felt helpless and angry at the gods that caused all this. He did not deserve this. He loved Caroline. The only sunshine in his life, as he watched his marriage to Margaret crumble into pieces day by day, neither of them liking each other, and yet, hanging on to a union that was maneuvered by her Navy parents to further his Navy career. He was the begotten protégé of her father, Admiral Benjamin Jonas. She was the spoiled daughter of the old Navy bloodline. It seemed a perfect arrangement to climb towards a command of his own Navy ship, which he had wanted to achieve, when he joined the Navy.

Two years and many marital fights later, the blight of depression nearly consumed his body and mind. Divorce was not an option. He knew it would ruin his career and his dream to command a warfighting naval ship. Gaston found himself leaving the house frequently. He didn't want to deal with his unhappy wife. And she didn't want to get help, even when she discovered her pregnancy by accident, whining and complaining through the nine months of carrying their unborn child. He had been thrilled with the news of a baby, but he knew that Margaret did not even want their child, only relenting to the pregnancy with the promise of a nanny to care for the child. It had been hard on her to keep her promise not to drink throughout the pregnancy. In consolation, she had started to smoke a few cigs a day, which may have compromised the baby's immune system.

And through all their hostilities and verbal assaults over the long years of their marriage, he had learned to block out her complaints and temper. Finally, he gave up on her.

Two months later, the beautiful, feisty Sharona entered his life.

Chapter 9

Her tears spent from her bloodshot eyes, Senefreya sat cross-legged on the faded and splotched wooden floor in the hallway, staring blankly at the distressed wallpaper of faded yellow and green flowers all around her. The bright rays of morning sunshine filtered through the living room window upon the blanket spread out on the floor, as if to wipe away the horror of the past few hours and grace the apartment with a blessing.

Her parents were gone. She was all alone, a stranger in her homeland apparently.

And yet, she was Papa's child. From a far-away time and a far-away land, his homeland. What he called "Egypt".

She was stuck in this dismal city of Berlin with no one to ask for help. Where everyone eyed each other with distrust and malevolence.

And soon, like Papa said, the STASI will come after her and the crystal he called the Merkabah.

So yes, her life was in danger.

Groaning softly, Senefreya picked herself up from the floor. She walked towards a mirror hanging on the wall in the living room. At first, she could see nothing. And then she saw her reflection. Only for a moment, before her reflection disappeared again. Back and forth. Like Papa had said, her control over invisibility was weak.

"I need that crystal Merkabah. Papa said to use it to learn to control my abilities."

Senefreya returned to the corner in the hallway where her Papa had passed away. It was no longer dark. It no longer felt heavy with grief. It only felt lonely, being all alone in there.

But still, that was a good sign.

Senefreya searched for that wooden plank. Papa had said it was on the opposite side. She bent down and inspected its surface. There was this small wooden plank surrounded by the larger ones. But it was smooth and tightly mortared to the other planks. How was she going to uproot it to find the crystal?

Senefreya smiled. She stroked the small plank with her fingers. Papa said I would know what to do. What if?

She had to try.

Sitting on her knees on the floor beside the small wooden plank, Senefreya focused her mind on the plank, closed her eyes, and concentrated mightily, the beads of sweat appearing on her forehead just like Papa did. After several seconds, a buzzing energetic hum emerged inside her head, causing to her ears to ring. She ignored the tiny, stabbing pain, persevering with focused concentration on that stubborn plank.

Open, damn it! OPEN!! Her mind screamed.

Soon, the small wooden plank gave way and lifted itself off the floor, clattering like a broken cover of a toy chest and landing a few feet away.

Senefreya yelped in delight. It worked!

Looking down inside a black hole, she could see the outline of a medium-sized wooden box, its smooth surface densely covered with fine wisps of dust. She lifted the box and brushed the dust off its surface revealing a shiny gold lamination on all four sides. The box felt slightly heavy in her hands.

A heritage box.

Placing the shiny golden box gently on the floor, she tried to find a way to open it. There wasn't any. The box was smooth and seamless all around it. Not even a keyhole.

For a moment, she felt helpless.

"Ok." Senefreya whispered to herself. "Seems like I need to use my mind again."

Her eyes wide with amazement, Senefreya ignored the tiny, stabbing pain inside her head and focused her mind on the box. She watched the top surface of the golden box slowly disappear to reveal the sacred jade-colored Merkabah crystal resting on its royal purple velvet bed. Once out in the open, the crystal lit up the hallway like the golden rays of the sun.

Senefreya squinted her eyes at the blinding brightness.

She carefully picked up the eight point Merkabah and cradled it in her hands. It felt warm and comfortable. Soon, she could feel an instant burst of power and energy from the crystal entering her body through her hands.

"I have the Merkabah, Papa." Senefreya looked up. "I understand."

Senefreya stood up from the floor with the crystal still in her hands and quickly walked towards the mirror, where she had earlier taken a look at herself flitting in and out of invisibility. Focusing on the Merkabah with all the might of her mind and willpower, she concentrated on controlling her invisibility. Soon, she saw herself fluttering less and less until her body became solidified, a human vessel.

She stared at herself in the mirror, stunned at the transformation.

She was exactly like Papa. Elongated head and large, feline eyes so blue with a vertical slit, not to mention her seminal abilities.

"Oh, Papa." She wailed softly at the mirror image. "What do I do now?"

The Merkabah glowed softly in her hand.

Chapter 10

The garage door slowly raised up from the ground. Gaston drove in and parked the Land Rover. He was tired. All through the drive from the naval base near Coronado Island, he had become lost in his thoughts of the next few days. Days so momentous and so secret, he felt truly alone with the intelligence imparted towards him from the brasses at the Pentagon.

He often wondered. Why me? And the only consolation was to escape to that bunker and spend precious moments with Sharona.

Moments later, he entered the house and closed the door quietly. In a split second, the kitchen lights abruptly flooded the room startling him. Gaston quickly turned around, his hand still holding the doorknob and gasped softly. It was his wife, wide awake and furious. He had thought she was sound asleep, it was dead of night, 3:00AM, with not a sound outside in the Willowbrook neighborhood. He had been deliberately careful entering the garage and into the kitchen, but there she was in her robes, her arms crossed, the glints of anger in her eyes like shining knives pointing at him. An eyebrow arched and her mouth was grim.

Time seemed to pass interminably in the short distance between them.

Not wanting to instigate a fight, Gaston waited. A million thoughts raced in his mind as he prepared himself to battle once again with his wife. Breathing carefully, he realized that now was the time to hash it out, whatever Margaret may have found to her detriment.

He waited.

The first to break the silence, Margaret glared at him, waving the tiny, crinkled paper she had gripped in her hand. "Tell me, who is this "S"?

"S?" Gaston asked perplexed. He knew "S", but decided to play along with her, hoping for the best.

"The answering machine, you moron."

"And what does the answering machine say?"

"Just these three words, See you later. S." Margaret could see the glint of recognition in her husband's eyes. "Something I should know, darling?"

Quickly recovering his stance, Gaston willed himself to act bored. "No one you know. Could be any number of people I know at the base. What kind of voice was it?"

"It was a strange voice. Can't tell if it's male or female. It was rather blurred, as if someone was talking through a cloth. How odd, hmmm?"

Gaston nodded. "That's odd, indeed. Crazy. I don't know what to tell you. It's not enough information."

"Okay, then." Margaret cocked her head defiantly, both eyebrows highly arched in suspense. "What about "See you later? Are you on a mission that I do not know of?"

"I can't talk about it, Margaret." Gaston replied firmly. "You, of all people, should know that." He looked at the phone answering machine on the smooth, white, porcelain, kitchen counter. "Whoever did this seems to be asking for trouble and believe me, I have no idea who."

Margaret nodded. There seemed to be a measure of truth in his words. He really did not know who left that cryptic message or so he says. There seemed no point in arguing some more. She turned towards the kitchen cabinets. "Fine. I'm going to get a drink."

Gaston rolled up his eyes. He was hoping she would go back to sleep. He brushed past her, his emotions a mixture of relief and disgust. There was one person in mind, who could have made that bizarre phone message, but the only way to find out was to ask. If true, this lapse of judgment on her part was dangerous. He would have to have a talk with her. Shaking his head at the near miss, he headed towards the stairs to check on Caroline.

As he approached the banister of the stairway, he suddenly felt the urge to enter his private office and went in, closing the doors behind him. Gaston spied a medium-sized, dark blue, canvas satchel lying neatly on the seat of the dark-brown, leather Lazy Boy recliner armchair, the Bora Bora series. The well-worn armchair had been and is still his favorite niche of peace and relaxation, where he could simply push himself back, place his legs up, and enjoy a shot of cognac in front of the window overlooking the backyard.

The previous day that Margaret had sat on it, on top of that satchel, a drink in her hand, was a need to irritate him, to frustrate him, by taking over and desecrating his beloved sanctuary. He hated her for doing that, but he could do nothing but wait, until she released that chair. His naval career mattered. Caroline mattered.

That ubiquitous canvas satchel. He needed to put it away. She was welcome to hound his favorite armchair, if only to bedevil him time and again, but no way was she going to put her ass on that satchel. The information in there was too important for the next few days ahead.

He glanced at the ornate 19th century grandfather clock, its pendulum circle swinging back and forth in perfect cadence, the soft ring of the bell announcing a new hour.

It was now 4:00AM.

Margaret entered the office, fully buzzed, whiskey in her hand, her red lips curled in an unhappy sneer.

Her eyes glanced at the canvas satchel in his hands. She walked closer, her forefinger touching it.

"What's in there?"

Gaston looked up, annoyed. "A new assignment, Margaret. Like I said, I can't talk about it."

Margaret shrugged. "Of course. Whatever. I'm not stopping you from reading it, am I, darling?" She poked with her finger at the heavy-duty canvas material. "How in the world do you open this curious briefcase. And what is this contraption?" She pointed at the embedded steel codex."

"That's how you open it." Gaston offered warily. "The code are the 6 letters and numbers, only I know."

Margaret laughed. She took another drink and put the glass on his desk.

"Darling Gaston". She toyed at his hair.

Gaston looked away, silently gagging at the ever-present stink of the liquor around her. Margaret chose to ignore his reaction.

"How long will you be gone this time?"

Gaston glanced back in surprise. Margaret generally did not care how long he was gone on assignments. Why now? He pushed her away and looked at her with suspicion. She was still his wife and yet, it would seem she deserved to know.

"Several months, Margaret. At least six months, I'm told. The reason it's not clear cut is because it's not certain. There are too many variables at play."

"Not certain?" Margaret's eyes narrowed. "How odd for the Navy to say that. The Navy is always certain. My Admiral Dad is always certain." She picked up the whiskey glass from his desk and swallowed the last drop of the amber liquid. "Hmmm, I wonder why it is uncertain. Odd, don't you think?"

Gaston shrugged. "Even I don't know all the information myself. All I can tell you is I have been assigned to command a brand-new aircraft carrier, the USS Arcanus." He defiantly crossed his arms, as he watched his wife pour another glass of whiskey, the bottle whisked out from a cabinet. With all that drinking and unhappiness, no way was he going to allow Caroline to be alone with her mother, while he was gone.

"I have already reserved a full-time nurse for Caroline. It is non-negotiable, Margaret. Non-negotiable."

Margaret chuckled, lifted her new whiskey glass to him, and settled herself on his armchair. She crossed her legs seductively. "No problem, darling." She sighed and moved her forefinger slowly on the side table next to the armchair. Eventually, she looked up at her husband.

"You know, I would rather you don't go, though. For Caroline's sake."

Gaston narrowed his eyes. "What do you mean?"

Margaret chuckled softly, her lips once again in a curl. "The thing is, I do know about that ship and to be honest, I don't like it."

Gaston stood frozen, stunned at the words coming out of her mouth. He walked towards her and quickly grabbed the glass of whiskey from her hand, placing it on the side table. He gripped her arm towards him, pulling her up from the armchair.

"What do you know, Margaret?" He demanded in anger. "There is no way you could access this briefcase, only I know the codes."

"Let go of me, Gaston! You're hurting my arm!"

Gaston released her arm, waiting for her response. She walked a step back, her head held high. Gaston took a step towards her.

"How the hell do you know about the ship and more importantly, what do you know, Margaret?" He could barely contain himself.

Margaret walked further back, slowly, until she felt the wall behind her. She placed herself against the wall. She had never seen Gaston that angry in all the years of their marriage. It was quite frightening to see him angry.

"It was Dr. Breslov next door, Gaston, darling. He knows things. Lots of things. He told me one day. I was just sitting on the porch. Caroline was upstairs with her nanny. He was there in the yard and kindly waved at me. I invited him in for a drink. I was lonely, you know."

Gaston groaned inwardly. Dr. Miroslav Breslov. The creator of the USS Arcanus. They had the unfortunate happenstance to have him as their next door neighbor. Why couldn't the goddamn physicist just settle down and enjoy his retirement without announcing to the world about his creation.

Why did they have to be neighbors?

"You invited him for a drink, Margaret?" Gaston shook his head at her. "We had an agreement with the Navy. You know we're not supposed to be friendly with him or talk with him. We can't stop him living next door, but we can't hang out with him. There is a reason for that. He is a crazy lunatic."

"Of course, the reason." Margaret responded with a smirk. "You all had to do that to him? Force him to retire? Make his life a living hell telling all the world what a crackpot he is? As a matter of fact, I do not find him crazy at all. He was quite petrifyingly sane and smart when I spoke with him that day, so yes, I do believe what Dr. Breslov had to say. I had to. It all made sense to me, this utter secrecy surrounding you and the ship and now this assignment. You are going to get yourself killed, my darling, and what would we do without you?"

Gaston was stunned.

"You need to tell me what he told you. All of it. Now, Margaret."

Margaret smiled, her upper lip curled in a scowl. Biting sarcasm laced within her voice. She lifted the glass again towards him.

"Of course, Gaston, darling. Do sit down. It may take a while."

Chapter 11

Senefreya firmly stood her ground, feet apart, her hands clutching the Soviet-issued AKM rifle she had earlier grabbed from the wall near the apartment door upon leaving the building. She had waited in silence alone in the apartment until nightfall. She was sure that the darkness of the night would shield the heavy weapon hidden inside her coat from the eyes of the border soldiers. She would just cross her arms, as if shivering from the cold. Thank god for the blustery winter wind that continued into another day and night.

Thirty minutes later, there she was exactly where she had planned to be.

The end of the rifle pointed at a portly and frightened bald man, who had just taken a shower. He had heard a noise coming from the front door into the living room and stepped out to investigate. Only a towel covered the lower half of his stout body, barely holding on to the round folds of stomach fat that glistened with water. He had both his hands in the air, his eyes round with fear at the hole of the rifle. Then his eyes quickly glanced at the telephone nearby on a side table.

It was close enough for him to reach out.

"Don't bother." Senefreya ordered him, her finger closing in on the trigger. Her body now visibly tensed, she was ready to shoot the moment his hands touched the telephone.

The man gave up and looked back at her.

"What do you want?" Sweat appeared like tears on his forehead, dripping down his round, red cheeks. He stared at Senefreya.

"How in hell did you change your head?" He demanded surveying her now abnormal head, elongated from behind her forehead just like her father, her raven black hair dripping down on her shoulders like waterfall. She did not bother to hide it from him. He was irrelevant and yet, she needed something from him. Now.

Senefreya breathed in sharply. Her lips curled. "I need a letter written from you, Mein Herr Greboschwitz. A letter authorizing me to leave Berlin immediately, no matter what and how. I have held my bargain for as long as I could. I want out now."

"And if I won't?"

Her fingers tightened on the trigger. "Then I will shoot you, of course. My Papa has taught me how to use this weapon very well. I will not miss, rest assured, Mein Herr Das Greboschwitz. You are pretty hard to miss."

The man laughed and laughed, his belly shaking. "If you shoot me, people will hear it. Soldiers will come and arrest you! Hah!"

Senefreya smiled. "I'm not worried about that at all. Not at all." She took a step forward, anger flashing in her dark eyes. She pushed the weapon at him again touching the fat folds of his stomach. "Now, that letter."

Astonished at her lack of fear and her strong will to shoot him, the man nodded at her and proceeded to take out a piece of paper and pen from the drawer of the side table. After scribbling a few words on a piece of paper, signing it, and stamping it with his personal government logo, the man folded it neatly and put it in the envelope, handing it to her promptly. He wasn't going to risk getting killed. She meant every word she said. To his dismay, the weapon looked quite comfortable in her hands. The moment she was gone, he would make a telephone call to the STASI to capture and kill her.

"Get out now." He hissed at her, hanging on to the towel just about to loosen itself onto the floor. "Get out."

The envelope now safely within the inner pocket of her coat, Senefreya backed slowly, still pointing the AKM rifle at him. She knew that he would have a hard time overcoming her with all that weight on him. And he would be dead before he had a chance to yell for help waking up all the neighbors. As of right now, she no longer had to sleep with him.

Soon she will be free. Soon.

By the time she reached the open front door behind her, Senefreya quickly ran outside.

Herr Greboschwitz gasped as he watched leave his house, her body slowing became invisible against the dark of the night. "Mein Gott! She is a witch. She must be killed! Mein Gott!"

Ignoring the cold blast of wind that suddenly blew inside the open front door, Herr Greboschwitz quickly turned around and picked up the telephone and dialed. His mind roiled with anger and fear. There was no question what must be done.

"Sie verhaften!!" He yelled into the telephone after describing the encounter with Senefreya and nearly getting killed by that woman, that witch. "Sie muss sterben!! Vorsatzlich mord von regierungsbeamter!!"

Slamming down the telephone receiver, Herr Greboschwitz suddenly realized the stark reality in his mistake. How in the world are his soldaten going to find a woman that had just disappeared into thin air? They will laugh him into der irrenhaus. He shook his head vehemently, staring at the open door, the wind blowing in more of the cold air. It was all so surreal. He had been planning a nice hot meal, a shower, an apres dinner drink, and then to bed.

"What the hell just happened?"

"Nein, nein, nein. I must think." He growled to himself, tightening the towel around his stomach. He closed the door and pushed the deadlock through. "Ja, think. Ja, but, first, a strong drink."

Herr Greboschwitz stumbled towards the glass cabinet in another room, still holding on to the damp towel wrapped around his thick waist, and leaving a trail of wet footprints behind. He quickly grabbed the first bottle of the Stolnichskaya vodka in the middle shelf.

A glimmer of thought appeared in his mind. His eyes squinted with understanding, as he frantically gulped some of the vodka from the bottle. The moment Senefreya turned around to leave, he had noticed a backpack strapped around her shoulders, slivers of light appearing at the edges just before she became invisible.

Could it be?

He lifted the vodka bottle towards the door in a gesture of toast.

"Ja, she makes an excellent weapon, ja, Senefreya. No need to kill the witch, ja. She could be very, very useful." The man chuckled with malevolent glee. She was his ticket to bigger things. A promotion to General Secretary of the Marxist-Leninist Party. A red Ferrari!" Raising the vodka bottle in the air, Herr Greboschwitz shouted in the air, "Gluckwunsch!!" and gulped the entire clear liquid.

"Ahhhhhhh." He sighed in satisfaction, as the warm liquid slowly burned down his throat.

Seconds later, his body stiffened, his eyes becoming wide with fear. Something was wrong.

In an instant, Herr Greboschwitz gasped loudly, dropping the vodka bottle, the glass crashing into smithereens on the floor. He grabbed his throat in terror. The towel dropped to the floor. His naked body now convulsing, he struggled to walk a few steps towards the telephone to call for help. Unable to maintain his balance, his body soon crashed helter-skelter among the shards of broken glass on the floor, his arms splayed and bloodied.

In a second, his wide eyes stood still, staring at the ceiling, as he let out his last breath.

Out in the dark of the night, Senefreya kept on running, hanging on to the hidden AKM rifle, a hint of smile curling in her lips, as the wisps of each breath flowed out of her warm mouth into the cold air. Behind her, within the backpack, tiny slivers of light beamed out from within the cover.

Chapter 12

October 14, 1962

It was time to go now. To activate what had been planned for months by the highest levels in the U.S. Navy. He had been waiting for several months and finally the Navy contacted him.

It was time to go.

"Yes, Admiral." Gaston replied formally, "I will leave as soon as possible."

"Good. We expect you here promptly for the briefing." Admiral Jay Clarkson reminded him. "No one is to know of this assignment. No one."

"Of course." Gaston agreed. "You have my word."

"Excellent, Captain Caine. Excellent. Goodbye for now."

"Goodbye, Admiral Clarkson, sir". He placed the telephone on its cradle and left his hand on it for a moment. He sighed and closed his eyes. All of a sudden, that fateful conversation he had had with Margaret several months ago now appeared in the corners of his mind, as if warning him not to go.

But he had his orders now. It was now or never. His career was at stake.

Gaston set his mouth in grim determination. Never mind what he now knew what he hadn't known before, even if he wished with all his might he didn't know, because he didn't want to know. And yet, it was better he knew, hard as it was to understand something so strange and so convoluted, as what he had heard from Margaret, who had heard from Dr. Breslov, that mad scientist, who created the ship he was soon to command.

It was better, because even though the situation tied to his assignment appeared inevitable and dangerous, at the very least, he knew enough to be control.

To be ahead of the game.

Perchance to survive this assignment that was so much on the outer limits of rationality that only the brave could muster the courage to go through with it.

And he was their leader, whether he wanted to or not. It was time to go.

The shiny, dark Lincoln Continental limousine hummed smoothly on the Virginia highway in the direction towards the Newport News Naval Yard, after a full five hours flight from his home in San Diego, California. Settled lazily in the luxurious comfort of the spacious back seat covered in soft brown leather, he turned his head towards the side window to watch the passing bucolic scenery of horses and cows munching on the rolling grasses, amidst the picturesque cottages and mom and pop stores dotted here and there along the road.

Listening to the droning hum of the Lincoln Continental, Gaston let his mind wander back to the past eight hours of this day.

Just before he left for the airport, he had kissed his beloved Caroline on her chubby cheeks, while she slept inside her crib, being careful not to wake her up. It had been early dawn, almost twilight outside. It was too early for her to wake up and he knew she would get fussy, if he woke her up. After brushing her cheeks softly with his fingers, he quietly placed the velvety soft, pink blanket up towards her chest and walked away, leaving the nursery room door slightly ajar. Soon the live-in nanny he had hired would arrive to take over Caroline's care for the duration of his assigned six-month mission. He had no choice. Since the birth of their daughter, Margaret had not expressed any maternal instincts towards taking care of the baby or even loving the child. The psychologist she had seen had remarked it was highly probable she was suffering from post-partum depression and to give it time, but he knew that it was not going to happen.

She simply didn't care.

The Lincoln Continental softly thrummed on. Gaston shifted his position on the seat. His thoughts moved back to another time in the past, further back.

A time when Admiral Jay Clarkson had informed him of his orders.

"Yes, sir." Gaston had replied over the telephone. "How soon are we to deploy on the ship?"

"Unknown at present." Admiral Clarkson had explained. "The ship needs to be outfitted with special equipment first and foremost. It will take at least 8 months. Just stand by until further notice."

"But sir, what special equipment?"

The Admiral brushed it away dismissively. "It's actually on a need-to-know basis and affects national security. I simply cannot reveal it over the telephone. You will receive by special delivery, a secure canvas satchel with all the information about the ship and its mission. Look for it. Study the information, while you wait. I cannot speak any more. Just wait until further notice."

"Of course, sir". Gaston was puzzled. "Before you leave, may I inquire as to the name of the ship?"

"An older aircraft carrier that served in WWII, The U.S.S. Jaguar. It has been renamed the U.S.S. Arcanus."

"Why, sir? I thought it would be a new aircraft carrier."

"Goodbye, Gaston. Read the file."

"Goodbye, Admiral Clarkson." Gaston's sense of puzzlement grew, as he placed the receiver on its cradle.

What an odd name.

Back to his present time, Gaston looked at his watch. There was one hour and half left of driving. He turned his head away from the window and laid back against the seat. He closed his eyes. His thoughts once again returned to the past, just when he was leaving his house for the airport.

Carrying his suitcase in his one hand and the dark-blue canvas satchel under his arm, he had encountered Margaret standing at the open front door, indicating a taxi has arrived for him. She was smoking her favorite Marlboros, while the morning glass of bourbon whiskey rested in her other hand. A flimsy silk robe barely covered her body and it reeked of cigarette smoke. The hallway also reeked of cigarette smoke. He coughed for moment and stared at Margaret briefly, feeling a sense of disgust overcome him. This seems to be the permanent constant of Margaret and at this point, it has now become depressing and tiresome to see her like that day after day after day. He will have to do something about their damaged relationship upon his return from the mission. This façade simply cannot go on any longer. Reluctantly kissing Margaret on the cheek, he opened the screen door to let himself out.

Outside the house, he breathed in the fresh air. It was invigorating. With a renewed sense of responsibility, Gaston firmly walked towards the Lincoln Continental parked on the curbside, the back door held open by the driver. Settling himself in the back seat, Gaston felt compelled to look at his neighbor's house next door. To his stunned surprise, he found himself face to face, eye to eye, with the eccentric Dr. Miroslav Breslov, his wildly disarrayed, gray-white hair framing his tired, wrinkled face. His eyes, though heavy-lidded with age, stared back at him as if forewarning him that he was heading towards unknown territory where, according to Margaret, he could get himself killed. He shook his head, dismissing the fears.

For now, he was glad to be away from the both of them.

Soon, he found himself falling asleep, the bucolic scenery passing him by.

"Sir?" The driver called out.

Gaston opened his eyes. "Yes, what is it?"

"Thought you would like know. We will arrive at your destination soon in twenty minutes."

"Thank you, driver." Gaston nodded and quickly sat up straight on his seat. He rubbed his eyes and placed the white Navy cover hat on his head. "Please carry on."

"Yes, sir. Would you like to read this magazine? It will pass the time."

Gaston reached out for the proffered reading material. Suddenly, his curiosity was piqued, interlaced with a growing sense of alarm. His body tensed at the thought of the unfathomable. Gripping the magazine on his lap, Gaston stared at the plain, yet ominous cover with the title written in large, black, block letters, "The Bulletin of the Atomic Scientists". Nestled below the title, there was a picture of the famous Doomsday Clock.

It showed three seconds to midnight.

"Get a grip." Gaston admonished himself. He tapped the driver on the shoulder. "Do you mind if I keep this magazine?"

"Of course not, sir! It is an excellent choice for reading."

"You have no idea." Gaston whispered, as he put the magazine away in the canvas satchel along with the other information he had been required to read for the mission.

Ten minutes later, Newgrange Gate loomed ahead of them, its grey stone security building a striking contrast among the velvety green grass and shrubs surrounding it along the roadway.

The iron gate slowly lumbered away, allowing them in.

The Lincoln Continental was greeted, inspected, and waved on by the military security guards standing at full, crisp salute.

"Enjoy your stay, sir!"

Gaston saluted back and smiled. He closed the window. "Take the long route, driver. I want to see it."

"Yes, sir." The driver nodded and maneuvered the Lincoln Continental towards the road that ran parallel to the ship dockyard situated along the bay.

Chapter 13

OCTOBER 14, 1962

Senefreya put the key into the lock and opened the door to the apartment, where several months ago, she had been happily living with her parents. Now it was dark and empty, her parents gone, brutally killed by the STASI and she was all alone. And like her Papa, she was now a stranger in a strange land. With a sigh, Senefreya entered the kitchen beyond the living room and placed the grocery bags on the small table surrounded by three small chairs. She pulled apart the curtains from the window next to the table and looked outside, pulling the ledge open to let the air in.

It was nearly midnight and she had just come in from a pitch-black, night sky dotted with a few twinkling stars in a town so quiet beyond belief, there were only the crickets chirping amidst the cool night breeze. Yes, it was easier to go out in the dark night than the bright day filled with people going about their daily routines. Hardly anyone here in Berlin dared to go out at night and the less people she interacted with at this point in her life, the better she could move on to what Papa had said she needed to do.

"I do hope I know when the time is right, Papa." She whispered to the air.

She looked at the moon just beyond the horizon, a calm iconic presence in this strange land of awful people and awful deaths. Even now, that pompous, avaricious neighbor that had reported her parents to the STASI eight months ago, causing their horrific deaths, was snoring in bed with his equally horrible wife, neither of them caring about anyone, except themselves in all their creepiness and narcissism, not to mention their love of money. And all Senefreya needed to do every time she went out at night, was to become invisible and quickly pass their apartment door on her way out to buy some food and supplies and on the way back home upstairs.

And during the days of sunlight and blue skies outside, interspersed with alternate rainy days, with all the people milling about in all directions, the door to the her apartment stayed locked and the windows locked with the curtains drawn together. From then on each and every day, Senefreya stayed inside the apartment, venturing out only in the darkness and silence of the nights. In that way, no one will ever know she was still around, still a stranger in a strange land. "More of an alien in a strange land." Senefreya smirked at her reflection in the mirror, her hand reaching up to caress her elongated head crowned with the beautiful, raven-dark hair.

"It's true." She sighed turning her head sideways. "I don't look like them. I really stand out like a sore thumb. What am I to do?"

A thump resonated around her in an instant and a voice whispered in her head. "Follow Papa's lead. Get ready. You know what to do."

Senefreya smiled softly. "Of course. I only hope I know when I'm ready."

"You will." The voice faded away.

Infusing herself with all her courage and will, Senefreya turned away from the window and reached out for the grocery bags. She put the food away in the pantry closet, grateful that the shopping was over. Grateful that one of the small neighborhood grocery store owners not far from the apartment building was a friend of Papa's. Somewhere in the past just before Senefreya's birth, the owner had learned of Papa's secret and had promised to never speak of it to anyone. And Papa would often go there at night to pick up beer and milk and whatever Mamoshka needed at that moment. The only safe place for him. The kindly grocer and Papa had struck up a friendship that forged into a brotherly bond. He became Senefreya's godfather, promising Papa to keep silent what was now her secret.

"Oh, Pate Bauer, Papa is gone now. Mamoshka also. I am alone." Senefreya had confessed to her godfather one night, her anxieties steeped inside her about to burst out. "And I am afraid, so afraid."

The portly old man with the white beard and twinkling, hazel eyes hugged his goddaughter to his heart. "Anything I can do for you, his tochter, also my tochter!" He cried, holding her hands in his, tears building up in his eyes. "Do not worry about your secret. It will never leave my lips." He hugged her again. "Always come here for anything you need. Anything."

"Danke, Pate Bauer, danke." Senefreya wiped away her tears. "I need food and supplies. I can only come here at night, just like Papa did, as you well know by now. I will pay more for your troubles."

"Nein, nein!" Pate Bauer brushed away her tears and hugged her once again. "Of course, I will open the store for you at night. I will wait for you. You do not need to pay more, not one deutschmark at all. Food and supplies are free for my tochter, jah. And you are my tochter, Fraulein Senefreya". He soon pushed her out the door. "Quickly. Now go home! Come back later at night when it is safe, jah!" He patted her hand.

Senefreya smiled through her tears. "I am so grateful, Pate Bauer. Danke Schon!" She hugged him and cried out. "Papa would be so grateful!"

"Bitte Schon, mein tochter!" He waved at her as she walked away from the store. "Bitte Schon! Come back again."

And so, the months passed by quietly. Senefreya soon felt a sense of being safe and unnoticed, hidden in the sanctuary of the apartment with the door locked and the windows locked and drawn.

Even so, she knew that danger always lurked nearby in this town every day with the rising sun. Always there causing her to look behind her shoulder, even in her own home. Causing her to stay on guard no matter if it was day or night or even in the sanctuary of her home. And then there was just a matter of time when she would be ready.

Papa said so.

After putting away the groceries, Senefreya removed the black scarf and hat that covered her elongated head. She shook her head and her raven-dark hair tumbled down onto her shoulders framing her heart-shaped face with large cat like eyes and high cheekbones. She smiled remembering her face in the mirror. The spitting image of his beautiful mother, Queen Nerilka, Papa had said.

Only way to accept how different she was in this town, where everyone was white-skinned with blond hair and blue eyes. And some with brown hair and brown eyes.

"Stay strong and be proud of yourself, Solnyushka." Papa often consoled her with a twinkle in his eye, as he brushed away her tears. "Even in this town of the hackneyed ones".

"Always, Papa." Senefreya whispered softly. "Always." She switched off the light in the lamp by her nightstand, pulled up the downy blanket to her neck, and went to sleep in the early hour of morning twilight, the window curtains drawn close together. The room as dark as it can be.

Several hours later, Senefreya felt the urge to wake up. She opened her eyes slowly. She could see the golden ray of the morning sun appearing from the distant horizon through the small gap between her curtains casting a circle of light upon the wooden floor. One could see dust dancing throughout that beam of light. It seemed so holy, amidst the ordinary surrounding of her bedroom.

She yawned softly. "How tiresome to wake up right now. And yet, I'm not able to go back to sleep." She turned over and sat on the bed. "I might as well start the day."

Stretching her arms, Senefreya walked towards the window. Carefully peeking through gap in the curtain, her eyes took in the bright, blue vista of the sky with numerous birds flying all around the bleak, gray buildings. Below, in the park across the street, the squirrels hastened here and there looking for nuts and berries among the fallen leaves. An elderly woman wearing a heavy woolen coat with her hair covered in a cotton scarf sat on the iron-clad bench. She was tossing out pieces of peas and nuts around the park for the squirrels and birds, who were gathering in flocks around her to feed. To her right away from the park, Senefreya watched parents standing proudly, as their little girl proffered a bouquet of wildflowers to the military police on their way to the Berlin Wall zone, their AK rifles blatantly snug on their shoulders. She smirked with disgust. The hypocrisy is everywhere. Our lives frozen by the brutal few.

When will we learn to fight for truth and freedom and our sanctity? When will we destroy that horrible wall?

Shaking her head, Senefreya stretched her body upwards, her arms reaching to the ceiling. Closing the curtains back together, the room she was in soon dimmed in the twilight, as if protecting her from those who do not understand. She turned around and picked up the velvet, purple robe from the old, faded, black and brown, striped armchair standing in a corner adjacent to her bed. Tightening the matching, velvet purple belt around her waist, she placed her feet inside the warm, grey colored cotton slippers.

With an air of determination, she left the bedroom and proceeded down the hallway towards the kitchen.

After gulping the last few drops of dark, espresso coffee, its fragrant aroma of chocolate and hazelnut still wafting throughout the small, hobo kitchen room, Senefreya turned on the sink faucet and proceeded to wash the old ceramic coffee mug. Shaking the water off the mug, she placed it to dry on the small, gray-green, cotton towel spread out on the countertop near the sink. Brushing her hands on the robe, she headed back to her bedroom to change her clothes.

The coffee was refreshing. She was wide awake and energized.

Fully dressed in dark-blue jeans and a navy-blue, pullover sweater with a high-collar covering her neck, Senefreya pulled up warm, fuzzy socks into her bare feet. Leaving her bedroom, she emerged into the living room down the hall. It was now time to meditate, the way Papa tried to teach her long ago. She had been surprised that she was able to remember the process clearly, the minute she needed the guidance. She suspected that Papa's spirit had a hand in it, jogging her memories.

Even so, it was now time to cram her daily exercises to connect with her inner soul being, her seven chakras, all of them separating her, no, shielding her, from the harsh reality of life outside her body. It was now time to reach out inside herself to conjoin with her DNA powers that had been dormant since her birth. Her 21st birthday was soon to arrive and just now her fledgling DNA powers were stirring ad hoc time and again, even against her will. Only on the day of her birth, propelled by the magic of the shiny, jade Merkabah in her hands, will her DNA abilities finally burst out in all their might and power.

And so, for now, she must prepare her metamorphosis that day, her training guided by the indefinable spirit of her Papa, his voice whispering in her mind, as she sat cross-legged and silent, her eyes closed, in the middle of the living room surrounded by darkness.

Time was of essence.

But no matter. She was still going to try to harness the powers of the ancients by the day of her birth, October 28, 1962.

"Good, good, Solnyushka. Good. Keep going." Papa had encouraged her in a little voice in her head. "Give yourself a chance in life. So much danger now surrounds you."

As the months passed by slowly and she practiced her exercises, Senefreya soon felt small increments of energies becoming stronger and stronger, especially now in the eighth month of October 1962 with her 21st birthday soon approaching in two weeks.

She could hardly wait for that day.

The only problem was she was in the wrong place at the wrong time, constantly in danger, as she already had observed since Papa's warnings.

What was she to do with her powers that day of her birth?

She shifted her body slightly and breathed in deeply, firmly brushing away her worries. There was no point in worrying. It only added to the stress of the danger lurking in the corner every day.

And yet, there had to be a purpose behind all this happening to her. First of all, why did Papa come here from the past? From thousands of years ago. Why was she born here in this awful city of Berlin, surrounded by danger?

What was she supposed to do now?

And then it became clear, crystal clear. "Of course." She reminded herself feeling foolish, her cheeks burning with embarassment. It seemed so long ago when he had said that. Papa did say to go that beautiful place of freedom on the other side of the ocean. A melting pot of diversity, of inclusion.

A place where she could be herself unfettered by prejudices and danger.

"And things will fall into place thereon." Papa had assured her. "You will know to find your way, Solnyushka. Just keep practicing your exercises."

Senefreya closed her eyes and took in another deep breath. She softly gripped the crystal Merkabah snuggled in a silver-patterned spiral enclosure attached to a silver necklace. It glowed warm and shiny in her hands. Soon, her mind was cleared of the relentless self-remonstrations and reached a point of clarity and calm. At the same time, the grew in power brighter and warmer, its shimmering energies entering her body through her hands like electricity, fueling her DNA abilties.

Senefreya quickly opened her eyes wide, still gripping the Merkabah crystal tightly against her breasts.

Things had quickly changed to her dismay.

A gnawing sensation was now slowly building in her stomach. A sense of dread. Senefreya tried to push it away in her mind, focusing on her meditative practice. But the dread refused to go away. Instead, the sense of ominous uncertainty grew and grew inside of her and soon she felt an even worse sensation taking place in her being.

An overwhelming sense of doom.

Something was coming. Inevitably coming. But she did not know what. It was still too early in her training to be able see what was coming. To know what was coming. And yet, she could feel it coming. A feeling so strong and so terrifying, it had to be devastating.

What was she to do?

Senefreya quickly stood up from the floor and walked towards the window in the living room. She carefully drew open the curtains. The desolate, grey, infrastructure of the city of Berlin was peculiarly encapsulated in the brightness of the shining sun, cotton clouds, and clear blue skies.

And then…

Senefreya gasped standing back from the window, her hands closing on her mouth in horror. In just that few moments, she could see the sky slowly changing in a menacing, gray color that apparently only she could see. Everyone else down there on the streets and in the park were going about their business nonchalantly in their normal day-to-day routines. The military guards were also walking about among the populace, holding their AK rifles in their shoulders, some chatting among themselves, others scrutinizing their surroundings. They were all oblivious to the change in the weather that only she could see.

She looked behind her at the clock on the wall, its pendulum rocking back and forth ominously. It was now 10:45AM. She looked back at the window, again, searching the skies, hoping the blue color had returned along with the bright yellow sun.

It had only gotten worse by now…

The twilight grayness was coming from over the horizon like a monstrous beast approaching Berlin, shutting out the light of the sun.

Slowly, but surely. It was coming.

"I must flee!" Senefreya whispered frantically. Making sure, the cherished Merkabah was still safe in its enclosure attached to her necklace, she picked up her go-to bag filled with spare clothes, food, and emergency kit and dashed out the apartment door.

And stood frozen in place.

"Oh, no…" Senefreya wailed softly, her eyes locked to someone ahead of her just beyond the landing. It was her nasty third floor neighbor on his way to the 10th floor to visit a friend.

"Ahhh…" His evil eyes and furrowed brows narrowed in recognition. He stood akimbo with arms on his hips, not letting her move past him, his tattered, old clothes providing a glimpse of irony and disgust. "How long has it been, heh? You should have been dead and gone, hah!"

Senefreya said nothing.

He laughed malevolently, pushing his head back in glee. "Oh, yes, oh yes, now I will get me some more money, heh?" He shook his finger at her. "Don't move." Still laughing at his unfolding draw of luck, he turned and disappeared down the stairs to make that phone call.

Senefreya stared at him, trembling with fear. It had been too late to turn invisible. In her rush to escape whatever was coming, she had forgotten to turn herself into invisibility, the moment she saw the darkness appear in the sky. She still had not mastered full invisibility, the power still flickering on and off, but no matter, she still had that ability. Every effort counted and she did not want to be seen by any more people.

She knew what her third-floor neighbor was going to do. Why he was quickly running down the stairs. A call to the STASI, still looking for her, still papering the buildings of the city with her picture. The strange girl with the dark hair and elongated head. A phone call from Herr Greboschwitz to the STASI had identified her as his killer eight months earlier. Worst still he had also identified her as a "wunderwaffe" that must be captured alive. It was non-negotiable. She was too valuable to them.

She found herself outside, solidified, barely escaping the clutches of her avaricious neighbor. A thousand thoughts raced through her mind. She needed to leave quickly, but where? How?

With her heightened sense of hearing brought on by the energy of the Merkabah nestled against her chest, she heard the clop, clop, clopping of horse hooves upon the gravelly, stone road located just outside the open, corroded iron gates of the apartment building.

That noise was getting closer and closer. Clop, clop, clop.

Of course! Gripping the straps of her backpack, Senefreya eagerly bounded towards the open, iron gate in her black, hiking boots, her invisibility flitting in and out, until she finally solidified back into her human form.

Chapter 14

Two hours passed.

The two black, draught horses were still clop, clop, clopping down the earthen trail on the Wansee district just parallel to the Nuthestrasse Road, moving away from city of Berlin. Behind the horses, the elderly driver held the reins, his body relaxed, as if he was in no hurry. He wore a tattered, brown winter coat and cap to protect him from the cold air of October, while he sat on the driver's seat up behind the horses. Behind him, the horses were pulling the 13-foot long, old wooden cart that were filled with medium-sized pallets of black wooden boxes piled on top of each other, bouncing against each other with each clop, clop of the horses' hooves.

In this bright, sunny day, the driver was in no hurry. The horses continued to clop, clop, clopping on the earthen trail away from the city.

Senefreya peeked up from within the center of the pile of black, wooden boxes, her nose sniffing at the stale, damp smell. She could see that the sky was still slowly dispersing into a form of darkness that now terrified her. And neither the driver nor the horses could see it, nor all the citizens milling about the city. Whatever it was that was coming was definitely coming closer and closer by now.

She only wished she knew what.

No point in frightening the driver with her worries. He had already been startled at how strange she had looked to him, a beautiful woman with light-brown skin and shiny, raven-black hair, and odd cat's eyes, not to mention her head was in an unusual elongated shape. How startled he must have been to see her approach him with desperation, probably thinking she was going to kill him. Funny, her appearance had no effect on the horses.

And yet, after hearing her pleas and seeing her tears, he had been most kind in allowing her to hide within the pallets of black wooden boxes in the broad daylight out in Berlin. The only way to avoid those pesky military guards and the horrible STASI, all of them still looking for her.

And everyone, she knew, hated the STASI, but loved the money.

"And where you be going, young lady?" The driver had asked scratching his head. He was puzzled at her insistence to hide herself in the back of the wagon within the pallets of dirty empty boxes. The horses neighed impatiently, their hooves striking the stones on the road. They wanted to leave now. Senefreya smiled. Even the horses understand something was coming.

"Come sit with me up there, no?" The driver offered, his hand pointing to the upright bench behind the horses.

"No." Senefreya whispered desperately, already climbing into the back of the wagon, pushing her body into the deepest midst of the black boxes. "I can't do that. You must take me to the Glienicke Bridge. Please, you must". She rifled through her backpack and took out several deutschmarks. She offered the money to the driver, a lone hand reaching out of the collection of boxes. "Here. Take this for your troubles, please. The Glienicke Bridge. Bitte jetz!!"

"Ja, ja, ja, Fraulein, kein problem!" The flustered driver reached out and quickly accepted the deutschmarks, stuffing them in the inner pocket of his faded, brown coat. "Danke!" He proffered his cap to Senefreya and clambered up the bench, lifting the reins.

"We be going now, Fraulein. It be a long ride. Sit tight."

Senefreya nodded with smile. "Danke, my freundin, danke." At that sound of the clop, clop, clopping, she felt the wagon being roughly pulled forward into a rhythmic stride. Feeling relieved, Senefreya let out a deep breath and settled down to relax within the dark cover of the black boxes.

Minutes later, Senefreya shifted her body slightly, moving the black boxes surrounding her. She was careful to make sure the boxes did not fall off the horse-drawn wagon carrying her to her freedom. But something was happening and she could not make sense of it. A feeling of dread. A feeling of apprehension manifesting itself as a sense of fear growing bigger in her body, her solar plexus, the most powerful area of emotions, other than her heart.

That was her Papa had taught her.

"Your heart is not the only place to listen, my Solnyushka. There is another place within you that you must also listen to." Papa had placed his hand gently on her stomach area. "This is called your solar plexus. Your heart is powerful, but not as powerful as this place in your body. Listen to it carefully."

Senefreya understood.

"Good." Papa had responded with satisfaction. "When the time comes, you will know what to do." He smiled. "You will fear it first, Solnyushka, the bad feelings. It is like nothing you have ever experienced, but it is there to help you, not hurt you. Learn how to work with it."

"Why do I have it, Papa?"

"It's in your DNA. My DNA. From our long-forgotten ancestors."

"Why long-forgotten ancestors, Papa? Here everybody has memories of family. Pictures of family. As far back as they could." Senefreya had questioned, her eyes bright with confusion. "Don't we have that too. Memories and pictures of our ancestors?"

Papa laughed gently. He opened his arms to his little girl, who went straight into the warmth and safety of his hug.

"It is complicated, Solnyushka. Too complicated to explain to your little inquisitive mind. It is not so easy to tell you what happened to our ancestors. Why they are now long forgotten. It would be such a burden to your little heart."

"But why, Papa?" Senefreya had demanded. "Tell me."

"I cannot, Solnyushka. Not at your tender age. Too long. Too complicated. Do not worry your little head about it." He rubbed her head playfully. He kissed her hair and hugged her harder. "Perhaps in time you will find out on your own the story of our ancient ancestors and why they are long-forgotten. In your time. When you are ready to see it better. When your heart can handle it better with open eyes."

Senefreya smiled, her head softly resting on his strong shoulders in the warm embrace of his arms. "Of course, Papa. I hope I know it when I feel what I'm supposed to feel."

Papa hugged her tighter, again. "You will know it, Solnyushka. You will know it."

Returning to the present, hidden under the safety of the black boxes in the horse drawn-carriage clopping onwards to the freedom, as she had hoped, but now it was happening. In her solar plexus.

That sensation was growing stronger and stronger. An ominous sense of doom, once again. Almost nauseous. Quite frightening.

What was she to do? Senefreya moved a couple of black boxes, careful not to dislodge them off the tilting, moving wagon. She looked up at the sky.

She gasped.

The sky was turning into a smoky, grey color, as if in twilight, becoming darker and darker, and yet it was only late morning. How can that be?

"We are coming near the Glienicke Brucker." The driver shouted carefully, bending behind to reach her, knocking on the top of the black boxes above her. "Be that your destination, Fraulein?" He looked up warily. "Best to leave quickly, Fraulein. Be rain soon. Maybe thunderstorm. Das gehwitter, yah!"

From within the black boxes, Senefreya called back to the driver, her eyes still scanning the smoky, gray sky, now changing into a charcoal, grey sky, "Nein, nein, nein. Keep going. Where are you going past the Glienecke Brucke?"

"Ah, we be going to my home town. Kromlau. Be welcome you come with me, Fraulein. My family will take you in and take care of you. Be worried out in this schlechter regen. Must hurry home." The driver warned pointing at the darkened sky. The horses whinnied, wanting to go faster, as the wind ominously arrived from nowhere, whipping the air around them.

"Go. Just go. Go home. We must hurry." Senefreya responded loudly, fear gripping her body, as the wind became stronger and stronger around the wagon, bustling the boxes around her. "Something is wrong."

"Aye, Fraulein, aye." The driver lifted the reins. "Gehen mein Rosses. Gehen!"

The horses picked up speed approaching and passing the Glienicke Brucker bridge, its olive-green steel braces and suspension cables presenting a haunting appearance against the darkened sky. The driver shifted the reins once more and the horses turned away from the bridge, going south towards the well-worn earthen trail running parallel to the road.

And there it was.

Bright points of lights appearing out of the darkness of the sky. So many of them. Some big. Some small. All of them bright and fiery. All of them coming out of that darkness of the sky falling towards the earth.

Towards Berlin.

"Oh, no...." Senefreya wailed softly. "Oh, god, no...." She turned around carefully. "Hurry! You must hurry!"

"Yah, Fraulein!" The driver responded already in fear himself at how dark the sky had become and the wind getting stronger by the minute. "Gehen mein, Rosses. Gehen mein!"

The horses whinnied loudly, their hooves picking up faster and faster.

Balancing herself against the speed of the ride, Senefreya watched some of the great balls of fiery light and rock drop down into Berlin, one by one. She winced at each drop. Soon, spires of smoke appeared at a distance.

And still more of those balls of light and rock landed in Berlin. More clouds of smoke appeared, dispersed all around like the aftermath of a volcano eruption.

And all of a sudden, a great ball of light and rock whipped down towards the Glienieke Brucke, where a gathering of persons and soldiers quickly scattered away in their desperate attempt to escape the bombardment.

Senefreya braced herself in silent shock. A loud, thundering noise boomed in the air, forcing the horses to run ever faster towards the bridge, the driver holding on for dear life, the black boxes spilling over the wagon, exposing Senefreya, who clambered to the far corner of the wagon desperate to hide herself.

Then she remembered her training. What Papa had taught her to do.

Senefreya closed her eyes, her body stumbling at the corner of the fast-moving wagon. By then, spirals of dense, grey smoke appeared amidst the shock wave emanating from the damaged bridge, its force strong enough to tear apart the fabric of the wagon and kill the living souls upon it.

With all the might of her mind and body, Senefreya called upon the Universe to wrap the entire wagon and everyone around it and in it, inside a protective shield and armor.

Use this power sparingly, Papa had warned. It will drain your energy.

Protected by the invisible shroud of armor magically called upon by her, the horses and the wagon and the driver and Senefreya all safely passed the barraged bridge, now a mile down the trail. Passed the explosion and the shock wave and the shoving wind.

All of them alive and unscathed.

The driver still in shock at being alive, breathed deeply saying prayers of thanks to his gods. The horses had settled into calm composure, as if knowing they were being protected by higher powers. Pulling the reins to the right, the driver guided the horses to clop, clop, clop towards the less traveled, unmarked, gravel path that would lead the wagon to Kromlau.

To home.

Suddenly, a loud voice yelled out of the empty air and smoke.

"Wait! Wait! Please wait! Please help me! Please help!"

Chapter 15

From her corner of the wagon, Senefreya opened her eyes. Balls of light and rock were still bombarding around Berlin, but the wagon and its occupants were now far, far away from the epicenter. The wagon was still safe and sound, amidst the smaller rain of fire and rocks, the horses now clop, clopping forward with confidence, as if nothing had happened a few minutes before.

She gasped.

There was a dark figure in the smoke-filled air ahead of her on the trail, desperately running towards the wagon, arms flailing out to reach it.

Desperately waving at her.

"Wait! Please help me!"

Behind him, Senefreya could see two more dark sfigures, dressed in stiff STASI uniform trench coats and boots, both of them brandishing their powerful rifles, running after the bedraggled, lone figure crying for help.

Senefreya quickly pulled hem of the driver's coat. "Slow down. Please slow down."

"Nein! Fraulein Verruckt! On to home!!" He pushed the horses forward. "Nein!"

"You must." Senefreya insisted. "We are safe. I promise. We are safe. Look at us!"

The driver looked around shocked at the sight. It was true. Small debris of fire and rocks were still falling down, but they were untouched, as if the debris simply bounced off them. The horses were fearless, as if they were not aware of what was happening right now.

He pulled the reins to stop the horses.

"Fraulein still Verruckt. How be this?" The driver scratched his head at the seeming calmness of the wagon in the chaos of the falling rain of fire and rocks.

"I know what it looks like." Senefreya responded with a smile. "Just trust me. We need to help that poor man coming towards us."

The driver looked up. Someone was clearly running and limping at the same time towards the wagon. Waving his hands wildly. His clothes were tattered and he appeared charred from the rain of fire and rocks bombarding him and the two STASI behind him.

"Help, please!"

Senefreya waited until he got closer to the open back end of the wagon, now empty, all the black boxes gone. She closed her eyes and chanted a mantra for the protective shield to stand down. She waved at the running man.

"Get in now! Now, you only have 5 seconds. Get in now!"

The lone, dark figure hurried with all his might and screaming loudly, as he finally reached the back end of the wagon and heaved himself inside, landing painfully on his back, his arms flayed out, gasping for breaths. At that moment, a large ball of fire and rock struck the two STASI soldiers closing in on the wagon, quickly obliterating their bodies to the ground.

"Good riddance" The stranger yelled back.

Unfettered, Senefreya closed her eyes again. At her silent command, the turbulent chaos disappeared a few feet away the wagon, willing the protective shield to raise up and cover them all. And all around the designated space, a sense of calm was restored to the wagon, the horses, and its inhabitants. In shock at Senefreya's manifested power and yet, desperate to leave from this awful cataclysm happening before his eyes, the driver called out to the horses to move forward. All around them, the blustery wind, dusty smoke, and falling pieces of fire and rock continued to batter the surroundings.

Senefreya looked up. A gigantic swirl of smoke was circling up and up forever into the sky after an enormous piece of fire and rock slammed down at distance creating an ominous mushroom cloud above Berlin.

She blinked her eyes at the horror before her. The city was destroyed, perhaps gone.

The Glienicke Brucke was also gone, its mighty steel fortifications torn apart and tumbling over and down, disappearing into raging waters of the mighty Irina River, already swollen and turbulent.

"No matter." Senefreya thought as she watched the iconic bridge, often used for prisoner exchanges between nations, disappear under the river.

"There is always another way. Another way to freedom. I'm not giving up."

She looked down at the lone, dark figure lying still before her, who had been chased by the STASI, her staunch arch-enemy. She wondered who he was and why the STASI was after him. Unlike her, he seemed normal. His body was quiet, but he was still breathing, his chest heaving slightly with every breath.

She hugged her knees, still watching the lone figure before her, as the clop, clop, clop of the horses continued onwards. Eventually, she found herself falling asleep.

The wagon driver, still in shock at the turn of events, at the luck that he was still alive, the horses still alive and now seemingly fearless pulling the wagon with fervor. The driver took in deep breaths and shook his head in disbelief. "Fraulien verruckte. Sehr Verruckte!" Patting his sweating forehead with his small, grimy bandanna, he urged the horses to trot faster.

One hour later.

Senefreya slowly opened her eyes. She looked at her watch. One hour had passed. She looked before her at the world outside. The sky was still dark, a kind of shadowy dark, where the sun is trying to light the sky, but the charcoal cover of clouds keep passing over it, pushed on by the busy, gusty wind, barely letting any light peer through.

All was quiet. All was dim and melancholic. Hardly any life to see around the dusty, sooty surroundings. The silver energy of the protective shield was still crackling around the wagon, only Senefreya could see.

There seemed to be no need for it now. Senefreya closed her eyes with a silent command for the shield to let go.

"Hello?" A tired, male voice broke the silence.

Senefreya opened her eyes. "Huh?"

"What time is it?"

"Half past one". Senefreya responded, warily eyeing the stranger now struggling with his hands to lift his body up. "Are you all right?"

The stranger nodded. Grunting loudly, he pulled his scratched and bloodied body to the other corner of the empty wagon opposite of Senefreya and laid his back against the seat. The driver, at the center on the bench, was still oblivious to his passengers, coaxing his horses to continue the trot.

"Here. Have some water." Senefreya offered a water flask she brought with her. "I have some biscuits and cheese and dried meats, if you want."

The stranger accepted the food and water graciously. "Thank you, Fraulein." He proceeded to munch voraciously on the proferred bread, cheese and some dried meats, gulping the hearty meal down with water to its last drop.

"Ahhh." The stranger sighed wiping his lips with the back of his hand. "Sorry. Don't mean to offend your sensibilities. I do not have a napkin in front of me." He grinned.

"De nada." Senefreya laughed, brushing away with her hand. "Are you all right now?"

"I would think so." The stranger tried to get up and winced with pain. "Ah, I may have hurt my knee trying to jump on this floorboard. Damn wooden planks are hard as rocks and I got splinters." He settled back down, nursing his bruised, bloody kneecap. "Damn. I kind of feel it swollen."

"May I?"

"What?"

"Look at your knee. Perhaps I can help."

"By all means. I could use some help."

Senefreya grabbed her backpack bag and slowly crawled to the stranger at his corner. She pulled out a pair of scissors and cut open the area of his pants exposing the knee. The blood was already dried and caked. Senefreya examined the knee with her hands. It was indeed swollen and tender to the touch. She poured in some hydrogen peroxide.

"Ouch! It burns."

"It hurts, I imagine." Senefreya joked, dabbing the wound with a cloth immersed in the hydrogen peroxide. "Your right knee took most of the brunt with you getting on the wagon. The skin is open and bruised. The cartilage and muscle appear sprained a bit, which is why it's swollen."

"Oh, great." The stranger groaned. "You did ask me to jump in and jump in fast."

"Oh, yeah, I did." Senefreya retorted hotly. "What was I supposed to do? Let the STASI get to you? You did ask to be rescued, if you remember yelling at us. I had no choice. It had to been done quickly."

"Why that fast?" His eyes became angry.

"Another time." Senefreya applied the last dab of the peroxide. "Too complicated to explain. You got in in time. Be grateful for that."

The stranger's eyes softened. "Well, yes, I did yell at you. I do remember that. Thank you very much, Miss. Much appreciated, however complicated."

"Apologies accepted. And my name is Senefreya." She rummaged inside her backpack bag and pulled out a white shirt. She ripped it apart into long stems of material.

"Stay still." She ordered.

"Of course, ma'am."

"Senefreya."

"Senefreya. Pretty name. Do you have a last name?"

"It's Vogel after my mother's family. My father has no last name."

"Now you are mystifying me." The stranger laughed. "How the hell is that? Your father has no last name? Does he have a first name?"

"Nope to the first and yes, to the second. Please stay still, while I wrap this material around your knee."

The wrapping around the wounded knee done, Senefreya tied the ends of the material into a hard knot and patted it. "There you are all set."

"What was your father's name?"

"Another time." Senefreya voiced her frustration. "We will soon arrive at the crossing of the bridge at the narrow point of this area. Right, driver?"

The driver nodded, urging the horses onwards.

"Bridge? What bridge?" The stranger asked his eyes surveying the environment. There was nothing but dust and pulverized earth ahead of them. "Look behind you. Almost everything is gone. Maybe even the city of Berlin."

"You don't know that." Senefreya retorted. "Berlin is a big city. It may still be there. Just destroyed here and there, who knows."

"Yeah, who knows." The stranger agreed. "So what bridge are you talking about?"

"That bridge we are going towards in this wagon. It's not that far now. A half hour more of riding, I would think."

"Does it go across to the American side?"

"Of course, it does. Precisely why I want to go there. I do hope with all my heart it still stands. I'm pretty sure it might. I feel it." Senefreya clasped her hands against her chest tightly.

The stranger smiled at her fervent hope. It was so contagious that it made him feel hopeful himself in all the danger surrounding them from the past two hours of a sudden apocalypse of fire and brimstones falling from the sky, the black, black smoke trailing the fiery debris at each pounding on the earth, like the aftermath of a nuclear disaster.

After all that, it would seem nothing was certain now. Not even a standing bridge anywhere around them. "Yeah, I do hope it is still standing if it does go to the American side. Does this bridge have a name?"

Senefreya nodded. "The locals call it the Devil's Bridge."

The stranger raised his eyebrow. "Devil's Bridge? Interesting. How did they come up with that name?"

Senefreya looked up, her eyes becoming dreamy, as if lost in a memory. "It was built around 1860 by a knight from the nearby town of Kromlau, where we are heading right now." She gestured towards the driver. "His home is nearby." She looked back at the stranger. "Anyways, the builder, well, his name was Friedrich Hermann Rotschke. He loved nature and would spend most of his time outdoors, often riding his horse in the countryside. So, one day, he saw what looked like a small bottleneck of the Irina River and a vision appeared in his mind. A beautiful, unusual bridge made of stones sprawling across that lower neck of the river."

"And did it?" The stranger asked becoming interested in the story. "Become unusual whatever that means?"

Senefreya smiled. "Indeed. Beyond his wildest dreams. Of course, he had help from an equally unusual group of knights."

"Oh, really?"

"Yes, you know them as the "Knight Templars".

"But how's that? The stranger was puzzled. "I hear they were supposed to guard the Christians who traveled on pilgrimages to the Holy Land during the Crusades? Right? That was their job, huh?"

Senefreya laughed. "Oh, they were much, much more than that. Of course, they guarded the pilgrims from marauders and thieves on their way to the Holy Land. But they were also a military group, a Catholic military battalion sponsored by St. Bernard of Clairvaux of the Roman Catholic Church."

"Go on…"

"Well, the Knight Templars also created the banking system and were powerful moneylenders and recordkeepers. But most of all, for this bridge, they were the ones that Sir Rotschke hired to build, because they can. They were the experts in building with stones."

"What do you mean?"

"Apparently, the knights knew what to do. They knew the secrets to building incredible stone structures, like the Chartres Cathedral in France and Lalibela in Ethiopia. In fact, they were almost like gods in their secretive knowledge, not allowing anyone not a part of their battalion to learn the secrets. So, one day, they had an idea they presented to Sir Rotschke. A semi-circular bridge made of stones. Haven't you noticed, they always use stones, all kinds of stones in building each and every medieval cathedrals and ancient bridges and so forth. Stone lasts forever, you know. Stone is everywhere to build."

"True. That is amazing." The stranger remarked. "Tell me more. How did they build this circular bridge, as you say?"

Senefreya shook her head, smiling. "Semi-circular. And, no, no one really knows how they built it. Like I said, they guarded the secrets to their knowledge. And, they expressly forbade anyone to watch them work day or night."

"Kind of hard to do, huh?"

"Not really. They mostly worked at nights. They had outposts with guards."

"Whew!" The stranger whistled. "How in hell do you know all that?"

"My father." Senefreya smiled. "Education was important and he took care of all that."

"So you were home schooled, huh?"

"Something like that."

"Why?"

"Too complicated to explain." Senefreya smiled. "Another time."

"I can't wait." The stranger rolled his eyes. "This is utterly mystifying, your life and your schooling."

"I know. Sorry." Senefreya joked. She sighed deeply, looking ahead at the melancholic view of destruction ahead of her. "It was awful watching that monstrous ball of fire and rock hit the Glienicke Bridge. Worse still, watching it go down the Irina River."

The stranger nodded. "Yeah. But how the hell did you manage to get away so fast? Just as the balls of fire and rocks, as you call them, arrived."

"Back then at my apartment home, I felt something awful growing inside me. I sensed something so awful about to happen and it was becoming worse and worse as time passed by. So, I packed up and ran out my apartment building. I was lucky to find this wagon going my way towards the Glienecke Brucke."

The stranger nodded. "Yeah, you were lucky. Why the Glienecke Brucke?"

"To cross over to the American side."

"Are you kidding? You would have shot on sight. It's only for prisoners like me."

"I know. But I have this letter from a member of the government." Senefreya ruffled through her backpack and brought out an envelope. "Not quite useful now, huh?"

"Nope." The stranger chuckled ruefully. "Anyways, you were lucky to find this wagon."

"Yes, I am." Senefreya smiled. "It's not too late to find another way to cross over."

"Yes, and, I'm damn lucky to find this wagon right when I needed it, although, believe me, I don't get why I have only five seconds to jump."

"Another time." Senefreya responded in a sing song. "Sorry. Anyways, why were you at the Glienicke Brucke?"

"Ah, yes. I was supposed to be crossing that bridge. An exchange for the Soviet spy the Americans captured a while back." He sighed. "And then all of a sudden, panic ensued. Damn STASI pulling me back from that bridge got me all worked up and I fought them and fought them and finally escaped. I didn't want to go back with them and I couldn't figure out why the hell they changed their mind.

"Scary." Senefreya nodded. "The STASI are awful."

"Yeah, and then I looked up at the sky. And that's when I realized why they were all going crazy. Of course, I had to run like hell to get away from them."

Senefreya nodded. "I know that bridge. You were not the only one crossing it to the American side when we have to make the exchanges of prisoners or spies or whatever there are. I figured you were an American."

The stranger laughed. "Smart. But you could have gotten in trouble letting me on this wagon. Why did you do that?"

Senefreya shrugged. "I just wanted to help you. And, I would need your help to cross to the American side." She pointed at the burning city. "There is no room for trouble now, is there?

"Nope". The stranger lifted himself up, his eyes shining. He extended his hand. "And you got it. My help. We will help each other. Quid pro quo."

Senefreya grasped it firmly. "Quid pro quo, whatever that is."

The stranger laughed heartily. He shifted his body and smiled at Senefreya. "Hey, if the good guys built this awesome semi-circular stone bridge as you say, how come it's called "Devil's Bridge?""

Senefreya laughed. "I told you. The Knights Templar would not allow anyone to watch them work. And you know, the locals being extremely superstitious decided among themselves that the bridge was the work of Satan and the Templars were Satan's cohorts."

"Good grief. Is that true?"

"Of course not!" Senefreya protested. "Nowadays, though, we all know better, but that name stuck. Oh well. It's really a beautiful bridge, you'll see."

"If you say so. Say…." The stranger's eyes became wide, as he assessed Senefreya's face, his mind becoming clearer as the seconds passed. "What happened to your head. I never noticed it before. Why is elongated?"

Senefreya grasped her head with her hands, combing her hair with her fingers. "Oh, nothing. I was born like that. My Papa had a head like that, too, even long hair too. All his ancestors, my ancestors, had heads and hair like that. We are just different, you know. Nothing to worry about." Senefreya paused, holding her breath.

The stranger smiled. "No worries. Maybe different, but really, you are incredibly beautiful and that beautiful, dark hair falling down like a waterfall. You are certainly different from any woman I have known in my life."

Senefreya blushed, her cheeks burning. "Thank you. I only wish I could manifest it differently."

"Huh?"

"Make it become normal like yours. I can do that, but it's just so hard right now."

"Come again?"

"I'm going to tell you a little bit of my complicated secret. See, I'm in a training phase, like my Papa said. It will take time to develop my abilities. So much work to transform myself back to a human with a normal head."

The stranger arched his eyebrows. "If you say so. That should be interesting. You are becoming quite a mystery to me more and more. How in hell are you going to do that?"

"I have abilities."

"And you are in the training phase?"

"Yes. For several months since January, when my parents were killed by STASI. I have been meditating and training my mind. My abilities are supposed to be fully strengthened on October 28, the day of my birth."

"Yikes! That's not far along. Not sure what to make of it. Perhaps hide myself? Are you becoming a witch?"

Senefreya laughed merrily. "Oh no, it's nothing like that, believe me. Although, it may have contributed to the paranoia of what you call "witches". Like everything else in this universe, there are good witches and bad witches. Take your pick."

"Well, then what are you?"

Senefreya sighed. "I'm not sure. It's a long story. Like I said, too complicated to explain now. One day, when we cross over to the American side and all goes well, I will tell you the long, complicated story, as best I can. You do need to keep an open mind, you know. It will probably upset you."

The stranger grinned. "Can't wait. After all I had just gone through, nothing really upsets me."

Senefreya laughed and extended her hand. "Deal."

"Deal."

Senefreya smiled. "Okay, so, for now, you have to trust me, okay, whenever something goes anomalous around us, around me. Please don't freak out. Just trust me. We will do this together. Like you said, quid pro quo. I already gave you my name. What's yours?"

"Lieutenant Commander Beauregard Faninus, U.S. Navy." The stranger kissed the back side of Senefreya's hand. "At your service, ma'am. You can call me "Beau"."

"Beau."

"Let me ask you again, how come your father doesn't have a last name? Like I said, nothing surprises me by now."

Senefreya laughed. "Okay. My father's ancestors don't use last names like humans do. They use the names of nature or places or affection following their first birth names. I'm actually Senefreya Ra-Azeris. Senefreya of the Sun God."

"More like the moon, if you ask me." Beau joked. "No offense. You have a dark, beautiful appearance you know with that beautiful dark hair that makes me think of moonlight."

Senefreya blushed softly. "Thank you. But, my Papa often called me Solnyushka."

"That's a pretty name. What does it mean?"

"My little sunshine."

"Very apt." Beau agreed. "I'm sorry you lost him."

"And my mother too." Senefreya's eyes saddened. "Both my parents died brutal deaths at the hands of the STASI. I found them when I arrived home one day."

"Oh damn." Beau remarked. "I am truly sorry. Why in the world would the STASI want to murder them?"

"They want me, my abilities." Senefreya stroked the necklace. "And this Merkabah, which I use to strengthen my powers."

"Yikes."

Senefreya shook her head. "Anyways, like I said before, I will tell you more later, when we have the time. Right now we must focus on getting to the American side and I just know what to do."

At that moment, the horses stopped, jerking the wagon wheels in a shudder. The driver turned around and looked down at the bedraggled couple seated behind him in the back of the wagon.

"Why are we stopping?" Senefreya turned to face the driver. "Bitte?"

The driver set down the reins. He jumped off the wagon to attend to the horses, patting them affectionately. "My horses. They tire now. So much happened down there. So much. There, there, there." He crooned softly. "We be going home soon. I must give them water."

"Bitte, driver." Senefreya pleaded. "We are running out of time. STASI know we escaped and will be following us."

The driver smiled at Senefreya and shook his head again. Fraulein still verrukte. May God shower her with his Grace. Patting the horse's flank, he turned to Senefreya, pointing at the field of blue waves of flowers nestled against the lush, verdant trees and brambly raspberry bushes, just a few feet beyond the wagon. One of the only places not touched by the fire and brimstones from the sky just a few hours ago. The trail leading to his village seemed to be a boundary, the right side, the beautiful forest miraculously untouched by the bombardment. Of course, the village, being on the path of the fireballs, the left side, is most likely gone. His family gone. His sad eyes followed the finger pointing towards the forest.

"Fraulein Senefreya, geh dorthin, past the cornflowers just there ahead into the forest. You will find a small footpath. Follow it and that will take you and your companion to the Devil's Bridge, which is what you want, no?"

"Vielen Danke! Mein fruendin! Danke!" Senefreya jumped off the wagon happily. "Come, Beau, we must be off. Before more STASI arrives."

"Gladly!" Beau crawled towards the edge of the wagon, allowing Senefreya to help him stand on the ground. He winced, bending his badly, bruised knee slightly. "Damn knee. I hope it's not too much trouble for you."

"Not at all." Senefreya reassured him. "You will soon get better, I promise. We must hurry towards the Devil's Bridge. We must go that way."

She turned to the driver. "You do not happen to have a bit of vodka? Whiskey?"

The driver shook his head.

"Aloe, garlic, basil? Honey?"

The driver lighted up nodding his head. "Yah, Fraulein, I be have honey for you. Be in that bag up there. Bought it for my wife. Take it." He eyes saddened. He clasped his hands in prayer. "Oh, my family. What becomes of them in all this?" He eyes looked at the destruction on the left side of the boundary. "The village is surely gone."

Ignoring him, Senefreya scrambled up the driver's seat and ruffled inside the heavy, sand-colored, canvas, potato bag, the edges already ripping apart.

"Here it is!" She exclaimed pulling out a bottle of thick golden liquid. "Perfect." She placed the bottle of honey inside her backpack bag.

Senefreya jumped down and walked towards the driver, still chanting in prayer for his family, hoping they are still alive and well. She hugged him tightly.

"Vielen Danke, mein freundin! Do not worry about your family. Your house is gone, true, the village too, but your family has gone to that cave you showed them, the cave between the rocks, where they need to go when bad things happen. There they are waiting for you. Your wife, son, and daughter. Go now! To the cave between the rocks."

A glimmer of hope appeared in the driver's eyes. He flashed his teeth grubby with brown stains and bad breath. He hugged Senefreya with vigor, shaking her body off the ground with glee. "Truly, Fraulein? Oh, I must go now, oh yes! Oh yes, I know that cave. My family waits in that cave. Danke, Fraulein. Danke! Oh, I must hurry!"

"Geh!" Senefreya waved. The driver picked up the reins and urged the horses to move.

Chapter 16

The wagon now gone from her sight over the horizon, Senefreya adjusted her backpack, turned, and walked towards Beau, sitting on a stone boulder not far from her, nursing his knee with his hand. "You made the guy happy. I was wondering what was going on."

Senefreya lifted him from the stone boulder. "It was the least I could do to tell him his family was alive and safe and waiting for him. Believe me, he was so brave to take me on, considering how I look. You even called me a witch."

Beau winced.

"Come, Beau. We must go now. To the bridge. We got to wash your knee at the river. Put your arm around my shoulder. Try to walk."

Beau struggled to lift himself from the stone boulder. He groaned with pain. "God, I feel awful, being this heavy burden on you."

"Nonsense. We are not far from the river, where the bridge is. But, we must hurry, please. I am afraid of the STASI. They are relentless. They are after me."

"And now after me, also. So, lead the way! To the bridge!" Beau jumped up and skipped each step forward, as Senefreya hung on to him.

The couple quickly moved towards the wispy waves of light-blue cornflowers a few feet ahead. Soon, the bright blue and green meadow converged into the ominously dark forest thick with trunks of trees. Once inside the forest, the couple found themselves surrounded by multitudes of thick, gray brown branches sprouting thicker leaves of orange, gold, brown, and red. Walking a bit further on, the couple soon found themselves enveloped by the soft ambience of sunlight and shadows, breaking through gaps in the branches, the wispy, warm light dancing all around them, hushing them with awe and splendor. Norway spruce, beech, pine, and oak trees abounded everywhere, embracing them in the solitude and safety of their abundantly leafy arms.

Steadfastly holding on to each other, the couple trod slowly forward, searching for that elusive trail somewhere on the darkened, graveled earth in front of them. At times, the couple found themselves entertained, when the silence was broken by the soft chittering of insects and the lilting songs of the nightingales among the fairytale woodland.

"Wow. This is nice." Beau remarked, gazing at the beauty of the woodland around them. "I hope we are not lost."

"There!" Senefreya cried out, pointing at a muddy footprint-marked trail several feet ahead of them. A ray of sunlight was shining over it, as if by order of the gods. The long-sought trail was riddled with hardened footprints of long-trod shoes and naked feet, old and new, over the passage of time, since the Devil's Bridge was built in 1860.

"See over there where the earth is broken apart by all those footprints. That must be the footpath the driver was talking about. So many people have trod here for decades, I imagine, to get to that bridge."

"Must be a popular bridge." Beau agreed, his mouth in grim determination, as he limped in line with Senefreya's walk. "If they want so badly to see it."

"Oh, yes, indeed." Senefreya agreed. "It is quite unique, that bridge. Everyone who finds out about that bridge wants to see it. Especially now, after the bloom of summer has passed in these parts. Oh, yes, you will know why when you see it. Come. A little bit further now."

"Alright." Beau pushed himself further, his feet now trudging over the dry earthen soil of embedded footprints and shoeprints. "So, how did you know about that bridge? Just curious."

"Papa took me there one time, silly. On one of those days he dared to venture outside." Senefreya explained, pushing herself ahead on the footpath. "It was a birthday picnic with Papa, Mamoshka, and me, when

I was a little girl. At this time like now. When summer has passed, just after the fall equinox, when leaves start to change. And then also, the Devil's Bridge is so, so beautiful at sunset at this time of changing leaves."

"You have certainly piqued my curiosity about that bridge." Beau remarked with a grin. "Hopefully that bridge still stands. I am anxious to cross over into the American side. I'm not going to feel safe until I do."

"Me too, Beau. Me, too. Only way to find out."

Suddenly, the earth trembled below them, forcing their bodies to jerk off-balance. Senefreya and Beau hung on to each other mightily, waiting for the tremor to pass.

"Oh my god. Another fireball hit." Senefreya cried. "I thought it was over?"

"Must be a second wave now." Beau pushed himself further. "Asteroids do that. We really need to get to that bridge."

In a second, after the earth stopped shaking, the couple suddenly broke out from the trail and stepped into the outdoors, their feet now trod upon the embankment of sand and pebbles in front of them.

"Wow..." Beau exclaimed softly, his eyes settling upon the mysterious bridge. "Just wow..." He stepped forward out in the open, heading towards the river, pulling Senefreya with him.

"No!" Senefreya hushed, pushing him back into the darkness of the trees and bramble bushes. "See, there's a military guard by that entrance. We mustn't be seen."

Hidden behind the brambles, Beau exclaimed softly, admiring the half-circle design of the stones making up the bridge. "Just wow...they did that in the 1800s? Looks impossible at that time. What did they do?"

"I honestly don't know. It's their secret." Senefreya sighed with joy admiring her favorite place for birthday picnics, the only time Papa agreed to venture out. "We are lucky to see it now, just past the bloom of summer".

"Indeed. And look, it's still standing. Yes!"

"Indeed." Senefreya surveyed the bridge. "It appears that the destruction is all at the other side of the trail to Kromlau, unfortunately. Those poor people."

The couple stood for several moments in silence, gazing with awe and wonder at the miraculous testimonial of human ingenuity in front of them from long ago in the 1800s. Still standing. Still powerful. As if the powers that be had shielded it from the wrath of nature in the form of the fire and brimstone from the skies.

Still standing.

Spanning 115 feet in length in a semi-circular arrangement of large, grey boulders and basalt quarried from the East German side, the bell curve, stone path crossing the Irina Lake towards the American side, the 150-year old bridge stood as a testament to a time long past, its builders long gone.

Outside the arch bridge, the stone walls at each side were thickly adorned with bursts of royal purple creeping Rock Cress flowers, mandarin hummingbird petals, and white and blue hydrangeas. Days of rain during the summer had filled up this small neck of the Irina River, becoming a sparkling, reflective mirror, in which the identical reflection of the flower-draped bridge continued into an endless circle of stones and flowers.

Above the bridge all around, the umbrella of red, green, and gold leaves from thick branches of the surrounding forest added to the amazing spectacle of the October fall tableau.

"Just wow…" Beau shook his head. "Can't believe I never heard of this place. This bridge."

"And now you have." Senefreya smiled. She pointed at the unique standing group of stones. "See those tall stone spires at each end. That's man-made, too. Friedrich Hermann insisted on adding the spires, so it looks like rock outcroppings and the bridge would look more natural, as if Mother Nature herself built it."

"I still wonder how they did all that work, the Knights Templar. It can't have been easy in the 1800s".

"Well, like I said before, the local legend maintains that it was built with the help of Satan, hence the name, Devil's Bridge."

"Yeah, and do you believe it."

Senefreya shrugged. "Not really. But the builders knew a secret, only I know passed on to me by my Papa."

"Seriously? So, what's the secret?" Beau urged. "I am dying to know."

"You'll laugh."

"I won't." Beau promised. "Cross my heart."

"It's possible, one of my ancestors found his way here, like my Papa. Perhaps the knight, Friedrich Hermann, bumped into this ancestor of mine and sheltered him. And so, perhaps a collaboration happened and he commissioned the bridge. The Knights Templars were only an afterthought. Perhaps to assist my ancestor."

"I really don't follow." Beau insisted, confusion reigned in his eyes.

Senefreya's eyes glinted with the secrets hidden behind them. "See, my ancestors, as my Papa tells me are from a different time and a different world. They were so advanced in science and technology that anything is possible with them. Only they would know how to build that bridge, not the local townspeople."

Beau thought for a moment and grinned. "No wonder."

"No wonder what?"

"No wonder the townspeople called it Satan's Bridge. The technology you speak of was too advanced for them to wrap their heads around it. It seemed a right place, but the wrong time."

Senefreya laughed. "Of course! That's funny." She grabbed his hand. "Look, there, the sun is going down."

Beau nodded quietly. Standing side by side so still and quiet, Senefreya and Beau watched the sun slowly blossom into soft hues of gold and red and purple and yellow painting the sky beyond the horizon, embracing the flower-draped bridge in its bosom of kaleidoscopic colors.

Senefreya looked into his eyes and smiled. She suddenly mustered her courage and dipped her head on his shoulder. Beau did not protest. Something about this strange, beautiful, eloquent woman stirred deep feelings inside him. Feelings no other woman had been able to illicit and, all of a sudden, he understood why.

He had met his match. With a smile of satisfaction, Beau bent his head against hers, the both of them enjoying the last painted streaks of sunset.

Hoping against hope, Senefreya impulsively reached out for his hand and clasped it softly. Again, Beau did not protest. Feeling contented, Senefreya wondered if he was the one. The sign from her recitation under the supermoon weeks ago.

Her one true love.

Time stood still, as the couple watched the waning sun slowly disappear beneath the far, distant line of the horizon.

And then, in an instant, the charcoal-dust of twilight streamed over the dimming red-gold hues. A sudden chill wafted through the air enveloping their bodies. Shivering with the cold, Senefreya let go of Beau's hand and blew into her hands, rubbing the palms. She rubbed her arms as more of the cold air and dark shadowy hues arrived to announce the beginning of nightfall.

"It's getting dark now, Beau. Look the stars are coming out." She pointed at the small scattering of tiny, twinkling lights, a comforting blessing after hours of enduring the cataclysm behind them.

"Yep, they are coming out. Pretty." Bo agreed, mightily shaking off the intense feelings of desire she had sparked inside of him. He wanted to kiss her badly. But, now was not the time. He didn't want to frighten her. She had enough on her plate right now, including his bruised knee.

"How do you propose we get to the American side? Is that bridge safe to walk on? In the dark?"

Senefreya shook her head. "No. Like I said before, there should be a lone guard at the entrance just over that side. It's been that way, since the Berlin Wall went up. Probably survived the fireballs like everything else here. I was going to suggest we swim under the bridge, when it gets really dark. It's just under the steps leading to the bridge itself."

"You're kidding me? It's damn cold now." Beau narrowed his eyes, as he once again surveyed the bridge and the River Irina, now fully swollen from the impact of the cataclysm, the water itself rushing furiously downwards toward the verdant, shrubbery surrounding the man-made rocky outcroppings. "I'm not relishing the thought of getting in that cold water. I'm not sure I can properly swim in that cascade of water with my lame leg, but hey, I'm not Navy, if not dogged like a SEAL. I only wish I had some weapon with me." He let out a determined breath, his mind working hard to find a solution. "All right. Let's do it your way first, Senefreya. Let's see if that damn guard is still there."

"Good. Stay here. I'm going to take a closer look up there myself first."

"Damn leg."

"Hush. You'll only make things worse."

"Sorry." Beau responded in a whisper. "I hate being helpless". He leaned against a large, stone boulder and let out a frustrated sigh. "Go ahead, but be careful. He's got a weapon."

Senefreya grinned. "Yup. So do I."

Beau grinned back. "I keep forgetting. But, hey, just be careful there. You told me you're not fully strengthened with your powers until your birthday."

"I can always try, you know. Sometimes, it works!"

"Let's try stay alive, huh?"

Senefreya grinned. "Watch me."

Standing still with her eyes closed and her hands open, Senefreya murmured the chants of the ancient ones that she had studied and memorized during her lonely months in her apartment before the cataclysm.

Beau watched, sitting still and mesmerized by her striking presence at creating cryptic commands in the air, standing like Hecate, goddess of the night, centered in a pentagram of fire. It only served to increase his nascent longing to make love to her, the only woman who managed to find her way into his heart with her strange, but beguiling looks and personality.

Seconds passed. The chants finally ceased and with a wave of her hand towards Beau, Senefreya stealthily moved towards the bridge, turning invisible.

Chapter 17

"HALT! Who goes there?" The sentry guard appeared from the edge of the trail, where the earthen soil became the gravelly stones and pebbles lining the way to the bridge. A light shone from a flashlight. His other hand gripped the AK bayonet rifle.

Distracted by the light from the flashlight, Beau scrambled towards the brambles and boulders, his eyes searching for Senefreya, desperately wanting to warn her about the bridge sentry guard approaching with the flashlight and bayonet rifle. The light reached where she would have stood by herself, her arms raised, chanting in the dark air, and then later walking towards the bridge. Except she was not there.

She was gone. Into the air. There was nothing there where should have been.

"Agh!!!" A yell rang out.

The sentry guard fell over in an instant all by himself, the AK bayonet rifle knocked to the ground, apparently pushed away, but by what? Something had pushed him. And pushed him. And pushed him, until he fell to the ground. Fear had now gripped the guard, unable to see what was there pushing him around, throwing him to the ground. Casting the flashlight away, he picked up the bayonet rifle and started gunning the attached sword all around him, making sure to cover all bases, including the lame intruder hiding behind a boulder.

Bo ducked, waiting for the moment to escape. The spray of bullets seemed to go on forever, the sentry guard still gunning his bayonet rifle all around him, hoping to hit the unknown and unseen terror that had pushed him down. He swore an oath to prevent anyone from crossing that bridge at all costs. No one was allowed to walk to the American side, not even from the Devil's Bridge.

And then the AK rifle started to falter, the bullets becoming nearly spent. The guard threw the rifle away, standing on guard, searching all around him. Suddenly, something unseen kicked the rifle away on the ground, terrifying the guard. The guard quickly sprinted to the rifle. It was still something he could use to hit the unknown assailant. But it was no use. Again and again, the rifle was kicked away, this time lost into the shrubbery. The guard panicked, searching for that rifle.

Beau narrowed his eyes at the scene, a thousand thoughts running through his mind on Senefreya's unknown whereabouts. But first, the moment had come, never mind his lame leg.

It was now or never.

Running from behind the boulder, grimacing at the pain digging into his leg, Beau lunged at the sentry guard, hastily removed the helmet, and gave him several strong punches to the head, finally rendering him unconscious.

Gasping with his breaths, his legs splayed against the still body of the guard, Beau heaved himself up and took a good look at the guard. He shook his head. It was a young man, too young, still a teenager, all on his own guarding the Devil's Bridge.

"Beau?"

He turned around.

Senefreya was now fully formed and solid, her hands gripping the AK bayonet rifle. She was grinning at him.

"So, that was you, huh, the almighty weapon?" Bo asked, flashing his teeth in a grin. "Pushing him around and kicking that AK here and there, you were damn hard to locate!"

Senefreya laughed. "Pretty good, huh?"

"You are something." Beau shook his head, searching the body for the additional bullets. "Let me have that AK. We need to fill it up with the rest of the bullets." Beau deftly removed the belt of bullets from around the chest of the still body of the unconscious, young guard. He waited. No movement from the guard.

"Is he awake?" Senefreya glanced at the body. The guard was still breathing softly.

"No. Not likely for a while. Let's leave him be. I'm not interested in killing him." Beau readied the AK bayonet rifle and slung it over his shoulder. "Come on. Let's cross the bridge."

"Wait! We do have a small problem." Senefreya objected. "We're still far from the American side. It will not be easy to get there from here and the bridge."

"Oh, great!" Beau groaned. "Now you tell me." He limped towards the boulder and slowly sat on it, wincing from the pain on his leg. "What do you propose we do? I hope you know the layout around here. I don't."

Senefreya smiled ruefully. "I'm so sorry, Beau. Truly. For myself, it was the only solution to get away from the STASI up north amidst the conflagration. It had been a split decision on my part. You just happened to show up on the way."

"Right. I did do that." Beau agreed. "Can't blame you a bit. It seemed a good idea at that time, yeah." He scratched his head in frustration. "Any ideas on how to get to the American side?"

"I do." Senefreya suggested, crossing her arms. "But it would require your effort and my powers."

"Huh? How?"

Senefreya opened her arms wide. "Remember when you couldn't see me a while back. You lost sight of me, just before that fight with the guard."

"Yeah, yeah, I did." Beau remarked. "How did you do that? Just up and become invisible?"

"Exactly!" Senefreya declared. "Like Papa said many times, it's in my DNA. I became invisible and that will be our solution! You only have to hold my hand and my powers will cover you, too, through my hand. You will be invisible, also!"

"And, just like that, we both surreptitiously hike through the countryside to the American side." Beau looked up in glee. "That is genius, Senefreya. Genius. Come on. What are we waiting for?"

Senefreya shook her head slightly. "There is another small problem." She pinched her two fingers.

"Again? What?"

"I won't be able to hold that power of invisibility long. A few hours are the most I can hold for the both of us. Until my birthday, October 28, several days away, when my abilities become fully activated in my body. A DNA process of transformation, you know, but only on the day of my birth at age 21."

"Oh, boy, can't wait for your birthday." Beau sighed grimly. "Well, it's the best we got for now. It's better than nothing. We can still walk invisible at nighttime together; the less to bump into STASI and anyone else affiliated with them."

"That was my intention." Senefreya agreed. "Plus, some of the fireballs may have hit certain areas out there. Less focus on us. But, be forewarned, people will be all over the place trying to save their skins, including the STASI and soldiers."

"That's true." Beau sighed for a moment. "Regardless, let's do this. How long to the nearest border?"

"Ten days." Senefreya calculated in her mind. "We can sleep in hiding during the day and we can forage for fruit and berries and nuts along the way. Maybe steal a piece of bread, if we can, huh? I have some food left in my backpack."

Beau laughed. "Just picturing the STASI chasing after me for stealing bread. Like in Jean Valjean in Les Miserables."

"Les what?"

"Never mind, can we go now? It is getting dark already and the guard will certainly wake up soon."

"Totally agree!" Senefreya burst out. "But first, we need to clean that bruise on your knee. Then we will slather the honey on it."

"Honey?"

"It's an ancient healing remedy. A potent disinfectant."

"And it works?"

"I promise. Come, to the river."

Fifteen minutes later, Senefreya put the finishing touches on the bandage covering his bruised knee. "There. Feel better?"

"Indeed. You are a miracle worker."

"Hah, hah. Come on, let's move. We will follow the stars."

Beau smiled, readying himself with a thick branch for a cane. "After you!"

He wrapped one arm around Senefreya's right shoulder, his other hand holding onto her upraised hand. Senefreya wrapped her other arm around his waist.

In that moment, time stood still, as Senefreya closed her eyes and murmured the chants of the ancient ones from long ago. After several seconds, Beau looked down at his feet. They were already becoming invisible, fading into nothingness, and yet, he still felt invincible, solid, and fully himself. Soon, the rest of their bodies became invisible from the soles of their feet to the top of the heads. Looking at his feet again, Beau realized he could now see his feet enclosed in the shield of invisibility surrounding their bodies. Turning his head towards her, Beau could see Senefreya's sapphire-blue eyes, with the beguiling vertical slants, smiling at him. Her forehead was glistening from the effort of her chants.

He found himself falling ever more in love with her. What a woman.

"Let's go." Senefreya urged quietly. "Not a moment to waste. My invisibility powers can only last so long."

"Onwards." Beau agreed. "Onwards and forward to the bridge."

The couple moved slowly up the granite, stone steps leading to the rock spire outcroppings, just before they merged with the curved arch bridge. Beyond the stone-covered bridge, the rambling, dark forest beckoned with promise to envelope them into its protective umbrella of leaves and shrubs, while they were still in a parcel of land ruled with an iron fist by the Communist Soviets and East German Budwarei.

Up above, a lone meteor flew swiftly across the night sky, its tail of light gleaming behind it, heading towards the earth in their direction.

"Oh no, another fireball."

"Get down." Senefreya urged. "And pray it doesn't hit us."

The fireball sped past above them, its powerful blast of wind shaking their bodies.

"That was close. Let's move now." Senefreya urged. "I don't have long to hold this power."

By the time the sun was ready to peek above the horizon, the couple were already fatigued, bedraggled, and dirty from the two days journey since they crossed the Devil's Bridge. Hunger and thirst tested their patience.

Letting go of her powers, Senefreya's body slowly materialized in the glow of the morning sunshine, followed by Beau's body, his hands still holding hers. Bo grimaced with hunger pains, as he set his body down on the ground. He rubbed his leg. The honey seemed to do its trick after all. He glanced at Senefreya, shaking his head.

What a woman.

Watching him, Senefreya scolded loudly. "Don't do that, Beau. You will cause an infection. Let the honey do its work. God, I feel badly for you and that leg. I wish I could heal it. But I don't yet have that power. Not until…"

Beau smiled. "Your birthday, right. So, you can heal?"

"Yes, I should be able to. That's what my Papa said."

"So, your strange mix of powers converge that one special day…" Beau nodded in contemplation. "Oh, well. Can't do anything about it now." He groaned softly. "I hope I can make that nine days walk. Nine days, right?"

Senefreya did not respond, her eyes becoming glazed, her mind in deep thought, her breathing becoming soft and forced.

Beau became worried.

"Senefreya?"

No response.

Beau called out louder. "Senefreya? Are you there?"

Senefreya's eyes blinked, her mind quickly coming to the present.

"Shhhhh, be quiet!" She shook her head excitedly and grabbed his hand with both of hers. "Beau, there is another way. Oh, I so hope it works!" She clapped her hands with glee. "Oh, I just remembered what I can do!" Her arms reached out to the sky in gratitude! "Oh, thank you, Papa!"

Beau stared in confusion. "Huh, come again?"

Senefreya looked down at him. She grinned mischievously. "See, I may just be able to cut down the 10 days walk into 3 days, maybe one day! Oh, I hope it works!"

"You hope it works?"

"Yes, it may not work either. Not until…"

"Your birthday, again…Oh, boy. You are full of surprises."

"But we can try, right, Beau?" Senefreya cried out. "We can try. It just might work. I have to give it my all, I think."

"You think?"

"Come on. Let's try!" Senefreya reached out for Beau's hand. "Come on, what have we got to lose?"

"Our lives?"

"Don't be silly. It either works or not."

"Heh, only one way to find out." Beau reached out and nervously clasped Senefreya's hand, his eyes wide with anticipation and uncertainty.

"Now close your eyes."

Bo dutifully closed his eyes, finding Senefreya's grip becoming stronger and stronger, even painful, the flickering electricity from her hand flowing into his hands and strangely tickling him. Her grip was getting too painful.

He groaned softly.

"Now open your eyes."

He found himself in Senefreya's tight embrace and she was laughing mirthfully. "We did it, Beau! Oh, yes, we did it! Yes, I gave it my all! It worked!"

"Huh, what worked?" Beau nervously surveyed his surroundings. Nothing seemed to have changed so far. It was still all forest and brushes and brambles. But the oft-traveled muddied trail was no longer there.

"Huh, where are we?"

"Oh, no!" Senefreya grasped her stomach and stared beyond the trees at the small opening between two giant oak trees. All of a sudden, the sense of doom that had warned her about the coming cataclysm had returned to warn her yet again. "Not again."

Beau sighed miserably, watching her mood change abruptly. "Okay…so let me ask again. Where the hell are we?"

"Heh, we are still in East Germany." Senefreya pointed at the opening. "Something in there bothers me. All my senses tell me it's getting dangerous. Oh, god, and we are so close to the American side."

Beau touched Senefreya's shoulder.

"Senefreya, you have truly lost me…what is going on?"

"I have no idea, Beau. But this awful feeling I have, it is telling me that danger is lurking just beyond…"

Beau sighed, still confused. "Okay, let me take a look. You stay here."

"Be careful!"

Beau limped towards one of the two large, twin trunks with the gap between it. He quietly hid behind the trunk and scoped beyond the gap.

"Damn." He breathed softly. "That was fast."

Senefreya caught up with him. "What is it?"

"Looks like and airport. Do you know it? And how the hell did we get here so fast? It was supposed to be nine days. No, no, no, no, no need to explain. I think I got it all figured out by now."

"Good." Senefreya blurted out. "It's too complicated to explain."

"One day you are going to have to tell me just what you are capable of." Beau mused thoughtfully. "I can't keep up with your surprises."

"No problem." Senefreya nodded. "Except I seemed to have brought us here into another danger."

"Not again." Beau commented with a sigh. "What danger?"

"There is this one dreaded airport in all of East Germany in this sector. Oh, I can't believe I brought us here. It was not intentional. You must believe me."

"I do believe you, Senefreya. I have no choice but to take your word." Beau stared back at the opening with interest. "What's the airport's name?"

"Kamenz." Senefreya shuddered. "I am so sorry. It was not intentional."

Bo stared thoughtfully through the gap for some time, his eyes narrowing, as his mind worked rapidly with the information from his past experiences. From his training in the United States. The maps. The airports. The flights.

He turned towards Senefreya, a wide smile on his tired face. "Definitely intentional, Solnyushka, whether you like it or not. Once again, you found a way to cut the ten days walk to cross the border to the American side." He lifted Senefreya up in glee and danced in circles with her, ignoring the pain on his bandaged knee. "Yes, we did it! You are amazing, Solnyushka!"

"Put me down!" Senefreya laughed. "And please don't call me Solynushka. That's reserved for my Papa now gone."

"Okay. Okay." Beau apologized, putting her down.

"Thank you." Senefreya brushed her jeans and straightened her backpack. "Look, I don't get it. I just brought us to our certain deaths and I am amazing? These are elite East German kamikaze pilots in training and most certainly some STASI hidden among them. Have you lost your mind?!"

Beau laughed, stroking Senefreya's cheek. "Believe me, I am as sane as ever. Don't you see, I can fly! I can fly us to freedom!"

"Now, you have truly lost it." Senefreya laughed. "You don't have my powers. I'm not sure I can fly myself."

"No, no, no, that's right, I don't have your powers, but that's not what I meant." Bo declared and turned towards that yawning gap between the two trees, his mind deviously creating a plan. He turned back towards Senefreya. "But see, I can fly a plane and look!" He pointed at the airfield.

"So many planes. There are a few I know so well. How did you know that about me?"

Senefreya pushed him away. "I most certainly did not know that about you at all. It was pure luck."

Beau scratched his head, staring at her. "Well, somebody did, for sure. How else are we guided here in one fell swoop, cutting down ten days walk and here we are among the airplanes, where my expertise lies?"

Senefreya looked up towards the wide grid of branches and leaves above her, where the sky was slowly changing from pink and orange to the blue canvas of the dawning day. "Papa…was that you?"

"Senefreya?" Beau reached for her shoulders. "Are you ok?"

"Yes, yes, I'm okay." Senefreya stared into his eyes. "I think it was Papa's doing. He is helping us escape."

"How so?"

"Another long story." Senefreya took Beau's hand. "Come. It is almost daylight. We must wait until nightfall to enter that death trap. I hope you know what you are doing."

"I do. But hey, it doesn't have to be nightfall. We can do this now just by being invisible."

Senefreya eyes widened. "Of course! That would drive them crazy! But first, I have a nice surprise for us. Come." She offered her hand.

Beau relented and grasped Senefreya's hand, his body becoming invisible along with her. Together, unseen to the wider, solid world, they backtracked deeper back into the forest.

"It better be good." Beau responded. "I am damned tired. My leg hurts now."

"There!" Senefreya pointed.

All of a sudden, a pristine turquoise-blue lake appeared in front of them, several feet away, beckoning them to come into its waters. The small rays of sunshine coming down from the gaps among the treetops formed glints of stars shimmering on the water's clear, glassy surface.

Senefreya let go of Beau's hand. Her body first solidified into being, followed by Beau's body. The couple stood silently admiring the stunning view of the lake. Just beyond, a small, gushing waterfall splashed into the lake from an opening in the embankment.

Senefreya shrieked loudly, as she ran towards the beckoning lake. She was soon taking off her clothes, becoming completely and utterly nude.

"Oh man…" Beau groaned.

Once at the edge of the water, she let herself wade in with the gusto of a hungry child, ignoring the chill temperature, as befitted the month of October. His body transformed back to solid, Beau only stood still, shaking his head with admiration and love, as he watched her swim like a dolphin all around the perimeter of the small lake and disappearing behind the small waterfall.

"Come on! Time to wash ourselves!" Senefreya called out, waving her hand, as she swam towards the shore. "The water's great, just a little bit cold. But so clean! Come on, Beau!"

Unable to resist her invitation, Bo grinned and took off his clothes in place slowly, being unable to run like she had only a few seconds ago. Utterly nude and dirty himself, he mustered all his strength and limped toward the lake, where he slowly waded into the water all the way into the deep, where he finally joined her.

Senefreya laughed, swimming around him, splashing him with the water.

Beau laughed splashing water back at her. Soon, he went underwater and stayed there for a minute. Senefreya looked around, as she waited for him to come out. When he broke into the surface, he let out a great sigh of relief and happiness, feeling the water wash off the grime and frustration of the past apparently nine days of hiding from the STASI day and night.

Senefreya eagerly swam around him. "So…how are you now? Water good, huh?"

Beau laughed. "Yes, it is good. Feels good to clean up. Energizing."

Senefreya splashed at him again.

"Hey!" Beau splashed back. "What are you doing?"

"Having fun!"

"Not yet!" Beau called out.

"Oh no, you don't." Senefreya swam away as fast as she could.

Being the faster swimmer, Bo managed to catch up with Senefreya, his arm grabbing her waist under the water. Senefreya found herself wrapped up in his arms, her eyes locked into his. Her cheeks suddenly flushed with hot, warm feelings that slowly spread to the rest of her body. Beau placed his hand under her buttock in the water, bringing her body ever closer to his body, now hot with desire. Senefreya wrapped her arms and legs around him, enjoying the warm feeling of the two bodies joining in unison, his maleness firm and hot inside her. Beau slowly put his mouth into hers, softly pressing her lips, urging them to open. Senefreya yielded, opening her mouth with a passion, allowing his tongue to reach hers in deep longing, their bodies finally shattering in the depths of their burning love.

Seconds passed.

Their eyes opened. Their faces glowed with the passion of their lovemaking, their bodies feeling the invigorating cleanliness from the waters of the lake.

All was quiet around them in the high noon of the day. Above them, surrounded by the rays of the bright sun cutting through the dense treetops, the nightingales sang their haunting melodies among the trees, a testament to the couple's newfound love.

Chapter 18

One hour later.

"Okay, Beau, which plane?" Senefreya asked, peering around a large tree trunk through the gap of the two, giant trees. Kamez Airfield, the death trap, was just ahead of them, not too far to sprint through the grassy field adjoining the long runway. Beyond the runway, two uniformed sentry guards holding AK bayonet rifles were in slow, regular motions, pacing back and forth in front of the apron near the hangar and the way station.

Behind these two buildings were small, rectangular bunkers housing the sleeping local pilots enrolled in the infamous kamikaze flight training program of East Germany.

Senefreya shuddered at the ominous sight, deadly sight. "Are you sure you want to do this?"

Beau nodded vehemently, staring at his corner of the tree opposite Senefreya. "I've done this before. I told you. I'm a pilot. This is genius. We can do this, Senefreya. Look, it's only a hop and skip towards the American side with that plane." He pointed at a large, lone silver airplane sitting near the forest, seemingly abandoned. "I know that plane. Illyushin 11-12. The Russians gave it to the Germans, when they built the updated

Illyushin 11-14. This plane is great for cargo. Easy to maneuver. Let's hope it has fuel."

"How do you plan on getting in?" Senefreya whispered.

Right at that moment, a door opened at the far hangar beyond the two trees, directly in front of where Senefreya and Beau were hiding.

"Wait." Beau put a finger on his lips. "Let's see what's going on."

Senefreya nodded. "Okay."

As the couple watched from behind the trees, several East German guards walked out from the hangar, each two carrying large, wooden, pallet boxes, joined by the pilots from the adjoining sleeping bunkers. To their surprise, the guards and pilots were slowly approaching in their direction followed front and back by two sentry guards, all of them carrying the AK bayonet rifles.

"They're coming this way." Senefreya hissed. "I'm not feeling good about this. Ugh."

"Shhhh…" Beau commanded firmly. "Let's see what they are going to do. Likely more weapons in these boxes. I wonder why."

"Berlin just got hit by the fireballs, duh." Senefreya reminded him. "Maybe they need whatever is in those boxes."

"Perhaps. Not likely to accept help from anyone else outside the Iron Curtain."

"Except the almighty Soviet Union. Good luck with that."

"Precisely."

A moment passed.

"Look, there's our answer!" Beau whispered excitedly.

The couple watched with fervent hope and excitement, as the contingent of East German soldiers and pilots and sentry guards approached the Illyushin 11-12, not realizing Senefreya and Bo were only 50 feet away hidden behind the two giant trees.

"They're loading the boxes in that plane. Our plane!" Bo declared with optimism.

"Now what?" Senefreya asked. "How do we get in there?"

Beau offered his hand to Senefreya. "We become invisible, darling Senefreya, and hijack that plane. It's that simple. These scumbags are not going to know what hit them."

Senefreya laughed and grabbed his hand. "Let's do it, my love! We must hurry. I can only hold this power so long. I have spent too much of my energy last time."

Beau nodded firmly. "Let's do it."

"And don't leave my hand."

Senefreya closed her eyes and chanted an ancient mantra for a few seconds. Together they faded slowly into the nothingness of air. The invisible couple ran towards the plane.

In five minutes, chaotic pandemonium ensued all around the plane. Both Senefreya and Bo pushed away the guards and pilots loading the pallet boxes into the door near the tail end of the plane. Bayonet rifles were knocked off the sentry guards, one by one, and kicked away repeatedly, frightening them to dash away from the plane, yelling in fear.

At last, the couple reached the open door of the plane and shut it abruptly, as if only the wind shut door by itself. The dazed guards and pilots were looking all around themselves on the ground for the perpetrators, unable to see anything that caused them to fall down and let go of the boxes, splattering the contents all over. What worse was the door of the plane shut all by itself in a sudden motion.

"Mein gott! What is going on?" The leader of the group yelled.

Soon the propellers rumbled in circular motion on each end of the wing and slowly the plane moved, turning slightly, and heading towards the long runway.

"Move!" The leader of the contingent ordered loudly. "Kill those bastards commandeering the plane! Kill them!"

"But Mein Capitan!" A soldier whined plaintively. "There is nobody at the cockpit! Look!" He pointed at the cockpit window. No one was visible in there at all. It was empty and void, and yet, the plane was moving in an intelligent manner. "The plane is alive!!!"

"Yaaaaaagggggghhhhh!!!" All the men stared at the plane slowly moving on its own, slowly increasing in speed.

"Mein Gott, it is possessed!!" The leader wailed. "Mein gott!"

"It's the Drudes!!! We are cursed by the Drudes!!!

In an instant, as the plane stopped by the starting line of the runway to prepare for the takeoff. All the men, by now enveloped in fright and confusion, stared in awe at the propellers, which still continued to move at the stop. Soon, they could hear the rumble of the jet engines becoming louder and louder, the propellers moving ever faster and faster.

Soon, the Illyushin 11-12 sped forward in faster and faster velocity down the runway, its wheels lifting up into its underside, its wings elevating towards the heavens.

And soon it was gone.

"Run for your lives!!!!!" Hastily leaving their scattered boxes and weapons on the ground, the guards and pilots dashed desperately towards the buildings beyond the apron.

"Hahaha, idiots!" Beau exclaimed with a grin, watching them run like scared rabbits from his cockpit window. He turned towards Senefreya and winked.

"We did it, darling!"

Sitting in the captain's chair on the left side of the cockpit, Beau was held tightly by the seatbelt strapped over him, as he checked the cockpit instruments to ascertain the altitude, attitude, and speed of the plane.

Senefreya, in the co-pilot's seat on his right, watched him work deftly on the instruments with astonishment and awe. She had let go of his hand the minute the plane lifted into the air and banked towards the left for the American side. They soon reached 20,000 feet in the air and settled down, their bodies fully solidified and held in their seats by the seatbelts. After flipping one last switch above him, Beau settled back on his seat and sighed with relief, his eyes locked lovingly with Senefreya. They both smiled.

They were on their way to freedom.

Chapter 19

Six hours later.

The table had been set for two, a sumptuous meal of German potato salad, sauerkraut, and bratwurst. The soft, red-gold light of the candle flame twinkled at the center of the table, held in place by a small glass candleholder shaped in the form of a swan. Two wine glasses stood at each end of the table. A bottle of Chateau Lafitte added the finishing touches of the beautiful table and meal arrangement.

Beau picked up his wine glass.

"Cheers, my darling, cheers!" He exclaimed with a beaming smile. "We are now safe and sound here in the American side. West Germany. Never thought I'd get here, finally. What a relief."

"Indeed, my love, as also am I feeling relief. It had been too terrifying a journey for words!" Senefreya responded, holding up her wine glass. "I am so indebted to you for flying us here. I really had no idea how to bring us over in the end. I was stuck, totally stuck. And you came through, my darling. Thank you!"

"You are welcome, darling. Like you said, your Papa somehow up there knew about me and somehow nudged you to bring us there at that airport."

Senefreya nodded thoughtfully. "Yes, I really think that Papa knew. It all worked out beautifully."

"So…here's to a brand new life. I can't for you to see America, my homeland!" Beau and Senefreya clicked their glasses once again, sipped their wine, and carefully placed their glasses on the table. They began their hearty meal with gusto, having been hungry far too long.

Several seconds later, Senefreya looked up at Beau. "Darling. Tell me. How did you come to be with the East Germans, unless of course, you do not wish to divulge?"

Beau laughed heartily. "No, no. I'm happy to tell my story. You see. I was near Potsdam at an American air force base there. A friend, who is an Air Force pilot, invited me there. I managed to wrangle a plane from the base to fly around West Berlin."

"And…"

"Hah…something showed up in the sky. A circular disk or some sort. It had a smooth cover, almost silver with lights flashing around the center in regular rhythms, and a dome at the top. Very unusual. And it moved so quietly. I searched for any kind of propulsion around that disk, but there wasn't anything. And yet it moved."

He poured more wine into their glasses. "Oh, I was fascinated. It moved so fast this way and that, without even turning around. Even our most powerful planes could not do that. I was determined to find out who these pilots were. Where that disk came from."

He lifted his wine glass for a sip. "So, I followed that disk. It seemed to be playing with me, as if dangling a carrot in front of me, daring me to follow it. It flew slowly, of course, but oh, so quietly, while my plane with its propellers was beyond noisy." He shook his head. "It wanted me to follow it. Like an idiot, I did just that."

"What happened?" Senefreya asked in fascination. She sipped her wine glass.

"All of a sudden, the disk disappeared, as fast as it appeared back there in West Berlin and my plane was hit by shrapnels from some sort of missiles exploded upwards from the ground." He gulped the wine to its last drop.

"Of course, I managed to eject myself, but I had no idea where I was landing, until I dropped down on the earth, the parachute fluttering behind me and all of a sudden, I was surrounded by STASI."

"Oh, no…." Senefreya eyes became wide. "That's awful. STASI are terrible people."

"Yeah, totally agreed. It's been a year of jail, almost had to do hard labor, but the East Germans deemed me too valuable with intel, so they kept me around, instead of shipping me off to the Russian labor camp."

"You got lucky, huh?" Senefreya smiled softly.

Beau laughed. "Yeah, I got lucky, phew. Lots of waterboarding and other torture, though. It's like being between a rock and a hard place."

Senefreya nodded. "I'm sorry…truly…"

"Yeah." Beau nodded. "It's been like that for a year. I wasn't really sure I would get out and I have been beating myself up for stupidly following that disk, not realizing I was crossing the no man's land into East Berlin."

Senefreya smiled empathetically. "So…you were about to be traded with someone else at the Glienicke Bridge? The one that fireballs destroyed?"

"Some timing, huh?" Beau shook his head. "I was about to be traded for that Russian spy, Oleg Zinobayevich. I heard the Russians wanted him back badly and I was the only solution. The Americans wanted me back badly, too." He grinned. "Of course, the East Germans had no say in this."

"Of course." Senefreya laughed. "You got lucky you found me. Or rather I found you. Or we found each other?"

Beau laughed. "Your Papa was smart to do that, bring us together. Look at us now." He finished off his meal and put the fork back in its place.

"Although, I would love to know where that mysterious disk came from. It has dogged me, ever since I was in that jail."

Senefreya looked at him thoughtfully for a moment, placing down her knife and fork. "Beau, I might know the answer, but it has to be between us. It is too dangerous, the information. It cannot fall in the wrong hands."

Beau stared at Senefreya. "You are full of surprises, my darling. My lips are sealed. Do tell me."

"Okay." Senefreya took in a deep breath. "When I was a little girl, Papa would sit me on his lap and tell me stories of the ancient ones, from where he came…"

"From where he came?"

"Something happened at his homeland long, long ago and he ended up in the future here. It's a whole another story and is complicated. Another time, maybe?"

"Sure." Beau agreed, wiping his mouth with a napkin. "Lots of complicated stories, so far, boy. We have plenty of time, though. So…tell me about that disk."

"See, in his time long, long ago, there was flight everywhere in the skies. Everywhere. And they all looked like smooth, silvery disks. His people called them discoidals. They are so fast and can cut corners and move back and forth without even turning around. Very powerful flying machines. I believe your people call them UFOs?"

"Yes, you would be right. UFOs." Beau smiled. "That's it. I saw a UFO. So…how did it end up here in that sky above West Berlin, of all places? It just came out of nowhere and disappeared just as fast into nothingness."

He shook his head in wonder. "That is a wunderwaffe of sorts, right?"

Senefreya laughed. "Yes, a wonder weapon. Except the Germans did not create it. Papa's people did long, long ago." She took in another breath. "Not a word of this to anyone, darling, bitte?"

"My lips are sealed, darling." Bo responded. "Go on. I'm dying to know."

"Okay…when I was sitting on Papa's lap, one day….he spoke about this phenomenon his people from long ago studied and somehow managed to leverage it for their purposes. Including flying their discoidals in and out at will. From your perspective, it looks like they appeared and disappeared, but actually, the discoidals are entering another dimension, a form of time and space dimension, a wormhole, perhaps, as your scientists call them?"

"Wow…" Beau whistled, stunned at the revelation. "That is powerful! They could win wars that way, huh?"

"Nonsense. They are a peaceful race, my Papa's people. But, yes, they were powerful in so many ways."

Beau looked at Senefreya thoughtfully. "And your Papa was a pilot on one of the discoidals?"

Senefreya nodded proudly. "Yes, he was. There were several discoidals at that time long ago. Some were in Atlantis. The others were in Egypt, where Papa was born. Then one day, his mother, Queen Nerilka, my ancient grandmother, assigned him as ambassador to Atlantis and my Papa piloted a discoidal towards the island."

"Go on."

"Well, Papa had said that something happened in Atlantis that created a time portal just as he was arriving towards the island. The discoidal was sucked into that time portal and Papa ended up in a time warp. His discoidal crashed in the Harz Mountains near Berlin."

"Who found him?"

"My mother. Mamoshka. She was hiking by herself and found him barely conscious. She brought him home with her to Berlin making pretend he was a long, lost cousin she found in the woods. She covered his elongated head with a scarf." Senefreya sighed. "The thing is, the discoidal was so damaged, Papa had no way to return to where he came from. He just left it there."

"A stranger in a strange land, huh?" Beau remarked sympathetically. "What happened next?"

"Papa and Mamoshka. They fell in love with each other and got married. Papa managed to find a way to transform his look with his powers, so he looked more like us without that long head. Anyways, they had a baby, me, and we all had a great life together until now." A tear appeared at the corner of her eye and fell down her cheek. "I miss my parents, Beau, dreadfully. They were all I had."

"Come here." Beau wiped the tear from her cheek. "I'm sorry, truly. But you are not alone, darling. You have me now and I promise to watch out for you and your powers. See, you saved my life and it falls upon me to take care of you."

"Don't be silly. You don't have to do that." Senefreya brushed her hand. "I can take care of myself."

"Oh, but you do need me. You have no idea how people will react with your powers and that elongated head covered with beautiful, black hair. At least, let me help until you know your way around, okay? I have never met anyone as beautiful and beguiling as you. I love you, Senefreya."

Senefreya smiled, snuggled in his arms. "I love you, too."

He picked up his wine glass. "So…you and I…we are off to a grand adventure in America!"

"Yes, we are." Senefreya lifted her glass. "Cheers, my darling."

Their glasses clicked. The telephone rang.

Beau put down his wine glass. He looked at Senefreya with a question. She shook her head. "I don't have anyone in my life to make that call. No one is going to miss me."

Beau nodded and stroked her cheek.

"Be right back, darling."

"Of course." She watched him walk towards the side table and pick up the telephone.

A few minutes later, Beau placed the receiver back on its cradle. He paused for moment.

"What is it, darling? Senefreya frowned. She had been watching her lover talk excitedly over the telephone and now the curiosity had overcome her.

"All good, my darling!" Beau offered his hands to Senefreya. She reached out to grip them. He pulled her against him tightly, kissing her with a passion.

Senefreya smiled. "My, what was that?"

"You are not going to believe this, darling, but that was my old friend, Gregory Myles, from my flight training days. He is now a test pilot and guess where he is?"

"I have no idea…"

"Paris! He is there in Paris at the Annual Paris Air Show! I have not seen him for years! And guess what?"

"I'm dying to know…." Senefreya laughed. "What?"

"He invited me to join him at the Air Show tomorrow. He is going to return America's beautiful new aeroplane, the Boeing 747, aka the

"Queen of the Skies", after the show. And I'm to be his co-pilot!" He picked up Senefreya and twirled her around. "You should see that new plane, darling! Magnificent!"

"How wonderful, my love." Senefreya laughed. "What does the aeroplane look like?"

"I'll show you a picture." He set Senefreya down and picked up the newspaper on the couch. "There is nothing like this aeroplane nowadays. Nothing."

Senefreya looked at the photo on the front page of the newspaper. "She's huge! And look at the smaller airplane next to it. So small. So different. Why is that?"

"It's the Concorde, darling. The British and French built it and wanted to show it off. It's supposed to fly at twice the speed of sound. That's why it's built like so. Aerodynamics they call it."

Senefreya nodded. "Twice the speed of sound. That's fast. Look, aren't they cute, next to each other? Like big and little brothers."

Beau smiled and hugged Senefreya. He kissed the top of her head. "How about we get married here at the embassy. It will be easier to get you in the United States as my wife."

Senefreya gently put her hand on her mid-section. A new life for the two of them and a child on its way. Except she wasn't sure how he would take the news of her pregnancy. Still he needed to know."

"Beau…" Senefreya started to speak.

Beau put his finger on her lips, shushing her and hugging her once more. He rifled through his pant pocket and picked up a ring.

Senefreya gasped. He went down on his knees and held her hands.

"Senefreya, darling. We had gone through so much and you have saved my life numerous times. You are an amazing woman and I'm not about to let go of you, now that we are safe and free. I want to spend the rest of my life with you." He paused hesitantly. "Will you be my wife?"

Tears spilled down onto her cheeks. He truly loved her and wanted to take care of her. Now it seemed so right tell him the news.

"Why are you crying?"

"Oh, my love. It's tears of joy." Senefreya smiled nodding her head with excitement. "Yes, I will be your wife. I think you are amazing yourself. Putting up with me. You know I'm not normal as you've seen already."

"No matter, darling." Beau stood up and put the ring in her finger. "I love you with all my heart and that's what matters come hell or high water."

Her eyes wide open and laughing. Senefreya's eyes gleamed at hearing those beautiful words from his mouth to her ears. She hugged him tightly. "I love you too! And guess what, I have news for you. We are expecting a child, my love. I hope it is not a burden for you. I do want the child."

Stunned at the revelation, Beau laughed. "Burden? What burden? Why, this is wonderful news, Senefreya darling! Absolutely wonderful! It's my child too! Oh, hah, hah, hah, I'm going to be a DAD, wow! Look at me already thinking lots of things to teach him or her."

He lifted Senefreya in the air joyfully and twirled her around twice. Then placed her on the floor, holding her tight to his heart. After all they had gone through in the past few terrible hours, so much has showered them with luck and love in this moment. Now a baby is on its way and life is good. Yes, life is good.

"Come, let's take our wine glasses and head to the balcony."

The couple stood outside in the chill of the evening. The sky was midnight black and black shadows of clouds passed by, pushed on by the October winds. One cloud revealed a jewel.

"Look!" Beau pointed. "A blood moon!"

"Indeed, it is." Senefreya murmured. "So pretty." She laid her head against his shoulder, her thoughts a thousand miles away.

"Beau?" Senefreya looked up, a sudden memory appearing in her mind. "Do you remember that supermoon the last few weeks before the cataclysm? Before we met? Did you ever see it?"

"What supermoon?"

Senefreya smiled sadly. "Oh, nothing, darling. It's not that important." She laid her head back on his shoulder. Puzzled, Beau kissed the top of her head. She smiled, warmed by the love and protection that Beau offered for the rest of their lives together. It didn't matter that he did not see that supermoon; that he did not hear that wish she had made under the powerful grace of the supermoon, the way other people make a wish at a beautiful, gushing water fountain.

Clearly, Beau was not her true love.

But no matter. He was a good man and they had both declared their love for each other for the rest of their lives as man and wife.

The sense of time slowed down for that precious moment between them and Senefreya felt a huge sense of relief wash over her. The couple both hugged each other in loving warmth, standing in the hotel suite balcony under the soft, white gleam of the full, dazzling moon, nestled against the velvety-dark sky.

Chapter 20

After staring through the glass surface for what seemed like several minutes lost in thought, Gaston finally opened the door and exited the red brick building, where he had already attended a mandatory top-secret meeting with the big brass of the U.S. Navy, just before he was due to take command of his ship. Ensconced among the navy-blue suits, all of them multi-endowed with numerous stripes and bars denoting years of experience and rank with gravitas, it was a briefing where Gaston was duly reminded once again of the seriousness of his official responsibilities towards Project Tesla.

He shook his head as his hand released the doorknob. Project Tesla. Having agreed with reluctance to take on the mission of this ultra-secret project, he was now finally on his way to take command of the USS Arcanus, where he and his motley crew of sailor volunteers will soon venture into unknown territory, fraught with uncertainties at the outcome, and yet, here they are again. The brand, new mysterious ship and its brave crew. The U.S. Navy starting over once again after the last massive, incomprehensible failure of the project's prototype, the USS Eldredge on October 28, 1943.

Only a few people knew what happened to the USS Eldredge and its crew.

And Dr. Miroslav Breslov, his next-door neighbor, the alleged mad scientist, was one of them. Barred from speaking to his neighbor by his superiors, Gaston smiled ruefully that his wife was nonetheless allowed to speak with the scientist on a daily basis.

Gaston looked up at the sky. The glowing, bright yellow orb was cushioned against the azure canvas almost blinding him. He squinted his eyes, his thoughts racing back to the present.

Yes, here they were. All of them. This day of October 28, 1962, 19 years to the day the USS Eldredge was speedily decommissioned after the catastrophe and never spoken of again.

Taking a deep breath for a moment, he mentally beseeched the Archangel Michael to protect and guide this mission, wherever it may lead them. Expelling his breath, Gaston placed his white naval cover hat on his head and straightened it.

"Let's do this." He whispered grimly, clutching his canvas briefcase, his feet moving forward away from the door and towards the ochre-brown town car waiting for him at the curb.

A naval ensign in crisp, white uniform bent down to open the back passenger door for Gaston. Holding the door, the ensign stood up and sharply saluted. "Sir!"

Gaston saluted back and entered the car with the utmost confidence befitting a ship commander. The ensign slammed the door firmly and stood back, again in salutation. "Sir. Good luck, sir! Godspeed, sir!"

Gaston nodded by the window. He tapped his white cover hat. "Thank you. Ensign. Appreciate it. Goodbye."

"Goodbye, sir!" The naval ensign saluted, as the town car's engine thrummed into action.

The town car slowly moved along the concrete apron towards the main road. Several seconds passed, as the town car picked up speed on the main road heading towards the shipyard.

"Be nice to know what is going on with the world right now." Gaston commented, as he looked through the tinted passenger window at the passing panorama of grass, trees, and buildings housing naval facilities and offices and residential homes. He had always prided himself with knowing many things ahead of everyone and everything. But today, with the enormous job he was expected to carry on his shoulders for the next few months, he somehow felt inadequate with the task at hand, if not helpless. There was so much at stake now, so much uncertainties and he did not like that at all. And the conversations he had had with Margaret, prior to his departure from home, had only served to increase his apprehension.

"Get a grip." Gaston firmly whispered to himself looking down at the black canvas briefcase holding the intelligence he needed to prepare himself for the mission. "Just do it."

"Yes, sir." The town car driver responded briskly. "Do what, sir?"

Gaston laughed. "That was not for you, driver. Carry on."

"Of course, sir!"

"What is your name, driver?"

"Benito, sir. Benito de la Garza at your service."

"Benito, my friend, I wonder, would you know any news from the outside world considering?"

The driver nodded and pointed at the newspaper sitting on the passenger seat behind him.

"It's all in here, sir." He shook his head. "I read several newspapers every day, sir, to teach myself English. To learn what is going on in the world. Every day, sir."

"Excellent!" Gaston replied. "How goes it for today, the news?"

"Bizarre news, if I may add. Quite bizarre."

"Spill it out, Benito." Gaston asked, his curiosity piqued, his ears perked.

"Of course, sir!" Benito exclaimed, his hands firmly guiding the car to its destination. "Let's see, the big news of the day is that fragments of a certain unnamed comet had hit Berlin, huh, East Berlin, and destroyed pretty much most of the city infrastructure and the outlying lands, not to mention hundreds of people dead or dying. Terrible news, sir. Terrible."

Gaston lifted his eyebrows in surprise. "Must be the Taurid meteor showers. It's the right time for it."

"If you say so, sir." Benito nodded, as he made a right turn in the intersection heading towards the dockyard. "The paper did say to watch out for the Taurid meteor showers for the past few weeks."

Gaston nodded. "Too bad we can't go in there to help out. That area is most definitely the Soviet Union's problem. Perhaps the United Nations can do something about getting help there."

"Good luck with that, sir."

"Of course, my friend. Anyways, go on, what else?"

"Well, as the paper says, that same day, same time, we were supposed to get our POW pilot back home through that bridge, where the exchange was supposed to take place."

"Ah," Gaston nodded. "The Glienicke Bridge. Was it successful?"

Benito fervently shook his head. "Hardly, sir. It was supposed to be a quick exchange. Their spy for our pilot. Never happened. The paper says, several pieces of a large meteor hit the bridge and nearby areas. The bridge itself is completely destroyed, sir. Everyone apparently dead and gone in the blast. Even our pilot."

Gaston nodded grimly. "That is terrible news, indeed. Tell me, what was the name of our pilot, we were supposed to collect in the exchange?"

"The paper says Beauregard Faninus."

Gaston thought for a moment. He shook his head. "No, I don't know him. Anything else?"

"Yes, sir! Well, the paper talks about this Cuban crisis that is still ongoing and getting nowhere after 34 days so far, sir. It I may add, it appears to be escalating at this moment."

Gaston was reminded of the Doomsday Clock, its hand at 3 seconds to midnight. He nodded slowly. "Escalating, my friend? How so?"

"It's all in here, sir." The driver pointed to the newspaper column. "These words. All politics. Too technical for me, but I do get the gravity of the message. A complicated turn of events, I may add. I do not envy our President." The driver picked up the newspaper from the passenger seat and handed it to Gaston. "The paper says that this Nikita Khrushchev had some nerve stationing nuclear missiles and bombers in Cuba. If you ask me, it is too close for comfort. Only 90 miles between us and their weapons, God help us." Benito crossed himself several times.

"Agreed." Gaston nodded taking the paper and spreading it on his knees. "That is serious business." He sighed. "Benito, I'm telling you this, good man, so you are fully informed. See, we are also at fault. We initially started the problem by placing our nuclear missiles in Turkey and Italy, specifically the Jupiter MRBMs, not to mention the failed invasion at the Bay of Pigs last year, all of which is public information. So yes, we are at each other's throats, so to speak. The gift of the Cold War, indeed."

"Indeed." Benito agreed. "I do not like it at all." He crossed himself again. "90 miles between us. 34 days of talks and no knows what the hell they are talking about. Not even the newspapers. Hell, we might get nuked in the end." Benito shook his head, "My poor family. We come all the way here from Cuba to get nuked? Is not what I dreamed of."

Gaston placed his hand on the driver's shoulder and gripped it. "Take it easy, Benito, just take it easy. Let's hope our President makes a smart move. That he knows what to do." Gaston glanced at the article on the open newspaper page on his knees. "See, the paper talks about this quarantine. Listen. The President proposed two weeks ago of a quarantine, as an option."

"Quarantine, sir?"

"A euphemism for a blockade, Benito." Gaston explained.

"Very good, sir." Benito replied. "That I like."

"Not so fast, Benito." Gaston commented. "See, the word blockade in the world of politics infers to an act of war, which the President doesn't want."

"Yikes, sir." Benito groaned. "Are we doomed, sir?"

Gaston shrugged his shoulders. "No one is certain about that. Not even me." He laughed softly. "And I certainly am going to a place of doom myself right now. Wish me luck."

"But of course, sir. Me and my family, we will pray for you and your crew, but like I said, I think it could be getting worse. The talks." Benito added vehemently, pointing to himself. "I feel it in my bones. And my bones never lie."

Gaston closed the pages of the newspaper and placed it beside him. "I do hope for all our sakes that your bones are wrong, Benito." He let out a breath, as he shifted in his seat. "And yet, my friend, who knows what the future holds, even at the last 3 seconds of the Doomsday Clock."

"Doomsday Clock, sir?" The town car was now approaching a sign with big block letters and an arrow pointing at the dockyard among the waters, where several naval ships were berthed. "We are getting close to your ship, sir."

"Huh, never mind." Gaston smiled. "It's not important. Know this, Benito, for myself, in this mission, I have no idea what I'm doing. That is real terror in my bones."

Benito nodded gravely. "Understood. Good luck, sir. All of our prayers are with you and your crew, whatever you are doing out there on your ship. Hopefully you all come back in one piece."

"Hopefully." Gaston smiled. "Many thanks, my friend. We certainly do need all the luck we can get."

"You are welcome, sir!" Benito pointed in front of him at a distance. "And there we are, sir. Your ship, I believe." He slowed down the town car. Gaston took in a deep breath, exhaled slowly, rolled down passenger window and turned to look outside.

And there she was.

Standing strong and immobile, and yet so dynamic, on the dark, brooding waters lapping beneath her. The first U.S. Navy nuclear carrier to have been built in 1959 to launch multiple aircraft to fight in the brutal war against the Viet Cong, she was finally brought home battered and damaged carrying her tired, distraught crew, all of them emotionally assaulted permanently by the brutality of the ten-year war.

For three years, the ship had undergone massive repairs and retouching to bring her back to form as the shining, fully capable, massive, aircraft transporter she was originally created to be. Ready to take on another mission.

The USS Arcanus.

Waiting for him to take command.

The town car stopped gently. Benito reached for his driver's cap and adjusted it on his head. Opening the driver's side door, he crisply stepped out, closed the door, and walked around towards the other side of the town car. Opening the passenger side door, Benito stood sharply in salute.

Gaston stepped out smartly, clutching the canvas briefcase. Standing tall in his 6'2" frame, he stretched and adjusted his white, naval, cover hat. Ignoring the small palpitations of anxiety in facing the unknown before him, he felt the enormous responsibility of watching out for his crew of 800 manning the ship. 800 souls. The ship was capable of at least 4,000 crew members, but because this was a special, secret mission into the unknown, the reduced number of volunteers was much more practical in the eyes of the Navy brass.

Benito saluted. "Godspeed, sir! Be well and safe. Try to return."

Gaston nodded and tipped his hat. He extended his hand towards Benito. "Many thanks, Benito. I enjoyed our conversation on the way to my ship. You have been very helpful."

Benito shook hands tightly. "My pleasure, sir. I do not envy your mission, but I know the ship and its crew are in good hands with you."

"Thank you, my friend. Goodbye."

"Goodbye, sir."

In a few seconds, the town car slowly drove away.

Gaston turned to face his ship. It was an odd name for the ship and yet, so fitting. A ship of secrets. Of mystery. Soon to embark into unknown territories with her small, brave crew. None of them were allowed to know what had happened to the USS Eldredge on October 28, 1943. All they were allowed to know was that the mission failed and now it was time to start again, this time with a galaxy-class, nuclear-powered, aircraft carrier.

All anyone knew was that the prototype frigate, USS Eldredge, had been commissioned to fight in WWII against the Axis group with her special powers that had eventually caused dangerous unintentional consequences, her crew either killed or rendered mentally disabled for the rest of their lives. The secrets to the ship's story have since been suppressed to all, except the rare few with a need to know.

"Goddamn!" Gaston whispered angrily. "I have a need to know what the hell I'm getting myself and my crew into." He looked down briefly at his canvas briefcase. "This will have to do. And Margaret's outlandish talk. And Benito's helpful chat. Bit by bit by bit, as much as I can collect to prepare myself for this mission."

Gaston looked back at the ship. The USS Arcanus having been refurbished in all manner befitting her status as a nuclear powered ship, looked as if nothing had touched her in the war against the Viet Cong. From stern to bow, the USS Arcanus (CVN-65) stood tall and proud against the calm, blue sky, its displacement at 85,600 tons, its length from stern to bow at 1,101 feet, its width at 252 feet, with a beam at 133 feet. The shining silver-gray color only served to lend an air of boldness, power, and strength, not unlike a group of mighty, chivalrous knights of the Crusades, pushing forth on steeds of speed, their deadly lances upraised into the air, their powerful voices emboldening each other on to continue towards their quest of war against the enemy.

Only this time, the enemy is unknown. Even terrifying.

The dread of this mysterious mission was only made worse by the sight of huge, black cables secured to the USS Arcanus, all around the ship's surface just below the hangar, where the aircraft were to debark during the mission. Like the monstrous 60 feet long Titanoboa that lived 60 million years ago in the dark, humid jungle of Colombia, the dreaded, thick, black cables, intertwined altogether, appeared to merge as one entity to slither and grasp on the body of the ship, ready to slowly crush it to its death.

"Get a grip." Gaston reprimanded himself. "This is no time to fall apart. Only one focus now and everything else to the back of my mind.

His resolve strengthened, his courage empowered, Gaston straightened himself crisply and took another long, look at the ship towards the flight deck. There, he could see the long line of crew member of various designations facing him, standing sharply with their properly colored vests and uniforms, and their hands in a crisp salute.

And there in the middle of the line stood Sharona Belladottir, a beautiful name befitting a gorgeous woman in her flight suit. One of a small number of women who joined the naval aviation program. He did not want her on this dangerous mission and expressly had voiced his objections over and over at every trysts they had encountered to express their love for each other. Clearly, she wasn't going to listen to him, not now, not ever.

He noticed that she did not even acknowledge his presence.

Gaston nodded briefly. The firewall goes up now between them. Blocking them from each other for all the time of this mission. He knew it was the one thing that Sharona had expressly agreed to follow through. She had no choice. The outcome would be disastrous. Both of them losing their jobs and reputations, not to mention their respective families. Although, Sharona did not keep in touch with her parents, her only family, Gaston wasn't going to lose his beloved little Caroline, even though it meant staying in his unhappy marriage to a drunk bitch. And yet, for both of them the arrangement seemed perfect. The lovers would spend time with each other now and then at the bunker in the forest. Time that would recharge their feelings and thoughts and imbue them both with a sense of happiness and vigor, ready to get on with their separate lives, knowing they would soon see other again.

But not this time. Not here. The firewall had to go up.

And it was time to go now.

Expelling a breath of air, Gaston pushed away the anxieties in his mind, distracting him from thinking clearly. Looking up at each and every one of the brave crew of 800 souls willing to share the unforeseeable danger with him, he mustered every ounce of courage and fortitude, firmly stepping on the plank towards the ship's flight deck.

Chapter 21

IT WAS TIME TO GO HOME.

Arm in arm in loving embrace, Beau and Senefreya stood on the hangar apron at Le Bourget Airport, this beautiful, sunny, warm day, their eyes resting upon America's gift to the world, the incomparable Queen of the Skies, Boeing 747. The massive aeroplane with its iconic front hump had dominated the air trade show for the entire week, where hundreds of businessmen, pilots, and spectators examined with utmost admiration and awe over its amazing design and capacities proven in a testing flight, both in Washington and Paris. Only the equally, iconic supersonic aeroplane, dubbed "Little Brother" standing next to the gigantic shadow of the 747, managed to equally dominate the awe and wonder of the Paris Air Show attendees with its supersonic speed and grace.

The future has arrived in 1962.

"Science and technology are wonderful, aren't they, my love?" Beau remarked.

"Indeed, my darling." Senefreya breathed. "She is beautiful, your 747."

"I am told she is very safe to fly." Beau shook his head in wonder. "And she is so big. I wonder about the aeroplanes after her. In the future, I mean. How much bigger they can get."

Senefreya smiled secretly for a moment. "You have no idea, my darling, no idea." She hugged him lovingly, keeping her thoughts quiet. Not now. He doesn't need to know the future as I do. Having seen it in her dreams, it would seem the future is more astounding than he could possibly wrap his mind around. Not really ready for its implications. So, baby steps are all he needs, or anyone needs, for now, starting with this amazing, gigantic Boeing 747.

And Beau had been invited to co-pilot her.

"Let's go, baby." Beau took her hand and guided her to the mobile steps towards the 747's cockpit section door. "Let's go home." He gently placed his hand on his wife's mid-section. And then kissed her forehead lovingly.

"I'd almost forgotten. Happy Birthday, Senefreya, darling."

"Thank you, my love. Today I am a witch..." Senefreya smiled brightly, her hand over his on her baby bump. "Yes, let's go to our beautiful new home. I can't wait to be safe and free on my birthday in a new land far, far away. To raise our son in the land of Lady Liberty." Papa had told her stories about the gift of France to the young United States, her outstretched hand holding the lamp, her book of justice held tight against her chest, inviting the poor, the persecuted, and the downtrodden to live in the land of the free and the brave.

She had waited all her life for this. To see the Lady Liberty raising her torch of freedom.

Precious freedom...

Fifteen minutes later, the Boeing 747, Queen of the Skies, the trailblazing prototype of hundreds of descendent 747s to adorn the international skies of the future, roared to life at the start of the runway, its engines at full speed and power, its landing gear heavily mobilized to move the massive rubber wheels, now rolling ever faster and faster to finally lift its entire silver-lined body and wings into the infinite, blue sky with its awesome grace and power.

The cockpit door opened with a blast with Beau standing upright with all the excitement coming from his eyes, his smile so wide and bright.

"Senefreya! Quickly!" He gestured to his wife. "I want to show you something! Come quick before it's gone."

In a second, Senefreya joined the four pilots in the cockpit, all four of them staring through the window ahead of them, frozen in awe and wonder. At 30,000 feet, a rare spectacle had unfolded before them bringing forth the miracle of the Universe and of life in all its colorful form and substance.

The Universe' gift to life…red, orange, blue, green, yellow, indigo, and violet, all in their own pathways in a half-circle above the dark-blue ocean and another half-circle plunging under the ocean waters, creating a rare spectacle of a circular rainbow.

Nestled against the bright, blue sky, a golden glow emerged as a soft dewy essence behind the circle of colors, enhancing the awesome power of its beauty and majestic splendor. All in the cockpit stared at this rare natural phenomenon with quiet reverence.

"So beautiful…" Senefreya whispered. "So, so beautiful…I'm quite blessed to even look at it. It's so rare."

Beau nodded, feeling overwhelmed by the strength and beauty emanating from the colorful, circular rainbow. He wrapped his arms around Senefreya's waist bringing her closer to him, one hand resting on their unborn child. She was his miracle. She saved his life. And now she is carrying their child. For the first time in his life, he was actually looking forward to being a husband and father.

And then the rainbow faded into nothingness.

All of a sudden, a turbulence shook the plane, everyone in the cockpit quickly holding on to safe harbor. Again, the plane shook and rattled, this time harder than the first shudder, threatening to throw their bodies helter-skelter in the cockpit. Beau quickly sat back in the co-pilot seat.

"Go back to your seat, darling!" He motioned to the door. "Lock yourself in your seatbelt pronto."

Senefreya quickly exited the cockpit.

"Damn it." The Captain remarked, struggling with the instruments, his hands gripping the yoke that was stubbornly pushing itself to turn left. "I can't make it go straight. What the hell…" Another turbulence destabilized the momentum, forcing the yoke to quickly move to the left, forcing the Boeing 747 to bank away left from the normal flight path towards New York City.

Banking south towards where?

Missing her Papa and Mamoshka in this major turning point in her life path, Senefreya sang softly. "And yet, in her soul, she is like the sea… calm and wild and so, so free…and yet, like the wind, she moved on and on, when she loses in love…"

Now sitting firmly in the seat near the cockpit with her seatbelt locked, repeatedly adjusting to the tumult of the turbulence from time to time, the liquid tears slowly bubbled up in Senefreya's sapphire blue eyes, now back to its normal form with normal pupils. All the memories came rushing back in her mind, the memories of the hard journey she had taken, since the STASI first showed up in her family's apartment in Berlin, including witnessing the awful deaths of Papa and Mamoshka, and all the desperate attempts to get herself to freedom.

Where she was free to be herself, to live in peace and joy, to no longer be a target of the STASI, who wanted her powers for their evil deeds.

Chapter 22

One hour later...

The massive, silver-lined leviathan lumbered powerfully along the deep, blue waters of the mighty Atlantic Ocean, its majestic profile only slightly marred by the intertwining black cables embracing the ship all around below the deck like double braids.

Above, the sun was shining among the white, cotton-candy clouds, its rays providing an unprecedented warmth in this oft-chilly month of October 1962. The pleasant weather was only marred by the lingering shadow of the Cuban Crisis, which had started in October 16, 1962 and continued to escalate to this day, October 28, 1962. No one was sure what to do with themselves. Many prayed this would soon be over through diplomatic means. Others prepared for what could be a cataclysm of enormous proportions, stockpiling food and personal items at places they felt would be safe to hunker down and save themselves.

Such was the daily grind among the peoples of the world, watching the crisis unfold in their very eyes.

Enshrouded by the relentless albatross of fear and uncertainty far, far away from the safety of the mainland, the restless, powerful, momentum of the USS Arcanus demonstrated nerves of steel, as she plowed forward into uncharted territories with her Captain, XO, and crew. All of them facing one more challenge to deal with. Unflinchingly.

Those were their orders.

From the Captain's bridge above the deck of the ship, Gaston eyed the skies with apprehension. Every day, he felt the weight of his responsibilities towards his ship and crew. And today, it felt the most ominous of all. His eyes narrowed, as he spotted a flock of seagulls flying lower than usual, all of them heading in V formation towards the US mainland. Too low for his comfort. Captain Gaston Andrew Caine shifted in the seat of his chair. He let out a breath.

"How much further, XO?"

"Navigator, position?" Commander Marcus Jean DeLaCroix ordered with a swift, short bark from his throat.

"Sir, we are directly on target to approach Point Nemo, coordinates are at 48 degrees south and 123 degrees west. One hour, give or take 15 minutes."

"One hour, sir, give or take 15." XO swiftly replied to his Captain. He walked towards the chair and stood beside the Captain, silently sharing with him the strain of facing the unknown. Now filling his mind with regrets, he wasn't sure any longer that he made the right decision to follow Captain Caine in what now seemed to become more and more a truly dangerous mission. What had seemed before a challenging distraction of boredom pervading his life, he was now beating himself up for not thinking this through. And yet, it was too late. He already accepted the mission. He already was on the ship. As second in command, he accept his responsibilities towards his Captain and his ship.

And now, as all of them were staunchly facing the uncertainties of their mission, as they headed towards Point Nemo in the middle of the Atlantic Ocean, the XO determinedly placed himself squarely front and center of the ship, providing all the strength and support he could muster to his Captain and crew.

"We are on schedule, sir."

Gaston nodded. "Take a look at the skies, XO. What do you see?"

"I'm not sure, sir. I do see several clouds approaching from the south."

"Dark, aren't they?"

"Affirmative, sir. Normal, sir."

"And yet, something is wrong." Gaston pointed at the birds. "They are fast moving away, south to northeast. Away from what?"

"I'm not certain, sir. Perhaps a storm is coming. Birds tend to fly at low pressure in an approaching storm. A warning of sorts."

"I know. I know." Gaston brushed it away. "I just have this gut feeling that something. is. wrong. I wish I could put my finger in it." His hands gripped the arms of the chair.

Commander DeLaCroix nodded astutely, watching the birds fly away. "That would make the two of us, sir." He faced the Captain. "Do you wish to change coordinates?"

"No." Gaston shook his head, his eyes locked with determination at Commander DeLaCroix. "No. We must fulfill our mission, come hell or high water. The brass had made it clear to me at last briefing. Damn it."

"Yes, sir. Agreed, sir."

"Sir?" The navigator's voice cut through the conversation. "We have an approaching storm coming from the south? A force 9 storm. Severe gale category."

"There you go." Captain Caine asserted.

Commander DeLaCroix nodded in agreement. "Continue forward, navigator. Full speed ahead to the exact coordinates of Point Nemo. We will hunker down and ride out this storm at all costs."

"Sir, yes, sir!" The navigator swiftly turned to attend to his post, the other crew of the bridge also turning to their posts within the bridge, all of them determined and steeled to ride out the approaching mix of severe high winds, gale, and pouring rain, all of them following the tenacious leadership of their Captain and XO.

"Shall I, sir?" Commander DeLaCroix reached out for the ship-wide communication phone behind him with the intent to warn all on board the USS Arcanus to swiftly batten down all planes and cargo and get themselves all hunkered down to ride out the looming threat approaching the ship's vicinity.

"Do it!" Gaston nodded firmly, staring apprehensively at the oncoming dark clouds, mentally preparing himself to lead the way.

Seconds later, Commander DeLaCroix slammed the phone back on the wall receiver. They were so close to Nemo Point to begin the process of invisibility, if not for that storm. It only served to delay their mission, but what the hell. They were not in a hurry and better to ride out the storm than fail their mission. No one had any idea what could happen when one becomes invisible in the midst of the storm's turmoil.

Not a good risk to take, in any case.

The XO turned to head towards the Captain's chair. In that split second, the phone rang. "Oh, hell." The XO turned around to pick up the phone.

"XO speaking?"

The conversation lasted for a few seconds. Slamming the phone back on the wall receiver the XO faced the ship's captain.

"Sir, you are wanted on the red phone."

Surprised at the announcement, Gaston quickly rose from his chair and headed towards the red phone at a private corner of the bridge. It was a phone call that very rarely happens, if ever. All crew and officers working on the bridge turned around and held their breath, watching their Captain pick up the red phone.

"Mr. President?"

The conversation did not last long and while it lasted, the air in the bridge became heavy with a sense of doom. All it took was a look at the Captain, as he placed the red phone back on its receiver. He did not look happy at all. His mouth in a grim façade, his eyes narrowed, his mind thinking a thousand thoughts, Gaston could not hide his trepidation from his crew.

That order from the President only served to compound the challenge posed by the oncoming storm. He shook his head and closed his eyes.

Why? Why now?

"Sir?" The XO asked. "Is there a problem?"

Gaston opened his eyes. Everyone in the bridge was staring at him, their eyes wide with apprehension, all of them holding their breath, not knowing what to think or do. Waiting for him to say something to release their frozen stance and move forward. The Captain was in frozen in a state of indecision.

"Sir?"

"Yes, XO." Gaston broke from his thoughts. He started barking at his crew with firm, clipped words of urgency. "Congress has made its approval clear. The President had announced war with the Soviet Union and Cuba. We are at war now."

All in the bridge tensed, waiting for their orders. Gaston resumed his duties forthwith.

"XO, order the engineering room to begin the generators. Start the invisibility process. Now."

"Yes, sir!" The XO headed towards the ship wide communications phone.

"Navigator!"

"Yes, Captain!"

"Change the ship's position and route from Point Nemo to head towards Cuba forthwith! Relay the changes towards the Junior Officer and helmsmen to point the ship's direction south to Cuba now and tell the engineering room manning the generators to induce invisibility and teleportation!"

"Sir, yes, sir!" The navigator bent down and quickly picked up his tools to plan the redirection towards Cuba. Time was of essence. Every other staff and officer returned to their posts, this time with an air of determination and urgency.

It is now war.

Slamming the phone back on its receiver, the XO quickly moved to stand by the Captain. So much needed to be done and quickly.

"Sir, the storm?"

Gaston shook his head firmly. "No time to worry, XO. Invisibility and teleportation appear to be the fastest route to getting ahead of the goddamn Soviets and their quarrel with us. At this position, we are the closest to Cuba and the President demanded we get to Cuba fast and put up a wall, a battle even. The frigates and warships will follow, but we can get there faster from where we are now."

"Are you certain, Sir?"

"No, I'm not. But what choice do I have?" Gaston sighed. "This is a first for us and for the US Navy. Unprecedented. The storm and the invisibility and teleportation process altogether is quite a maelstrom and at this point, I have no idea what we are getting ourselves into". He turned and grimly locked eyes with the XO. "But as I see it, we are at war, a war too close to the mainland and that is not acceptable. No." Gaston pointed at the floor.

"This here and now is our real job. And it is a risk we must accept, come hell or high water."

"Of course, sir. Agreed. Perfectly clear. No arguments from me." XO nodded.

At this point, the ship's gigantic rudders began to rumble and quickly move the massive, silver-lined behemoth, displacing over 86,000 tons of water, in a smooth circular wave-encrusted trail towards the south of the Atlantic Ocean.

Towards Cuba. Towards war.

Waiting for the invisibility and teleportation process to begin with all the fear and uncertainty decisively suppressed in the backs of their minds, both the Captain and XO stood firmly next to each other before the panoramic view of the bridge window, their hands behind the strong lift of their backs, their postures perfect, as they faced unknown territories by order of the President.

All around them the naval staff and officers were hard at work in their duty posts.

As the shadows of the storm clouds gathered just above the ship, the skies becoming darker and darker, the flight of the seagulls gone, all aboard the USS Arcanus waited in trepidation and fear, as a new reality closed in upon them. In the engineering room, the generators were being powered up to higher frequencies and capacity, causing the outer steel casings to tremble with the ever increasing intensity of the powerful thrust of electromagnetic flow going through towards the external, overlapping thick cables below the deck.

And all of a sudden, amidst the loud noise of the exhausted generators still rumbling powerfully, a haunting foggy mist of blue and green appeared out of nowhere to surround the ship and its crews, fully embracing them in its frightening potency. And all of a sudden, several electrical lightnings emerged out of nowhere, flickering, crackling and lighting up the blue-green darkness of the skulking, foggy mist.

Watching the mist of doom enshrouding the USS Arcanus, Gaston suddenly yelled out loud, "Oh, hell!"

Time was of essence. This cannot happen again. No time to explain to his XO.

He swerved quickly towards the ship-wide communications phone and picked up the receiver. "To all of you ship-wide, wherever you are and whatever you do, DO NOT MOVE! REPEAT. DO NOT MOVE!"

And then the ship disappeared into oblivion…

Chapter 23

Not far behind and high above the roiling waters of the Atlantic Ocean, the Boeing 747 continued its persistent journey towards the south, the yoke still frozen in place. as if something unseen was gripping it harder than the pilot himself, Captain Gregory Myles.

"What the hell!" Beau yelled, as he gripped the yoke in front of him, desperately trying to keep it from turning a hard left. "I have control now, Gregory."

The Captain nodded surrendering control to Beau. He was so tired. And yet, even under Beau's skillful guidance, the yoke refused to budge from the left turn going southwards down the eastern seaboard coastline.

"The autopilot is messed up, perhaps. It's not working. It appears to have disconnected just like that." Captain Gregory Myles yelled out. "Something is pulling the plane hard left."

"Come on! Pull right! Together! Pull right!" Beau gripped with all his might on the yoke again, which still refused to budge. "Captain, help me out, now."

"I'm trying! I'm trying, Beau! This thing is stubborn as a mule!"

"I can't get comms to work! We are dead in the air. Nothing's working!" The engineer behind Beau shouted helplessly, manipulating the instruments in front of him and above him.

Beau let go of the yoke. He was so tired, beads of sweating trickling down his forehead.

"Oh hell, I give up, Gregory. This is too hard and too stuck. We just have to face where we are going and deal with it?"

"There's nothing we can do with this aeroplane. It's got a mind of its own." Captain Myles breathed out in frustration, letting go of the yoke in front of him.

"Guys, I'll be back. I got to go check on my wife."

"God help us…" Captain Myles crossed himself. Both his hands were red with bruises from his battles with the yoke.

At LaGuardia Airport, the tower controller looked aghast at the circular, electronic map panel in glowing, green lights before him, the blinking code identifying the Boeing 747, which, instead of heading straight towards the airport runway in a regular flight pattern, was now deviating away from the flight path towards the south of the mid-atlantic coastline.

He reached for the emergency phone appalled at the turn of events showing up in his electronic screen.

The Queen of the Skies, seemingly controlled by an unseen, unmitigated force of unimaginable strength and power, had slowly banked left from her normal flight path to New York City, its massive engines thrumming loudly on both wings, as the aeroplane itself at 30,000 feet slowly descended in increments of 1,000 feet down and down southward towards the Caribbean Sea.

Chapter 24

Gaston found himself floundering, the USS Arcanus bucking back and forth against the foam-encrusted, giant squalls buffeting her. Outside the bridge window, the skies were filled with huge, dark cumulonimbus clouds expelling large swaths of rain and hail and flash lightnings on and on.

For all its power and strength in the mighty seas, the USS Arcanus appeared reduced to a small ant of vulnerability in the relentless turmoil of this stormy seas. The relentless storm Gaston personally ordered to enter in their diversion from Point Nemo to Cuba by order of the President. They would have to accept whatever outcome the storm imposed on their process of invisibility and teleportation. It was the only way to reach Cuba speedily, ahead of the Soviets and their almighty MIGs and warfighter ships.

Steadying himself against the unyielding, erratic convulsions, Gaston yelled out. "XO, where the hell are we?"

"I have no idea, sir." The XO looked out the bridge window, hanging on to the instrument panel in front of him. "It appears we have materialized promptly and yet, we are still at sea. All I see is water everywhere. Like water back then. Navigator?

"I'm trying, sir. I need time. My instruments are not functioning well at the moment! Apparently, we are being played out with the gremlins of technology."

"Funny. Never mind that. Get to it and report back!"

"Sir, yes, sir!"

At that moment, loud terrifying screams were bombarded all around the ship, reaching the bridge. Screams of terror and fear mixed with groans of pain and agony.

"XO?"

"Right away, sir!" He reached for the ship-wide communications phone. "Report! What the hell is this godawful noise coming from below?"

After a few seconds, the XO slammed the phone back on the wall receiver. He leaned against the wall for a second, stunned beyond belief. "Oh, my god…" a whisper came from his mouth.

"XO!" Captain Caine demanded loudly.

"Sir, it's the men, at least some of them. They're…how do I say it… they're embedded in the walls of the ship?!"

"Come again, XO? Embedded?"

"That is what I heard, sir!" The XO repeated his words. "Embedded into the walls and dying. Our men."

Realization instantly hitting him, Gaston groaned. "It's all my fault. I was too late. Too late for it."

"I don't understand, sir." XO asked.

"Never mind. I will explain later." Gaston responded, heaving mightily to right himself on the floor and resume command. He knew right now, right away, there was nothing he could do. "Take the bridge, XO. I'm going down to my men. I am responsible for this."

"Yes, sir!" The XO headed towards the Captain's chair. "Navigator, where the hell are we?"

Gaston rushed with all his might towards the below decks, where the screams continue to pound the air with terror and agony. It pained him to hear it, knowing he really could do nothing about it. The least he could do was to show up and comfort his men. Be there in their final throes of inevitable death.

Jumping down from the stairs, two at a time, to the first below deck, he saw two men screaming in pain, their bodies clearly embedded into the steel walls of the ship, their hands flailing in pain and pressure, their eyes crying from terror. Around them, their mates quivered in fear not knowing what to do.

"Jesus Christ…." Gaston whispered in horror. "It is as Dr. Breslov had warned. I was too late. Jesus Christ, I was too late…"

"Ten hut!" The air boss yelled. All the mates stood at attention mustering all their strengths to allay their fears amidst the unrelenting screams behind them.

"Stand down. Relax." Captain Caine raised his hand. "At this point, I'm not interested in ranks. Please relax. We need to help our men."

"How sir?" One of the mates turned around staring at the pitiful sight of the two bodies embedded, the victims' face already red with pressure and pain, unable to breathe.

They were all now gasping for air, the awful specter of death closing into them.

"Just hold their hands, men. Pray for them. Be there in their final moments." Gaston explained, his face racked with guilt at his complicity in their deaths. He was too late. "One of you start a prayer group for them. That's an order. I'm heading downstairs for the others."

"Yes, sir!" The air boss saluted, as Gaston headed towards another round of stairs towards the below decks. "Gather round, men. Two of you, hold hands with the casualties. Now."

Thirty minutes passed. In that time, Gaston had dutifully covered all the below decks, where the victims were embedded in the steel walls, the floors, and even the steel doors, giving the surviving mates and sailors and officers his orders to form a prayer group to facilitate the passing of the victims in love and peace for all their pain and agony.

He hoped doing that would mitigate the horror of the events, even though he himself no longer believed in the teachings of the Church. He knew the men needed this, the calming rites of passage for the awful deaths of their shipmates.

Heading back upstairs towards the bridge, Gaston reprimanded himself to let go of the guilt. There was no room for it. He needed to muster all his strength and will to lead his men in the here and now and right now they all had no idea where they were…".

And still out there, the massive, dark, powerful storm battered the USS Arcanus no end.

"XO?" Gaston yelled, as he appeared at the bridge, still fighting against the rolls. "Where the hell are we, now?"

The XO jumped from the Captain's chair. "Navigator still has problems with his instruments. Seems the storm is interfering with its operation. He is working on it."

Gaston nodded. There was nothing he could do for the navigator. All he had right now was time and the means to ride out the storm, wherever the hell they were. The USS Arcanus was built for this storm. She can ride it out.

"Man overboard!!!!!"

Captain Caine groaned, his face looking up at the bridge window being pummeled by the rapid turmoil of hail and rain. It was hard to see outside.

"Now what, someone fell overboard? In this weather?? Get to it, XO!"

"I'm on it, sir!" The XO grabbed the ship-wide, communications phone. Seconds later, he slammed it back. "Sir, there is someone on a sailing boat a few clicks ahead of the hull. That boat is sinking fast. This person, a civilian, is waving for help."

"What are we waiting for?!?" Gaston yelled back. "Go get him onboard!"

"Yes, sir!" The XO disappeared from the bridge.

Chapter 25

Four hundred feet away up north near the coastline of Connecticut, still descending in 1,000 feet increments, the Boeing 747 was stubbornly and quietly on its way to enter the darkly, omnipresent fog and stormy clouds, booming with the incessant noise and darkness of thunder, hail, rain and lightning.

The yokes were still stuck in place. Still unyielding to the pilots' desperate attempts to turn the aeroplane around. The autopilot shut down by an unseen force. The instruments functioning wildly all over the avionics panel, as if that same unseen force was playing games with them.

Unable to take back control of the 747 with all the desperation and might of their beings, the pilots had all, but gave up hope, having let go of the yokes and instruments, back then, breathless with their hearts beating ever so fast, sitting back on their cockpits in terror and fear, all of them allowing themselves be taken by the aeroplane to god only knows where.

Beau and Gregory locked eyes. Still going down at 1,000 feet in increments, the aeroplane now slowly approaching close to the surface of the Carribean Sea engulfed by the horrendous thunderstorm, they were now at the point of no return. Perhaps a crash in the waters. Perhaps a smooth landing on the waters.

There was only one way to find out.

Still gripping the arms of her seat behind the cockpit door, Senefreya steeled herself for the next few minutes of pandemonium, knowing what she knew she would finally end up. Back to where she belonged. There was no point in explaining to Beau and his pilot friends what she knew. It was too convoluted, too confounding to wrap their heads around and most likely will dismiss her back to her seat and get real.

And yet, the plane going down slowly through that maelstrom of wind, rain, and lightning, she knew they would have to depend on her magical knowledge every step of the way, once they all arrived at a different place and time.

Papa's place and time. A place and time where she truly belonged.

It has been Papa's wish in all the bedtime stories she had grown up listening. He had told there were two possibilities. Either she was going to the land of freedom or she was going home. His home. And there it was. It was finally happening.

She was going home. To Papa's homeland…

And on and on, the mighty 747, bounced around by the turbulence, droned lower and lower towards the darkly, looming clouds pummeling rain and hell ahead of the aeroplane.

Chapter 26

The bridge door slammed open.

Commander DeLaCroix dragged the rescued civilian into the bridge, gripping him by the shoulders and thrusting him to stand before the Captain. Gaston was aghast. Portly and bearded with his clothes already ripped and torn, his hair disheveled from mud and rain, his hands ripped and bleeding from holding on to his deteriorating boat, the civilian they vowed to rescue in this confounding storm was now standing before him, barely alive and yet, there he was.

Not speaking at all.

"XO?"

"I can't get him talk, sir." XO replied. "Every time I said something, both his hands fly all over the air. Very odd, sir."

Gaston looked back at the scraggly civilian, his hands now desperately flying in the air, his mouth making all the motions of articulated words, yet no sound came out.

"Speak, man!" Gaston ordered the civilian. "What are you saying?"

The ship roiled back and forth, the rain and hail pounding mightily outside.

Nonplussed, the civilian again motioned wildly with his hands and silent mouth. He crossed his arms stubbornly, his feet firm against the floor, as the ship rolled back and forth. His brown eyes glared from under the unkempt wet hair.

"He's deaf, sir."

Captain Caine turned around quickly, facing the helmsman, whose hands still gripped the steering wheel, eyes staring ahead, not willing to let go of it in the storm.

"Deaf?" Gaston turned back towards the XO. "And how do you propose we communicate with him?" He stared at the civilian, still talking wildly with his hands and pointing towards the bridge window. "What is he saying? Why is pointing at the window?"

The helmsman shouted above the din of the storm, "Captain, sir! I know someone below decks, who knows American sign language. I believe that is what our rescue is doing. Signing words."

"Well, what are you waiting for?" Gaston yelled at the XO. "Get this person! Forthwith!"

"Yes, sir!" The XO headed towards the ship-wide, communications phone, having armed himself with the name of this sailor and his duty station. "Right away, sir!"

A minute later…the bridge door opened and a woman entered. Amidst the rolling movements of the ship, she stood firmly in front of Captain Caine with a crisp salute.

"Petty Officer 3rd Class, sir! The woman yelled out among the roar of the waves lashing against the ship. "At your service, sir!"

"At ease, now! What is your name, Petty Officer?" Gaston yelled out not caring about ranks and protocols. They were already in a crisis and danger abounded without having to worry about who was what and where and when.

"Joanna, sir!" Petty Officer 3rd Class stood her ground, her body and feet working with the rolls of the ship. "Joanna Pettigrew at your service."

"Joanna Pettigrew. Good!" Gaston yelled back. "I'm told you know American sign language. Is that correct?"

"Yes, sir!" Joanna yelled. "My whole family is deaf, sir. I grew up learning sign language, in addition to speaking English."

Captain Caine looked at Joanna with relief in his eyes. He sighed wearily, his hand rubbing his forehead. This is better now. He looked up at his XO, who nodded firmly and at once moved the nervous and weary boat rescue towards Joanna Pettigrew.

Joanna turned around to face the boat rescue. Again, his hands flailed in the air, his silent mouth filled with articulate words. Joanna's hands responded, flying enthusiastically and fluently in the air. The both of them spoke fluidly and vividly with their brilliantly expressive hands and arms, their eyes understanding with luminous clarity every silent word spoken between them, both of them nodding their heads in tandem with the dance of their hands.

Beyond the bridge, the hail and rain and lightning relentlessly pounded the ship all around. Gale force winds now whipped the foamy waters into giant waves battering the ship, each wave becoming bigger and bigger over time.

"Well?" Captain Caine barked impatiently.

The dance of the signings stopped.

"Yes, sir!" Joanna responded ready to impart the translations. "According to our deaf friend here, his name is Barto Jepson, well, he is saying that the ship is now in the vicinity of what's known as the Bermuda Triangle, in the exact coordinates where the 5 Avenger torpedo bombers, aka as Flight 19, and the Mariner rescue plan, disappeared 18 years ago, never to be found again. All of them Navy."

Gaston sighed, scratching his head. "Bermuda Triangle, huh?" He looked at the XO. "How in hell did that happen?"

"I don't know, sir." Commander DeLaCroix shook his head firmly, his hands behind his back, standing tall against the buffeting of the ship. "I do know for certain that we entered the right coordinates for Cuba prior to invisibility and teleportation. I can personally vouch for that."

"And yet, here we are materializing in the wrong place! Wrong time!" Captain Caine barked with annoyance. "XO, go find out what happened with the coordinates. Forthwith! This needs to be fixed. We are under orders of the President of the United States!"

"Yes, sir! Forthwith!" The XO hastened towards the bridge door.

"Wait!!" Joanna yelled out, her hands flailing in the air. Barto nodded excitedly. At that moment, everyone in the bridge froze in their place, all eyes focused on Joanna animatedly signing with Barto. "He knows what happened, sir. He knows."

"Ah, a breakthrough…" Gaston yelled back. "Grab rails! Now!" In a second, the ship abruptly rolled deep left, causing them all to hang onto whatever was there to place their hands and feet and bodies, all of them working hard to stabilize themselves in the turmoil of the giant, angry waves battering the ship. And the waves were becoming stronger and stronger.

Balancing himself with all his might, Gaston spoke out, "So he knows?"

"Yes, sir!" Joanna responded. "I will be translating his sign communications as he speaks. It appears to be quite complex, but I will try my best."

"I'll be the judge of that. Now, speak!" Captain Caine ordered, glaring intently at Barto. They were now very, very late and running out of time to reach Cuba. By now, the Soviets surely would surely have gotten closer to Cuba and the mainland.

Gaston heaved again. "Go on. What does he know?"

For several seconds, Joanna and Barto each signed animatedly with each other. Barto nodded happily. "Okay, Barto, go ahead. I will translate your words to the Captain." Everyone in the ship watched the silent conversation progress with suspended breath, each of them not daring to utter a sound. So silent was the bridge, it could be said that a needle could be heard falling down to the floor.

"Go ahead, Barto." Joanna smiled with her signage. "Don't worry."

Nodding his head with relief, Barto smiled broadly. He was now at least being taken seriously for once, ever since he was hoisted up into the safety of the USS Arcanus, his long-time boat now gone into the cold depths of the Caribbean Sea.

After taking a couple of breaths, Barto excitedly signed and signed, imparting all that he knew what happened to the ship, his hands and arms flying all over in the air and his mouth spouting word after word without a sound. And standing steady as a rock, Joanna put all her efforts and linguistic knowledge into translating each and every word, what Barto had been trying to tell the Captain all along, since he was hoisted up into the ship.

"Sir," Becoming baffled and, yet, still standing steadily, Joanna translated with her firm, enunciating voice directly to the Captain, her confidence expressed in every word translated from Barto's signage to her spoken vocal cords. "Barto is saying that from where you were coming in the north, your ship has crossed a core point here, where there is a legendary giant crystal machine buried deep within the mud and silt of the sea below. Miles deep. He is saying that your ship's generators, upon entering this core point, activated the power of the machine, causing your ship to solidify prematurely and keeping her stuck here, where she is, like a magnet to an iron bar."

"Whoa…" The entire crew within the bridge listened with fascination. It was all so bizarre.

Captain Caine groaned, his hands against his hips, giving his crew the glare in his eyes. "What giant crystal machine? And how does he know about my ship's generator? It wasn't supposed to be public knowledge."

"Ooooo…" The ship's crew whistled and listened, all of them still holding their breath.

Captain Caine glared again, shushing them all.

Joanna turned to Barto and signed some more.

"Sir, he is saying that he is friends with a famous scientist. Long-time friends sharing a deep common interest searching for Atlantis."

"Atlantis?"

"Um, sir, that's another long story." Joanna continued to translate. "Barto is saying that this famous scientist worked for the Navy on a secret project."

"No wonder." Gaston whispered. Damn if he is standing in front of a friend of Dr. Miroslav Breslov, that crazy mad scientist and creator of the USS Arcanus. He looked at XO and sighed. XO only shrugged his shoulders, not knowing what to make of all this inexplicable talk coming from Barto, who seemed a simple, deaf man from a fishing boat."

"Okay, fine, so he knows about our secret project." Gaston admitted glaring at Barto. "So, go on, what is he doing here all by himself, lost in the storm in the Caribbeans?

Joanna smiled awkwardly, shrugging her shoulders. "As best as I could translate, sir, Barto is saying, he is looking for that giant crystal machine, the key to finding Atlantis."

The entire bridge crew stopped their work and listened, hushing their voices, their eyes staring at Barto, who was now grinning like a

Cheshire Cat from the Adventures of Alice in Wonderland. It was getting more and more interesting. The XO now crossed his arms and sighed, rolling his eyes with impatience at his crew, all of them absorbed in the three-way conversation among the Captain, Joanna, and Barto, all of them oblivious to the riotous tempest of rain, hail, wind, and giant roiling waves buffeting the ship apart.

"The key to finding Atlantis? But why?" Captain Caine asked, his forehead wrinkled in confusion. "More to the point, how in hell are we going to get out of here and back on track to Cuba? We are wasting time now. There is a war going on. We are under orders of the President, for God's sakes."

"Yes, sir!" Joanna turned and watched Barto signed speedily, trying to be helpful, knowing that his conversation appeared extraordinarily preposterous and bizarre at each and every second.

"Barto is saying that he believes that the logical step is to shut down the generators in your ship causing the invisibility and teleportation, his words, and that should cut off the crystal machine below the sea, thereby cutting off their intertwining energies. And then, only then, you can move your ship ahead a few feet and then start over to become invisible and then finally, you are on your way. But first, cut off your generators. It is causing the crystal machine to go crazy. His words."

Captain Caine rubbed his chin thoughtfully. "Seems too much work, but then again, it does make sense." He looked at the XO and lifted his chin in agreement. "Do it."

"Yes, sir!" The XO headed towards the bridge door.

"Sir!" The navigator shouted, staring at the lighted, green panel, now showing a moving blip from the north. "We have imminent danger in our sight! Level red, sir!"

Stunned, the XO stopped his tracks and turned to the navigator. "What is happening, navigator, what do you see?" Captain Caine turned around, waiting for the updates. Joanna, Barto, and the rest of the crew waited with bated breaths. It was all going so fast.

"Sir, it is a huge blip on the panel north of us and heading speedily towards us at 12 meters per second and man, it is huge!"

"Speak, navigator! What do you mean, huge?"

"Hard to say. It is a blip. Could be a plane of sorts. I suggest we look out the window. I'm telling you, whatever this is, it's going to hit us in approximately 3 minutes, give or take a min."

Astounded at the inexplicable updates, Captain Caine and the XO tried hard to search through the bridge window for the strange anomaly now heading towards them with the speed of a rushing train. And all around them, the rain, hail, wind, and waves continued to block their view, even with the window wipers on.

"I don't see anything, yet." Captain Caine asked, becoming worried. He did not like being helpless. "Do you?"

"Not really, sir, but it's hard to see it in this storm, sir." The XO responded, his face pressed against the glass window. "The navigator said in 3 minutes from the north. It shouldn't take too long to show up, sir, and then, we can see what it is."

Gaston felt a strong touch on his left shoulder. He turned around. "Yes?"

"Sir?" Joanna asked the Captain. "Barto would like to speak with you, again. I believe he has something he can help you with."

Annoyed once again, Captain Caine looked up at Barto, who was still grinning ear to ear like the Cheshire Cat. Closing his eyes, he shook his head trying to push away the irritation of dealing with the bizarreness of it all. All around him, his men and women had no idea what was going on each second of each minute, and yet, here in front of him was this simple, deaf man from a fishing boat armed with all the technical knowledge of an erudite scientist from Harvard.

The irony was not lost on him.

"What does he know, Joanna?" Gaston ordered. "This better be good."

"It is, sir." Joanna responded, watching Barto's animated signage. "Barto says your ship caused it. The thing that is coming at us in 3 minutes."

"We caused it? Come again?" Gaston sighed. "What is that "thing"? Does he know?"

"Well…" Joanna struggled to understand more of Barto's signage. It was all too fantastic to absorb in her own logical mind and yet, the Captain needed the information. "Barto is saying the ship's generators not only activated the giant crystal machine below us, but that same machine is most likely overwhelmed, transmitting its electrical power for miles without anyone there to control its mechanisms. In other words, the power was getting stronger and stronger causing an earthquake down below. We just can't feel it yet in this storm, but Barto is sure it happened."

"Earthquake?" Gaston was astounded. "Down below?"

"Yes, sir. We can't feel it, because it's miles underground and we are surrounded by the noise and din of this thunderstorm, but the effect is…" Joanna paused watching Barto sign some more. "The effect is the power from the crystal machine has most likely created a phenomenon we all know as a rogue wave."

"Is that the blip on the panel?" Captain Caine asked XO.

The XO looked back through the window. "Sir, I see a dot now. Very black and distinct moving in our direction. Perhaps it is what Barto said it should, a rogue wave coming at us."

Barto nodded excitedly, finally getting through them. Gaston groaned, becoming even more irritated and tired. He combed his fingers through his hair in frustration. "How big is it, XO? Can you see?"

"Not yet, sir, but they are known to rise hundreds of feet high."

"Enough to overturn this ship and drown us." Captain Caine nodded gravely, multiple thoughts and memories racing in his mind, trying to figure out the best way to escape from the monster wave intent on destroying his ship. He wasn't taking a chance on facing this colossus head on. It was very rarely a ship, any ship, survived the rogue wave, even one as big as the statue of Lady Liberty. He knew from experience that the Bermuda Triangle has long been the zone of rogue waves for centuries with multiple theories abounded on its sudden and swift development in that sector of the sea. Some of the ships hand ended up sunk and buried deep inside the waters and others had disappeared forever.

And apparently this fantastic theory of the giant crystal machine explained by this simple, deaf man, the key to famous, lost city of Atlantis, had caused this rogue wave coming at his ship. And his ship was responsible for activating the crystal wave in the first place.

Reeling with mystification at the order of events, Captain Caine exhaled forcefully. He gripped himself with resolve and barked orders. "XO, tell engineering to shut down the generators. Helmsman, you are to turn port and move south speedily at the top speed at once. We need to get away from this core point that's causing all this exasperating ruckus around the ship. We need to get to CUBA! Forthwith, never mind invisibility and teleportation!"

"Yes, sir!" All the crew returned to their posts and duties, their eyes focused on their instruments and tools, their concentration heavy with anxieties and forethought, putting all the years of their naval technical and boot camp training to full use. Joanna stood next to Barto, putting her arm around his nervous shoulders, giving him a reassuring smile. "Don't worry, Barto. This is normal for us. You did well. We just wait and see now. Ok?"

Barto nodded. He wasn't sure if he should let the crew know that he knows. That something else was going to happen, if his mental extrapolation was right. For surely, it was the very reason the giant crystal machine, now buried miles deep under the sea, was built for. He looked at Joanna with a wan smile.

Should he?

Joanna smiled back. "What?"

"Nothing." Barto whispered, shaking his head ever so slightly, showing his famous Cheshire grin. Not now. Now it was just wait and see and go with the flow. His eyes fervently looked through the bridge window towards the north, his left hand behind his back crossing his fingers for good luck. If by any chance he was right about what he knew, what he extrapolated based on all the series of circumstances already encountered by them all, he knew he could do nothing about it.

God help them all.

By now, the black dot was becoming bigger and clearer, a darkly, silver-blue, concave shape in its race directly towards the ship. A rogue wave the height of the Lady Liberty, its white peaks foaming like thick bubbles. Its stark beauty under the gray, stormy skies, belying the danger of its arrival.

And yet, it seemed in all this organized chorus of chaos and control by all the occupants within the ship under level white defcon status, and all manpower available at battle stations focusing on the oncoming potential nuclear war, no one seemed to be paying attention to the yawning shimmer of air showing up in front of the ship.

Except for Barto.

Barto quickly signed towards Joanna. His hands flying with words in the context of fear and desperation.

"Oh my god." Joanna gasped, her hands covering her mouth. She turned to look at the bridge window, the ship heading southwards, her eyes narrowed as she searched for that shimmer of air that Barto was talking about.

Yes, it was there. And it was growing…

She turned towards the Captain, now seated on his chair, his commands leading the bridge crew to their assigned functions, expertly and efficiently, through the relays from his XO.

"Yes, Joanna?" Gaston barked. The XO stepped forth to stand beside the Captain's chair, the both of them looking at Joanna with exasperated interest.

"What now?" Gaston gripped the arms of his chair tightly. "This better be good."

Joanna eyes expressed outright fear as words poured out of her mouth, translating the next several conversations from Barto to the Captain.

"Sir, we are about to enter a time portal." Joanna shouted firmly under the roar of the storm still pounding the ship. She pointed at the window. "See? Look closely."

Captain Caine and the XO turned towards the bridge window, their eyes becoming wider with incredulous anticipation. What had been a slight shimmer, as Barto was watching it, was now becoming a twirling vortex of clouds, rain, hail, and wind. Soon, purple and green colors and clouds appeared, streaking through the inner swirls, as the shimmer became a full blown vortex tunnel, the clouds moving in counterclockwise direction.

Everyone on the ship gasped awe and terror. The front hulls of the USS Arcanus was already touching its surface, already on the throes of entering the chaos within it.

Gaston was fed up. "How in hell did this happen?" He stared at Barto, his frustration growing by the minute. He was not entirely prepared to manage this brand, new conflict that seemingly appeared out of nowhere and just when they were trying to escape the horror of a giant rogue wave coming from behind the ship, already closing in on the ship. There was 1 minute left of this monster wave, now dead astern, ready to come crashing down and capsize the USS Arcanus into smithereens and force it to sink into the depths of the Bermuda Triangle, killing them all.

No easy task to call out for rescue in this frenzied squall of wind, rain, and hail. It is highly likely they would all drown like the unfortunate souls of the HMS Titanic.

Captain Caine set his mouth in a grim position, analyzing the situation carefully with all his experience and expertise. He resolved to try to save his ship and crew, come what may. Whatever this supposed pseudo-archaeologist keeps saying is showing up time and again, each one worse than the previous one.

And this one was the worst of all.

Captain Caine glared helplessly through the bridge window from his chair, as the swirling vortex of purple and green, the clouds following the momentum of the swirl deeper and deeper into the diminishing tunnel itself. Three quarters of the hull was already entering the vortex, as if pulled by a giant magnet ahead of the ship, no matter how hard the helmsman steered the ship away from it. No matter how anyone in engineering applied all the might and power of the engines and generators below deck to force the rudders to move the ship away from that vortex. Right now, right this moment, they were all helpless against its powerful pull, the rest of the ship slowly entering purple-green darkness.

"Agh!" Gaston slammed both his hands on the arms of his chair. He got up in frustration. "Explain, Barto! What the hell is this, again?" He pointed at the purple-green darkness already enveloping the ship in its deep bowels, its eerie colors dimming the lights in the bridge. All in the bridge stared at Barto. Right now, he was the only solution to the incongruous, fantastic anomaly appearing before them, its claws attached to the ship, dragging it inside.

Right now, they all depended on him.

Again, Barto signed in rapid speed, Joanna working hard to understand the complexities of his conversation. She translated towards the Captain.

"Sir, Barto is saying that this anomaly we are entering in now is a time portal, triggered by the crystal machine, which was triggered by the ship's generators the moment the ship entered this core point. That is how I understand it to be as he says it."

"Logical, once again." The XO muttered softly. "I would agree with the assessment. We are being hounded by too many inexplicable events one after another coming at us. The question is how do we get out of there and still not be killed by that oncoming rogue wave?"

"Good question." Captain Caine agreed. He stared at Barto. "Yes, how? Do you know?"

Barto signed speedily. Joanna translated.

"He says we have to go in that vortex. We have no choice. This time portal has a certain power that is pulling, uummmm, it's stronger than the ship, forcing the ship to go in, invisible or not." Joanna shrugged helplessly. "He says it's just the way it is. We have no choice but to go in."

Captain Caine stared for a moment at Barto. He did not like this at all.

"Sir." The XO asked firmly. "May I suggest that it may be auspicious in our favor to enter the portal." He pointed towards the navigator's panel. "Look! The rogue wave is about to crash soon from the aft of the ship. We will not survive its onslaught."

"Agreed, XO. As Barto says, we have no choice." He turned towards Barto.

"And where will we end up in there?" He pointed towards the singularity point of the yawning purple-green vortex. "Do you know?"

Barto shrugged his shoulders helplessly. He signed again towards Joanna.

"Sir, he says it's anyone's guess. Barto does not know the mechanisms of the crystal machine and where we will all end up in. He only knows that the crystal machine was built for this purpose by the people of Atlantis. It is a time machine."

With a sigh of exasperation, Gaston sat back on the Captain's chair, his hands gripping the arms, not knowing where to start with all the mayhem and confusion surrounding him. The rogue wave in the back and this mysterious tunnel to god knows where in the front. Except they were being forcefully pulled towards that tunnel.

That he was sure of. Mercifully.

The ship-wide communications phone rang. The XO picked it up speedily. Seconds later, he slammed it back on its wall receiver.

"Captain." The XO yelled. "It's Pry-Fly. The Air Boss is saying his group wants to mutiny. They're not willing to go with the ship into that anomaly, your orders notwithstanding. They did not sign up for that. In fact, right now many of them are running towards the deck with the intent to jump off the ship into the waters."

Stunned by the news, Gaston got off his seat heading towards the bridge window. All within the bridge followed him, all looking down through the bridge windows.

Below them, hundreds of volunteer shipmates were running towards the hull edges of the flight decks, already jumping off the ship, half of its massive body slowly gliding within the horror of the purple-green swirling vortex, moving like a giant open mouth about to devour them, ship and all. Deeper inside the vortex, the swirling coils of the cotton-candy clouds still moved in a relentless counterclockwise direction into infinity.

Already consumed by fear and terror going into the unknown, half of the hundreds of the ship's officers, sailors, and workshirts, resembling a large group of dark ants, altogether were running towards the edges of the ship, all of them jumping off the decks without hesitation, their arms and legs flailing into the eerily, ominous darkness of the tunnel only to disappear in an instant the minute they were in the air.

Not realizing what was happening at the bow, port, and starboard decks, more of the hundreds jumped off into the fading environs of their diminishing reality, their world, at the stern of the ship, now slowly entering the darkness of the electronic purple-green fog. It was a complete chaos of mayhem and fear bursting out all over the flight decks, all the hundreds of souls desperate to escape the inevitable act of the USS Arcanus being forced into the monstrous void ahead of it.

And alone among the hundreds running in terror, a lithe figure in gray-green pilot jumpsuit jumped into the water, her blonde hair tied in a pony-tail, her arms and legs flailing, her uniformed body disappearing instantly the minute she bailed out from the deck with the others.

Captain Caine instantly recognized her.

"Sharona!" Gaston yelled with all the might of his voice, the shock enveloping his body, not caring that his secret was out for all to know. Head lowered, his eyes brimming with tears, his hands slamming on the bridge window. "Sharona! Don't go! Please don't go. I need you!"

All of a sudden, the bridge became still and quiet. So quiet one could possibly hear a pin drop.

Their bodies and minds in abject shock witnessing the horror of the sudden mutiny of their fellow shipmates, all the crew within the bridge stared with a new sensation of utter shock at the Captain for what seemed like forever.

Gaston found himself lost in desperation, not able to find a solution to their dilemma, to his dilemma. At this point of shocking revelation, he did not care if they all watched him. Puzzled and mystified, the bridge crew turned towards the XO.

He shook his head ever so slightly, making the motions of a knife crossing his throat.

We all did not ever see this.

Then the quiet mood was interrupted by a commanding voice, the Captain still lost in his thoughts, his slumped body sitting on the Captain's chair, his eyes blankly staring through the bridge window at the now empty deck of the ship, half of his crew gone overboard.

The mutiny was now over.

"Man your stations!" The XO ordered, taking over command at the bridge. "And stand on guard for potential anomalies ahead. Use all your training and experience collectively. I myself have no idea what we are getting ourselves into right now."

"Yes, sir!" All returned to their duty stations, as the ship now fully entered the purple-green swirling vortex bedecked with cotton-candy clouds moving counter-clockwise.

At that moment, Gaston sighed wearily, his hands over his eyes, trying not to let a tear drop. It seemed so unmanly, so undignified in his status as Captain of the naval nuclear carrier to cry. Even if she was his beloved, more than his cold fish of a wife. Drunken wife. Unhappy wife. God, he needed her and now, she was gone, propelled by her fear of entering whatever caused her and all the others to disappear the moment they all jumped.

Gaston knew as Captain he had to maintain an appearance of strength, fortitude, and confidence to the remaining ship's crew and workshirts and pilots.

There was nothing he could do about it. It was now time to move forward.

After several seconds mustering all his strength, Captain Caine sat upright on his chair, his mouth grim and determined, his brown eyes blazing with unwavering courage, as he assumed command of the bridge from XO. He was determined to sally on and try his mightiest to save his ship and crew, wherever they are inexplicably and inevitably being forced to go in this equally inexplicable time portal, as Barto was wont to say.

A time portal in the middle of their secret mission. Who knew?

"I'm sorry, Mr. President…" Captain Caine whispered softly, as the USS Arcanus wholly and fully entered the time portal. "I have no choice. We are being forced to go in there. May the gods from above preserve us."

Only one image stayed in his mind, as Gaston gave in to the pressure of the anomaly, giving up his control of the ship, allowing it to go into unknown territory, tears brimming in his eyes.

"Goodbye, Caroline…"

Chapter 27

Several seconds later, the Boeing 747, still stubbornly gliding down the final 1,000 feet, its flight crew now aghast at the sight of a US naval aircraft carrier ahead of them, just entering the blue-green swirling vortex, all four of the pilots in the cockpit, fighting with all their mights against the pull of the yawning mouth of this strange anomaly in the Caribbean Sea.

But it was useless. Inadequate. Even hopeless. The 747 simply would not respond to their desperate measures to control the plane's approach towards whatever was there that wanted to swallow them all.

"Guys!" Beau declared checking the barometric altimeter in front of him. "We are about to lose cabin pressure. I'm starting to feeling faint."

"Same here!" Shouted the engineer sitting behind Beau. "You want to bet whatever is controlling the direction of this goddamn plane is also messing with our pressure systems?"

"Where are those goddamn oxygen masks?" Captain Myles yelled out searching around his seat.

"Can't find them, yet, looking at the manual now." A third pilot muttered angrily, looking around his seat behind the Captain. He flipped the open manual on his knees. "It says they are on the cockpit side console."

"All right! Found them!"

All four pilots quickly donned their masks. Beau went into the cabin to check on Senefreya's mask, which had flipped down from above her seat.

Five minutes later, he returned to his seat.

"She's okay." Beau said with a sigh of relief. He stared at the cockpit window, the wipers furiously battling the slashing rain. "What's going to happen to us in there?" He pointed at the yawning dark-green vortex.

Captain Myles shook his head and let go of the yoke once again after a final try to yank it back in place. He placed his hands on his lap. "It's too late now, men. Whatever is controlling this aeroplane has more power than us four can handle. I can do nothing now." He crossed himself.

"May God help us all."

All four pilots stared blankly at the cockpit window in silent dread, not one saying a word. In that critical moment, time seemed to come to a stop, the world moving in slow motion.

Each of the pilots waited with hushed breaths, as the 747 finally entered the blue-green swirling vortex of the electronic fog and cotton-candy clouds, following the inescapable path of the lost USS Arcanus.

Behind the cockpit, in the quiet loneliness of the cabin, Senefreya suddenly felt a strong sense of a different future unfolding before her. Her mind was racing and yet, she could not clarify what would happen in the now and then. She only knew that she was finally going home. Looking forlornly at the door of the cockpit just in front of her, Senefreya knew there was nothing she could do for the hapless pilots in the cockpit facing their fates, whatever they may entail, including Beau, the father of her unborn child.

Today, on her birthday, October 28, 1962, her powerful DNA structure was finally activated, still nascent, its budding powers leaving her tired and nauseous. She knew it was yet to mature to full strength. A few days needed to pass before she felt better and in control of her DNA powers.

For an entire year, since Papa unfolded the secret of her existence, she had been training herself day by day for this very day her DNA would awaken imbuing her with extraordinary powers. Her powers needed to awaken at a certain frequency customary to all of Papa's people from the ancient past and that took time from the day of their births.

At that level of strength in her DNA structure just becoming nascent, she only had enough energy to save herself and her unborn child against the inevitable doom approaching the Boeing 747.

A voice inside her head whispered. "Take off the mask now. It is interfering with your abilities. Just take it off. You know what to do."

Senefreya nodded, releasing the mask from her face and throwing it away.

She gasped. The cabin had been losing so much air. It was getting so hard to breath at first. She laid a hand softly on her stomach. Her baby was already growing ever so subtly. Senefreya marshalled all her inner strength and quickly sat up in her cabin seat, breathing hard. She checked the lock on her seatbelt and gripped the arms of her cabin seat. Laying her head firmly against the head rest of the chair, she closed her eyes and let her mind enter into oblivion. It was now or never.

"Goodbye, my love…" She whispered.

Once the tail end and elevators of the 747 disappeared into the blue-green darkness of the tunnel, following the path of the USS Arcanus, the time portal abruptly closed into a flashing singularity, leaving only the roaring waves, golf ball-sized hail, whiplashing wind, and bolting lightnings, all of them furiously intermingling within the tumultuous thunderstorm thrashing outside the singularity.

And finally, the foamy-white capped, monstrous wall of the rogue wave, now a hundred feet high, a fearsome legend among fishermen and sailors at sea for centuries, having relentlessly traveled behind the USS Arcanus and the Boeing 747, quickly crashed with a thunderous roar into the surrounding roiling waters of the Bermuda Triangle.

Chapter 28

Gaston opened his eyes. He found himself gripping the arms of the Captain's chair, his entire body rigid with determination to save himself, as his ship entered the anomalous presence at sea all on its own veracity. He knew that the only way to help his ship and crew was to keep himself alive and stabilized staying in one place in one piece.

Speaking of one piece…

He looked around the bridge. All the bridge crew and Joanna and Barto were still there in their places, alive and clearly well as can be in this manner of existence, having entered a time portal. All of them just awakened, each of them trying to adjust with awe and wonder and a lot of questions in their minds. Each of them wondering if they were alive or dead; in heaven or hell.

Relieved that all the bridge crew were still there, alive and well, Gaston faced Commander DeLaCroix.

"XO? How many have we lost?"

"Checking, sir!" The XO grabbed the ship-wide, communications phone and barked orders.

Seconds later, he slammed the comm phone back on the wall receiver, shaking his head. "As of now, it appears we are short 400 men and women, all of them having gone over the ship back then, when we entered this anomaly."

Gaston nodded with a sigh, sitting back on the Captain's chair. He placed his hand on his chin, his mouth set in a grim line, thinking hard. "what's left of 400 is far too few to man this ship. But no matter, we have to make do where we are with what we have."

"Agreed, sir. Again, we have no choice."

Gaston nodded. "We have no choice." He breathed in deeply, narrowing his eyes at the unusual dark waters of the strange ocean their ship landed upon. "So…where in hell are we, XO, and what are those mountains over there?" He pointed at the rocky, twin peaks just appearing in front of the bridge window. Huge twin peaks set miles apart from each other and rising ominously above the unknown, dark waters in an unknown terrain.

And yet, Gaston couldn't help feeling that somehow this place seemed familiar. As if he had been there before.

All in the bridge stared through the window at the gray and black, rocky twin peaks forming two promontories standing guard over the narrow opening 8 miles wide into what appeared to be a large bay or sea miles beyond.

One of the two promontories appeared to be the bigger peak, over 1,000 feet high.

"Pillars of Hercules, sir." Joanna piped up. Barto was excitedly nodding his head, his forever Cheshire grin becoming bigger in his face, lighting up the freckles in his cheeks.

"Explain." Gaston turned and glared towards Barto, suppressing his own frustration at being thrown in unknown situations for all his naval experience and yet, fascinated at what this simple man, a fisherman no less, had to say.

"Barto says it used to be called "Pillars of Hercules" back then in ancient times and beyond that is actually the Mediterranean Sea, sir."

"Ancient times, huh? Navigator? How far back??"

"I'm trying, sir." The navigator looked at the data and instruments in front of him, trying to discern the ship's position, place, and time. "From what I see, it seems we have just returned back to where we had come from in the north back then, a distance past point Nemo further east. And looking at the promontories ahead of us, it does appear we have reached the far eastern portion of the Atlantic Ocean back up north and right near the Mediterranean Sea. That one I know for sure, over 1,388 feet high, it's the Rock of Gibraltar!"

"Come again?"

"I'm saying that's where we are now. The time portal apparently brought us back to the north on the opposite side of the Atlantic Ocean. But the strange thing is, sir, I can't locate any civilization in the system. At least not the ones we know back then."

"XO?"

"He's right, sir." Commander DeLaCroix asserted firmly. "There is no way to communicate to any known civilization around here. The comm systems just won't work anywhere here. I can only speculate that we have been taken back in time, far back to a time before early civilization appeared, perhaps the Neolithic times by the looks of it."

"I agree with the XO, sir." The navigator nodded vehemently. "From my extrapolations, there only appears to be small villages of huts and boats built from bamboos and reeds. Perhaps, hunter-gatherers?"

"Hunter-gatherers?" Captain Caine groaned. "How far back is that, anyone?"

Barto excitedly raised his hand. Gaston glared at him.

"Yes?" He looked at Joanna. She signed quickly and Barto responded quickly pointing at the two colossal, rocky sentinels on the one side and then pointing to the west of the ship on the other side.

Joanna nodded, brushing away her growing bewilderment at his responses. "Okay, sir. This is going to sound strange."

"At this point, nothing surprises me anymore." Captain Caine shook his head in mystification. "Speak."

"Well, Barto says we have been thrown into the past, way back into the past, thousands of years into the past."

"Specifically?"

"9632 BC, give or take a few years."

Stunned at the revelation, Gaston tried to maintain his composure, as he sat back on the Captain's chair. 9632 BC was a lot to take in. Of course, there were no civilizations around to contact for help. The ship was now alone in the time of Paleolithic origins, if he could remember his history lessons. Of course, the navigator was right. It was the time of the hunter-gatherers. The Cave of the Neanderthals.

Not much help at all with their current dilemma. What to do now?

He tried to think again. He looked back at Barto. "Tell me more, Barto. Why the hell are we that far back?"

Joanna signed. Barto responded.

"Sir, he doesn't know, but he does know this. Atlantis is right there on the western side hundreds of miles away. A civilization, no less. We can get help there."

"Atlantis, again?? Help from the mythical, imaginary Atlantis? How is Atlantis there right now? We don't even know it existed."

Joanna signed. Barto responded in a lengthy conversation. Joanna spoke, as he signed word for word.

"He says Plato mentioned the lost island of Atlantis in his dissertation, "Timaeus and Critias". Plato actually spoke from the story handed down by an ancestor, Solon, who existed before him in the year 600 BC about a spectacular kingdom land of gods and humans living among each other in an area larger than life existing between 9000-10,000 years past in Solon's time. For thousands of years, this sovereign island existed in peace and prosperity, becoming an advanced, utopian civilization and a naval power, until its destruction in approximately 9600 BC, give or take a decade or so."

"Naval power, heh?" Gaston rubbed his chin. "Perhaps we could get help there."

Barto nodded excitedly, his hands still signing in the air.

"He says that that's where we should be going." Joanna spoke in finality.

"Sir!" The navigator shouted. "We have an anomaly forthwith!"

Captain Caine sighed. "What now?"

"A blip on the screen, sir. It's becoming bigger and bigger, as it approaches us. Looks like a plane. Moves like a plane. A huge plane."

"A plane in 9632 BC?" XO asked. "That is impossible. Check again."

"Agreed, sir, double-checked. Triple-checked. But there it is. Right above us about now." He arched his head to look above the bridge window.

At that moment, a thunderous roar filled the air, as a dark, mysterious shadow of a giant birdlike shape flew closely over and past the bridge window, darkening the bridge cabin momentarily with its shadow. All in the bridge clasped their hands against their ears, the mighty roar and boom adding to an increasingly painful pressure in the bridge cabin.

And then it was over. The rumble and roar over and gone. The light returned. The pressure ceased. Everyone slowly released their hands. All eyes looked through bridge window again and quickly they all instinctively clasped them back against their ears. The pressure was building again in the bridge.

And at that moment and all at once, there was an explosion of enormous magnitude at a far distance of the ship, with dark smoke and frothy white waters rising up from the core into the air, higher and higher until only a sliver of dusty-gray smoke was left, as it wafted down back into the waters.

"What in hell was that?" Captain Caine asked around. "Anyone??"

"The navigator suggested a plane, sir." Commander DeLaCroix explained. "I would go with that extrapolation and assume it was a plane, even in this time and place. All that had happened so far explains the logic behind it. I just don't know why we are strictly in 9632 BC, close to Atlantis' destruction."

"Barto?" Gaston glared. Barto raised his shoulders helplessly.

"He doesn't know." Joanna responded. "He is as befuddled as we are."

"Oh well. Perhaps, he'll know more later." Captain Caine nodded. He turned back to the bridge window. "At any rate, I agree with Barto. We should all head there. It is, after all, civilization. But first, we head towards the plane crash. There may be survivors."

"Of course, sir!" The XO turned. "Helmsman, turn north and head towards the source of the explosion full speed ahead."

"Yes, sir!" The helmsman shouted, his hands quickly spinning the steering wheel to the left and north. The massive bow of the USS Arcanus slowly turned to face the fading strands of smoke still enshrouding the waters far in the distance, the ship's colossus propellers now pushing the mighty carrier ahead at full speed, leaving behind frothy white-capped waves in its wake.

Twenty minutes later.

"Oh. My. God." Three underlined direct words, palpable with dread and apprehension, now floating in the minds and hearts of every man and woman in the USS Arcanus looking out towards the north of the Atlantic Ocean from the ship's bow and from the bridge above the deck.

All around them, multiple, shattered cockpit and cabin debris and broken pieces of silver-blue, carbon composites and aluminum alloy were scattered helter-skelter in the dark waters. Here and there, seats already dislodged from the cabin were floating aimlessly above the water.

Where were the clothes? The luggages? The shoes? Human remains?

"Look!" A member of the bridge crew pointed at a large, silver blue cockpit/wing and engine piece floating at a far end of the perimeter of broken plane debris. "It looks like a hump." He squinted his eyes. "There are blocks of words written on it. Trying to read. BOE…that's all I can see. And there's another word above it in smaller letters in cursive. Perhaps Queen?" He scratched his head. "And then over there is a 7 and a 4. How odd."

Captain Caine was stunned. Boe 7 and 4. Queen. It can only be one thing. A thing he had read in the newspapers given him by his driver on the way to the ship at docking port in the mainland. A thing that did not belong there in this time and place just like his ship. Damn if he knew what it was doing there along with the USS Arcanus.

His hands on his hips, staring at the broken, silver-blue plane debris scattered far and wide in the waters, Gaston announced with a strong, assertive voice belying his confusion. "Listen up. I know what it is. It's an aeroplane. Our aeroplane built in the USA, in Seattle, Washington. Brand new. A prototype called Boeing 747." He pointed at a large debris. "Look at its hump, where the "BOE is written on. This aeroplane was brought to LaGuardia Airport to fly to the Paris Air Show. Imagine! And what's more, that plane was supposed to return to LaGuardia just now."

"But what about that word, "Queen"?" A voiced piped up.

"Queen of the Skies". Gaston explained with the air of a college professor leading his class. "She is very big and elegantly assembled from nose to tail, including that unusual hump, which becomes a second floor above the cockpit, a lounge room so to speak. Yes, that's what our people called her. Beautiful aeroplane, but hell if I know why it's here with us in 9632 BC." He shook his head. "Well, there was supposed to be at least one pilot, most likely two on the way to Paris and back. No passengers, as far as I'm aware of. I do not see any bodies floating. Do any of you?"

"No, sir!" All voices chimed back with certainty.

"Get back to looking for bodies now. That's why we're here."

All eyes in the bridge scanned the widely scattered debris. No one dared to stop the search, until at least a body was found. Minutes passed, eyes still searching, breaths still holding, even from the men and women who had gathered at the bow and side decks to search from their positions.

Suddenly a commotion broke out from the crowd gathered at the bow decks.

Two hands waved towards the bridge from the bow deck. Gaston picked his binoculars. He saw that one hand repeatedly pointed at a debris further north and then pointed to his ear indicating a phone communication.

"XO?"

"Yes, sir!" Commander DeLaCroix headed towards the comm phone and picked it up. Seconds passed as the conversation quickened.

Dumbfounded at the news, the XO slammed the comm phone back on the wall receiver and turned to the Captain with the news.

"Sir, I don't know what to tell you, but clearly there is a body. One body." The XO stood firm. "But it is not the pilot, at least as we know of."

"No? Well, then who is it?" Captain Caine became curious. "If not the pilot, then who?"

"A woman, sir." The XO responded, his eyes expressing mystification. "She is splayed out face down on a broken plane wing, hugging the edges of the engine turbine. She is not moving, sir."

"A woman?" Captain Caine was stunned. "Unheard of. Damn strange one to fly on the prototype 747. Not even mentioned in the news. Anyone see the pilot nearby?

"No!" A chorus yelled out inside the bridge. "Still looking around."

"Keep looking." Gaston ordered loudly. "XO, have someone bring her aboard and to med bay. Check to see if she is alive. I want to know what the hell she was doing on this 747 and where are the goddamn pilots."

"Yes, sir!" The XO headed towards the bridge door.

Thirty minutes later.

Commander DeLaCroix slammed the comm phone back on the receiver, shaking his head. He rubbed his hair. He wasn't sure how to explain this to the Captain. Only what was appeared to be a blunt truth that had come out of the mouths of the rescuers bringing aboard what appears to be the only survivor of the plane crash and a woman at that?

He expelled his breath and walked to the Captain.

"XO?"

"Sir, they found the woman. Clearly, not dressed to pilot the plane. More likely dressed as a passenger. Checked her pulse. She is alive, but barely breathing. They are bringing her up to the med bay forthwith."

"Excellent." Captain Caine responded firmly. "Anything else?"

The XO hesitated. "They can't find any other bodies. Only her." The XO hesitated again. "All I can say is the rescuers mentioned that there is something strange with her."

"Explain." Gaston asked surprised.

"There is something wrong with her head." The XO shook his head. "As if it has swollen up like a balloon to the back. Not sure how to explain this."

Gaston's eyes widened. "A blown-up head. That is certainly peculiar. But then we don't even know where the hell we are after coming out of that anomalous entity. He shook his head. "Well, the important thing is she is alive. Let Dr. BanMinh deal with her head." He looked back at the XO. "So, that's it? Did they find anyone else? Any pilots, for god's sakes? We can't leave them behind."

"No, sir." The XO explained. "Just that woman they're bringing in. The only body among the thousands of pieces scattered about in front of us. I have no answer for this myself and I doubt Barto does." The XO looked at the fisherman, who grinned, showing his teeth.

With an exasperated sigh, Gaston looked back through the bridge window at all the silver-blue, broken pieces, large and small, of the lost Boeing 747 prototype, The Queen of the Skies, now floating forlornly like flotsam in the water, never to return to LaGuardia.

He shook his head.

"She couldn't possibly be the pilot." He declared to himself. "And yet, she could. Just like Sharona, but…that is an odd choice of clothing to fly with."

Feeling desolate at the loss of Sharona, Captain Caine looked up at the XO quizzically. "So, what was she wearing? Those elegant, passenger clothes?"

"A white sheath dress with large, green polka dots, torn to shreds, sir. No shoes, nothing else. Just that dress. Not exactly pilot dress uniform, sir. At this point, I'm certain she is only a passenger of the 747. Perhaps a stowaway?"

Captain Caine mused for a moment. "Not good. Even worse, we can't find the bodies of the pilots, whether one or many. I would dare say it is safe to say we did the best we could trying to find their bodies."

"Agreed, sir." The XO responded. "Extremely odd. It would seem that only she knows the answer to this question, assuming she was the passenger or stowaway in that downed aircraft." The XO pointed at the debris.

"Had to be. It only fits the logic. She's wearing a dress, for god's sakes, and it is torn and she's hanging onto a piece of the wing with engine turbine attached, I'm certain by the looks of that piece." Gaston expelled his breath, brushing through his hair. He picked up his white, naval, cover hat. "So, it would behoove that I'm going to go talk to her right now at the med bay. Joanna, you and Barto are with me." Captain Caine placed the naval cap on his head firmly and made a move towards the bridge door.

"You have command, XO."

"Yes, sir!"

All in the bridge stood up and saluted, as the Captain headed towards the bridge door followed by Joanna and Barto.

Chapter 29

Senefreya's eyes slowly opened. Pinpoints of pain throbbed inside her head like sharp knives piercing the skin. She tried to move her hands to rub her forehead, but they both were stuck in place at the sides of her body, as if frozen to whatever she was laying on. Closing her eyes, she could feel something soft and warm wrapped around both her wrists, holding her arms in place, unable to move.

Again, the piercing knives stabbed her brain, forcing her to close her eyes in grimace. From out of the air, she could hear a voice suddenly breaking the awful silence.

"How is she, Doctor?" Captain Caine demanded, brusquely opening the door to the med bay, followed by Joanna and Barto, all of them in anticipation of the news of their unexpected rescue.

Curious at the sound of the strong, assertive voice amplifying in her ears, Senefreya opened her eyes again, searching for that voice. And then, the voice was gone. Silence. Only this time, she could hear a humming sound all around her and coming from above her. What was it? Pain emanated from within her ears. She moaned softly, turning her head slowly back and forth. Where was that awful hum coming from. Please stop it. Her eyes looking up towards the ceiling, Senefreya found herself staring at a mid-sized, silver-white steel box, bigger than her head, with levers and dials all around it. Multiple cables were attached to the steel box and to an even bigger standpost nearby, the rest of the cables fully extending towards a wall beyond it. Looking closer above her at the bottom end of the steel box, she could see a glass cover the color of black and green staring into her eyes.

The humming sound grew louder.

Afraid of the hum focused at her head, Senefreya tried to right herself up, tried to release her hands from whatever strong folds of clasps were holding them in a tight grip on both sides. Again, she shook her head trying to erase the relentless, daunting pain of knives stabbing inside.

"Ohhh…." She moaned softly, giving up the effort to fight for herself. She laid her head back on the surface, her eyes staring at the mysterious black and green glass above her head once again, before closing her eyes.

She prayed for mercy. "Help me, Papa…wherever you are…"

In a second, the humming stopped. All of a sudden, the pain in her ears went away, leaving her free to breathe and relax. The steel box moved away from above her head and, free from its visual obstruction, she could finally see the grayish-white paint of the ceiling above her and all around her. Dull, white and gray color. So boring and yet, she felt relieved she was where she was right now and not lost in the vast, cold, dark-blue ocean, hugging a remnant of the 747 she could not save with all her DNA abilities.

She looked around once again. Where were her husband and the three other pilots?

Here and there were the similar grayish-white cabinets covered with glass windows. Cabinets filled with bottles and boxes and canisters of all sizes. She stared at the containers. What were they? More to the point, where was she? The whole gray and white room looked and felt terribly sterile. She breathed in deeply and coughed. Even smelled sterile. Ugh.

Lifting her head a bit and looking down at her body, Senefreya again tried to discern where she was. What she apparently was laying on. Something long and solid and yet soft and comfortable. Again, she tried to right herself up, only to be held back by the strong, ropelike clasps around her wrists.

Two hands touched her shoulders, gently pushing her back onto the med bed.

"Relax." Dr. BanMinh asserted with a smile. "You are in a safe place with us. We will take care of you. No need to get up now. Please, relax."

The voice was soothing and self-assured, releasing the fears inside her mind. Senefreya nodded slowly and let her body relax. She still wasn't sure, where she was, but she trusted that calming voice. Laying her head back once again, she closed her eyes.

Dr. BanMinh covered her with a sterile, white, medical sheet.

"You may speak with her, if you wish, Captain Caine, but only for a few minutes. She needs rest." Dr. BanMinh turned around, his hands clasped behind his back, graciously nodding at the presence of his Captain. "I will now go check on the X-rays."

"Of course." Captain Caine responded firmly. Both Joanna and Barto stared at the woman of the med bed, her head elongated with dark hair spilling on her shoulders. They were fascinated at the mystery of her survival from the 747 crash. She appeared normal, even human, and, yet, so unlike them with that long head.

Removing his white, naval, cover cap and placing it under his arm, Gaston walked up to the med bed and looked down at the strange woman they had pulled from among the wreckage of the Boeing 747. In their communications with the ship, the rescuers had called her strange. In every other respect, she seemed a normal, human woman to them all, except for one incongruity that made no sense to them. Even frightened them. Her head.

And, yet, they had a fiduciary responsibility to rescue her from her fate, being stranded all alone in the vastness of the ocean.

Having strapped her wrists to the med bed, Dr. BanMinh felt assured that he had done all he could to prevent any frenzied activity or behavior that could occur, a major risk with this curious, unfamiliar woman lying helpless and quiet.

For now, he had X-rays to examine in the next room in the hopes to answer the questions of her.

So far, so good.

Still holding his white, naval, cover cap under his arm, Gaston looked down at the strange woman lying still, her large, eyes closed, her breathing soft and regular, her chest rising and falling under the medical sheet. He could not believe at the essence of her. She was so beautiful.

So Serene. Hair so raven-black spilling like waterfall on her lissome shoulders and covering a gorgeous face with high, regal cheekbones and a soft, full mouth, her head resting on a long, elegant neck.

Where had he seen that face before?

He gazed along her body. Her skin was a warm, olive hue, typical of people living in the Mediterranean Sea sector, but what was she doing all alone on the prototype Queen of the Skies going from the Paris Air Show to New York's LaGuardia Airport? His eyes warmed at the beauty and stillness of her. And yet, there were so many questions to ask of her. Stepping back a bit, Gaston felt hesitant to wake her up, the ship doctor stubbornly asserting she needed rest from her terrible experience in the crash.

Gaston watched a hand slowly move inside its clasp, her long, graceful fingers stretching out. He looked back at her.

Senefreya's eyes slowly opened, revealing sapphire blue eyes with a cat's eye vertical slits. Gaston was stunned.

"Where am I?" She whispered softly. "Where am I?" She turned her head slowly to the right.

And gasped.

In an instant, their eyes locked, oblivious to everything around them, the med bay room dimmed into a romantic tableau. Senefreya found herself staring at Gaston's strikingly brown, intelligent eyes, his face rugged with a dimple on is chin, his hair a sandy color unknown her, having seen only shades of blond where she used to grow up in the city of Berlin.

Gaston and Senefreya.

Their eyes stayed locked for a long time in the dimmed romantic hue surrounding them both, each exploring the other with their eyes. For Senefreya, she had never encountered one so tall, so masculine, so muscular, so self-assured, so superior to the visage of her missing husband, Beau.

She could not understand why, but somehow, she felt safe in his presence.

And yet, somehow, she was meant to stumble across him, one way or another. The power of connection between the two of them was too formidable. Compelling.

A fretful voice broke the silence in the air.

"Captain Caine, are you all right?" Joanna piped up nervously, hesitantly touching his shoulder. Both she and Barto had witnessed the entire spectacle of the dance of the eyes between her Captain and this strange woman lying on the med bed. It was going on too long for her comfort level. Barto was fascinated, she could see. He appeared bursting to say something. "Wait." She touched Barto on his shoulder firmly. "Later."

Barto nodded. He stared back at the couple in front of him, their interlocked eyes still rhapsodizing in the discovery of each other.

"Captain?" Joanna asked again, in a louder voice, rapping on his shoulder.

"What?" Gaston woke up from his reverie, shaking his head in shock at his behavior. He straightened himself firmly and turned towards Joanna.

"What's happened?" The Captain broke away, brushing his white, naval shirt, alarmed that he may have done something unbecoming to his rank. "What the hell is going on?"

"I'm asking you." Joanna declared bluntly with a grin. She pointed at the woman, the pull from whose siren eyes he had broken off. "Is she all right? She looks awfully strange."

Captain Caine nodded, reassuring Joanna. "Yes, she appears to be all right from where I am. Just needs to rest, as the Dr. says. I don't know what to make of her strange appearance myself, but it is not relevant now."

Having satisfied Joanna's concerns, Gaston turned and gently placed his hand upon Senefreya's hand. He finally found his voice.

"How are you doing?" He gently asked in an assertive tone. "What happened out there?"

Senefreya blinked her large, cat-like eyes. She shook her head vehemently. "I don't know. I was supposed to go to the land of freedom."

"Land of freedom?"

She sighed. "Why am I here? I was supposed to go home."

"Of course, you are." Gaston hesitated, confused at her choice of words. "But even I myself am not home. We are all in a strange place and time and we found you lost in the waters, hanging on a piece of aeroplane made in my country. Can you explain that?"

Senefreya shook her head. "It all happened so fast. I had no choice." She groaned softly. "I am so tired…." Her large, leonine eyes slowly closed, her breathing slowing down softly.

"No choice?" The Captain scratched his head.

"She needs rest, now." Dr. BanMinh ordered, gently pushing Captain Caine to move away. "Exhaustion is keeping her memories at bay. That is normal and indicates the need for rest. Perhaps, later. I will let you know."

"Of course." Captain Caine responded quickly, pushing his need for answers to back burner. "Tell me, what are your thoughts so far, Doc?"

Dr. BanMinh moved towards a far side wall and pointed to the clipped X-ray films in that section of the wall. "These films are of her head and body. As we all can see, her body appears normal, but her head is quite abnormal compared to ours. Very elongated. I was trying to find out the cause of the elongation."

"And?" Gaston held his breath.

"Nothing." Dr. BanMinh. "Her long head is normal in every respect like ours. She was definitely born with it. Perhaps an unknown race of people. I need to do further research to determine if it is caused by a genetic deformity."

"Of course." Gaston replied. "Anything to help us out. So, her head is normal and, so, she is normal like the rest of us?"

"As far as I'm aware of right now. I only wish we had the technology to test her DNA. Her blood tests indicate that something is going on. I can really pinpoint it with what tools I have here."

"So, let me ask you, she is not of any danger to us?"

"No, not as far as I'm aware of right now." Dr. BanMinh repeated himself trying to assure the Captain, in spite of his misgivings. "From the X-rays I have, I could see that she has the coronal and the metopic sutures, just like us."

"But?"

"But, and that is a big but, she has no sagittal suture." He pointed at a section of Senefreya's skull in the X-ray. "That, to me, is quite an abnormality compared with our skulls. Perhaps a different race of people."

"Perhaps." Gaston nodded in agreement. "Perhaps put her in the closed quarters, when she wakes up, just to be careful."

At this point, Barto jumped up and shook his head vehemently. He signed quickly to Joanna, whose eyes grew wide at his signings. She turned towards the Captain and the doctor.

"Sirs, Barto says, this lack of sagittal suture is normal for her. For her people. We need to return her home to her people."

"That's what she keeps saying. And how would you know that?" Gaston demanded, turning towards Barto. Joanna continued to sign his responses.

"I just know. All my research with my friend, Dr. Miroslav Brezlov, can confirm this." Barto pointed at his mind. "I remember it all. Only, I can't prove it here and now. We should ask her when she wakes up."

"Oh, God." Captain Caine commented, his hand upon his forehead. "Never mind that for now. We will worry about that later."

Barto signed furiously. Joanna raised her hand.

"Barto says once we know where we are, and we will know where we are one way or another, we will also know where to bring her home."

He looked at Barto briefly. Somehow, he was relieved to have Barto around.

The med bay comm phone rang. Gaston quickly lifted it up from the wall receiver.

"Captain speaking, yes?" Gaston barked into the phone. "What now?"

After a few seconds, he slammed the phone back on its wall receiver and headed towards the med bay door. "We will discuss all this later, Doc. Joanna, Barto. You both are with me. To the bridge. Now."

"But, Captain." Dr. BanMinh quickly called out. Gaston turned around, holding the open door. Joanna and Barto followed his move.

"What?"

"Based on my examination of the X-rays, it appears she had been with child."

"What?" Gaston was appalled. "Had?"

"She lost the child." Dr. BanMinh explained. "The trauma of the plane crash caused internal injuries affecting her pregnancy."

"How far along?"

"A few days, a week at most."

"So, on top of her strange appearance, there's something going on in her blood and she had a miscarriage. Interesting. Well, we'll know more later when she wakes up. Keep an eye on her, Doc. I got to return to the bridge."

"No problem." Dr. BanMinh watched the Captain storm out and down the hall followed by Joanna and Barto.

Chapter 30

"**T**en hut! Captain on the bridge!"

All in the bridge stood up and saluted at the direction of the bridge door, which had opened brusquely, the Captain rushing in and nodding gravely, hiding all the stress he had accumulated, as each fantastically inexplicable occurrence, one after another, continue to upend his reality.

Joanna and Barto followed suit, ever ready to assist the Captain.

"At ease." All in the bridge relaxed and returned to their duties.

"XO?"

"Sir, we are seeing an anomaly ahead of us, approximately 4.5 klicks. The navigator discovered it on his screen a few minutes ago and just now we see it out there beyond the bridge window, just there over the horizon."

Lowering the binoculars, he pointed his finger towards the window.

"Explain." Gaston asked, narrowing his eyes and peering through the bridge window. He took the binoculars from the XO. At 4.5 klicks distance with the naked eye, he could only see what looked like a pinpoint of light shining at the far horizon, where the sun normally rises and set each day.

Viewing that same pinpoint of light anomaly through the binocular, it became a bigger globe of light so mesmerizing, so bright, it hurt his eyes, and yet, he felt strongly drawn to it, like a sailor to a mermaid's deadly song.

Calypso's song.

"Sir?" XO asked, concerned at the frozen reaction of his Captain to the anomaly. "Are you all right?"

Placing down the binoculars, Gaston shook his head, forcing himself to come to grips with his reality, blinking his eyes to brush away the blinding brightness. "Yes, I'm fine at the moment. XO, what is that anomaly? Does anyone know?" He gestured at the sparkling pinpoint of light. "Would that be a light from a lighthouse?"

"Not entirely, sir." XO responded. "Lighthouses have a ray of light that moves around, especially at night. This light only stays in one place. Doesn't even blink. Just glows. It is quite peculiar. No one here has an answer."

"Barto?" Laughter spread all around the bridge. All looked at him in rapt amusement waiting to hear what he had to say.

Barto grinned his famous Cheshire grin, wildly waving his hands in the air. Joanna called out. "Sir, Captain, Barto says he does know!"

"Of course he knows." Captain Caine responded, his hands on his hips, facing Barto and Joanna. He shook his head in wonder at how much this little fisherman knew of the here and now. "I would now dub him the ship's oracle." He scratched his chin. "I do wonder who is speaking to him to answer our questions, hmmm." His eyes glared at Barto.

More laughter erupted.

Unfazed by the laughter and entirely self-aware, Barto signed furiously again, nodding his head and smiling broadly. Anything to help the Captain return them all home.

"He says thank you! Several times!" Joanna interpreted. "He said you found Atlantis! That light over there..." Joanna pointed at the pinpoint of light still shining brightly at a far distance. "That light is the lost city of Atlantis. We are just too far to see it clearly, but it has historically been known through generations of oral traditions to be a city that glows brightly for all to see its glory and welcome them to its ports. A beacon of sorts."

"This is astounding." XO remarked.

"Indeed." Captain Caine turned to stare at the dazzling pinpoint of light for several seconds, begging him to dock his ship at its ports. He wasn't comfortable docking at an unfamiliar port and a strange one at that, lost in the annals of history, and yet, he had no choice.

Being that it was also one more puzzle to decipher on top of all the others still not yet resolved, the Captain took a deep breath and let it out, his mind working hard to think. Priority was of the utmost need right now. First, that rescued lady, who apparently had a miscarriage, is now recovering and must rest, according to Dr. BanMinh, and yet, the good doctor is baffled at whatever else is hampering her well-being.

Regardless, he will check on her later within a couple of hours.

Perhaps, like Barto, being a strange one himself, the lady would know something about the conundrum facing them all right now. Perhaps not.

At any rate, it would not hurt to find out.

Secondly, there was nothing he could do about the broken pieces of the prototype Boeing 747, its numerous wreckage now floating aimlessly in a strange ocean environment not found in their database of maps and grids and charts. Worse still, there was no investigative agency like the National Flight Safety Unit (NFSU) from his world anywhere in this strange otherworld that his ship somehow ended up after drifting into that anomalous, electronic fog. He had no choice but to leave floating debris there to sink forever in the depths of the dark waters, rusting away and collecting algae, mosses, and krill, and no one ever knowing what happened to the venerable, prototype Queen of the Skies in his homeworld.

No one, except his crew and him. And Barto.

Breaking away from his reverie, Gaston turned around and stared at Barto grimly. "Joanna, ask Barto to start at the beginning. How in hell is this Atlantis? It was supposed to be a myth."

"Yes, sir." Joanna responded firmly, turning to Barto. "We have to help the Captain."

Nodding happily, Barto signed furiously, his face animated with all the experience and knowledge coming out of his mind and mouth and hands. Joanna watched breathlessly, aghast and yet curious and excited at the signing responses coming from the even more excitable Barto.

"Sir, Barto says one at a time. Maybe you heard it before…"

"Never mind that. Repeat. End to end." Gaston ordered. "I want to know it all step by step, word by word. I need to see the logic behind the words."

The bridge became quiet, everyone in there listening.

"Yes, sir!" Joanna turned and signed to Barto. Again, he signed with all the excitement of discovery and epiphanies and memories that his mind could conceive from all the years of research work with his good friend, Dr. Breslov, and wanted to share what he knew with all around him, the Captain especially.

The only way to pacify their anxieties. And figure out what to do from hereon.

Breathless with the strange responses coming from Barto, Joanna turned to Gaston, "Sir, he says from the beginning, your ship's generators for invisibility and teleportation had activated the crystal machine buried deep below in the ocean mud and silt, the one that he was looking for in the Bermuda Triangle…the crystal's energy caused that monster storm and big wave coming at us, not to mention the earthquake in between… the crystal also caused your ship to become stuck in place at that section of the Bermuda Triangle, acting like a magnet…"

Gaston paused for a moment and then nodded, remembering th events one by one. "Yes, it would seem like a domino of effects that we had caused. And then, following Barto's suggestion, we had to shut down the ship's generators to release the ship from the crystal machine's grip and move on. Doing that, we inevitably lost invisibility. Agreed. Go on."

Joanna translated.

"Well, as you can see…it was too late…the crystal machine was built there by the ancients, Barto says they were the Atlanteans. The Atlanteans built it there to activate a time portal leveraging the earth's magnetic field in that sector. See, Barto is saying that that area where we were stuck, the Bermuda Triangle, is one of the 12 vortex points around the earth containing very high electromagnetic properties in that sector. The ancient ones, the Atlanteans, built the crystal machine there thousands of years ago to leverage that magnetic power and create a time portal."

"Clearly, they were successful." XO remarked. "Lots of ships and planes disappeared there."

Gaston placed his hand on his forehead. No matter how he looked at it from different angles, he still could not find solutions to get them all out of this mess of time and space. And now it was becoming a headache.

Nothing he had ever learned at grammar schools or high school, or college or even at the Naval Academy had ever prepared him for this utterly inexplicable, yet fantastic journey. He had to drop all that he learned and trained for and think with a new frame of mind. A new clarity of thought.

And this simple, deaf fisherman working with his crazy, next door neighbor was now the one he had to work with to build a new foundation of potential solutions.

"Okay, okay…let's see…magnetic properties…12 vortexes around the earth, time portal, crystal machine…all of them… to what purpose? Why the hell are we here of all places?" He looked at Barto pointedly.

"We just went through it, sir." Joanna shrugged helplessly. "That was the purpose. It's a time portal, remember, and we lost a lot of people jumping off the ship in there."

Barto nodded excitedly, also shrugging his shoulders.

"He really doesn't know the purpose of the time portal. He is very sorry about that."

Feeling defeated, Gaston looked at his XO, both of them nodding with their eyes. There wasn't much to go on being stranded in the past in unknown waters. They had to use every bit of knowledge Barto had in his mind to find a way home.

Gaston turned back towards Barto and Joanna. "Keep talking." He pointed at the ocean. "So this is still the Atlantic Ocean, correct?"

"Yes, sir, the Atlantic Ocean, sir, it's where we ended up from the time portal. Specifically, we ended up near the Straits of Gibraltar, no, wait, Barto says in this timeframe they were called the "Pillars of Hercules.""

"Go on."

Joanna spoke slowly consumed by the excitement of the discovery they all just made stranded in the distant past of the ancients. "Barto says that with a 95% confidence level, he is certain that bright light 4.2 klicks ahead of us is most probable the lost city of…"

"Atlantis again. Of course…and he could be right." Gaston agreed, placing the binoculars back on his eyes. "He could potentially be right."

"Sir?" XO asked, tapping his shoulder. "What are your orders?"

Captain Caine looked at Barto for a moment, still on the fence. "Perhaps he knows something…"

Barto nodded excitedly at the Captain. He walked towards the bridge window and sighed with joy, raising his hands in the air, yelling with gratitude at the gods above for the privilege of this amazing discovery in his life.

He finally found the lost city of Atlantis. And Barto had waited for this privilege his whole life.

Gaston pondered for a moment at his impulsive sense of happiness. This strange, deaf man has baffled him time and again, but somehow he felt compelled to trust him. He had to. So, for now, he must know something about Atlantis, the only one on this ship who does. He clearly wants to go there. No hesitation about it. No fear in every cell of his body, only certainty and joy.

It seemed a risk worth taking. He had no choice.

"All right. Let's go." He looked up at XO and nodded. "Let's move on. Medium thrust ahead. Alert everyone ship-wide to be on battle stations. I have no certainty that these so-called Atlanteans are friendly or inimical. We could end up at war with the inhabitants, us being foreigners in a strange land. Their land."

"Yes, sir! Medium thrust ahead, helmsman." XO barked. "29 knots ahead towards that light." Turning around, XO headed to the ship-wide communications phone.

Barto excitedly clapped his hands. He gave the Captain a two thumbs up gesture. "This is so exciting! You won't be sorry." Joanna interpreted.

"I'm counting on that." Gaston sighed feeling apprehensive, as the XO ordered the bridge helmsman and engineering operators to turn the ship towards the bright dot of light at medium-thrust.

Several seconds later, the two, giant, thick propellers of aluminum and stainless steel burst with a mighty rumble and roar, propelling the USS Arcanus towards the pinpoint of light, now only 2.6 klicks ahead, and leaving in its wake the remnants of foamy, white-capped waves on the dark surface of the waters.

Chapter 31

"Wow!"
"Oh, my God!"
"Holy Crap!"
"Whoa!"
"Good heavens!"
"Yowza!"
"Zounds!"
"God Almighty!"

A loud cacophony of all kinds of emotional epithets burst out from the mouths of the ship's crew, their first impression of the mysterious, shining light now seen at a closer viewpoint, as the USS Arcanus slowed down to impulse speed in her journey to reach the mysterious lost city of myths and legends.

Atlantis.

For, as Barto had asserted over and over, it was a definitely a city. A city of bright light shining all on its own, all around its environs, the light coming from nowhere, and yet, shining everywhere.

All in the ship instantly dropped their guard and stared out from the deck and bridge, all of them wanting to be the first to step onto this marvelously lighted metropolis.

Atlantis.

But first, they had to find a way to surmount an intimidating obstacle all around in front of the ship, daring the ship to confront their deadly surfaces in a life and death maneuver.

That damn obstacle.

At closer view, the ambiguous obstacle from a distance soon emerged as a rising, formidable fortress enclosure of razor-sharp, dark beach rocks encircling the beautifully lighted city sitting a half mile away at the center.

Upon even closer scrutiny, one could see the green, brown, and yellow patches of slippery seaweed and sea moss sprinkled upon the cragged, rocky surface.

"Look!" All in the deck pointed ahead of them, looking up at the bridge, where the Captain and his crew were ensconced. All in the bridge followed the pointed fingers of the crew on the deck, staring ahead through the bridge window, speechless and mesmerized.

There, between the only seen, widely-balanced gap of the rocky enclosure at approximately 300 feet wide in between, stood two massive columns of pentellic marble and solid granite, the one column sculpted in the image of a Greek warrior or military leader. Beautifully sculpted larger than life in human form wearing a Greek military outfit of red tunic and outer gray armor, a long, flowing, red cape attached to his shoulders behind him.

And there was more.

Golden strapped sandals covered his muscular feet and a prominent thick beard enveloped the lower part of his handsome, rugged face, his thick hair crowning his head endowing the statuesque figure with an air of royalty.

He was sculpted in a sitting posture of self-assurance and pride, sitting on a chair and showing his powerful thighs, his right hand holding the iconic, three-pronged trident and a globe of light in his upraised, left hand.

Clearly the image of a god. Only a god could look that spectacular and intimidating.

"Barto?" Gaston asked, his mind enlivened with curiosity. "Who is that sculpture, do you know?"

Barto nodded excitedly. Joanna interpreted.

"Sir, he says it is the image of Poseidon, the founder of Atlantis."

"Poseidon, of course." Gaston nodded sagely, his memories hearkening to the mandatory Greek studies he had to take in his boarding school, all those Greek myths and legends subtly influencing his growing desire to join the US Navy. Poseidon. That name was ubiquitous in the annals of Greek mythologies he had collected in his studies. The second son of Cronus. The brother of Zeus. The god of the sea. And now, according to Barto, the founder of this mysterious city of Atlantis just ahead in his view through bridge window.

Could any of this be real? The lost city of myths and legends?

Gaston shifted his eyes towards the second pentellic marble and granite column across from Poseidon. The other column was also impressively carved, the image of a beautiful, long-haired woman dressed in long, white Greek toga, empress style, her feet enclosed with golden-strapped sandals, peeking out from the dress. Carved in a sitting position facing Poseidon, her left arm rested on her swollen mid-section, her right hand holding a globe of light.

"Who is she?" Gaston pointed at the female monument.

Barto signed excitedly. Joanna interpreted.

"Sir, Barto says that female monument you are pointing at was his wife. His human wife. See, Poseidon created Atlantis as a sanctuary for his young family. His wife was with child."

"Interesting." Gaston nodded. "I never knew that. I wonder why that information was suppressed, if true."

"Sir, Barto says only a handful of people knew that. It was a well-kept secret over eons of time. Perhaps to protect his family from primitive people like Neanderthals?"

"Perhaps." Captain Caine agreed. "And now, here we are."

"Yes, sir." Commander DeLaCroix responded swiftly. "Perhaps we'll find out what really happened, if the story of Atlantis is true."

"I would love an answer." Gaston nodded. "But first how do we get in?" He gestured at the imposing gateway between and behind the two massive monuments of Poseidon and his wife.

Just behind the individual monuments, at each end, rising from the waters, giant slabs of granite and marble were seen attached to the monuments in precisely cut, standing blocks, half in and half out of the waters, extending back a couple of feet away. Attached to blocky extensions at each end are massively thick, solid double doors, also of granite and marble, beautifully washed in the color of lapis lazuli.

Or in layman's terms, midnight blue.

On the double doors' entire smooth, shiny, midnight blue background, one could see the golden and amber colored images of lions and tigers and lizards and birds, all of them beautifully carved among the curving arabesque lines intersecting each other all around the square parameters of the double doors. Dotted here and there with the animals are the images of lotus flowers, the entire picturesque tableau adding to the special mystique of the mysterious, sparkling, white city behind them.

The mythical, ancient city of lore and wonder that the razor-sharp, dark rocks and the two feet thick, double doors gateway were obviously protecting.

From what? From whom?

As the ship slowly approached the imposing double doors, all in the bridge and on the bow decks of the USS Arcanus, the 400 strong left after the unexpected mutiny the past few hours, all of them stood frozen and mesmerized, as if a spell or curse has been sprinkled upon them from out of nowhere, beckoning them to enter the city at their own risk.

Gaston shook his head in wonder. He looked at his XO.

"What do you think?"

"I have no idea what to think, sir." XO responded in a whisper staring at the double doors. "This is beyond anything I have ever been trained for or experienced in my career in the Navy. I do not even know where to begin."

Gaston nodded. "Where to begin…"

"At least, it appears to be a form of civilization, however odd it may seem from our perspective." Commander DeLaCroix commented. "And yet, in my assessment from here, Captain, this civilization does look quite advanced, likely sophisticated. Perhaps, we can get the help we need."

"Or end up in a battlefight." Gaston stared ahead. "No doubt they have their own military." In all of his naval career, he had always held the mantra to never judge the book by its cover. Even the most beautiful entity could cleverly hide the most ugly, the most evil of intents, whether primitive or sophisticated.

He wasn't taking any chances.

"Let's find out if we can get help." Gaston gave the order. "Steady as she goes."

XO nodded and barked. "Steady as she goes. Move at slow impulse, so the city can see us approaching it. We need for those doors to open."

"Hopefully." The Captain remarked looking at Barto, who nodded in head in excited agreement, two thumbs up in the air.

The helmsman gripped the steering wheel in a steady motion, staring with amazement ahead of him through the bridge window. It was unlike anything he had ever seen in his entire life in the Navy. The curiosity that was imbued within him and his shipmates was growing every second they slowly approached the massive, beautifully decorated double doors gate, the globes of light held by the human monuments becoming bigger and brighter.

"Look!" A bridge crew member cried out pointing his finger at the bridge window. "The double doors gate. It's opening for us."

And so, it was…

All in the bridge and on the bow deck stood immovable, watching the slow, lumbering motion of the massive, granite and marble gate, both doors pushing against the heavy, dark waters in opposite directions inwards towards the city. Wide open between the 300 feet gap space enough to allow the ship to enter. Beyond the open gateway, the shimmering mysterious, ancient city shone twice as brightly like the sun now only 600 feet away from mortal eyes.

Atlantis…

"It's remarkably huge." XO commented. "As I see it, there are three circular terrains of the city with what looks like canals in between. Each terrain smaller than the previous outer ones. The biggest one I would approximately 30 miles in circumference before the canal and the next circle of land. They are just as Plato had foretold. Amazing."

"Agreed." Gaston responded. "It really does fit the description Plato gave of the Atlantis metropolis design. There are buildings and bridges and even ports all around the outer, circular terrain and all of them in bright, white colors, shades, hues, what say you. Perhaps marble and granite."

"And limestone." XO added. "Reminds me of Santorini, the design of this place. All these blocks of white, shining buildings stacked on top of one another interspersed with pathways."

"Interspersed with winding pathways and roads." Gaston agreed. "Remarkable builders, these people in the city, considering Barto tells us we are in the distant past towards the end of the Last Ice Age. How far back, do you know?"

"The Ice Age started 100,000 years ago and only started to melt 17,000 years ago." XO shook his head. "That would still entail the Palaeolithic period just before the onset of the Neolithic period. At least, as I learned from my geology class."

"The times of early man, Neanderthals, again, huh, XO?" Gaston asked. He shook his head vehemently. "No. Not possible. These stone age group of people could not possibly have built this magnificent city in front of us with their primitive tools and primitive minds." He shook his head firmly. "Not possible."

"And yet, there it is." XO raised his hands towards the city. "A modern city in the Stone Age period. Who would have thunk?"

"Come, let's ask Barto some more questions." Gaston urged XO, his curiosity increasing with the need to resolve the uncomfortable uncertainty of unfriendly, and perhaps hostile, reactions from the city's inhabitants, all of them now gathering at a port nearby. "Perhaps he knows more than the both of us about the citizens of Atlantis. We need to be prepared, if they are hostile."

"Perhaps later, sir." XO commented, his eyes wide with the same equally uncomfortable feeling of uncertainty, staring through the bridge window, not moving from his position. "We are being approached at their port ahead. Look."

All within the bridge and on the bow decks stood silent once again, watching the immense gathering of the city inhabitants upon the concavely carved granite and marble circular port embracing a quiet bay. One member stood out with his haughty demeanor standing up front of the gathering crowd. He was dressed in white, linen toga, feet enclosed in golden sandals. Soon, he diverted himself from the group to stand next to a marble, standing post, his hand gesturing to the ship to dock in there.

Gaston nodded. "Follow his order, XO. Have the ship dock at that standing port."

As the silver-colored, leviathan aircraft carrier lumbered slowly and carefully towards the assigned port docking, passing the giant beautifully colored, double doors gate, Captain Caine gestured to Joanna and Barto to stand beside him.

"Ask Barto." Gaston looked at Joanna firmly. "Are these people normal? Friendly? Anything? Can they help us get home to our normal time frame?"

Barto signed excitedly. Joanna turned to Captain Caine.

"Sir, Barto says he truly believes they are friendly. He could see by their clothes and attitude, and he knows the mythical story from all the sources he had read in his research work with Dr. Breslov. He says, these people standing there are the elite members, the group standing in the front with their long, white togas and golden headbands and tiaras. They are clearly the leaders of the Atlantis. Perhaps priests, also. Behind them are their military. And the rest, I guess, just people who live in the city. They are gesturing at us to dock this way. They are welcoming us, actually, Barto says. They are just as curious of us as we are of them."

"Apparently. All right, I have no choice but to take your word for it." He turned to Commander DeLaCroix. "Let's follow their direction. And make sure to maintain battle stations readiness, regardless."

"Yes, sir!"

The irony was not lost among the ship's crew and among the city's inhabitants standing at the docking port, all of them still observing each other with heightened interest and curiosity, as well as guarded optimism.

And, yet, what lies ahead…

His curiosity enhanced, Gaston assessed warily beyond the elite group of pristinely dressed leaders towards the military legion standing behind them at readiness, grimly holding mysterious lances, no, tridents in their right hands. Just like the trident the Poseidon monument was holding.

He did not like this at all. Still assessing the military group, Gaston noted the soldiers were outfitted in the familiar, steel-armored shoulder and chest plates strapped over their red-colored tunics, their heads hidden within the steel-armored helmets reminiscent of the Roman legions in the time of Christ.

His sense of confrontation heighted at that moment of realizing just how powerful they could be, if history was right about them, the Atlanteans. Gaston hoped he would not have to deal with them. He wasn't sure which side was more powerful in this potential conflict between the modern military from his time and the legions of Atlantis.

He rubbed his chin, thoughtfully. Funny, Barto did mention just how very powerful Atlantis was with all its numerous kinds of crystals used all over the island. The crystals were to them as nuclear power were to humans living in the 20th century that they had inadvertently left behind going into the electronic fog.

Powerful crystals. Barto had emphasized. Captain Caine did not like the sound of that.

He looked back at Joanna. "I would need Barto's help along the way communicating with these people."

"Of course, sir. I'm sure he's happy to help." She signed to Barto, who responded with glee, nodding his head in pure happiness, his Cheshire Cat grin for all to see. He could not wait to disembark the ship and greet the people he had studied about for most of his life with the help of Dr. Miroslav Breslov, his friend.

He could not wait to step foot on the mythical, lost city of Atlantis…

And yet, something was wrong.

Something he could not, would not, bring up with the Captain for fear they would leave this beautiful city that he wanted to explore. Something was clearly wrong. For Barto could not dismiss the nascent glimmer of an awful sense of doom that was appearing in his mind. As if the city's inhabitants were letting him know by their silent words coming into his mind the truth of their reality. They were welcoming the ship, he could see that, but clearly, something was wrong. And only he knew how they also felt. The connection was too strong. A mixture of happiness and fear. Oh, the feeling was too confusing to him now, to be able to disclose what was coming into his mind from the city's inhabitants to the Captain and to the others in the ship.

Especially now that they were lost and looking for help.

Now was not the right time to disclose.

Still listening to the silent, telepathic words of the standing group at the docking port, Barto stared at the white city coming closer and closer, as the USS Arcanus prepared to dock sideways along the port. He smiled and waved at the motley group of elites, military, and city residents, mentally imparting to them that he understood their mixed feelings. Mentally communicating to them that the Captain needed their help. And all in the standing group at the docking port waved back at the ship, their hands upraised, many of them gesturing an invitation to step on the shores of their city.

And still, the yawning sense of doom and doubt troubled him…

Chapter 32

"Ahoy there!"

Rolls of thick, twisted manila rope and wooden planks embarkation ladder was heaved over the USS Arcanus, now securely parked in its assigned post of the docking port.

A haughty, lead member of the group of elites raised his arm, nodded his head, and pointed to the extensive length of the ladder being hoisted down. In an instant, two military soldiers standing behind the elites extricated themselves from their legion and headed towards the embarkation ladder, as the last ledge of the long, ladder hit the bottom of the port deck.

Standing at opposite ends of the ladder, the soldiers held it firmly in place and waited.

"Not necessary, but we appreciate it!" A yellow workshirt crew member shouted.

Gaston in his full naval regalia appeared at the top of the ladder followed by his XO, also in his full naval regalia, both of them resplendent in their white, jacket uniforms covered with medals and bars and wearing their white, naval cover hats befitting the first contact with a new unknown land and its inhabitants.

Joanna and Barto followed behind the Captain and XO, all of them looking down at the groups of elites, military, and island residents, male and female, standing on the deck close to the ship, their upraised heads staring with awe at the massive size and height of the USS Arcanus.

The air was pervaded with feelings of excitement, uncertainty, and curiosity. What will happen next?

"All right." Captain Caine ordered. "Only the four of us only will go down and meet these people. For now." He positioned himself to debark down the rungs of the embarkation ladder step by step in a swift and sure manner befitting a highly trained naval officer. Commander DeLaCroix, Joanna, and Barto followed suit, Barto a bit ungainly due to his weight, until all of them were standing together on the deck, all of them facing the collective Atlantis groups standing only 20 feet away from them.

The past and the future staring at each other.

Seconds passed.

Gaston waited in silence. He wasn't sure what to do. Normally, in his world back in the 1960s, the host party was expected to make the first move of customary, diplomatic greeting, extending a hand to shake and welcome, or even a bow of his or her head and perhaps a warm hug, depending on the circumstance and nature of the first contact.

Seconds passed some more. Not a word was heard from both sides. It was so palpably quiet, one could most likely hear a pin drop on the white, coralline limestone floor of the docking port.

"Silim-Sha!" A basso, melodious voice rang out. The leading member of the group stepped out, his right hand reaching upwards toward the sky and then touching his chest, where the heart rested, bowing his upper body and head. "Silim-Sha!"

Barto pushed Gaston from behind with both hands. "Sir, Barto says this man is saying "hello" in Sumerian. You need to respond the same. You are the leader of us." Joanna interpreted.

Gaston nodded. "Of course." He took a few steps ahead. "Silim-Sha." He bowed his head and body, removing his white, naval cover hat and placing it on his heart.

In that moment, that leading member of the elite group detached himself from his group and walked slowly with the self-assurance of a royal, as he headed towards the Captain, XO, Joanna, and Barto.

Barto could hardly contain himself, his body shivering with excitement, his eyes wide with anticipation.

Joanna had earlier told him that he was to do nothing, until the Captain provides instructions. That it was for his safety and that it was also to let the Atlanteans, whoever they are, know who was in charge of USS Arcanus and its crews, including Barto himself. Everything had to go through the Captain standing in front of him.

The Captain was now anticipating the auspicious approach of this mysterious Atlantean leader with the Greek-inspired garb. Several thoughts raced in his mind.

Really, these peaceful people standing in front of him; they couldn't be the vaunted Greeks or Romans. They were all too far back in time. The Palaeolithic time, according to the orthodox history studies at his boarding school. Worse still, they couldn't even be the hunter-gatherers, either, surrounded by advancement and sophistication.

So, who were they?

None of this made sense to him. But no matter, the focal point now was how to get back to the 1960s. Back to their homes and families. Back to helping the President win the war in Cuba.

Perhaps these so called Atlanteans have the answer. Only time will tell.

Gaston waited in silence, observing the regal solo march of the elite member, who had detached himself from the Atlantean group. The stately walk towards him left Gaston in awe, the long, flowing white toga rustling on the limestone floor like soft waves around two golden-sandaled feet, each foot walking in perfect, rhythmic synchronicity, like a ballet dancer in his time.

His eyes observed the man approaching closer.

A full circle of thick, white hair crowned his head and framed his robust, rugged face, almost resembling the Greek bust of Socrates. Two hazel eyes scrutinized the Captain with a sparkle of intelligence, the long, aquiline nose appearing to snub everyone in his way, the mouth grim with serious intent. He did not reveal any reaction on his face, maintaining a sense of neutrality and self-assurance.

Standing firm in his place, his cover hat under his arm, Gaston prepared himself to confront this leader come what may.

The elite member stopped in front of Gaston and bowed once again, this time deeper and with the highest intent, finally revealing his emotion.

"Silim-Sha… Welcome in peace, my friends." He placed his right hand on Gaston's left shoulder, grasping it firmly. "Welcome to Atlantis, our glorious island city." Turning around, he spread his hand towards the groups standing behind him. "We all are more than pleased to be your hosts. Welcome in peace, all!" He exclaimed loudly with a smile, bowing once again to the Captain and, then, turning aside, acknowledging the other three behind the Captain, Commander DeLaCroix, Joanna, and Barto.

"You are curious group here." The elite member asked with an engaging smile.

"Well…" Captain Caine started to explain. "Wait a moment, you do know English?"

"But of course! We know many languages of this vast universe." He raised his hand upwards in an arc. "All we had to was tap into your minds and voila, English is your language!"

The Captain and XO looked at each other with raised eyebrows.

"Interesting." Captain Caine whispered. "How in hell do they read our minds?"

"I don't like this." XO responded in a whisper. "Now they probably know more. That puts them in power over us."

"Agreed." Captain Caine responded. "We have to be careful with our thoughts around these people."

"Not easy, sir, but doable."

In that instant, Barto separated himself from behind the Captain and emphatically stood in front of the elite member, bowing deeply with gusto.

"Yassou, parakalo." He bowed with his hand placed on his heart. "Forgive my compatriots for they are not familiar with your ways of greeting. We are from the future."

"Of course." The elite member nodded. "And who are you?"

Commander DeLaCroix started to explain, only to be duly rebuffed by Barto, who stated excitedly, pointing at each member of the group behind him.

"This is the ship's Captain."

Gaston nodded. "Captain Gaston Andrew Caine."

"Commander Marcus Jean DeLaCroix."

"Petty Officer Third Class Joanna Pettigrew."

"Also, my interpreter. I cannot speak, only sign with my hands. My nom de guerre is Barto Jepson at your service." The elite member nodded sagely with smile. He put his hand on his heart. "Barto Jepson. Welcome. You seem to know who we are."

"I do." Barto signed. Joanna tried to interpret, but the elite member stopped her with his upraised hand.

"I am familiar with his signs, rest assured."

Barto smiled broadly and stepped aside, letting the Captain lead the way. All is well now. All was done to perfection. Nothing was amiss and no one seemed offended.

The elite member spoke out, his basso voice filling the air with confidence.

"I must introduce myself, of course. My name is Jor-Ahel, supreme leader of the island of Atlantis and High Priest of the Crystal Pyramid.

"Crystal again?" Captain Caine asked looking at Barto quizzically. "Is it anything like the crystal machine back then?"

Jor-Ahel nodded with an enigmatic smile. "You will see it soon, Captain Gaston Andrew Caine. You will see our magnificent Crystal Pyramid, when we all go to the Temple of the Council Elders to join the others waiting for us."

Captain Caine lifted his eyebrows, searching far ahead of him. "Where is it, this Crystal Pyramid? I do not see it from here."

Jor-Ahel pointed behind him. "Oh, it is far, far away inland at the center island ring of Atlantis. You see, our home island is made up of three concentric, land rings miles apart, as you will see soon see. We are standing in the third and largest outer land ring. Two smaller, yet massive, concentric land rings lie behind us. Now having introduced ourselves, we will all go to the inland center ring there by longbarge through our water canals and then a brief walk over a bridge. There, the Temple of the Council Elders is located right next to the Crystal Pyramid. You will see it. We are very proud to show them to you all."

"Fascinating." XO replied. "Why are we all going to the Temple of Council Elders?"

Captain Caine nodded in agreement. "Yes, why?"

"All in good time, my friends. Too long a story to tell." Jor-Ahel responded firmly, his eyes resting on the XO grimly. "It is a critical time now and you all have arrived at a most inopportune time. Still, you all must join us. It now affects you as well as us."

"Critical?" Captain Caine asked. "How so?"

"We are at war. A war that started at long time ago. A war between good and evil." Jor-Ahel replied grimly, his mouth set in a firm line.

"It doesn't answer our question, Jor-Ahel."

"Something is about to happen, my friend. Something evil. Even I know not what that is." Jor-Ahel nodded to the Captain sagely. "We will all discuss at the council meeting of elders from near and far. All will be there. All will find out."

"Good grief." Captain Caine whispered. "We came from war back then to war right now. This is not good."

"At least we have our ship." XO responded. "We are prepared for war."

Captain Caine nodded. "Yes. Our ship. Okay, then, let's find out what's going on."

Captain Caine bowed at Jor-Ahel.

"Jor-Ahel, we are honored to attend this meeting with you. Perhaps we can help each other in this war. My ship is powerful with nuclear capabilities."

He pointed at the USS Arcanus.

"We can certainly try. Your nuclear ship and our crystals." Jor-Ahel nodded. "But first, we must found out what is going on right now. That is important. That is the crux of the meeting. And then, only then, can we plan together on a strategy and tactics." He gestured to the USS Arcanus. "We thank you for offering your ship."

"Excellent, Jor-Ahel. Now…what about my ship and crew. We are 400 souls with nowhere to go."

"Do not worry, my friend. Your people in the ship will be well taken care of with food, water, and shelter and plenty of entertainment in our residential island ring not too far from here through the canal. The second inner ring." Jor-Ahel gestured quickly. "Come, we must all go in haste to the meeting. The others are waiting for us. The news is of paramount important, you understand?"

Captain Caine nodded. "Let's all go now. XO, inform the ship that they are to take shore leave."

"Very good, sir!" XO reached for the satdite phone in his jacket.

"Good! Good! Good! Come! Time is of essence. Let us all go to the Temple of the Council Elders at once!" Jor-Ahel's basso voice boomed in a forceful manner, his hand gesturing the others to follow him.

"Wait!"

All turned around to look up at the deck of the USS Arcanus. A loud male voice yelled from the deck near the embarkation ladder.

Dr. BanMinh was waving his hand desperately. "Wait!"

"Speak up!" Captain Caine ordered loudly from the docking port. "What is wrong?"

"The lady at the med bay." Dr. BanMinh shouted back cupping his hands around his mouth. "Something is wrong with her. I'm not able to discern what is happening inside her. Her heart is racing and her EKG brainwaves are becoming more and more irrational. I am not equipped to help her. You must ask them if they can help her." He pointed at Jor-Ahel.

Captain Caine looked towards Jor-Ahel. "We have a female passenger on the ship. A lady we rescued at sea from an aeroplane that crashed."

"Aeroplane? Crashed?" Jor-Ahel asked curiously, lifting his eyebrows.

"Never mind. I will explain later." Captain Caine brushed it away. "This lady, she is in need of medical help my doctor obviously cannot provide. Can you help her?"

"We can try." Jor-Ahel bowed his head. "We also have our own medical and spiritual healers with their crystals, herbs, and potions. Let us bring her to them. Quickly." He signaled to his group behind him. A lone member wearing the ubiquitous, white toga and golden sandals detached from the group walking towards Jor-Ahel.

"Silim-Sha." He bowed to the Captain and the group. He turned to Jor-Ahel. "I will be happy to help."

"My friends, this is our chief medical healer, Tal-Sharee. He will take the lady to the Abode of Healing established in the second island ring of our city. Where is she, this woman?"

Commander DeLaCroix looked at the Captain, his eyebrows raised.

"There seems to be a ubiquitous obsession with crystals from these people." XO whispered. "Is it safe? The crystals, I mean."

Captain Caine nodded. "It is curious that they use crystals. It was a crystal that brought us here in force clearly." He breathed thoughtfully. "But right now, we have no choice, XO. The people here, they seem civilized and helpful. Perhaps we can trust them."

"Agreed." XO replied. "Let's continue to be careful."

Nodding in agreement, Captain Caine looked up towards Dr. BanMinh, waiting hopefully by the embarkation ladder.

"Bring her down now, Doc. These people, they agreed to help with the lady. Bring her down and be careful with that ladder."

"No need!" Senefreya spoke out loudly appearing at the top end of the ladder, feeling nauseous, her hand holding onto the ship's deck rail. "I'm familiar with climbing ladders." She found herself groaning, clutching her elongated head. "Oh, it hurts. It hurts all over."

"Ya! Kirikazal! Kirikazal!" Jor-Ahel, surprised and amazed at the sight of Senefreya, formally bent down on his knee, his hand over his heart, his head bowed. "We all greet you in our most honorable repute. Welcome to Atlantis, my Queen. Welcome." All the groups behind Jor-Ahel followed his manner of greeting in hushed tones. Waiting for Senefreya to respond as their protocols dictated from the royals.

Nothing. Not even an acknowledgement. Senefreya stayed silent and confused.

Both the Captain and XO stared at each other in curious puzzlement and both then looked up at Senefreya, still gripping the deck rail in pain.

"Who is she?" Captain Caine asked.

XO could only respond. "I have no idea, sir. She must be important to them. They seem to know her."

"Indeed, they do."

After several seconds passed with no recognition from either side, Jor-Ahel finally stood up slowly, still looking up at Senefreya with astonishment. The sight of the lovely Queen struggling with her pain troubled him.

He turned towards the Captain.

"Ye gods! How come she to be with you all?" Jor-Ahel repeated. "How come she, the Queen?"

"Queen?" Captain Caine stared wordlessly at Jor-Ahel. "What Queen?"

"The Queen of Egypt, of course!" Jor-Ahel emphatically responded.

The Captain looked at XO, who shook his head, again. He did not have an answer, either. Finally, Captain Caine looked at Barto, who pointedly ignored him, staring with wonder at the woman above, who was dubbed a Queen of Egypt in the eyes of the people of Atlantis. His mind raced with thoughts and pictures from the past working with Dr. Breslov.

Finally, it dawned on him. "Boy, she does look like Queen Nefertiti. The one with that long, conical crown. The spitting image. Boy…"

"Queen Nefertiti. Not bad. So, they know her well." Captain Caine whispered in disbelief, looking up at Senefreya, already positioned herself down the first three rungs of the embarkation ladder. "I would really appreciate knowing how the hell she ended up in a downed 747 from 1962, our time. And where are the goddamn pilots?"

Also baffled, Barto shook his head with upraised hands. Joanna could only shrug. "Sir, Barto does not know. And Barto says now is not the time to ask questions. He says to follow the leaders of Atlantis. It is of utmost important. He does not have a good feeling about it. Follow them, he says."

"As soon as that woman comes down."

Senefreya had now moved herself halfway down the embarkation ladder rungs, still struggling with nausea and pain. She stopped briefly, gasping for breath, her thick, frazzled hair spilling around her shoulders, blocking her view.

"Anudja hara!" A chorus of sounds emerged from behind the Captain and XO. Barto and Joanna stared with curiosity at the Atlantis crowd, now standing upright in formal attendance, their hands upraised to the skies, their collective voices loud and melodious. "Anudja hara, blessed hail to the Queen of Egypt, truwa truwa! May the gods and goddesses of Atlantis bless you! Truwa truwa!"

Captain Caine, XO, Joanna, Barto, and all ship's crew standing around the upper deck above in the USS Arcanus watched in astonishment as all of Atlantis below on the docking port sang out over and over their hail of greetings to the lady from the sick bay now hanging on for dear life on the embarkation ladder, and who herself now appeared quite confused at all the commotion pointed towards her.

Senefreya shook her head free of the frazzled hair to get a better view. So many people down there. Who are they?

Captain Caine looked up at Senefreya, still in confusion and unsure what to do now, hanging for dear life on the ladder rung. "I need to go help her get down."

"No." The strong, basso voice of Jor-Ahel stopped him. "My men will do the honors." He gestured formally to the legion of soldiers standing among the Atlantis crowd, his eyes locked to a particular individual. Nodding in agreement, that soldier put down his trident and detached himself from the legion, running towards the ladder, still held in place by the two other legion soldiers.

"Let him help the Queen down." Jor-Ahel insisted. "You and your people are our honored guests and we do not ask our guests to do work."

"That's fine with me." Captain Caine responded amicably. "Thank you. Please do keep me posted on her progress. She has been my responsibility, since we found her in the seas out there. I have questions to ask of her. Important questions."

"Of course!" Jor-Ahel remarked, nodding his head sagely. "I understand. Like I said before, I, myself, am puzzled at how our most noble Queen of Egypt come to be with you from the past in your ship." He brushed his hand in the air. "Regardless, my friend, she is now our responsibility. Indeed, she belongs here with us" Jor-Ahel added. "Please, do not worry. We will let you know how the Queen thrives. I believe that she will be just fine in several hours of care in the Abode of Healing."

"Then, you know what is wrong with her?"

"But of course, we do know. It is commonplace and normal among her people. It will pass eventually, but she must be placed in the Abode of Healing for observation and care. Tal-Sharee has experience with her people."

"So, you know her people?" Captain Caine was shocked. "Who are they?"

Jor-Ahel smiled. "That is a long story, my good Captain. We will worry about it later. Fow now we must go to the Temple of the Council

Elders. Let us hasten there now. The elders, they are waiting for us. Every second counts. I do hope now no more distractions."

"Indeed. I'm aware of none at my end." Captain Caine remarked looking up at his XO, who nodded in agreement.

"Excellent!" Jor-Ahel boomed. "Come. We must all go to the dock of the first inner canal. It is a long journey, 10 miles in your parlance. From there we will embark in a longbarge for a 4 miles sail towards the second island ring and from there we will cross the channel bridge leading towards the Temple of the Council Elders in the center islet 10 miles in diameter. Big, no?"

"It certainly is big." Captain Caine remarked. "No problem. Please go ahead, Jor-Ahel and lead the way. I am just as curious as you are what the elders have to say."

"As am I." Jor-Ahel nodded sagely. "As am I. I am quite worried. Come, let us embark on the charachaise." He gestured towards the waiting perambulator behind the Atlantis crowd. "Come follow me."

As Gaston and his entourage walked behind Jor-Ahel marching in a stately manner befitting his position, the Atlantic crowd slowly split into two separate groups creating a pathway towards the charachaise that would take the entire entourage to its destination.

Gaston and his ensemble gasped at the sight of the charachaise they were to embark. Entirely open at the top end and configured with 4 ascending lines of seats behind the driver's station, it was unlike anything they have ever seen without wheels. Just a sturdy rectangular, box-like vehicle sitting on the limestone floor, a prominent bulge extending from the back end, perhaps for fuel and thrust power.

"Behold, our charachaise." Jor-Ahel gestured to Gaston and his entourage to take their seats. "You will seat yourself with me, my friend. The others behind us."

"Of course." Captain Caine replied, stepping aside to let the others scramble in to take their seats. "What about the lady?"

Jor-Ahel smiled, haughtily brushing his hand in the air. "She will be fine with our most esteemed healer, Tal-Sharee, rest assured. The Abode of Healing is nearby in the second inner island ring. My guards will accompany them. You may check on her later. But first we must hasten to the meeting."

Captain Caine nodded. "Thank you." He turned his attention to the chariot. "By the way, I am curious. What is this machine made out of and how does it work? I do not see any wheels."

Jor-Ahel laughed. "We do not need wheels. Wheels are destructive on these magnificent floors of our island city. No, we use thrust power and anti-gravity mechanism. Please do seat yourself, my friend. We must hasten."

Gaston finally entered the first level of the 4 ascending levels of the seats just behind the driver's station, the others all seated comfortably above him, all of them observing the resplendent panorama of the island city for miles around, white and shining brightly all over, the sun adding its golden rays for an added vibrant touch. Interspersed here and there with the shopping bazaars of myriad colors and flamboyant textures, the smells of cooking and perfumes permeating the air.

The third outer island ring was filled with raucous electricity, savory aromas, and the vibrant essence of love and joy, all the people milling about enjoying the day.

"This is amazing…" Joanna voiced her admiration. "So colorful… so beautiful and warm and sweet-smelling. I feel like I'm finally at home and I don't even know this place."

"What a buzz!" Barto signed excitedly.

"It does have an intoxicating effect." XO remarked with a grin. "It appears to be quite easy to be pulled into its magnetism. Be careful, you two. I myself am entirely absorbed with its pull to my dismay."

Jor-Ahel smiled broadly turning around to face them. "Yes, my friends. That is our purpose of this beautiful, island city. Let yourselves immerse in its beauty and warmth and safety. Let the people welcome you with joy in their hearts. We live in peace and harmony in this island with the locals and want nothing more than to have you and your people join us in our happiness."

"Except we do need to go back to our time and space, our homeland." Captain Caine interrupted the conversation. "You see, there in our homeland, we are at war and our country needs us. Hell, the President contacted us first. Jor-Ahel…can your people help us go back home?"

"I'm not certain at this point." Jor-Ahel responded, shaking his head sadly. "You see, we here at this beautiful, island home are also at war. Which is why we need to go to the temple and meet with the elders immediately. It is, as you say, bad timing, heh?"

Captain Caine nodded. "That is unfortunate, of course."

"Yes, my friend. It does complicate matters."

"Do you need our help, then?"

Jor-Ahel shook his head. "No, my friend, most likely no…we, the elites, along with the local people, are strong and resourceful in this war together. We have been fighting the evil ones for ten years, but now, unfortunately, the war, our war, is going in an ominous direction. Being lost and stranded in this island home of ours, my friend, we all are now responsible for your people's safety and well-being. That is the crux of our prime decree."

"Understandable. Our apologies. We had no control." Captain Caine nodded. "But, you have my word…we will help your people however we can, a joint operations of our resources, people, weapons, and transportation." He looked up towards XO, who nodded in agreement.

"Our many thanks, my friend." Jor-Ahel nodded graciously, his hand on his heart. "Now, shall we?"

"Forthwith." Captain Caine agreed. "Let's move on. We are at the ready?" He turned to his entourage behind him.

XO nodded.

"Readiness con Level, sir!" Joanna yelled, saluting her Captain.

"Off we go!" Barto yelled, his arms raised in the air. Laughter rang around him.

As the driver manipulated the controls in his station, a strong hum soon emerged from the bulge at the back. In an instant, the charachaise began to lift itself up 2 feet above the ground floor, the seated passengers holding on to their seats, all of them marveling at its anti-gravity capability, except for Jor-Ahel, who found it all amusing. The driver reached out to another avionic control lever and soon a soft roar emerged from the built-in thrusters, propelling the charachaise forwards in a smooth, gliding motion at slow speed.

One two miles later…

Still at 2 feet above the pristine, laminated marble floor of the third outer island ring, the charachaise continued to slowly cruise forward in a sure, steady motion, still humming softly from the back bulge. Joanna and Barto were still observing the city in awe and wonder, waving at the local inhabitants, who were walking around the buildings and pathways in their colorful, free-flowing clothes, bandanas, and hair bands. Many of them carried baskets of goods and food. Others held on to the hands of little children on a walkabout. All of them bowed graciously to Jor-Ahel with a smile and waved back at the unusual passengers in the charachaise they so rarely see around the city, which was primarily designed for walking and sailing.

"How odd." Joanna remarked. "There are no other cars like this one for miles around. I hope we don't hurt anyone on the way. There are so many people and children milling around this place."

Barto nodded profusely, both hands still waving wildly, his face smiling with gusto, as if he was a VIP on a colorful, ticker-tape parade.

"You are funny, Barto." Joanna laughed. "Get down. You could hurt yourself."

Jor-Ahel smiled genially. "This vehicle, the charachaise, is special and only used for infrequent purposes, very rare purposes, like now. Mostly, we all of us just walk around or take the longbarges in the canals to get to our destinations. Do not worry, my dear. The people know to move away, once they realize we are in motion. They know about this vehicle. They can hear the hum. And so…like I mentioned, this vehicle is used only rarely and just now, we have need to use it to transport us speedily to the temple for the meeting."

"Hello!" Barto waved, refusing to sit down. "Hello!"

Chapter 33

One mile left to go...

The charachaise thrummed softly still moving steadily towards its destination, a docking port where a longbarge awaited them. At the top passenger chair, Barto and Joanna laid back lazily, the great excitement having passed into a sense of laziness, neither of them saying a word, just laying back on their top chaise. Below them, Commander DeLaCroix, his arm resting on the side of the charachaise continued to stare out ahead of him, still examining every aspect of the island mile by mile. Impressive design and structure. Bold and beautiful people strolling under the hot, bright sun. So like Santorini in every way, that one would think Santorini itself was modeled after Atlantis.

Could it be?

There was hardly any proof, only conjectures based on geological and archaeological evidence in his time, the 1960s. Were he to go back home, he would have difficulty proving the truth of Atlantis and how much it resembled the beautiful, layered, white city of Santorini, Greece. People would be ridiculing him beyond belief for the rest of his life. So, no. Best to keep to himself all he was seeing in the here and now in the ancient past of Atlantis.

Meanwhile, as the magnificent charachaise thrummed softly onwards, the XO found himself listening ardently to the interesting conversation between his Captain and Jor-Ahel.

Too interesting to ignore.

"Yes, my friend." Jor-Ahel responded sagely, his hands resting on his knees, sitting next to the Captain of the USS Arcanus at the bottom passenger seat, just behind the charachaise driver. During the last few miles of the ride towards the waiting longbarge, the two improbable leaders had struck up a conversation. "Yes, we who wear the white togas and golden sandals, as you call them, we are the ones descended from the skies, from the outer, dark space beyond the thermosphere, and then beyond the solar system orbits of all your planets, all the way to the other end of this galaxy, the other side of sol, your sun, as we call. Yes, there were three groups of us descending from the skies in our starships."

"Three?" Captain Caine asked, his eyebrows raised.

"Three large starships, yes, each with its own leader. Our starships were designed to carry a few hundreds of colonists from our home world at the other side of the galaxy…called the Dur-Ayaa system.

"Interesting." Captain Caine nodded. "So, it seems your starship landed here and you are the leader. Why here?"

"Because it was beautiful. There were local people living here, of course, but they were suffering and struggling. Hungry and tired. We offered our knowledge and technology and taught them how to dress properly, farm the land, build homes and plazas, and animal husbandry. We became their gods, so to speak, nothing we can do about that, but it helps to be their leaders, you understand."

"Of course." Captain Caine nodded. "So, you all live together and work together."

"In peace and collaboration."

"I can see that." Captain Caine looked out briefly towards the people milling about, as if they all knew each other. "I'm curious. Where are the other two groups of starships?"

Jor-Ahel nodded. For a moment he was silent. Captain Caine waited, puzzled at the Atlantean leader's hesitation. He narrowed his eyes.

"Something wrong?"

"Oh, no, my friend, oh no." Jor-Ahel shook his head. "Just trying to find a way to explain the "other two groups". Anyways, so…better to just be direct."

Captain Caine raised his eyebrows.

"You see, my friend." Jor-Ahel began slowly, his voice marked with certainty and yet, with a hint of anger. "The second group of us, they found another island in the opposite side of us. There is a huge landmass between us and them, filled with ice miles high and miles wide. Freezing ice. Not a good place to settle, you see."

Captain Caine nodded. "Yes, the last Ice Age. I read about that. That landmass you just mentioned, it's called the North American continent in my time back home."

"Ah, of course." Jor-Ahel nodded. "Like I said, very hard to build homes in there. So, we, the first group of colonists, we found this paradise island with beautiful, but primitive people, who needed our help and it was a fertile island with fresh water and bountiful plants and trees." Jor-Ahel pointed towards the plants and trees dotted here and there all around the pristine, white city, their splashes of green and brown color enhancing the beauty of the environment. He turned back towards the Captain, "So, the second group found their own inhabited island on the other side of the continent you speak of. It is called Kalamuria. Much, much bigger than Atlantis. More people living there."

"Kalamuria? Island? On the other side of the North American continent?" Captain Caine asked looking at XO. "I have never heard of it, have you?"

XO shook his head. "I'll ask Barto." Reaching out towards Joanna and Barto, he initiated a lively conversation among the three of them sitting in the upper two passenger seats. Barto's hands danced vigorously in the air, his eyes effusive with certainty, as he responded to the XO's questions about Kalamuria.

"Thank you, Barto." XO smiled. "Very informative."

He turned towards the Captain. "Sir, Barto says, based on his research with Dr. Breslov, Kalamuria was a large island in the Pacific Ocean at this time right now, the last Ice Age. When all the ice melted, the rising waters flooded the island, causing it to sink below the Pacific Ocean."

"Entirely?" Gaston asked.

"Not really, only a small island survived the flooding." XO responded. "We know it as Easter Island, with all those giant stone statues Barto says are called moais."

"Easter Island?" Captain Caine exclaimed. "But I thought they were ruled by the Rapa Nui people. Are you telling me those giant stone statues were built by the ancient Kalamurians living in the here and now? The ones we are just talking about?"

XO lifted his shoulders. "That's correct, sir. They all drowned in the rising ocean, as Barto says it. The Rapa Nui people merely discovered the statues by chance."

"How can that be, the rising waters sinking that island?" Gaston asked puzzled. "When does that happen?"

"Sir, we are now in the last Ice Age." XO reminded him. "Jor-Ahel did mention rising waters occurring over time. Let's see, the melting started in 17,000 BC and we are now in 9632 BC. That's a long time for the rising of the waters."

"Yes!" Jor-Ahel agreed, nodding his head. "Our best scientists are keeping an eye on the rising of the waters." He pointed at a wall running into the waters pockmarked with lines and scribbles. "They are measuring the rising waters in that wall. Keeping track of it."

"That's good." Captain Caine responded. "That's smart. But is there something off?" He could not help noticing the hint of anger coming from Jor-Ahel, his countenance darkening.

"My friend, it is an unfortunate situation, but it does happen. Which is why we are at war. An uneasy war for the eons we have all lived here on Terra far away from our home planets in the Dur-Ayaa system."

"Sounds like a Cold War of sorts going on between, Captain." XO remarked helpfully. "Not unlike us and the Soviet Union."

"Indeed." Captain Caine nodded. "What happened, Jor-Ahel?"

Jor-Ahel sighed deeply, shaking his head. "At first, we were all in communication with each other, the three groups of us, wherever we landed, and we were all kind and diplomatic to each other, including our locals, offering our resources and our help as needed. We even visited each other in our disparate homes miles apart by boat."

"Interesting…then what happened?" Captain Caine urged. The XO listened intently, bending down towards them, the three of them huddled in deep conversation.

Jor-Ahel continued slowly, accentuating each word with gravity.

"The prime leader of Kalamuria was eventually murdered by his son, when his son reached the age of leadership. But he was hungry for power. He wanted to be the sole ruler of all of us, no, all of Terra." Jor-Ahel shook his head. "And the warriors followed the son and became also hungry for power. As such, a coup happened, the King of Kalamuria murdered and all his advisors also murdered. Much blood. Overpowering. The son took over the land and, believe me, such a nasty, evil one. The people living there are now his slaves, the warriors his servants."

"So, a coup happened and no one opposed?" XO asked. "That is hard to believe."

Jor-Ahel smiled sadly. "This group of the son and his warriors, too many of them in the land of Kalamuria. Very difficult to confront. We would lose many of our people in such a fight. Look at my legion of warriors. Not many of us, heh? And so, we forged an uneasy peace that mercifully lasted for eons, each of us acting as if the other did not exist. I am not happy about it. Any moment now, there could be an uprising from them, because they are so hungry to rule this planet of Terra. We are constantly on the lookout, my people and my legion of warriors."

"Of course." Captain Caine added. "That makes sense. That is terrible, indeed, Jor-Ahel." He looked at XO, who nodded in agreement. "We ourselves in our home back in the 1960s, we have our own uneasy peace, what we call the Cold War. Been going on for decades. The both of our peoples watching the other, always on guard. Not easy way to live, I know."

"Not easy." Jor-Ahel nodded. "It is not a favorable way to live. We all coming here from our homeworld of Dur-Ayaa made a pact to live in peace and help each other. That pact is now broken and I am angry."

"I don't blame you." Captain Caine added. "Many times in our homeworld back then, we came close to breaking our unspoken pact of the Cold War and start a fight to conquer. In fact, Jor-Ahel, a fight was about to break out between us, the Americans, and them, the Soviet

Union, the minute that time portal showed up and sucked the USS Arcanus in. We were supposed to be at the frontlines, as ordered by our President."

XO nodded.

"Ahh…." Jor-Ahel breathed. "You have your anger issues, too. Perhaps we can help each other get through this, what come may in front us now. I am much afraid that the meeting may be about this matter of what you say, an unspoken war, although I do not know much more than my own presupposition."

Captain Caine nodded. "We will find out then. Of course, we will help each other. That is our mission statement as the USS Navy in our home back in the 1960s."

Commander DeLaCroix nodded. "That's true. So, what happened to the third group. You did say there were three of your groups."

Captain Caine nodded expectantly. "Yes, the third group?"

Jor-Ahel smiled broadly, the warmth returning in his smile. "Ah, the third group of our colonists from Dur-Ayaa, they landed in a faraway land just beyond the two mountains." He pointed behind him. "You have seen the two mountains rising from the ocean, no? You have come from there, no?"

Captain Caine nodded. "Yes, we have come from there. Where we came from, in the 1960s, the sector of these two mountains were called the Gibraltar Straits."

"Also known as the Pillars of Hercules long before." XO offered helpfully. "Leads right into the Mediterranean Sea."

"The beautiful turquoise sea beyond, yes." Jor-Ahel nodded. "This third group landed on a fertile plain, where the beautiful, wide rushing river runs through it for miles downwards to the south. The River Roraima. The local people lived near that river in huts, collected plants and berries, and fished in the river for food. Beautiful people, but very primitive. So…there were beautiful trees and plants all over that land, very fertile, just like in this island of Atlantis, when we arrived. So, of course, the third group, they landed there in that bountiful land and mighty river and the local people welcomed them."

"River that runs for miles downwards in that land." Captain Caine said thoughtfully. "Hmmm, you know what I'm thinking, XO?"

"Yes, it's actually the Nile River." XO nodded. "It fits. The land is Egypt."

"Egypt, yes, that is correct." Jor-Ahel nodded brightly. "Beautiful land, beautiful people all living together in peace, just like us. We visited each other frequently and bring gifts of all kinds." Jor-Ahel sighed, shaking his head forlornly. "They too, in the land of Egypt, live in an uneasy, unspoken peace with the people of Kalamuria, just like us. We were in shock at what the son did to his father many years ago. We thought best to leave them alone."

"Except your group and this other group have been watching your backs for years". XO added. "Constantly on edge. How unfortunate."

"At least, you have each other." Captain Caine offered consolation. "That's two against one."

"Yes, we do outnumber them, but we are not interested in pursuing war with them. We just wanted to be left alone to live our lives in peace." Jor-Ahel nodded, fear and courage emerging in his eyes. "And so, it was decreed until now…and now, something is wrong. Very wrong. And we are going there now, to the Temple of the Council of Elders, to find out."

Jor-Ahel glanced at both the Captain and XO. "It must be predestined fate for you all to arrive in your powerful ship to our land at a time where…"

"Something is wrong…dreadfully wrong as you lay it out."

Both Captain Caine and Commander DeLaCroix nodded gravely, as they looked out beyond the driver of the charachaise. Their fun, driving transport was now slowing down bit by bit, like a locomotive train slowing down in its approach to the train station in all its grandeur. Ahead of them was the second docking port, smaller than the one they all had just left a few miles behind.

And there the longbarge awaited them.

Chapter 34

The driver of the longbarge sat in his station at the bow, his hands firmly grasped to the steering wheel, his eyes focused onwards to their destination. The blue-gray waters remained calm, as the longbarge cruised on in a steady speed from the thrusters in the back bulge, not unlike the charachaise.

The passengers settled comfortably in their seats, marveling at the pristine, aquatic beauty around them. Canal is not a word they would all apply to this magnificent creation of contained water channeling around each island ring.

The Captain looked ahead, trying to measure in his mind the size of the island from where he sat.

"Big island." Gaston remarked, seated in the front row of the three horizontal benches, each behind the other. XO sat behind him by himself. Jor-Ahel was seated alongside the Captain, the both of them just behind the longbarge driver. The last bench behind Commander DeLaCroix was occupied by Joanna and Barto, both of them acting like new tourists viewing the spectacular panorama the island.

A deep conversation continued among the Captain, XO, and Jor-Ahel.

"We are not into what you call timeframe, your atomic clock." Jor-Ahel responded. "We use the planets and stars and the sun above to let us know the seasons and time that passes by. So, you see, by the astronomical deductions of our most esteemed astronomers, as you call them, we are now in the age of the constellation of Leo."

The Captain nodded. "We know the Leo constellation."

"Then, you know about the earth wobbles, as you call it? 25,000 years back and forth? Good. Good. So, yes, yes, there is now a warm atmosphere change happening all around us, what you call climate change in your homeworld. And the seas all around us are rising ever higher, the ice glaciers in that big landmass to the east melting as a result of the climate change."

He shook his head. "As you can see, these rising waters are coming this way to our island. We all are watching, our scientists carefully measuring the rise of the waters day by day by day. Perhaps one day, it will be necessary to leave the island, who knows."

Captain Caine narrowed his eyes. He looked up at XO, who shook his head, not sure if they are supposed to be the harbingers of truth. Both of them looked at Jor-Ahel, both of them uncertain if they should tell him of what they knew already…that Atlantis was going to be destroyed, the entire island sunk beneath the seas.

What if by imparting the full truth of Atlantis to Jor-Ahel, the timeline changes…to a different future than the one they just came from?

For several seconds, no one spoke.

"Look!" Joanna pointed ahead. "A mermaid!"

And so there was. Not too far from the longbarge now slowed down to a still standing, the tantalizing mermaid was sitting on a rocky outcrop, her massive silver-gray fishtail with graceful overlapping scales wrapping around the smooth, crag rock jutting out of the waters, Her physique was described as a beautiful half-human, half-fish feminine form, her thick, shining, auburn hair spilling like waterfall over her shoulders. A heart-shaped face revealed sparkling, hazel eyes, soft red cheeks, and a full pouty, red mouth. Giant, green leaves covered her full bosom, her right hand resting on the rocky surface, her left hand brushing her left hip/fish scales in a seductive manner, her entire body glowing under the ray of the sun.

She opened her mouth…to sing.

"Should we worry?" Captain Caine asked, fascinated at her entire persona and her bewitching smile, not to mention her melodious singing voice that was coming out of her luscious lips. Never had he ever seen such a magnificent creature, if you could call this a creature.

Too tempting.

Jor-Ahel laughed. "No need to worry, my friends. Enjoy her musical singing. It is an inherent part of her being and does no harm to anyone. Please enjoy…it is like opera, no?"

The longbarge stopped still, bobbing softly like a buoy. The passengers all waited with anticipation, as the mermaid began her song.

A glorious, vibrato, soprano voice filled the air, soaring high like angels in a choir, like violins at play, each word a different melody arising from deep within her throat. All the passengers in the longbarge sat still and quiet, mesmerized at the beauty of her impressive singing.

"I never tire of her voice, when I pass her domain in these waters." Jor-Ahel sighed. "She is remarkable, no?"

"Indeed." Captain Caine responded. "Where we live back in our world, there is no such thing as mermaids. Just a myth, a fairy tale being in children's books. How did you come upon this creature?"

"I would not call her a creature." Jor-Ahel smiled. "That would offend her. She is half-human and the human part is very strong inside her. She is full of love, but unfortunately, her home will always be in the waters."

"Come again?" XO prodded.

Jor-Ahel sighed. "She is a by-product of terrible DNA experiments by our genetics scientists not too long ago. We had some very bad geneticists, on a path to doing dreadful experiments with human and animal DNA."

"What?" Captain Caine was shocked, his eyes towards an equally shocked XO. "Please explain."

"It was a genetics experiment gone awry creating the beautiful half-human, half-fish being you see before us. We put a stop to it before they have done any more terrible experiments mixing animal and human DNA." Jor-Ahel shook his head. "Terrible. They are now locked up in our underground cells."

"Are there others?" XO asked. "Other experiments?"

Captain Caine looked up reprovingly.

"Yes, my friend." Jor-Ahel responded sadly. "There are two others we had rescued from the science labs. We also have a being who is half-man, half-bull and another being who is half-man, half horse."

"My god…a minotaur and a centaur." Captain Caine remarked. "The Greeks spoke about them in their history annals. And here we thought they only exist in fairytales. Where are they?"

Jor-Ahel pointed beyond him. "They are both living in peace in the second island ring far away from the people. We set a section of land to be their sanctuary. We have good people taking care of them. Poor souls. They did not ask for this."

"Of course not." Captain Caine agreed. XO nodded. "And this beautiful mermaid there, the waters there, where she is sitting on the rock, are her haven, correct?"

"Yes, that is correct, my friend." Jor-Ahel nodded with a smile. "Below the rock is her cave and she swims with her water friends like the giant turtles and spotted seals. We also take good care of her."

"Any chance we can get closer." XO asked, feeling the rising temptation to touch her, to be with her, hell, to kiss her. "Can she talk?"

"Yes, she can talk, and no, we must go further on to that meeting with the Council Elders. It is of the utmost importance. Any delays will destroy any chance to provide remedies to any problems that may arise and trust me, I have no idea what we are all getting into. It is dreadfully worrisome." He rubbed his hands in impatience. "It is such a bother… such worries going on now. Come, we must hasten." Jor-Ahel tapped the shoulder of the longbarge driver sitting before him, waiting to proceed. "Move on, my man."

The driver turned a lever and the longbarge shifted its speed thrusting forward towards the center island.

"I am sorry." Jor-Ahel offered. "We must hasten, you understand?"

Captain Caine nodded firmly.

"Sure." XO replied, disappointed at not being able to get closer to this fantastic half-fish/half-female. He could only stare at her in remorse, her tantalizing visage becoming smaller and smaller, as the longbarge cruised steadily away towards their destination.

"Look! The mermaid! She is waving at us!" Joanna spoke up.

Chapter 35

"**M**y god."
"Beautiful."
"Wow."
"Brilliant."

Words of praise and admiration flowed from the mouths of the four wayward visitors in Atlantis standing with Jor-Ahel in front of a shining, white, temple building unheard of in their homeland, except for perhaps, the ancient Greek temple, the Parthenon.

But this building was different. Unheard of.

Made of the same materials, as all the buildings stacked like blocks on top of each other in each of the outer rings of Atlantis, the corraline limestone and pentellic marble and solid granite all combined to produce this magnificent edifice prompting all who viewed it with all kinds of beatific adoration.

The four visitors simply stood frozen in awe assessing its magnificent Grecian design.

Just in front of them at its very bottom, the crystalline, white stairs of 20 steps gracefully extended upwards to the heavily, fortified foundation, the portico, housing the giant, crystalline temple structure that somehow reached the skies forever. At 200 feet high each, four standing doric columns etched with arabesque lines, graced each side of the front portico, about 7 feet wide. At each side of the largely, rectangular configuration, there were 12 similar standing doric columns extending as far back as the eye can see, perhaps 100 feet long.

"Wow. That really looks like the Parthenon, huh?" Joanna remarked with a whisper of awe, stunned at the amazing size of the only building that huge in the entire island of Atlantis, save for the pyramid nearby, also a colossal megalithic structure, also made of corraline limestone, pentellic marble, and solid granite. Side by side not too far from each other, like two giants standing in alliance with each other, their resplendent manifestation in the center ring of Atlantis simply took one's breath away.

"It's bigger than the Parthenon." XO agreed.

"Absolutely." Captain Caine remarked.

Barto signed excitedly. Joanna laughed softly. "Sir, Barto says, now do you believe me? We are all standing on ATLANTIS."

Captain Caine laughed. "Of course, it appears we are in Atlantis, as we seem to be still solid human being forms existing somewhere in this universe." He shook his head. "I only wonder how the hell we ended up in Atlantis of all places going into that green, electronic fog."

XO nodded. "That has been my sentiment, also. Why Atlantis?"

They all looked at Barto, who could only shrug his shoulders. "Sir, Barto says that he had a working theory, but he needs Jor-Ahel to confirm it."

The group all looked at Jor-Ahel, who smiled broadly. "It's all in your thoughts, my friends."

"Not funny." Captain Caine replied. "Our thoughts?"

XO nodded grimly.

Jor-Ahel laughed softly. "Oh, yes, your thoughts. You really have no idea how powerful your thoughts are. Whatever you think and whatever you say based on what is in your mind and…." He gestured to the four visitors standing confused before him. "If all your thoughts are collectively gathered into one, then the manifestation will happen. Tell me, my friends, what were you all thinking and talking about at that time what you call the electronic fog opened for you all to enter? Tell me."

The Captain and XO stood silent, still confused.

Barto excitedly signed. Joanna interpreted. "Sir, remember, we were rescuing Barto in the Bermuda Triangle. Remember?"

"Yes." Captain Caine responded. "Of course, and we were asking him what the hell he was doing in the waters with the storm coming."

XO nodded. "And he started to talk about the crystal machine of Atlantis buried in the Bermuda Triangle area. Just near the Bimini Road."

Barto jumped excitedly, his hands dancing in the air. Joanna laughed. "Sir, Barto says you are getting warmer and warmer. Yes, that's it. We were all thinking and talking about the crystal machine and Atlantis."

"Just as the ship was entering the time portal." XO marveled. "That is an amazing theory. I would likely believe it. How else?"

"Yes, how else." The Captain nodded. "So, in retrospect, that would explain why the lady we rescued, what was her name again?"

"Senefreya." XO replied. "She identified herself as Senefreya to Tal-Sharee. I just happened to eavesdrop. Unusual name, if I may add."

Jor-Ahel nodded with a smile. "Not so unusual here. Senefreya is a name belonging to the language of the people of Kalamuria, the first colony, understand. It means "my beloved".

"So, if she was the only one in that plane, she must have been thinking about Atlantis." Captain Caine rubbed his chin. "It fits perfectly with this theory."

XO nodded. "Perhaps the missing pilots were thinking otherwise, other places?"

"And just disappeared into oblivion?" The Captain added. "Is that right?" He looked at Barto and Jor-Ahel, both of whom nodded in agreement.

"So, the lady Senefreya was obviously thinking about Atlantis. Why Atlantis?" XO asked.

"Yes, I wondered why myself." Gaston added thoughtfully.

"This is her home." Jor-Ahel replied. "Her rightful home. She thought to come home to her people and they are here, but not in Atlantis."

"Her people? But how?" Gaston asked. "She is from the time back as us. She is from the 1960s. She can't be that old. Impossible." He shook his head firmly. "Impossible."

"That I cannot answer for I do not know." Jor-Ahel smiled. "You will have to ask her."

"Of course."

"When she is well, my friend." Jor-Ahel warned. "Tal-Sharee knows how to work with her, to heal her. It won't be long and then, you can then speak with her."

Captain Caine nodded. "That's fair."

"Still, it would be nice to know what is wrong with her." XO asked. "Why our medic couldn't do anything. That is strange considering our exemplary medical technology."

Jor-Ahel looked at XO with a smile. "It has nothing to do with your medical technology, trust me. We know you tried."

"Then what is it?" Captain Caine prodded with curiosity. "What needed to be done?"

"Well…" Jor-Ahel responded cautiously. "It might likely be her day of birth this day. And also, she herself appears to be in the age of maturity common in her people. So…it is inevitable. Only Tal-Sharee can help her, notwithstanding your excellent medical technology and doctor."

"But still…" XO prodded. "Why not?"

"Look!" Joanna pointed up at the portico. "Someone's there."

Barto bent down on his knees, his hand on his heart, his head bowed.

In an instant, a 9 foot tall being almost transparent in its white essence, his face long and triangular with large, slanted blue eyes going back to the head, his head crowned with long, silky white hair, appeared in the yawning dark portico out of thin air, as if a genie coming out of the dark, dusty bottle.

Dressed in a flowing long white, silky garment overlapping around his body, slightly showing toned torso and limbs, the tall being slowly and royally gestured beyond the stairs below him with his large, graceful hand, the long, long fingers flowing through the air.

His eyes locked with the tall, white being's crystal blue eyes, Jor-Ahel slowly placed his hand over his heart in response, bending his head slightly in acknowledgment.

"Come, my friends." He gestured to the four visitors to climb the magnificent white, pentellic marble steps towards the portico at the top of the stairs, the 9 foot tall, snow-white being now turning slowly and disappearing into the dark recesses of the temple.

"Come. We must hurry to the meeting of the Council of Elders."

"Of course." Captain Caine acknowledged with a bow of his head. "Lead us on."

The four visitors followed Jor-Ahel up the marble stairs, each opposing banisters flanked by two giant marble statues of lions at the base, their gorgeous, sculpted manes crowning their heads held high and aloof, as they sat in perfect posture, their eyes gazing intently like sentinels guarding the temple building.

Joanna softly touched one of the sculpted beasts, as she walked up the stairs with the others.

Barto smiled at her. "I feel the same way…." He signed softly, his hand on his heart.

The dark recesses beyond the portico became a hallway, each side of the wall flanked by a row of what appeared to be brightly, polished, white crystals the size of basketballs, each of them a shining ray of beam lighting their path along the hallway.

"Crystals again. Interesting." XO remarked scrutinizing each passing bright, white crystals. "How do you make them work?"

"Not us. Our high priests do the work." Jor-Ahel smiled. "It is their what you say, their duty to make it work. They are the experts with crystals."

"But how?" XO prodded. "I don't see any wirings."

Captain Caine gave XO a warning in his eyes. Not now.

"We will explain. Later." Jor-Ahel responded patiently. "It is a complex process and requires much deeper thought than we can do right now. The meeting we are going to must be of higher priority and we are already a little late. Come, come." Jor-Ahel hastened deeper into the hallway.

The group of five finally reached a door at the end of the hallway. It was made of the same heavy stone structure as the magnificently, beautiful gateway double doors out in the waters by the rocky knolls that opened to let the USS Arcanus enter. The same lapis lazuli colors, the same lions and tigers and lotuses etched all around, interspersing with the beautiful arabesque lines.

Jor-Ahel stopped for a moment, his eyes focused on the double doors. Gaston could see there was no latch, no levers, nothing that they could manipulate to open the doors. Nothing. Just one long straight beautiful sets of slabs with a long, tight joint running down its center.

"What's he doing?" XO remarked. "How do we open this door?"

"I'm not sure, but I think that's what our guide is doing right now." Captain Caine replied, watching Jor-Ahel breathe firmly in and out, his throat emitting a soft hum, his eyes in a fixated gaze at the double doors.

"Wow…" Joanna whispered in amazement, as the double doors slowly creaked from the center line towards them, forcing the group to back away slowly letting the double doors take up the necessary space. "Just like that…wow."

Barto nodded. "Just like that." He signed. "These people…they are special."

"Boy, I would definitely be interested in knowing how our Jor-Ahel does this. We could definitely use it." XO commented.

"Definitely." Captain Caine agreed. "We'll ask him later. Let's find out what's going on that makes this such a rushed meeting of sorts."

"Agreed. Hope it's not bad news."

"50-50, XO." Captain Caine chuckled. "We'll find out soon enough."

"Do you think Barto knows?" XO fingered him walking with Joanna.

Barto, knowing how to lip read, only stared pensively at the Captain and his XO. Joanna watched him. "What is it, Barto?"

Barto shook his head. He smiled sadly at Joanna. "I just do not get a good feeling out of this, that's all. It is not for me to say. But it is not good."

"Why not?" Joanna implored. "What's happening, do you know?"

"I do." Barto signed. "But like I said, it is not for me to say. It would be like ruining the conversation. Best be said from their mouths, their truths, so no one is lost in translation, you know."

Joanna nodded. "I suppose so." She took Barto's arm. "Come on, let's find out."

The formidable double doors, smaller than the ones guarding the island of Atlantis at the rocky knoll enclosure, but nevertheless, no less intimidating, now fully opened, as if inviting the group to enter at last, no hesitation at all.

"Come." Jor-Ahel gestured. "Let us go in now. The others are waiting for us."

"Silim-Sha!" A warm, basso voice sounded from within the meeting gallery, a spacious, square suite, the walls a color of luminous pearl, the numerous white crystal balls lining each of the four walls, all of them emitting soft ambient light.

At the center of the gallery, ten cushioned throne chairs, the color of deep royal-blue lined with gold leaf decorations all along the edges, were arranged in a semi-circle, a couple of feet away from the center, colorful, mosaic artwork on the floor, comprised of a circular network of braids and triangles in a spiral arrangement. Upon closer look one could see the exquisitely designed pattern consisting of glowing, colored glass and tiles, interspersed with sections of white marble.

At the apex of the semi-circular rows of the ten throne chairs stood two giant throne chairs, also royal-blue with the golden leafy design edges. The two chairs immediately drew everyone's attention to its massive size.

XO looked at his Captain. "Giants?"

"Possibly." Captain Caine responded. "Hopefully of the good kind. Jor-Ahel would not possibly put us in danger, it would seem, but still."

"It is certainly massive." XO nodded. "Would not want to confront them directly. We must be prepared for the worst."

"Indeed." Captain Caine nodded, his hand massaging the gun he had surreptitiously hidden in his belt just before going down the ladder to meet the inhabitants of Atlantis. XO did the same.

Jor-Ahel gestured to the four visitors. "Please be seated anywhere you please, except the two at the front." His finger pointed at the colossal throne chairs.

"Of course, thank you." Captain Caine replied with a nod. He turned to the other three. "Follow me and stay close."

The four visitors all seated themselves together in a row, Gaston choosing the middle chair as far away from the giant chairs as possible, yet close enough to converse directly. Each of the other three, XO, Barto, and Joanna seated themselves next to the Captain, in that order, all of them still staring at the titanic size of the two chairs, wondering who will occupy them.

"Ah, excellent…" Jor-Ahel nodded, walking towards the chair just to the left of the Captain and much closer to the colossal chairs. He did not seem perturbed by the size of the chairs or the closeness of its proximity to him.

"He's not worried about who sits there." XO pointed out.

"I know." Captain Caine nodded. "But still, we don't know them, so be on guard."

"Of course." XO touched his gun firmly.

"Silim-Sha!" Jor-Ahel's basso voice rang in the meeting gallery, the beautiful, vibrato sound echoing against the marble and limestone walls, the reverberation of his words clanging like a bell in the tower.

"Silim-Sha!"

His heart firmly set on his chest, his head bowed deeply, Jor-Ahel repeated his intonations. "Silim-Sha! Patronas! Silim-Sha!" He motioned to the seated group to stand.

Captain Caine first stood up slowly, removing his white, naval, cover hat and placing it under his arm. XO did the same. Barto and Joanna quickly placed themselves in a standing manner following XO's move, Joanna lifting Barto's arm, the instant he faltered towards the floor.

All four of them stood in silence with Jor-Ahel.

In the far corner of the meeting gallery, a rectangular section of the marble and limestone wall slowly gelled into a semi-liquid form for a few seconds, before it disappeared in an instant, leaving behind a dark recess.

"Wow." Joanna whispered. "That is so cool."

"These people consistently surprise me with their magic of all sorts." XO remarked.

Captain Caine nodded. "We need to be quiet now. It appears to be a solemn ritual, as I see it. Look." Jor-Ahel now bent his body at waist level, his hand on his heart.

"Here they come." XO whispered. "Plus, two giants to be seen. Not sure how they'll fit through that door."

"Be quiet." Captain Caine cautioned. "Let us not offend them."

All four visitors watched with amazement and wonder, as one after another, each wearing long, white togas of silk, with long, bell sleeves and ample hoods covering their heads, their feet enclosed in golden sandals, the council elders appeared out from the mysterious dark doorway.

Each seated himself/herself on the royal blue throne chairs, as if that particular chair was marked for that elder.

All except the two giant throne chairs.

"I don't understand." Captain Caine whispered, bending down in respect, as each elder claimed his seat in the semi-circle. "Who's filling those two chairs?"

"Please seat yourselves." Jor-Ahel gestured to the group of four, as he seated himself gracefully. "It is time for the others to arrive."

"Others?" Captain Caine asked, looking at Jor-Ahel. "What others?"

"You will see." Jor-Ahel smiled. "It will take a little time, but they will arrive. Just wait in silence with us. There must be silence now for a moment."

The group of four watched in silent awe, as the six elders proceeded to make themselves comfortable seated in their royal-blue throne chairs. One by one in simultaneous motions, each of the elders removed the sumptuous white, silk hood covering their heads, revealing their true appearance, their true nature.

And two of them had the heads and faces of lions replete with golden manes for hair spilling on their shoulders.

"Yikes." XO remarked, stunned at the sight. "Can they talk?"

Jor-Ahel laughed softly. "They speak their own language. They are ambassador elders sent from our ally, Egypt. They are of the race called Puma from the Lyra Constellation".

"Right". XO was baffled. "And look, there are two that resemble our Senefreya, with her elongated head and cat-eyes."

"Yes, they are ambassador elders from Kalamuria." Jor-Ahel explained. "Unfortunately, they cannot go back to Kalamuria, when this cold war started. It is too dangerous for them. We are happy to offer asylum in our beautiful island home."

Gaston continued to analyze the contingent of the ten council elders, two of them ambassadors from Egypt and two from Kalamuria. He turned towards his XO. "This is getting so interesting."

"Indeed." Commander DeLaCroix commented. "They clearly appear not of our world, at least. I have never seen anyone in their manifestation. Are they even human?"

"That I wonder, also." Captain Caine replied. Turning to his host seated at his left. "Jor-Ahel, who are these elders? Where have they all come from?"

Jor-Ahel smiled, the tip of his finger on his lips. "Shh…not now, my friends. We are waiting for our two special guests to arrive." He pointed to the giant throne chairs still empty. "They will soon arrive. And then we can all introduce ourselves properly. You will see."

Joanna and Barto only stared in silence. Barto smiled. Finally, he can truly say to his mentor, Dr. Miroslav Breslov, that he, Barto, has seen them in person, in flesh and blood. With all the truth his words could muster, he has seen them and interacted with them.

If only they could get back home at all considering…

All at once, the ground trembled and shook, the sound of the groaning columns swaying outside becoming louder. The royal blue throne chairs swayed, its occupants desperately hanging on with their hands for dear life.

"What's happening." Captain Caine asked loudly.

"This feels like an earthquake." XO commented. "Is there a fault around here in this island?"

Jor-Ahel nodded, his body shaking with the trembling ground, his hands gripped on the arms of his throne chair. "That large landmass behind the island is actually a ridge, a tectonic ridge and littered with volcanoes. That land has been quiet for so long, thousands of years, it is virtually asleep. This is a sudden turn of events, even we, our scientists apparently have not been able to foresee." Jor-Ahel shook his head. "Incomprehensible. There must a reason."

"We need to go back to the ship." XO suggested. "We need to leave the island and move out into the sea. Now."

"Agreed." Captain Caine responded firmly. He stood up from the chair only to find himself pushed back by the shuddering floor. He eyes became wide with consternation, as the cracks appeared in the middle section of the circle of throne chairs, the mosaic floor plan. "Look, there are cracks now, that is not good. We must all leave. Now." His voice becoming loud and firm with resolve, his body once more attempting to stand up, followed by XO and Joanna and Barto.

Then silence.

The tremors stopped. The cracks ended, revealing ugly lines in criss-cross patterns across the mosaic floor itself, ruining the picturesque tiles.

Outside, the massive columns stopped groaning and shaking, not once moving away from their foundation.

All was quiet and still.

"This is not good." Captain Caine remarked. "This was a warning. More of that temblors are likely to show up."

"Agreed." XO responded. "We must leave forthwith."

"Jor-Ahel..." Gaston laid his hand on the host's shoulder. "Understand, we..."

"Whoa!" Joanna cried out, standing up and pointing at the giant throne chairs, her eyes becoming wide with interest. "They're here. Oh, my god. They're here!"

Barto signed furiously, waving his hands in the air as a gesture of clapping.

"Who are they?" XO asked, sitting back on his chair, stunned at the revelation appearing before his eyes. "More to the point, what are they?"

All others followed their lead, their eyes now focused on the giant throne chairs. Changes were happening before them as never have they ever seen in all their lives, be they at home in the 1960s or now in this strange land of the past.

This strange land of miraculous happenings.

The air, rather a portion of the air above the seats of the two, giant, royal-blue, throne chairs shimmered at first from a tiny singularity, becoming wider and thicker like soft waves of gelled water moving up and down the formation of the chairs, retaining the invisible tint of air for the moment.

All six elders loosened their grips on their chair, having fully recovered from the momentary surprise of the temblors appearing, their countenance becoming less shaken, more self-assured. All six of them brushed down their silky garments, smoothing the wrinkles, and making sure their sandals were firmly attached to their feet.

And then....one by one, each of them stood up from their respective royal-blue, throne chairs in a slow and gracious manner, until all of them stood in perfect unison, all of them focused on the giant throne chairs, the moving, gelled, watery substance making a transformation into solidified entities.

"Silimma hemeen-zen!" All ten elders sang out in chorus, their heads bowed, their hands on their hearts.

"What are they doing?" Captain Caine asked. "What's happening?"

"Do as we do." Jor-Ahel ordered firmly, bowing his head and placing his hand on his heart. "Just do it for now. It is a sign of respect."

Joanna quickly followed with a cute curtsy, her head bowed. All the ballet lessons she had taken instinctively told her that was the proper thing to do to what could be a sign of….royalty?"

Barto bowed deeply from his waist, all the respect and joy coming from his heart, his hand softly resting on his chest, feeling the quick beatings of his heart.

If only Dr. Breslov was here….

"Bow your head, please, my friends." Jor-Ahel insisted. "This is respect for our federated associates, one of them is from our comrades from afar, across the galaxy."

"No kidding." XO added breathlessly, now bowing his head, his hand on his heart. "Across the galaxy? How'd they do that?"

"It is our technology." Jor-Ahel responded softly, still bowing with respect. "We cannot divulge it to you and your people now. Too complex to explain. You must understand."

"Fine." XO responded with disappointment, rising back to his form, crossing his arms. "At least, we'd like to know who or what they are."

"In due time." Jor-Ahel responded softly. "In due time." He lifted his body with ease watching in the direction of the giant throne chairs. "They will now arrive."

Silimma Hemeen-zen!" The meeting hall resounded with the chorus of greeting from the six elders, bowing yet again in deep respect.

The ground reverberated again with another set of tremblings, the chairs clattering in tandem with the temblors. More cracks appeared going beyond the center mosaic floor. All the elders and the group of four with Jor-Ahel were suddenly thrown back to their chairs.

"This meeting better be quick." Captain Caine commented unhappily, gripping the arms of his throne chair.

"Either we go now and not find out what the meeting is all about or we stay and potentially get killed." XO remarked unhappily, preventing his body from swaying.

"Damn if we do. Damn if we don't." Captain Caine agreed. "Let's take this one step and a time and find out what the hell is going on."

The temblors soon stopped.

"Wow…that is so, so cool!" Joanna whispered, her eyes still focused on the giant throne chairs.

"Silimma hemeen-zen". The 10 elders once again sang out.

From out of the waves of thick, viscuous liquid moving around the perimeter of each of the two giant, royal-blue, throne chairs, the colorless fluidic form slowly changed from the monochromatic hue of air and water waves into a distinctly colorful, holographic form, each a well-defined individual entity from the other, each appearing already seated on the giant throne chairs, their arms resting on the arms of the chairs, their hands gripping the edges of the chairs' armrests.

On the left side, closer to Jor-Ahel, sat a giant, holographic, female figure with soft, smooth, olive skin. She sat gracefully with her head held high and her dark eyes gleaming with a graceful haughtiness befitting an opera diva or a prima ballerina, her eyebrows arched to reveal the strength of her individual personality as a queen, her high cheekbones gracing her strong, heart-shaped face with soft silent lips. Outfitted in a long, empress-style gown the color of crimson flecked with golden stars all the way down to the ankle hem of her dress, the holographic queen persona nodded with the utmost royal gesture to all around the council meeting hall, as if she herself was leading the meeting.

"What is that beautiful blue thing on her head?" Joanna signed to Barto, pointing at an elongated headdress, not rounded, but rather in the shape of an inverted, wide, cone hugging her forehead and extending high behind her head. One only saw the headdress on which a golden silk band surrounded the base and a figure of a reptilian snake ensconced on the band, just above her forehead. As such, no hair could be seen around her head and shoulders. "How odd, and yet, how beautiful."

Barto signed discreetly. "I wonder who they are. I'm beside myself with curiosity."

"Guess we'll know soon enough." Joanna signed back. "She really is beautiful." Barto nodded with smile. He pointed at the second chair. "Look who's coming now."

The chair on the left of the holographic queen was soon seated by a second holographic figure, this time a giant, male entity with blue skin, his body large and muscular all the way to his six pack torso, to his powerful thighs and calves, to his strong feet enclosed in thick silver snug boots hugging his calves and feet. His rugged square face was crowned all around and upon his shoulders with thick curly, blonde hair befitting the image of a Crown Prince. He had high cheekbones just below his obsidian green eyes that gazed in an arrogant manner around the council meeting room. An aquiline nose complemented his perfect features, while his lips pursed in a haughty manner depicting one who comes from the far, far ancient bloodline.

Seated in perfect posture with the Queen to his right, he wore a silver-blue unitard of strong, plastic material that clung to his perfect body. Two bronze brooches with his family crest logo rested on his chest at opposite ends just below his massive shoulders, attached to the long, thick, flowing robe behind him, the color of magenta. A silver-gold belt enclosed around his firm waist, a large brooch of the golden sun at its center.

Joanna was instantly besotted with a crush on this mighty, holographic, handsome giant from out of this world.

For a moment longer, they all stared at the mighty couple in holographic form, the four visitors awed at their appearance out of thin air just like that.

"He's certainly big." XO commented staring at the male holographic entity. "It would be a challenge dealing with him."

"Agreed." Captain Caine nodded. "I definitely want to know their technology; how they got here in that form". He looked at XO. "Anyways, they are here for a reason. Let's try to be diplomatic for the moment. I'm willing to bet those two are not of this earth."

XO nodded. "Would be great to know where they are actually from. Why in hell do they need to be in holographic form? Those are holograms, correct?"

"It would appear so." Captain Caine agreed. "Perhaps Barto knows...."

"Shhhh…" Jor-Ahel scolded from his seat. "We must show respect first. Then we will talk."

"Wow…" Joanna gushed, signing to Barto, ignoring Jor-Ahel's order, her heart still beating with the teenage crush that emerged and empowered her feelings. "He's so handsome, wow. So much bigger than the Queen. How tall is that? 10 feet?"

"Close." Barto signed. "If I'm correct, he is extraterrestrial from outer space, a specific race as I recall from the hieroglyphs in Egypt long ago, all of them, male and female, tall, at least 9 feet, with big muscles, even the females."

"The females must be awfully gorgeous." Joanna replied signing. "I can't compete with that kind of gorgeousness, huh?"

"Quiet!" Jor-Ahel ordered in a whisper. "We will talk later. Please show respect."

The clanging of the bell, sounding much like the clanging on a thin sheet of steel, reverberated once again, the four visitors once again covering their ears in pain.

A long creak suddenly sounded in the middle of the multiple bell ringing.

All eyes looked at the door of the council hall meeting. Two more visitors had arrived.

"Oh, hell." Gaston breathed in shock. "What is she doing here?"

"Beats me." XO responded, taken aback. "That was fast."

All the 10 seated council elders and the two giant, holographic entities found themselves nonplussed at the new visitor's presence, standing proudly at the center of the open granite door, the perplexed Tal-Sharee standing behind her, not knowing what to do in this important, sacred event occurring right before them.

The giant, holographic Queen slowly stood up from her chair and gestured with her graceful hand. "Come."

The lady Senefreya entered the council meeting hall with an air of determination, followed by Tal-Sharee, who bowed apologetically over and over to the seated council of elders, following her towards the giant holographic Queen.

"She didn't want to stay at the healing suite." Tal-Sharee explained to the council elders seated on their chairs. "I tried to stop her, but she insisted to come to this meeting herself right away. I chose to follow her. She does not know her way around Atlantis nor our people. She does not know our rules. She demanded to be here! I could not stop her."

"That is unfortunate…" Jor-Ahel sighed, shaking his head. "Now we have a distraction to deal with, when we should be heeding the message they have arrived to impart to us. An important message. Why else all this hurry for all of us to get here?"

Gaston and XO only stared at him for a moment.

"What is going on?" Captain Caine whispered to Jor-Ahel, who only shook his head once again, shrugging his shoulders. "How should I know? Look at them…the lady Senefreya with the mighty Queen of Egypt, both of them resembling each other."

Soon, the Queen stood up slowly and surely from giant, throne seat, still facing the lady Senefreya, now standing before her with a sense of pride and determination.

"Come…" The Queen of Egypt gestured gracefully. Still shaking with nerves, Senefreya knew she was interrupting an important meeting of the council of elders, a lost commoner among the elites and royals. She knew that she must have broken several rules just by showing up uninvited and unexpectedly. But she didn't care. She knew what her mind was telling her to do. Her mind was telling her that what only mattered was the urgent sense to go home, only she didn't know where home was, but it must be on this island, as she had hoped.

And the meeting was her only hope to find out where to go home. The Queen herself, however unreal she appeared, was the answer to her bewildering search.

"Turn around now…" The Queen commanded. Senefreya obeyed instantly, turning her body slowly in place, her head held high, her arms outstretched with open hands.

"Ahhh…as I thought so…" The Queen marveled softly, as if remembering a far-off dream, her eyes glazed with a glimmer of tears. "I thought so…you have the beautiful, long cranium reminiscent of my people." She pointed at Senefreya's head and body. "You also have the bodily appearance of my people, of myself." Slowly, the Queen removed her conical headdress, heavy in her hands. A long waterfall of raven-dark, silky hair spilled down her shoulders, revealing her elongated head.

Gaston, XO, Joanna, and Barto stood stunned. Jor-Ahel and the elders, however, were not surprised.

Senefreya herself stood shocked, uncertain what to say. It all seemed so unreal. Finally, she was not the only person in the universe to have the unusual head shape that mystified so many she had encountered in her life experience, since Papa caused a change that showed her real, natural head form.

"I don't know what to say." Senefreya whispered softly, tears brimming in her eyes. "I thought I was the only one with this awful head." The Queen understood. "I have many questions to ask of you, my dear." She placed her right hand on her heart and bowed her head towards Senefreya. "I am Queen Nerilka, most high Queen of Egypt. And your name?"

"Senefreya. Senefreya Vogel."

"Ahhhh, as I have expected. Senefreya, the beloved…and who may your parents be?"

"Papa and Mamoshka? They have passed away days ago."

"They know each other?" Captain Caine asked.

"They do look alike." XO commented. "Considering their long heads and black hair. Same body type. Interesting."

"Clearly." Jor-Ahel responded in agreement. "You are now understanding the difference of her. She belongs here with us."

"We do not have time, My Queen." The giant, holographic male turned towards the Queen and spoke with the highest authority. "People will die soon. We must act promptly."

"Of course." The Queen responded, her eyes reflecting the gravity of the situation. "I have been pleasantly surprised at this wonderful revelation in front of me that did distract my mission". Her eyes returned to Senefreya, who was now struggling to stand firm, her body shaking with tremors, her fatigue showing clearly in her face. "Senefreya, darling. Have you matured, yet? Are you at 21 yet?"

Senefreya nodded slowly, her eyes locked with the Queen, hugging herself tightly, trying to cope with the tremors enveloping her body. Tal Sharee quickly grabbed Senefreya just before she started to collapse, holding her body in his arms.

The Queen clapped her hands.

"Bring her to lie down at the foot of my chair. And cover her with a warm blanket quickly." The Queen commanded of Tal-Sharee, who obeyed without hesitation. A warm, fuzzy blanket made of white sheep's wool was proffered by one of the council elders. Tal-Sharee bowed with thanks, accepted the blanket and proceeded to cover Senefreya. After assuring himself that she was stable and her breathing stabilized, Tal-Sharee sat on the floor beside his patient, dismissing the obvious awkwardness of sitting on the floor in front of the esteemed council of the elders and beside the two, equally esteemed visitors from afar.

"What is the Queen talking about?" Gaston asked. "What is the age of maturity? 21?"

Jor-Ahel sighed. "This has to do with the passage of age condition prevalent among her people and the lady Senefreya clearly belongs to her people. To be exact, 21 is the age of maturation when her inner physique and her mind changes, in sum, her DNA changes, not unlike the process of the age of puberty among your young population. It takes time to stabilize the process and she is clearly in distress. She should be resting at the Abode of Healing." Jor-Ahel shook his head.

"Obviously." Captain Caine responded.

"My question, though, what is the point of the age of maturation?" XO asked.

"It is the beginning of her life's purpose, when she becomes of a powerful state of mind and body." Jor-Ahel explained sagely. "She will have abilities beyond the concept of your people, excuse me for saying that. I have no other way to put it."

"Abilities?" XO asked again.

"Explain." Captain Caine demanded.

"Telepathic abilities, invisibility, clairvoyance, and levitation among others. All of her people have these abilities. They are the very, ancient bloodline, the Kiru-Ashar bloodline, going back millennia of years. They are expert space travelers and often my ancestors joined them in interdimensional excursions."

Before the Captain and XO could ask more questions to allay their growing curiosity, the bell rang once again, louder than the previous intonations.

"Attention!" Queen Nerilka stood up firmly from her giant, throne chair. Her holographic state shimmering in the air. "Time is of essence. Please pay attention!"

All participants in the council meeting room ceased their conversations, turning to face the Queen, who was now seating herself back on her giant, throne chair.

The Queen, satisfied at the attention, nodded at the giant, male holographic figure seated next to her. "You must speak now."

"Thank you." He nodded at the Queen. Facing the entire entourage in the meeting room and nodding in satisfaction at the attention directed towards the Queen and himself, he took upon himself, a stance of authority, his voice booming with urgency.

"I am Amazari-Ah. I come from the other side of the galaxy, a representative of my people, the Zhuraxi of the planet Mayora. We have news to impart to our most esteemed friends, the Atlanteans, and their guests. Terrible news. To cut this short, you must tell everyone, no, warn everyone, and that is, everyone, on this island to leave immediately or you will all die a terrible death." He slammed his holographic lance on the floor, though no sound was heard. "Make haste immediately. Leave Atlantis!" He roared with emphasis. "Make haste!"

The lance slammed one last time.

The Queen nodded in agreement, her eyes reflecting the fear and the terrible knowledge of what was to come for all existing in Atlantis, both the elites and the locals and their wayward visitors from the past.

Senefreya could only stare in mystification at the news, her mind still grasping the revelation that the Queen somehow knew her as family, and yet, she did not know the Queen.

This terrible death that seemed imminent in its arrival had only added to her burden of worries. She just wanted to go home.

But where was home?

"You must leave Atlantis!" The Queen once again commanded forcefully. "The Horrodix-Tra have arrived! You must pay attention to our grave warning!" She stood up quickly and raised her arm in the air, moving her hand in an arc.

At the other end of the section where the Queen was standing, a holographic vision appeared, much like a movie display without a projector. In that motion picture view, several waves too massive to discern, perhaps thousands of feet high, could been seen, their caps frothed with heavy, bubbles of foam, their restless energy abounding in the waters, as the waves continued to move and move towards its destination.

"There!" The Queen announced. "There is your danger. Atlantis will be destroyed forever in just 24 hours from now, when these waves arrive. Make haste! Leave Atlantis! Now!"

A large resounding gasp could be heard among all seated in the council meeting room. Senefreya whimpered in terror, hugging her blanket. Tal-Sharee held on to her, trying to comfort her. Joanna put her hands to her mouth in fear. Barto smirked in the knowledge of that terrible feeling he had in his gut now finally coming to reality.

Finally, he knew what he knew. Atlantis was about to be destroyed. In 24 hours. Sunk into the sea like the myths of yore. Only he could not speak to voice his fears and Joanna, poor Joanna, was in a state of frozen gaping mood, vacillating betwixt her crush for the handsome Amazari-Ah and her fears of this "terrible news" no one is speaking of yet. The shock was palpable to all at this moment. He could not get through Joanna at all with his signings asking her if she was all right.

Fed up with the shock consuming her, Barto shook Joanna's shoulders.

"What?" Joanna yelled. "You're hurting me."

"I need to talk to the Captain!" He signed.

"Okay! Tell me!" Joanna pushed his hand away. "Stop hurting me."

Meanwhile, the Captain was deep in conversation with Jor-Ahel.

"What's Horrodix-Tra?" Gaston demanded of Jor-Ahel, glaring at him in frustration at yet another problem to deal with after all he and his crew had gone through the past few hours, ending up in this unimaginable place of all places in the end of the Last Ice Age of all times. "What's going on? I don't like this "we all are going to die a terrible death".

His anger manifesting inside him, the Captain was becoming worried about his people that he had left on the USS Arcanus. People he had given a shore leave approval earlier and all 400 of them were now scattered far and wide within the two, outer, circular, land rings of

Atlantis, the only jurisdictions allowed to them for their pleasure of wine, feasting, dancing, and music. "Explain!" He demanded of Jor-Ahel.

"Captain!" Joanna beseeched loudly putting herself in front of the Captain with a firm salute. "Barto says you must tell your crew to get back on the ship and get out of Atlantis! Now! No questions asked! Just please do it."

Startled at being ordered about by Joanna, he looked at Barto for a moment and saw deep fear in his eyes. Barto nodded his quickly.

"Barto says just do it. To trust him."

"All right." Captain Caine replied choosing to trust Barto with the need to act quickly. Then he will most sure ask Jor-Ahel what the hell is going on.

"You are saying for my ship to leave quickly?" Gaston asked again. "Where to?"

"Barto says…" Joanna gasped for breath, as words quickly poured out of her mouth. "Barto says to go back to the Pillars of Hercules, enter the Mediterranean Sea and head for Turkey as fast as you can. Pronto!"

"Why Turkey?" XO demanded. "That's pretty far for the ship to move quickly. Wouldn't the Pillars be a better place for safety?"

Barto responded quickly with his signings.

"Barto says…Turkey has the Duarokara Valley with thousands of underground caves. There are already people living in there, people who know the danger coming just now and escaped to the Valley. It is much, much safer there. It is not too far if you all go quickly now, right now!"

Captain Caine thought for a moment. "But it is too far for our ship to make it quickly. We'll never make it in 24 hours. Hell, XO and I can't even make it to the ship right now." He looked at XO. "Any thoughts?"

"I am at a loss myself." XO replied.

"Jor-Ahel?" Gaston turned towards their host, who was listening to the conversations in silence.

"There is a solution." Jor-Ahel replied calmly. "Your ship already was outfitted with the electromagnetic tools for invisibility and teleportation."

"That's right." Captain Caine replied. XO listened with interested.

"Then, you only need to activate the electromagnetic currents once your ship is 2 miles away from Atlantis going west. The currents will activate the same vortex that brought you all here in this timeframe. Just think about this place you call Turkey and our Duorakara Valley and hopefully you all should get there promptly and safely".

"Of course!" Captain Caine lighted up. "That will get the USS Arcanus to Turkey in 24 hours."

XO nodded in agreement. It could work.

"What is Turkey?" Jor-Ahel asked puzzled.

"Oh, right." Captain Caine responded. "It's the future name we give to that land you just mentioned that has the Duorakara Valley of caves. Good idea, Jor-Ahel." He patted his host's shoulders. "You have out utmost gratitude. We owe you."

Jor-Ahel nodded happily. "My friends, you are most welcome, but hurry, the ship must leave now. Right now."

Captain Caine turned towards XO. "Do it, XO. Send out the message and instructions. Shore leave is terminated effective immediately."

"Yes, sir!" XO reached for the satdite communications phone strapped to his thick leather belt and punched the buttons.

"God help them…" Gaston wiped his forehead. "One of us really need to be there. Huh, what is that?" The floor started to tremble beneath his feet, a rhythmic tremble that seemed so unfamiliar for an earthquake. No groaning and cracking of the tiled, mosaic floor. Only a rhythmic hum vibrating beneath the soles of his shoes entering through his feet into his body, causing his body to shake uncontrollably. "Why am I shaking?"

XO was also shaking, trying hard to hold on to the satdite phone, still loudly conveying instructions for the USS Arcanus to leave the island with everyone onboard, the ship's crew and the Atlanteans from the two, outer land rings.

"What the hell…"

Jor-Ahel smiled, his body flowing with the vibrations coming out of the floor, as if he was used to it, familiar with it. "Do not worry, my friends. This will pass."

"What will pass?" Captain Caine demanded, the vibrations and humming becoming louder and stronger, the floor shaking harder and harder. "Is this another earthquake? Damn strange, if I may say."

"I know." Jor-Ahel added. "It is damn strange for one who is not used to it. Our discoidals are leaving. This is only the beginning, the ramping up of the engines and thrusting power."

"Discoidals? You mean starships?" Captain Caine demanded. "Where?" The vibrations at that point slowed down, but the humming became louder and louder into a high frequency, a high musical note, as if from a giant flute, coming closer and closer to the building.

Jor-Ahel continued to smile. "Go, my friends. The front of this temple. You will see." He gestured towards the meeting room door. "You will see what I am talking about."

The Captain and XO, Joanna and Barto, all reached the terrace of doric columns and soon arrived at the front portico of the temple. Not seeing anything ahead of them, they all looked at each other, and then upwards towards the sky. The fluting sound grew so loud, both the Captain, his XO, and Joanna covered their ears in pain, searching the skies. Barto did not appear to care about the hum affecting the others. He was too excited, his eyes searching the skies with anticipation, knowing what he knew was about to happen. He wanted to finally see it or them or whatever was soon to show up above them all.

Dr. Breslov would be so excited to hear about it.

"What the hell?" Captain Caine exclaimed.

"Oh, my god!" XO replied. "It's true. They are starships! They're the UFOs in our time! Jesus, they are huge! They are real! Jesus…"

"I knew it!" Barto yelled, his body quaking in excitement, his joy unfettered and expressive in all its energy. He waved at the air.

"Hello! Goodbye! Safe travels!"

From the top, square roof of the granite, marble and limestone temple, three massive, disc-shaped spaceships majestically appeared, one following the other in a straight-line formation. All three were coated in all their gleaming, metallic-silver tint all over the round body with bulges at the top and bottom. Bright lights of various colors beamed rhythmically all around the slowly-moving, center edges of the discoidal body.

The three spaceships moved up further, the two of them soon deviated from the line, the three of them forming a triangle pattern in a steady state just above the temple, not unlike an aeroplane at the start of the runway, waiting to proceed. The humming grew louder and louder and then, in an instant the three discoidals, quickly zig-zagged into a singularity one following the other, disappearing at a speed of light into the skies.

And they were gone.

The Captain and XO only stared at each other, unable to voice their words, stunned at the reality of what they had saw with their own eyes. And what they had seen with their own eyes, forever changed their worldview. It would be so difficult to explain in their world in the 1960s, if they ever made it back home. For now, they only had each other as silent testimonies to a powerful, albeit harsh reality.

They were not alone.

Soon, a voice commanded from the darkness of the front portico of the temple, breaking their silent reverie.

"My friends, please hasten and follow me. We must leave this island. We have only 10 hours left and time is of essence, considering our escape. There are too many of us in there."

The Captain and XO broke from their reverie, both of them staring at Jor-Ahel, who had appeared at the portico entrance.

"What drives the discoidals?" Captain Caine demanded, still in shock at seeing a mode of flying weapon and transport far more powerful in speed, direction, and thrust than his own ship, the latest design of formidable dominance in the annals of the US Navy's aircraft carriers, using only nuclear capabilities, and now testing the addition of the electromagnetic capabilities to render invisibility and teleportation.

Jor-Ahel was now frustrated. He waved his hand wildly, gesturing to the Captain and XO to hurry up. "I will explain later, my friend. Come! We must escape immediately."

"In that temple?" XO asked, scratching his head. "I don't get it."

"You will in time." Jor-Ahel responded. "Just follow me or we will all die. The floods will destroy Atlantis completely. No question about it. It's many thousands of cubits high! Horrendous!"

Captain Caine nodded, remembering the visual display activated by the Queen. These waves that were inevitably coming to destroy Atlantis were impossibly gigantic and dangerous. "We got to do what he says. We have no choice. I'm not interested in dying. We still need to get home."

"Copy that, Captain. Me neither."

The Captain, XO, Joanna, and Barto, all quickly followed Jor-Ahel into the darkness of the temple back towards the council meeting hall, already empty and dark, its silence echoing across the vastness of the suite and the horror of the impending disaster.

"Where is everybody?" Captain Caine asked, his eyes searching the suite. "Where is the lady Senefreya?" He still felt responsible for her, no matter that she was now in good hands with what could be truthfully said, her people of Atlantis and Egypt.

"Just follow me." Jor-Ahel gestured. "Quickly. We are losing time. They are waiting for us down there."

"Down there?" XO repeated. "Where?"

Jor-Ahel pointed at a corner door, still exposed, where the council elders had come out at the beginning of the auspicious meeting with the two giant, holographic entities, now also nowhere to be seen. "In there…"

After scrambling down the stairs in the darkness, their hands touching the smooth, stone walls on both sides to stabilize themselves, the three men finally reached the bottom of the stairs. It was still dark, their eyes not yet adjusted to the dim fuzziness of the lack of light down there.

"Come." Jor-Ahel gestured. "We must go through that tunnel, see?" He pointed at a burrowed opening in the wall ahead of them, barely discernible in the fuzzy darkness, but Jor-Ahel knew the way. The four of them followed their host into the burrowed opening and through the tunnel comprised of thousands of stone boulders fitted together perfectly without mortar. The tunnel was huge, big enough to fit a subway track and train.

"What's this tunnel?" Captain Caine asked. "Where are we going?"

"Yes, where?" XO demanded. "We are supposed to escape from those waves. Is being underground the solution?"

"No." Jor-Ahel responded firmly. "It is difficult to explain. You must see it. Come, we must go to where the pyramid is located all the way down there."

"Ah, the pyramid, of course. I wonder why." XO remarked, glancing at his watch. "It's what, 4 hours left?"

"One hour left, my friend." Jor-Ahel added. "We must go quickly. The waves are supremely fast. We did not anticipate that much."

"That's true." Captain Caine looked at his XO. "Glacier melting water moves fast. Can be unpredictable with the currents and wind. Why the pyramid, Jor-Ahel?"

"That's where the energy comes from. Come! Hurry!" Jor-Ahel reached the other burrowed opening and exited through it, gesturing to the four to follow him. Suddenly, the ground shook and trembled, just as the Captain and XO exited through the other burrowed opening, the heavy stone boulders all collapsing in a massive landfall blocking their way back, the heavy, gray dust spiraling all over the air, adding to the dim fuzziness of the darkness.

"Jesus." Captain Caine cursed softly, steadying his body, brushing the grimy dust from his uniform. He already lost his white cover hat in all the melee going on the past few minutes. "No hat with me. I feel naked."

"Ditto, sir." XO dusted himself with gusto, coughing at the murky, gritty powder overpowering his nose and mouth. "We have no use for it, I would think."

Captain Caine nodded.

"Now what, Jor-Ahel?" Captain Caine asked, having brushed the last of the dust from his white, unform pants. "How in hell are we going to escape now?" He looked up in anger and frustration.

"Jesus, again…." XO whistled. "What the hell is that?"

Both men, Joanna, and Barto stared ahead in what appeared to be a huge yawning cavern, the domed ceiling at least a hundred feet high, the entire perimeter of the cavern enclosed by huge, stone boulders also fitted tightly without mortar. But what shocked the two men just standing behind Jor-Ahel was the giant horseshoe-shaped contraption they had no words for.

It did not exist in their world. At least, not that they were aware of.

As the two men scrutinized the giant horseshoe enigma, they noticed that each curving side was patterned with a delta sign of different colors all around end to end. The hollow center was filled with what looked like thick, viscous pale-blue, liquid, like heavy water, shimmering in place.

"What in holy shit is that?" XO remarked, not able to turn his eyes away from this apparent piece of machine.

"And look around." Captain Caine announced. "Everybody we know of is here."

Huddled around the base of the horseshoe apparatus of aluminum and molybdenum materials, the ten elders were standing in silent thoughts waiting for their orders. All of the elders were carrying baskets and handbags and metal containers, their bodies now enclosed in a grey plastic-like, skin-suit outfitted to the shape of their bodies, their heads enclosed in globular glass helmets. Next to them, Tal-Sharee was holding the lady Senefreya in his arms. She was still weak and tired, groaning softly.

"Something is missing." Captain Caine asked Jor-Ahel. "Where are the two giant ones?"

Jor-Ahel smiled. "They are not here with us. They were holographic images of their real personas, who are very far away. It is much, much safer that way for them, so our enemies do not reach them on their arrival here to meet with us. It would have prevented the warning, you see. Do not worry about them."

"That is impressive." XO remarked. "Their holographic technology is beyond my head."

"Indeed." Captain Caine agreed. "What's this contraption for?"

Again, the earth trembled and shook and groaned beneath their feet, this time worse than before and the rumbling noise louder than ever.

The ten elders all faced Jor-Ahel and bowed deeply. Jor-Ahel bowed in return, straightened his body and raised his arms upwards.

"Go, most high council of elders. Two by two. Go to where you can rebuild a new world all over Terra and preserve our technology and knowledge for the future. Go now!"

Tal-Sharee stepped back away from the horseshoe machine, letting the council elders march towards the convoluting, thick waters. Jor-Ahel was now standing behind a stone post in the corner, his hands flowing over the surface. The lights on each of the delta all around the horseshoe lighted up one by one in rhythmic fashion, at first slowly, then faster and faster, until it became a colorful blur of moving lights. The shimmering, heavy waters inside the stargate burst loudly in an explosion, and then receded in place.

"The portal is ready. Go now. Two by two."

"The portal?" XO commented. "Another one?"

"It would seem so." Captain Caine replied nodding. "That is apparently our escape route. Good thinking, Jor-Ahel." He saluted to their host, who bowed his head with a smile.

While the last two of the ten council elders prepared to enter the shimmering, heavy water substance within the horseshoe contraption, Gaston approached Tal-Sharee and scooped up the lady Senefreya in his arms. Feeling the deep connection resume between them, Senefreya laid her head on his shoulders and closed her eyes. She was safe in his arms, where she belonged.

Tal-Sharee nodded gratefully, following Jor-Ahel, the Captain, and XO, Joanna and Barto, all of them running up the ramp and entering into the shimmering, heavy waters…

Outside the temple in the ominous darkness of the day, the thousands of feet high roughly, contoured, frothy, dark, goliath waves coming from all directions in the ocean, pushed on and on by the terrorizing powerful rumbles of the earthquakes below, finally arrived to plunge aggressively over the island of Atlantis in all directions, in a roaring, clashing heap, one over the other, the few who could not escape on time to the USS Arcanus, becoming caught in its drowning spirals of death and destruction.

In a day and night, the howling wind, rumbling earthquakes, and giant, blustering waves soon broke apart the last remnants of Atlantis and the volcanic landmass ridge behind it, causing everything and everyone to sink into the ocean.

Gone forever…

Chapter 36

Three days later…

The evening sky was still twilight in shades of soft grey and pearl colors, the soft, streaks of grey clouds slowly, moving west, buffeted by the breeze of the seashore.

Gaston stood tall and assured with his XO and Jor-Ahel, the three of them facing the Mediterranean coastline beach, north of where six of them from that inauspicious meeting of the council elders days ago, had landed upon entering the thick, shimmering, heavy water of the stargate, just before the ill-fated city of Atlantis violently sank into the ocean.

The pristine, aquamarine saltwater of the Mediterranean Sea splashed softly on their bare feet. It had been awkward to take off their shoes, but their Egyptian hosts insisted, urging them to just relax and enjoy the beauty and warmth of their palatial beach resort they had named El Mayarina. The one place the Egyptian royal family insisted they all go, when it was finally safe to emerge from their place of safety and shelter, the minute the cataclysm ended.

Jor-Ahel, Captain Caine, Senefreya, XO, Joanna, and Barto had all exited from another stargate also located underground 200 feet below what would be famously known in the future as a dominant tourist icon of Egypt, second only to the Great Pyramid.

The titanic Sphinx.

Two hundred feet below its right paw.

Gaston shook his head wildly, letting his unkempt hair fly about his forehead and temples. That felt good against the sea breeze. He bent down to scoop the clear waters in his hands and splashed them on his face, its warm, healing liquid cleansing the desert dust from his skin. Feeling better and cleaner, his mind cleared from the confusion of the inexplicable series of events the past three days, he took a long breath and let it out slowly, enjoying the view of the pristine, sandy beach.

His XO just put his hands in the pockets of his white, uniform pants, now grubby from the dirt and grime from the escapade, letting the warm, sea waters wash over his feet. His analytical mind was still swirling with endless questions of what he had just experienced the past three days.

Gaston smiled with compassion at his XO and placed his hand on Commander DeLaCroix's shoulder. "Just breathe, XO. Only thing we can do now. Breathe. We appear to be in a good place. The danger is over, hopefully."

"Hopefully." XO nodded. "Can't believe Atlantis was real. Can't believe all that happened and it's gone under the ocean. Plato was telling truth. Atlantis existed."

"Indeed, we existed, my friend." Jor-Ahel smiled broadly. "We lived and breathed and died just like you and your people."

"But how?" XO asked. "How come we never found Atlantis. How come it was all from myths and legends with so many people saying it is just a fairytale spouted from a crazy Greek philosopher from ancient times long gone. Yes, he was said to be crazy many, many times. That's what they called Plato. Right?" He looked at Gaston.

Gaston gripped the XO's shoulder. "Apparently. Now we know better. Plato spoke the truth. Atlantis was where he said it would be, just beyond the Pillars of Hercules."

XO nodded. "Beautiful place. I'm really sorry to see it gone."

"Not entirely." Jor-Ahel interrupted with a smile. "You see, your Plato did not tell the whole story about the destruction of my home island. Of Atlantis."

"Explain." Gaston asked, his curiosity piqued. XO listened intently.

"Ahhhh…" Jor-Ahel turned to face the ocean before him, the warm waters still lapping on his bare feet. He breathed in and then out. "You see, my friends. Not all of us died in that horrible catastrophe of our beautiful home island. As you can see, some of us were survivors, us and the elders, two by two who had gone into the stargate to travel around Terra and rebuild new worlds just like Atlantis."

Gaston nodded. "I see. Well, Atlantis is destroyed. Hopefully, your people had better luck in other places, where they ended up through that stargate."

"But they have!" Jor-Ahel exclaimed. "Look into your future. There are ancient monuments, megaliths, pyramids, and stone circles everywhere you go to explore the past in your time. Everywhere. Don't you see? Those are our legacy that we left behind."

"And your people?" Gaston asked.

"Some of us left for home in another galaxy in our discoidals." Jor-Ahel looked up at the skies. "Others assimilated with the local natives, our DNA merging with theirs."

"I have question." XO looked at Jor-Ahel expectantly. "What…"

In that moment, a loud clang boomed throughout the air from behind the three men, their bare feet still wading in the warm, shore waters. Then another clang boomed out. And third clang before dying out.

"What the hell is that noise?" Gaston turned around, his eyes searching the area behind him, his XO following with his hands against his ears.

"You will see." Jor-Ahel responded with a smile. "Come, we must go back to the royal beach resort. The people are gathering now."

And so, they were. The three men, having walked away with reluctance from the warm, ocean waters and captivating conversation, towards the lush, green, plants and colorful flowers, just past the sandy border.

The three men meandered through a long, winding trail of cobblestones arranged among the panoply of date and fig trees, palm trees, papyrus, fountain grass, and all the flowering bushes of periwinkle, blue lotus, and yellow lantana, all of them adding a delightful and pungently sweet fragrance to the whiff of salt air wafting in the air.

Soon, the three men emerged from the blossoming mini-jungle dividing the ocean from the royal beach resort.

Just in front of them, a multitude of the local and elite people of the colony of Egypt, including the Puma, Kalamurians, and the

Atlantean survivors gathered around in front of the quartz and granite steps leading down from a magnificent resort temple portico, the color of ecru with two rows of giant, doric, columns painted in vibrant colors of red, gold, and blue with interlacing lines and symbols. The columns appeared to diminish into the far back of the temple, as far as the eye could see.

"That is some beach resort." XO joked.

"Indeed, it is." Gaston responded chuckling. "But what can you expect from the royals?"

"Hey, look there's Joanna and Barto." XO waved. "Let's join them."

"Go ahead." Jor-Ahel nodded with a wave, as he started to walk in another direction towards the temple. "I will be with my people. Please stay near the royal temple. Something is happening and we do not want to offend the royal family."

"No problem." Gaston replied. "See you later."

"Hey, Barto!" XO greeted, as the two men approached Joanna and Barto. "We have a question for you! Do you know anything about ruins in our time? Jor-Ahel keeps saying his people split into groups and spread out to the west and south of Atlantis. Jor-Ahel thinks you have the answer; that you know the names of those ruins in our time. He doesn't."

Joanna signed quickly. Barto responded with excitement.

"Sirs, Barto says, of course, he knows. The ruins in North America are in the southwest area like Chaco Canyon and Mesa Verde, away from those icebergs up northwest during the Last Ice Age through the ice-free corridor between the Laurentide and the Cordilleran glaciers. And then, there, in South America, oh boy, you have dozens of stone pyramids all over that continent, all of them huge like that Great Pyramid near the Sphinx, Chichen Itza and Teotihuacan. And also, you have Macchu Picchu, Bimini Roads, Angkor Wat, Borobudur, Mahabalipuram, and Dwaraka, all built by the Atlanteans!" He flourished his signings with a yell in the air and a jump up from the ground.

"No kidding." XO remarked stunned.

"Oh, yes, the Atlanteans are everywhere in this earth! Oh, boy, Dr. Breslov is going to love this when we get back, oh boy!" He started to dance around and up and down with joy.

Joanna giggled at his enthusiasm. He is such a dork and yet, they all depended on him every step of the way in this amazing and yet, utterly unfathomable adventure.

Gaston smiled at Barto's happiness. Good thing they picked him up in that storm back home. They would all be utterly helpless without his knowledge. His guidance in this strange new world in the ancient past.

If only he knew how to get back home…

Gaston placed his hand on his XO's shoulders. "Just absorb it, XO. I know the feeling. Best to keep it secret when we get back. Do you understand?"

"If we ever do, sir."

"Damn right." Gaston replied. "We should be finding the way to get back home right now. What the hell are we doing here in this time of nightfall?"

All of a sudden, the gathering of the people, some of the men outfitted with iconic, colorful shendyt-skirts made of thick intertwined fibers and other men wearing linen tunics and gallibayas, dipped in various shades of brown and beige, each sporting a belt at the waist.

The women all wore kalaris-sheath of various colors and design, adding on to their face, arms, hands, and bodies, the best and beautiful jewelry made from the vitrified stones and minerals collected from Egypt's hot desert.

The ecstatic crowd broke out in a tumultuous chorus of cheers and hails, their hands waving wildly in the air, all of them facing the royal beach resort with joyful anticipation, including Jor-Ahel in all his knowingness, standing out of the crowd in his white Atlantean tunic attire, befitting an elite.

Not fully comprehending what was going on, Gaston, XO, Joanna, and Barto joined the crowd. The throng of people were now acclaiming their royal family's arrival with uplifting gusto, their voices joining in a combined choir song.

"Karra Hadisha!" The cheers grew louder and louder, the sea of waving hands moving in rhythmic motion back and forth like a pendulum. "Karra Hadisha, Pharoah Ra-Azeris! Karra-Hadis, Queen Nerilka! Karra-Hadisha, Crown Princess Senefreya!"

"Crown Princess?" Gaston whispered, both he and XO looking at each other in surprise. "That's a long way from being a lost survivor of the 747 crash."

"Indeed." XO stared at the Princess.

"What are they saying, Barto?" Joanna asked. "Our Senefreya is an Egyptian princess?"

"Karra Hadisha, it means hurrah and hail!" Barto responded with signs. "Look!"

The four of them raised their eyes towards the portico.

From out of the darkness of El Mayarina, the portico in front of the stairs bathed in soft-dimmed gold and blue light against the backdrop of the evening twilight, a four-man military contingent appeared attired in what appeared to be an iconic Egyptian warrior uniform.

The four men were of average height and muscular features and each wore a thick, tight-fitting shendyt-skirt the color of sand reaching just above their knees in an upward swirl at both sides and fastened by a large belt buckle fitted with an assortment of tiny stones of bright neon colors. Spilling down from the belt buckle in a rectangle form, the material, also fitted with colorful tiny stones, covered their groin, reaching just above their knees.

Each of the men wore a skin-tight shirt, the color of dark magenta, befitting one who protects the royal family. On each of their heads, conical headdress, the color of gold and sienna, was fitted comfortably against their temples, adding to their height and mystique of their haughty presence.

On each of their right hand, their strong, brown fingers gripped a lance with a spearpoint. Once at the portico in full view of the adoring crowd, the four-man contingent solemnly divided into two, each two moving to stand side by side on either side of the portico, forming a pathway between them.

And all at once, they slammed their lances on the ground. One of the four raised his voice towards the crowd.

"The Royal Family from the bloodline of Ptolemy the Great arrives!" Each of them bowing to their knees simultaneously, pounding their lances on the ground.

"Look at our Captain." Joanna smiled. "He is certainly smitten with our Senefreya. God, she looks beautiful in her outfit."

Barto nodded with a smile as he observed the Captain from the corner of his eye.

"I wonder. Is she their granddaughter or their future descendent?" XO asked himself loudly.

"Be quiet." Gaston elbowed his XO. "We need to show our respect or we'll get in trouble with the crowd. We do stand out, you know."

"Of course, sir. No problem, sir. She is beautiful, sir."

Gaston nodded slowly, unable to take his eyes of what appeared to be no longer his responsibility, the lady Senefreya they had rescued from a 747 jumbo jet that had inexplicably ended up in the year 9632 BC and crashed not far from the island of Atlantis, of all places.

She had been lucky the USS Arcanus was nearby to pick her up. And he still had questions to ask of her. Where were the pilots gone? How in hell did she survive the crash?" He straightened his jacket uniform, now faded and wrinkled, wishing he had his white cover hat for this most auspicious event.

No matter. Time to focus on the present. The burning questions can wait for another time, another discussion. Now is the time to join the crowd in welcoming their princess home.

And there she is…in all her beautiful, royal regalia befitting an Egyptian princess, her grandparents/ancestors proudly standing on her left and right side, each holding her arms, as the three of them glided in majestic manner befitting their imperial heritage.

Pharoah Ra-Azeris, in a gold and blue shendyt-skirt, his upper muscular torso naked and adorned with a wide, beaded collar of jade, obsidian black, citrine, and turquoise, the arrangement shining brightly against his silky, brown-skinned chest. His slightly elongated head was bare, his brown skin sparkling in the dim light of the portico. Metallic curling bracelets the color of gold spiraled along both his forearms, the ends sporting the head of a serpent just below the shoulder blades.

Pharoah Ra-Azeris slowly ceased the stately walk and with his right hand reached out to the adoring crowd below the stairs of the portico, including Gaston and his group of three just behind the crowd.

"Let us welcome home, our beautiful Crown Princess Senefreya!" His voice boomed with a baritone resonance meant to reach out far and wide among the crowd. "She is home with us at last! The daughter of our beloved son, Crown Prince Basteteme, now long gone! Our Senefreya! Welcome her home!"

"Huh?" XO asked. "Basteteme?"

"Quiet." Gaston whispered. "Listen."

"Yes, do welcome her home, our Senefreya!" Queen Nerilka sang out towards the crowd, her voice resonant with a melodious tone not unlike an opera singer, also reaching out far and wide with the wonderful news.

Like the Pharoah Ra-Azeris, she had an elongated head, choosing this time to not wear the conical headdress to cover her head. Instead, her elongated head was fully shown replete with a waterfall of thick, raven-dark hair just like Senefreya. Her impossibly, high cheekbones was a remarkable feature on her face, emphasizing her royal presence, her wide feline, sapphire eyes with a vertical slit for pupils, only served to add to her mysterious persona, which belied her inner warmth, the minute she turned to hug the daughter of her long-missing son. The son she had regretfully sent to represent Egypt, who was on his way to Atlantis, when his starship encountered an accident propelling him into the past, never to return.

But his daughter, Senefreya, did return.

The Queen wore a long, flowing gold and blue kalasaris-dress designed in an empress style to emphasize her firm, full breasts and graceful shoulders, her arms enclosed with the same spiraling serpent bracelets, as her royal husband, her right ankle enclosed by small golden anklets, the nails on her feet and hands painted in coral color.

Her head held high, Queen Nerilka continued her story. "Long ago, my son Prince Basteteme, we sent him to be our ambassador to Atlantis governed by our dear friend and ally, Jor-Ahel." She pointed at the supreme leader of Atlantis, who bowed graciously to the crowd. "Long ago, in his starship, he disappeared from our world to never come back." She smiled at Jor-Ahel. "But we forgive you and your people. It was an accident, sadly. A terrible accident."

"What accident?" XO whispered.

"Later." Gaston elbowed again. "Just listen."

The Queen continued. "Our son, Crown Prince Basteteme has passed away to the realm of spirits, where he joined the earthly woman who rescued him in another time and space. He made her his wife and together they created our beautiful Crown Princess Senefreya. Welcome her home!" Her voice was loud and melodious. "She is home with us at last, the heiress to the throne of Egypt!"

"Welcome home at last, our Crown Princess Senefreya!" The crowd yelled in unison. "Long may our Princess live! Long may she rule our land of Egypt!"

"So…I am home?" Senefreya whispered to herself, watching the crowd applauding her with heartfelt joy, feeling a sense of homecoming overwhelming her. A feeling she had been waiting for, searching for, in all her complicated life in the here and there, since her unusual birth.

She had never felt comfortable in Berlin, Germany, where she was born. No, all her life she had felt she belonged somewhere else, that she had to find her home, her real home, being pulled, no, guided by forces beyond her knowledge, in her quest to find her real home.

Stunned at her ethereal beauty, a far cry from the sad, dripping, ghost of a survivor at sea that his crew had pulled from the ocean, Gaston's heart beat forcefully, as he stared at Senefreya's magnificent presence standing between two powerful Egyptian royalty, her grandparents, and yet, also her ancient ancestors.

He wanted her in his arms right now; it was all he was feeling right now. She was so beautiful, so haunting, and yet he could not shake the gut feeling that they somehow belonged together in a form of quantum entanglement. Only way he could describe the feeling. Somehow, somewhere he had known about it.

He just could not finger it yet. Not yet.

"Our Senefreya is home!" Pharoah Ra-Azeris once again announced with his booming baritone voice. "Let the festivities begin!"

The crowd yelled in unison, all of the people quickly walking and running past the four visitors still standing at the back, unsure what to do; where to go. The four of them were forcibly buffeted by the large throng heading straight to the community plaza not too far from the El Mayarina Resort Temple.

"Let the festivities begin!" Echoed the crowd.

Fires were ignited, fruits and vegetables and fish of all kinds, were displayed on the resplendently designed, ceramic bowls and platters. Large grey stoneware urns, their lips painted in gold and green, all of them containing sweet grape wine from the royal garden, stood next to the tables of gastronomic abundance.

Jor-Ahel, having waited until the crowd had dispersed, the Pharoah and his Queen following them, each of their arm interlocked with the Crown Princess Senefreya, sauntered up to the four visitors left behind.

"Come, join me, let us enjoy the festivities."

"But what about us?" XO spoke up. "How do we get back home now?"

"We will talk about that later." Jor-Ahel assured them, placing his hand on his heart. "It is a promise. Come, let us eat, drink, and be merry. The night is young! Come! Do not offend the royals. They have invited you all. You brought home their granddaughter and heiress to the throne."

"Lemme at the wine!" Barto yelled in signage, instantly dashing towards the large, pale-grey urns, a long line having just formed with people holding empty, ceramic cups. A young servant behind the tables offered him a cup.

Gaston, XO, Joanna, and Jor-Ahel all laughed at his antics, his joyful thirst for fun.

"Barto is such a dork!" Joanna commented. "I cannot for the life of me get how he knows stuff so much! I feel massively small around him, funny."

"I know the feeling." Gaston placed his hand on her shoulder. "We are lucky to have him around, considering what we just went through. Very lucky."

"And we are damn lucky you know sign language." XO added. "Out of the hundreds of us in that ship."

"Come, come, my friends!" Jor-Ahel impatiently gestured towards the three guests of honor, already walking towards the joyful revelry and feasting.

Soon, the sound of the rhythmic salsa and samba music filled the air.

"The dancing is just about to begin!"

Chapter 37

The shadowy, twilight soon morphed into the dark panorama of the infinite sky above them. One star after another appeared, each of them dotted against the velvety backdrop, each one lustrous and twinkling.

From the panoply of green, beach bushes and jungle plants and colorful flowers, one could see the moon's large presence peeking out from behind the tops of the abundant flora just feet away from the celebratory jubilee.

And the music and dancing continued on…

Gaston, XO, and Jor-Ahel each sat on an intricately-carven, dark-brown, bucket seat, its double lion legs ending in lion paws at the bottom. Behind each seat was a carving of a golden eagle about to spread its wings.

As honored guests of the royal family, they were offered the seating only afforded to royalty, council elders, and the elites. Each held a silver goblet in their hands of which the royal servants always made sure to keep them flowing with the sweet, purple wine.

Having satiated themselves with a hearty meal of roasted fish and vegetables and sweet, juicy figs, peaches, grapes and oranges plucked from the royal garden, the three men sighed with contentment, the goblets of wine in their hands, all of them watching the dancing unfold before them in the middle of a large circle of ordinary Egyptians, some seated cross-legged on the ground, others seated in mundane brown chairs, all of them paying homage to their beloved royal family, seated at the head of the circle.

Joanna and Barto chose to seat themselves with the ordinary citizens, both of them laughing at the paradoxical results of their attempted conversations with the local natives, both of them imbibing the sweet, purple wines with gusto.

And the dancing continued on, the rhythmic cadence of salsa and samba alternating with the tender, lyrical passages of love songs. At the center of the circle, the dancers, male and female, were all pirouetting, cavorting, twirling, and gamboling and finally ended with a slow dancing, as the music changed into a haunting, love song.

XO gulped the last drop of the sweet wine and placed the goblet on the ground. "Jor-Ahel, my man, I still have that question hanging in my mind. I'd like to pick your brain."

Gaston's curiosity was piqued, bending his head to listen, his hand grasping the half-unfinished goblet of sweet wine, his eyes following the beautiful moves of the professional dancers.

"Of course, my friend." Jor-Ahel responded with a smile. "Go ahead and pick my brain, as you say."

"What is the Horrodix-Tra? Never heard of them."

"They, my friend, are a terror in this universe. Very bad aliens. Huge reptiloids with the bodies of giants wearing heavy armor, their skins like reptilian scales protecting them from the pain and attack of weapons. They are mean, my friends. Very mean. You do not ever want to cross paths with them."

"Indeed." XO commented. "What the hell are these monsters doing in our earth home?"

Gaston nodded attentively. "Yes, why?"

Jor-Ahel smiled sadly. "They want to control Terra and all its inhabitants, local and alien, like me, for example, and my people. They are predatory, controlling, and aggressive. It is in their nature; has always been for millennia in the fabric of the universe. All of us out there, the good ones have always been and still are watching their every moves."

"And yet, this one was unexpected, huh?" XO asked.

Jor-Ahel nodded sadly. "Indeed, it was. The Horrodix-Tra were certainly sneaky and secretive with their plans to conquer Terra. We are lucky, the Amazari-Ah people sent their ambassador to warn us, albeit in holographic form. The royal Queen Nerilka offered to accompany the ambassador, lending her support, the Queen's ancestors, the ancient Kiru-Ashar people, having lived in peace with the Amazari-Ah's people for millennia in the planet Knomora, 120 light years away in your parlance".

"120 light years away." XO sighed. "Wow. That's too far away. How did they get here so fast?"

"What you call interdimensional travel with their starships."

"Huh?" XO asked puzzled.

"Kind of like a wormhole effect." Barto added with his signing and Joanna interpreting. "Manipulating and bending space and time with their ships to reach planets and stars at extreme distances."

"That is correct." Jor-Ahel responded, nodding at Barto. "Manipulating and bending space and time is a good example. It is an ancient technology well known among my people, also."

"But the holograms?" XO asked.

"That was necessary to protect the integrity of their beings. A technology best left quiet."

"I see." XO understood. "It was safer that way for them. So, it was the Horrodix-Tra species that destroyed Atlantis?"

"Yes." Jor-Ahel shook his head sadly. "That is how desperate and terrible the Horrodix-Tra are. They wanted to conquer and control Terra."

"But how did they do it?" XO asked.

"Yes, how?" Gaston added, watching with interest, as the Crown Princess Senefreya kissed both her grandparents on the cheeks, giving her goblet of wine to a servant.

Rising up from her throne chair designed to resemble the lotus flower at the back, she brushed down her silky, long, empress dress and slowly walked towards the group of dancers performing slow, undulating movements, expressing their connection to the mother Earth. Watching speechless at her natural dancing movements, he could not take his eyes of her and finally, Senefreya's eyes found their way locked into his eyes, both of them gazing unabashedly and oblivious to their surroundings.

"Hello?" XO snapped his fingers. "Do you still want to hear Jor-Ahel's story?"

"Go ahead." Gaston replied. "Don't mind me."

"Seriously?" XO asked. "You are quite besotted with the Princess, you know. Anyways, go on, Jor-Ahel."

"Very well." Jor-Ahel sighed continuing with his story. "You know that where we are, as our scientists have noted and recorded, the weather is changing, becoming warmer, all the icebergs and glaciers in all the lands surrounding Atlantis are melting, have been melting for a long time, the melting causing the ocean waters surrounding Atlantis to rise."

XO nodded.

"So, we have been watching the waters rise carefully over time. We knew we would have to leave the island city one day."

"But then the Horrodix-Tra arrived?" XO added. "What'd they do?"

"Ah, they did terrible things, my friend, only I know that. The Queen knows that. Amazari-Ah knows that. It was actually his people, who found out that the Horrodix-Tra were already on their way to Terra and, as such, tried to warn us at the council meeting, remember."

XO nodded. "Go on."

"Indeed." Jor-Ahel agreed. "But that peace and community of us all, Kalamuria, Atlantis, and Egypt, were shattered by the unexpected arrival of the horrible Horrodix-Tra with their powerful ships and weapons. Believe me, they have a weapon that can blow up a planet."

XO whistled in surprise. "No kidding! Wow. But they didn't do that, blow up earth, I mean."

"No, they didn't." Jor-Ahel agreed. "Because they wanted something more from this planet. Like I said many times before, the horrible Horrodix-Tra wanted to take control of Terra and turn all the people inhabiting this world, alien and local, into their slaves, their food. That much I know about them. They have done that in other worlds, sadly."

"That still doesn't answer my question." XO demanded. "How did they destroy Atlantis?"

Jor-Ahel took in a deep breath. "Well, you see, with their planet-destroying weapon, they somehow configured it to do something else. Something that was necessary to do in order to facilitate their takeover of Terra."

"Facilitate?" Gaston asked. "How so?"

"They had to get rid of us colonists, the Atlanteans and the Kalamurians, and all the local, indigenous people living among us, not so much the Egyptians, but us islanders on both sides of that big continent that you call North America. So, what they did was focus their powerful weapon and changed the energy into a kind of grappling capacity. With that on the ready, the Horrodix-Tra…

"Grabbed with the grapplers what we call the Tauriid meteors that show up on October every year…" Barto signed and Joanna interpreted.

"Yes, the Tauriids, as you call them…" Jor-Ahel nodded at Barto. "And the Horrodix-Tra just threw them all on the icebergs already melting on both sides of that massive central landmass, breaking them apart and adding fuel to their already melting capacity."

"And that caused the gigantic floods on both sides." XO finished the sentence. "It was certainly fast and furious."

"No wonder it was hard to escape." Gaston commented. XO nodded gravely.

"I only hope your ship and crew made it out safely." Jor-Ahel commented. "And my people with them."

"Hell, I don't even know if my ship made it out." Gaston remarked ruefully. "There is nothing I could do about it."

Jor-Ahel nodded. "We can only hope they did escape quickly, my friends. This has been a terrible, terrible time for us all. I am eminently grateful for our friends, the Egyptian royal family, for providing sanctuary in their homeland for us."

"Never could I imagine, we would end up beneath the Sphinx." Gaston commented. "For a long time, I had thought it was just a monument standing in the desert. It is an amazing sanctuary underneath it, miles of caverns and tunnels. Unbelievable."

"Indeed." Jor-Ahel replied proudly. "They were meant to last forever, these building blocks being the only resources our ancestors could scrounge up to build what they needed. Heavy impenetrable stones. Granite stone and pentellic marble and coralline limestones are perfect resources for building. For lasting as long as they did and still are into infinity."

"There's more…" Barto signed, Joanna interpreted. "Based on Dr. Breslov's research, he believes there is more to the Sphinx than meets the eye. He believed it is also a marker for all to see and know, now and in the future."

"What marker?" Gaston asked Barto, still not leaving his gaze upon the raven-haired Senefreya, now swirling around with a brightly-colored, silk shawl like an exquisite butterfly.

Jor-Ahel smiled. "It's true. The Sphinx is a sanctuary and, also a marker, for all times. You see, when my ancestors arrived from the cosmos long, long ago…it was the time of the Leo Constellation in the sky, and so, they built the Sphinx, his gazing eyes looking up towards the distant stars, towards the Leo Constellation, in commemoration of the arrival of our ancestors to Egypt, Kalamaria, and Atlantis. Excellent, Barto."

"That's amazing. Who would have thunk?"

"Indeed, my friend." Jor-Ahel chuckled. "Who would have thunk? Your people have many markers in your time, but few of them, as gigantic, and as complex, as our beloved Sphinx."

"I like better that the head looks like a full-fledged lion, the way Dr. Breslov believed it was originally set up." Barto explained in signage and Joanna interpreted.

At that moment in time, Senefreya disconnected her gaze with the Captain and dropped her shawl to the ground. Her skin glistening with small droplets of sweat, she ducked beneath the other dancers still gyrating to the music and slowly walked towards the cobblestone trail among the plants and flowers.

Gaston watched her disappear into the tropical, garden patch, her hands softly brushing the hanging leaves of palm trees, the soft luster of the half-moon glowing upon her thick, dark hair.

"Excuse me." Gaston apologized, rising up from his guest chair.

<h1 style="text-align:center">Chapter 38</h1>

"Hello."

Startled, Senefreya broke away from her dreamlike reverie, her eyes now opened and rising to lock with the handsome Navy Captain now standing beside her, a warm smile in his rugged face with the 5 o'clock shadow on his lower jawline. Feeling an instant, inexplicable sense of connection to him, as always, she smiled back, her dark eyes twinkling.

"May I sit beside you?" Gaston asked, feeling embarrassed, uncertain what to do with himself standing up and looking deeply into her eyes, wanting to envelope her in his arms. What is it about their eyes always finding a way to each other and lock themselves into a scrutinizing trance, as if they've always known each other?

"Of course, please do." Senefreya responded. "I have come out here to take a break from all that dancing and feasting."

Gaston settled himself on the soft, thick sand, crossing his legs. Turning towards Senefreya, he reached out for the unusual jewel enclosed in a silver clasp, resting just between her breasts. An eight-pointed star. "What is this? Do you always wear it everywhere?"

"Oh, yes, everywhere!" Senefreya declared, clasping his hand still holding on to the jade-colored, obsidian jewel. "Ever since my Papa bestowed it to me the day he passed away. He was saving this for my 21ˢᵗ birthday, already three days passed."

"Your birthday?" Gaston fingered the stone feeling it smooth, exterior surface in his hand. "Why is that?"

Senefreya smiled. "The 21ˢᵗ birthday was my day of ascension, the day when I finally entered a new phase of growth. Like Jor-Ahel explained before, it is common among my people, my race, as my Papa told me the year approaching my 21ˢᵗ birthday."

"But why?"

"My DNA changes significantly that day and it shows. You saw me becoming tired and nauseous, remember?"

Gaston nodded. "I was wondering what was going on with you."

"Well, my body was only just trying to adjust to the changes in my DNA process, but I end up feeling nauseous and dizzy and very, very tired." She took in a deep breath. "I'm okay now, I'm in full control of my abilities."

"Clearly." Gaston was impressed. "You must be quite omnipotent."

"Hardly." Senefreya laughed. "I live and die just like the rest of you. I'm just different, because of my abilities, which I inherited through my Papa, not my human mother."

"That is impressive." Gaston gently let go of the jewel. "Why the need for this?"

"It helps with my abilities." Senefreya fingered the jewel. "The crystal arrangement is called the merkhaba and you need only this very special kind of crystal, only found in the original home planet of my race."

She pointed at the skies above her. "From Proxima Centauri."

"Okay, why?"

"You ask too many questions." Senefreya giggled. "Like I said, it helps with my abilities. It's how I was able to put myself into another dimension, the minute the 747 crashed into waters. I managed to escaped death, mercifully."

"You certainly did." Gaston commented. "No one could possibly survive this crash. I wondered how you did."

"Now you know." Senefreya patted the merkhaba lovingly. "But be assured, this powerful little gem in my necklace can also kill me, so focus and self-control is very, very important."

Moments passed, as Senefreya and Gaston became quiet, the both of them watching the skies, a few more stars filling the yawning, dark canvas surrounding the star of the show.

Senefreya hugged her knees, sighing with admiration.

"Tonight is the night of the blood supermoon, did you know that?" She pointed at the massive size of earth's orbiting partner, now at its most perigee point.

Another rush of the ocean waves splashed their bodies.

"It's so warm, the ocean." Senefreya sighed. "The water is so healing. I love to sit right here and let it wash over me time and again, my mind lost into dreams."

Gaston smiled. "That must be nice. The water is certainly warm tonight. I cannot abide cold water myself, unless I have to."

Senefreya laughed. "The ocean is always so warm here, so inviting. You should see this place in the summers. White, white sands and aquamarine water, so clear you can actually see the bottom. It is heaven on earth."

"You were there at this beach? Back in the 1960s?"

"No. No. I couldn't." Senefreya responded. "But this ocean was always in my dreams. In fact, my dreams are so vivid I can actually feel as well as see the things in my dreams. As if I was there, out of my body."

"That's something". Gaston remarked.

"And so, I was always dreaming about this place and its beautiful colors and I was always wondering why am I dreaming about this place?"

"And…"

"It is my Papa's home. Back in the time of my ancestors, Papa's family, this was his favorite place to be, the beach. He spoke about his beach in my bedtime stories, how beautiful it is and how warm and comforting the waters are, when times are stressful." Senefreya sighed. "And so, I dreamed the dream of Papa's beautiful beach, as if I'm supposed to be here, the place that keeps pulling me, keeps telling me I have to come home."

"That is quite a beautiful story. So, you are happy here? On this beach?"

"Oh, yes!" Senefreya exclaimed, hugging her knees. "I am home the way I'm supposed to, I guess. Just doesn't feel complete, the way I expected it, if you know what I mean?"

Gaston nodded. "Maybe you need to look further for home, hmm?"

"Maybe…" Senefreya turned her head to look up at the darkened skies, sprinkled here and there with a few sparkling stars and the supermoon.

"It's big." Gaston commented turning to look at the moon.

"Yes, the supermoon is at its perigee." Senefreya whispered. "It's so big and beautiful. So magical."

Seconds passed, as the couple remained sitting comfortably next to each other.

"You know…" Senefreya began. "I saw this supermoon back then in our time in the 1960s, when I was trapped living in Berlin with my parents. I was just walking home in a snowstorm along that horrible Berlin Wall and its sentry guard posts and I tried to ignore the soldiers with their awful bayonet guns by focusing on that supermoon."

"Go on…" Gaston urged.

"So, as I was walking home to the apartment I shared with Papa and Mamoshka, not too far away, I did something unexpected. Must have been the pull of that supermoon. It was, it still is, so magical, so riveting, pulling my deepest dreams and desires into focus."

"And what were they?" Gaston asked. "What happened?"

Senefreya laughed softly. "I had this dream. This desire. And the words came pouring out of my mind and soul at that moment in time, gazing at that supermoon. I still remember the words to this day."

"I'd like to hear it, those words."

Senefreya closed her eyes, hugging her knees tighter, all sense of fear and embarrassment gone with this kind, handsome stranger listening to her deepest thoughts. "It goes like this…wherever you are, my love, my true love, whoever you are out there in the dark night. I feel you are watching this beautiful moon with me just now, whether you are near or far. Until we meet, my love, as the Fates have ordained by the power of our interwoven braids of life."

Gaston felt the hairs on his back rise.

His thoughts went back to that day he was driving home in his Land Rover on the Pacific Coast Highway. The last day of his secret tryst with Sharona. Feeling nauseous, he had felt compelled to pull over and try to stabilize himself, finding himself in some sort of trance…and the same words had appeared in his mind like a song from far away…he found himself chanting word for word:

"Wherever you are, my love, my true love, whoever you are out there in the dark night. I feel you are watching this beautiful moon with me just now, whether you are near or far. Until we meet, my love, as the Fates have ordained by the power of our interwoven braids of life."

Senefreya stared at him for a long time, becoming shocked herself.

"And get this…" Gaston continued in exasperation. "It was not the first time I heard those words. I heard it again and again. At home in bed, at the naval base. On this ship. It only stopped the minute you showed up hanging onto a piece of debris from the 747 floating in the ocean. Just stopped. Again, I really couldn't figure it out and chose to let it go."

"Until now…" Senefreya smiled, her eyes gazing at the handsome, rugged lines of his face. She wanted to feel the thick, soft tousle of hair on his head, beautiful sandy-blond hair, now growing towards his shoulders, his whole persona resembling Apollo of the Greek myths. He only needed to wear the iconic Greek tunic and sandals and it would a be perfect look.

"Until now…" Gaston repeated. "What was that all about, that poem? Sending me those cryptic words all the way from Berlin? Why me?"

Senefreya smiled, with a love growing inside her, soft and warm, her body feeling the need to get closer to him. "It's not a poem, Gaston, may I call you, Gaston? Or would you prefer Captain Caine?"

"Gaston is fine. May I call you Senefreya?"

"Yes. And well, it's not a poem, but it does sound like one." Senefreya mused, her hand playing with the sands, as it slipped between her fingers. She was trying not to look into his eyes. Right now, it was happening and it was becoming too, too personal and right now, she only knew him for several days, so far.

But, it was happening. The connection between them. That quantum entanglement no longer lost.

"I'm quite confused." Gaston asked, wondering why she looked away from him. Compelled by he knew not what, he put his hand on hers and clasped it softly. "Tell me more."

"It was a magic spell, the best I could say it." Senefreya explained, her hands catching the waves once again washing over their bodies. "My Papa taught it to me. He says thoughts are powerful and can be manifested under the right conditions. Some people have that power more than others, like Papa and me. It's all in our DNA. You have it too, but my power is stronger. I am supposed to be the future of you."

"But that still doesn't answer my question." Gaston demanded. "Why me?"

Senefreya finally dared to look up into his eyes, now darkened with a sense of desire, having felt the warmth and silkiness of the skin of her hand in his grip. Her heart was beating so fast against her chest, her cheeks blushing hotly, her body becoming warm all over at his touch on her hand.

She sighed deeply, still searching his eyes. "It was you, Gaston. No, it is you, right here, right now. It is you, my love. It has always been you."

"Come again?" Gaston asked.

"I was praying for my true love, the only way I could, from Papa's teachings." Senefreya whispered. "I was praying for my true love, wherever he was, watching that supermoon, near or far. The words keep coming out of my mouth time and again. And like you, it only it stopped when you came into my life, rescuing me from that crash. It was you. It is you."

Gaston pulled his hand away and faced the ocean, his hands grasping his face, his elbows resting on his knees watching the waves lap on the shoreline. "I'm lost. I have this strong feeling for you. I've always have, since you were pulled from that crash, but to be honest, I'm lost."

Senefreya smiled. "Don't be. I have strong feelings for you, too. Always have the moment our eyes locked in that medic bay. My heart was telling me it was you, but my mind was all over the place, my body and soul struggling to survive in a strange place in your ship and with your crew.

"Seriously?"

She placed her hand on his cheek, ruffling her fingers into his thick, sandy-blond hair. "Don't be afraid of me, of our feelings."

"Are you kidding." Gaston exclaimed, opening his shirt buttons one by one.

In that moment, he ripped his shirt away from his torso, throwing it away on the sands in a crumpled mass. He gently pulled her face towards him and kissed her full, red lips, diving into her wet mouth, feeling her tongue surround his.

He placed his hand on her right breast, his other hand around her back, enveloping her body towards him. All at once, he felt the sensual warmth and lustful feelings grow intensely in his body, his groin quickening at her warmth and nearness.

Together they ripped off the rest of their clothes throwing them in several piles on the sand, pulling each other on the sandy surface in the full embrace of two bodies intertwining in a dance of love and lust, their feet entangled, their arms grabbing their backs, in all their nakedness, feeling all the senses coming out from each of them, firing brightly their burning love for each other into an explosive state of completeness, the white-crested ocean waves tumbling over them, the exquisite light of the supermoon gracing them.

Chapter 39

The warmth of the dawning sun caressed her skin…

Senefreya opened her eyes, feeling her feet being washed over by the foamy waters of the ocean, now cooler than the night before. The tide was now low, the waters only splashing on her feet. Feeling a muscular arm holding her body in an embrace, she found herself resting against a warm, male body, her head nestled on his muscular chest.

A flood of memories spilled into her mind, the beautiful memories of their lovemaking by the high tide of the ocean, under the magnificent indigo sky and the vibrant supermoon.

Senefreya smiled, sighing contentedly, playing with the skin on the hairs on his chest.

She felt a hand go through her long, dark hair, brushing it down softly.

"Good morning, Senefreya, my love." Gaston whispered, enjoying the pleasure of her fingers exploring his chest. "It is morning, isn't it?"

"Oh, yes." Senefreya looked up into his sparkly, grey eyes, content in their lovemaking the night before. "Early morning, look, the sun is only just sneaking up. Look at the colors. It's just so glorious."

"Indeed, it is." Gaston smiled, kissing her forehead, as they both took the moment to enjoy the gold, pink, and orange hues surrounding the half-rising orb slowly moving up from the horizon line, its rays outstretched in all directions.

"If only this moment stays forever…" Senefreya sighed contentedly, her arm wrapping tightly around his body. "Just you and me and the ocean and the beautiful dawning of the sun."

Gaston laughed softly. "That would be nice. I want nothing more than that. The stark reality is we do need to eat in order to live, don't you agree?"

Senefreya laughed. "Of course, silly. We do. I'm quite famished myself. Shall we go back?"

She lifted her body up to look behind her towards the lush, green, jungle garden with the cobblestone trail inside it. Two palace guards in their royal purple and gold uniform garb, stood tall and firm, their hands gripping lances with the spear points, their eyes fixated towards the horizon, the both of them standing sentinel not far from the sleeping couple.

"Look, my grandparents apparently sent protection for us overnight. Oh. That is so sweet of them."

"Indeed." Gaston looked back. "You are very valuable to them, it seems. No objection either, to my being with you."

"No objection, indeed." Senefreya stroked his cheek. "Quo vadis, my love?

"And where are we going, my love." Gaston pulled Senefreya to his body, the both of them falling back into the sand, laughing, his mouth reaching for hers in another long passionate kiss.

Seconds later, a sound broke in the air…its haunting melody ringing out at full volume from somewhere behind them.

"What the hell was that?" Gaston remarked, irritated. "Why are we hearing it now?"

"It's the temple horn played by our musician. It's the call to wake up and gather for the morning feast. It is our tradition."

"Well, why didn't you say so?" Gaston exclaimed. "I'm famished!"

For a moment he started to get up, his hand reaching down to Senefreya's hand and pulling her up beside his body. "But first, I do need to ask you something."

"By all means, my love." Senefreya smiled warmly, her hand enveloped in his. "What is it?"

"One, how in hell did that plane, that 747, get here in this time and space. Two, where are the pilots. I know you couldn't possibly fly that plane, did you? And three, why are you the only survivor in that crash?"

"Lots of questions, my love." Senefreya laughed softly. "I will try my best. We were heading home to the United States in the plane, what you call the 747, towards New York La Guardia from Paris, where we escaped to from Berlin."

"Berlin? We?" Gaston asked.

"That is a whole another story, Gaston, my love. A story for another time, perhaps before a nice, blazing camp fire, no? Senefreya smiled.

"Of course, another time." Gaston agreed. "Go on…"

"Well, we were getting close, the 747, when all of a sudden something pulled the plane to the left. None of the pilots, including my husband, could control it."

"Your husband? You are married?"

"No, I'm a widow now. Yes, I had a husband and we were with child, when it happened. The crash caused the fetus to miscarry, unfortunately."

"I'm sorry for that." Gaston hugged her tightly. "Please do go on. Who was he, your husband?"

"An American astronaut and pilot. Beauregard Faninus. We fell in love, the both of us trying to escape from Berlin, and, like I said, it's a whole another story for another time."

"Of course."

"Well, my husband and three other American pilots tried to control the plane, but the force pulling the plane down south was too strong. The pressure in the plane too heavy. I could not get out of my seat to help them. I just let go in my seat. Waiting for the end."

"Go on."

"Well, I lost consciousness in my efforts to protect myself through my abilities and my crystal merkhaba and found myself floating in the waters, the plane broken up, the debris floating all around me. I crawled to the biggest one and just lay there, exhausted beyond belief."

"I see." Gaston commented. "That plane was heading towards the Bermuda Triangle. I'm guessing the force from the time portal pulled it in just like it pulled my ship in. Oh, Senefreya, I'm truly sorry this happened to you." He stroked her hair.

"Don't be."

"What?"

"I found you. My one true love."

Gaston nodded. "That's true. But, I can't figure out, though, why your husband and three other pilots disappeared. They should already be dead. We can't even find their bodies."

"It's simple, Gaston. Jor-Ahel already talked about that. The pilots, they all went wherever their thoughts brought them, either altogether or separately."

"Of course." Gaston nodded. "And your thoughts of Atlantis brought you here, right?"

"Actually, I was thinking of home, my Papa's home, and this beautiful beach resort his family often go to in the hot summer days and cool fall seasons." Senefreya added. "It just happened to be in Egypt, near Atlantis in the year 9632 BC."

Once again, the loud, melodious call of the horn sounded in the air. A flight of cormorants flew away close by towards the far end of the ocean for their morning meal of fish.

"Come on." Gaston gently turned Senefreya away from the ocean waters, still holding her against his body. "They are calling for us. Let's go have breakfast."

Chapter 40

Breakfast was a scrumptious feast with bread, fish, and vegetables galore accompanied by goblets of milk and beer to one's own desire. The palace musicians played joyful music on their lyres, lutes, castanets, and drums, providing a backdrop of uplifting energy for all to start their day.

And then it was over, the plates cleared away, the musicians leaving the breakfast hall, the sound of silence permeating the air. Senefreya had excused herself to spend time to refreshen herself with a spa session by the temple bath pool, just beyond the breakfast suite, surrounded by palm leaves.

"We never should have sent him to Atlantis." Queen Nerilka exclaimed with fervor and deep regret in her heart. "Then he would not have disappeared."

"And then I would not have existed." Senefreya gently kissed her grandmother's cheek, before heading to the bath pool.

Both of them seated on their carven throne chairs, Pharoah Ra-Azeris and Queen Nerilka, enjoyed the early morning relaxation under soft, rays of the sun. Two gentle lions side by side with Senefreya near the edge of the bath pool.

Senefreya smiled and calmly stroked one of the lion's head. The lion purred, butting his head in her hand. Looking up at her grandparents with love in her heart, she asked her grandmother to tell her the story of Papa. With a gentle nod, Queen Nerilka began the she began reciting about that fateful day, Crown Prince Basteteme, her Papa, disappeared.

Meanwhile, Gaston and his XO had sauntered lazily about the temple hallways towards the portico, where they had settled down on a bench, relaxed and full from the lavish breakfast offered to them.

"This will keep me full all day." Gaston commented. "I'm not used to this kind of breakfast."

"Imagine doing this, every day, sir." XO laughed. "Imagine beer for breakfast just before work."

"We would get fired in an instant." Gaston agreed, chuckling loudly. "So, XO, what did you want to relay to me. You said you had received a message earlier in the morning? From whom?"

"You'd never guess, sir." XO responded. "I'm still trying to wrap this around my head."

"Spill it out."

"They are alive and well, sir." XO explained. "Our crew and the Atlanteans escaping the floods. Not all of them made it to the ship on time, when I made that warning call, but the ones that did, they are alive and well."

"So, the satdite comm is working now?"

"Yes, sir, it's working. I got their message, in spite of the static coming through. I heard their words and I must tell you, I am still astounded at what is going on with them now."

"Go on." Gaston urged. "What's happening?"

"I'm told they found that warren of caverns in the Duarokara Valley, the ones Jor-Ahel mentioned. The people in there were hostile at first and a lot of talking and negotiations had been going on, but first, the lead officer who took over the helm, told us, that going through that time portal after disembarking from Atlantis was just like going through that time portal in the Bermuda Triangle. It was a creepy sense of déjà vu. And then the waves crashed, just like the rogue wave behind us in the Bermuda Triangle incident."

"Fascinating." Gaston commented. "What happened then?"

"Like I said…" XO reiterated. "The ship's crew and a motley of Atlantis survivors, they had to negotiate their way into the caves. Good thing there someone in the group of Atlantis survivors, who knows them, their language, their culture. God knows what would have happened to them, if that guy who knows them did not speak up."

"Sheer luck." Gaston shook his head. "So, the ship?"

"Gone in an instant, sir." XO shook his head sadly. "It was not built to sustain the height and power of the thousand feet high flood waves that just sunk Atlantis in 24 hours. Impossible to save her."

"God rest her." Gaston smiled. "She got us all through safely in this bizarre experiment I hope to never repeat. By the way, no one did what they were not supposed to do, once the ship started the generators?"

"As far as I'm aware of, no." XO responded. "No one is likely to forget what had happened the first time. It was gruesome to watch."

"Exactly."

"And so here we are…" XO commented.

"Yes, here we are…" Gaston repeated, his eyes staring ahead, his brain scrutinizing possibilities, still searching for an answer on how to get the four of them home. He could not do anything about the survivors at the Duorakara Valley. Best to leave them there to build a new life.

Once again, the two men settled quietly against the intricately, carved wooden bench not saying a word. The warm, morning breeze brushed against their skins.

A loud tap on the marble, portico floor broke the reverie. Gaston and XO turned towards the entrance of the portico.

A sentinel guard in full regalia was standing at post with his golden spear lance, his head held high and proud, nary a smile on his face, but a firm countenance of self-assurance on his mission. Once again, he tapped the spear lance on the floor.

"Okay, we got you." Gaston responded. "What is this about?"

"He doesn't know English." XO commented. "But he is telling us something. Something he wants us to do?"

"Most likely." Gaston agreed. Again, the spear lance thumped on the floor. The two men waited a moment more for the sentinel guard to at least say something. Instead, the guard bowed in deference to the naval officers, turned half-way around, and gestured with hand for the two men to follow him into the El Mayarina resort temple.

"Let's go." Gaston rose up from the bench. "Looks like we are wanted somewhere in there."

"No problem." XO commented, staying in line with his Captain, as they both followed the sentinel guard into the dark recesses of the temple.

Seconds later, Gaston and XO found themselves back in the breakfast suite, where Pharoah Ra-Azeris and Queen Nerilka were seated in their beautifully carven wooden royal chairs facing the bath pool and the garden, their granddaughter, Crown Princess Senefreya, at the edge of the bath pool, with the two lions lying beside her. Her feet were immersed in the waters of the pool, lifting her head upwards, the Crown Princess was enjoying the full warmth of the sun's rays upon her.

Their host Jor-Ahel also joined them, seated in his carven chair next to the royal couple quieting conversing with Joanna and Barto, who were also summoned to the breakfast suite by the royal couple.

Jor-Ahel smiled quizzically at the Captain and XO, as if he was hiding a secret he was dying to burst out. Joanna and Barto apparently were also bursting with the secret hiding in their minds.

In the far corner of the suite, a table was once again filled with platters of fruits and bread and goblets of wine, beer, and fresh drinking water. Two royal servants stood by the table patiently waiting to serve.

It was now mid-morning.

"Come, my guests of honor." Pharoah Ra-Azeris spoke in a welcoming tone. "Please be seated." He gestured at two additional carven chairs next to him facing the pool and the Crown Princess, who turned to smile at Gaston, the memories of their love-making rushing back in the corner of her mind, her cheeks blushing in the presence of the ones, who were not aware of their intimacy.

Gaston smiled back at the Crown Princess, his eyes glazed once again with the thoughts of their love-making on the sands, the white-crested waves lapping over their bodies. Not leaving his gaze with the Crown Princess, he walked towards one of the two carven chairs to seat himself, followed by his XO, who maintained his silence, who somehow understood what had happened between his Captain and the Crown Princess.

Queen Nerilka, watching the quiet, yet attentive and loving exchange between her granddaughter and the Captain, also understood, nodding in satisfaction.

The outcome was becoming better than she had expected. Hopefully, the Captain would agree to their terms.

Pharoah Ra-Azeris clapped his hand loudly. "Now we will have a mid-morning meal, my guests of honor. And then, we will have a heart-to-heart discourse of the utmost importance. A mission so to speak."

"A mission." Gaston repeated looking at XO with sarcasm. "Why does that sound familiar?"

"I don't know whether to laugh or cry." XO responded.

"Me, too." Gaston nodded. "Me, too."

An hour later, the platters of food and drinks taken away by the palace servants, Senefreya resumed her place by the bath pool, immersing her feet in the warm sun-kissed waters, the gentle lions purring beside her.

"Now…" Pharoah Ra-Azeris announced, as soon as the last servant closed the heavy, carven door. "We will discuss this mission."

"It is a good mission, do not fear." Queen Nerilka reassured them, her hand reaching out towards her husband's hand. Her eyes looking ahead at the bath pool, she smiled at Gaston. "My granddaughter will join the mission with you and help you."

"What mission?" Gaston asked perplexed at the suggestion. "I'm not interested in taking your granddaughter away from her home. She is not equipped for a mission."

"She most certainly is equipped." Pharoah Ra-Azeris objected vehemently. "You will need her in this mission."

Jor-Ahel nodded in agreement. "Listen to the Pharoah, my friends. This may be the solution to your dilemma."

"We are going home?" XO exclaimed. "Is that right?"

"Not exactly." Queen Nerilka interjected, her eyes capturing her granddaughter basking in the mid-morning sun. Sensing the Queen's attention, Senefreya turned slightly and bowed her head in deference.

The Queen continued. "It's a small, but important twist of the journey to go home. It's actually for the Captain and my precious Senefreya." She turned towards the Captain, her eyes shining with a sense of joy. "I know. I just know in my heart. I am happy for you both in your long life of being together as husband and wife. This will help with your mission."

"What mission?" Gaston asked in frustration, embarrassed that they all now knew what had happened last night at the beach, but thankful no one objected to their love for each other.

Just as the magic spell Senefreya had sent out at the night of the supermoon a few weeks ago had promised him, Gaston had finally found the love of his life in Senefreya. They were true soulmates.

"Okay, I'm all ears now." Gaston acceded.

"What happens to me." XO sounded out, feeling deflated. "I'm not even part of the mission. I cannot leave my Captain. You all know that."

"I cannot leave my Captain, either." Joanna piped up, fascinated at the turn of this captivating conversation, her hands signing each word uttered in this amazing conversation, towards the equally fascinated Barto staring at her dancing hands with due diligence.

Jor-Ahel smiled. "You will know your mission, my friends, soon. It is not that bad. In fact, you might even enjoy it."

"Fine." XO grunted unhappily. "Spill it out. We are all ears."

Pharoah Ra-Azeris took in a breath, watching his honored guests waiting in anticipation to hear about the new mission about to be discussed among them. The Pharoah looked beyond them towards his granddaughter softly absorbed in the warmth of the sun's rays. He nodded for a moment. Yes, it was time for her to fulfill her life' mission.

A mission that will take her away from them, but he knew she would be loved and safe with the Captain in this mission.

The Pharoah turned his attention back to the others still waiting for his dialogue of the mission. "Myself and my Queen, along with Jor-Ahel, have spoken with the galactic diplomats in our assembly room built to accommodate their holographic images, you understand?"

Gaston and XO nodded. They had seen it before in Atlantis.

"Ah, good. The discussion centered around what to do with you and you…" He pointed to Gaston and XO and Joanna and Barto. "And all your people now living within the caves at Duorakara Valley with the locals."

The Pharoah paused for moment. "My honored guests, the galactic diplomats from planets far, far away in this galaxy, have provided a solution agreeable to us all and we do hope that you and your XO and the lady Joanna and Barto will also find it agreeable."

"This solution…" Queen Nerilka explained. "It's actually a mission directive. You do not have to agree to it, but you do not want disappoint them. The galactic diplomats are supreme guardians of this galaxy. It is their job to watch over Terra. They have been doing this for millions of years, you understand?"

"Huh, you mean they'll get mad at us, if we do not follow the mission?" Gaston asked.

"Oh boy…" XO breathed out. "That should be one hell of a mission."

"No, they will not be upset." Queen Nerilka responded calmly. "They are benevolent, spiritual beings from the 9th dimension, beautiful and loving, and kind. They have the answer to your dilemma and we all like it, my husband, Jor-Ahel, myself, and even our precious Senefreya. We certainly hope you will like it. Do keep an open mind, no?"

"In that case." Gaston commented. "I'll try."

"Good." Jor-Ahel nodded. "I have a feeling you will like it."

"So…" Pharoah Ra-Azeris sat back on his carven chair and looked around once more. "We are in agreement to listen and keep an open mind. Good. Good. So…after a long discussion of potential advantages and pitfalls, we have all agreed to this decree that will now be your mission, Captain Caine…you will, of course, go home, but not to your real home in this universe."

"Come again?" Gaston asked.

"You will go back to what is called your alternate home in a parallel universe. You see, your actual home in your universe has sidestepped the nuclear danger thanks to your President's smart maneuvers. With the help of the galactic diplomats, a nuclear war had been averted. The world is fine and standing, and stable, but the ugly Cold War continues…"

"And my wife and daughter?" Gaston demanded.

"They are also fine. They have come to depend on the kindness of your good neighbor, the mad scientist, I believe?"

"But why can't I go back to my actual home, back to my family?"

"Because there is a need for you in your other home in a parallel universe." Jor-Ahel explained, taking over the conversation, trying to smooth out the anger and disappointment in the eyes of Gaston and his XO. "In that world, a nuclear war had happened and it was terrible. Terrible. There are very few survivors. And yes, your mirror doppelganger in that world is killed, as are your wife and daughter and many, many others. Don't you see, my friend? They have a need for you there."

"Yes, they have a need for you there, Captain Caine." Pharoah Ra-Azeris emphasized. "The survivors, they do need a leader, and you are perfect for that mission. To lead them to rebuild their new home world. Do you understand?"

"I don't know…" Gaston replied, realizing the logic of the situation. He was actually trained to do this his entire life. "My wife and daughter… they need me also."

"Do not worry…" Queen Nerilka gently spoke. "Your good neighbor will take care of them, I promise you that. They already think that you are killed. They know the President ordered the ship to Cuba in the first place."

"That crazy Dr. Breslov…messing up my wife's head." Gaston spoke softly. "I suppose I can accept that. My wife, she somehow became obsessed with him, while I'm gone on my tours. Loneliness does that to you, I would think."

Queen Nerilka smiled. "She will be fine. And your daughter will grow beautifully under his care, your neighbor. He knows what to do with her condition. So…will you do this, Captain Caine? Your new mission?"

Gaston thought for a while. "I suppose I can. XO will assist me."

"No." Pharoah Ra-Azeris spoke forcefully. "Your XO cannot assist you in this mission. He is not capable."

Gaston and XO looked at each other. "Not capable?"

Jor-Ahel chuckled at the irony of it. "Just wait until the end."

"No." Pharoah Ra-Azeris reiterated firmly. "But my granddaughter is capable. She has the abilities and powers to help you and the survivors build a new world. You see, with her DNA frequency, she will be the only who can access the Sphinx, where the Hall of Records reside with everything you need to rebuild the new world, all the technology, blueprints, tools, everything. You see, that is why we built the Sphinx. It is configured to match her DNA frequency, so only she can access it, no one else."

Gaston' eyes rested upon Senefreya, amazed at the revelation he was just hearing, the power of her.

Pharoah Ra-Azeris paused a moment. "You see, there is a reason for this. Our technology and tools, data, and records are powerful, very powerful, but very, very dangerous in the wrong hands. Of course, you need her there beside you in your mission."

"It should not be a problem, now?" Queen Nerilka asked softly. "Senefreya and you have bonded deeply, no?"

"We are in love." Gaston admitted. "But does she want to come with me in this apparently dangerous mission. I would be taking her away from her home with you both. I do not relish that."

"Hey, what about me?" XO demanded. "I'm just as capable as her in a way. And like I said before, I'm not leaving my Captain."

Pharoah Ra-Azeris lifted his hand. The suite became quiet for the moment. "I assure you, my honored guest, I too have what your Captain call my XO. I understand your predicament, but do remember, you are here and not in your actual home world, where everything is gone and destroyed. Here, our policy is different for you. You have a choice, my friend."

"Choice? What are you talking about?" XO demanded.

"You can either go back to your home world, now shattered and destroyed and try explaining how you came back from the past without your Captain to the bewildered survivors or you can join your crew, all of them safely sheltered in the caves of Duorakara Valley and rebuild their world. They too need a leader, the local inhabitants and your crew. Like Captain Caine, you are perfect to lead them."

"So, you are saying I absolutely can't go with my Captain to this other home world?" XO asked.

"You can, but it would be pointless and quite useless." Jor-Ahel explained. "You will be alone in another strange world trying to figure out your destiny, when the galactic diplomats agreed that your destiny should be better to lead the rebuilding of the Duorakara Valley. Will you do that?"

XO looked at his Captain. Gaston nodded, placing his hand on XO's shoulder. "You can do this, XO. We need to regroup and change our viewpoint. They need us to do our jobs. It all makes sense. So... you are henceforth released from the position of my second-in-command forthwith."

"Yes, sir." XO saluted. "As such, I will gladly comply and stand released as XO of the USS Arcanus. And from my viewpoint, you are henceforth released as Captain of the USS Arcanus. May god help us."

"He will go to the Duorakara Valley." The Captain smiled at his XO. "He knows what to do. You are right. We are both trained for this mission, as you put it."

"Excellent!" The Pharoah clapped his hand.

"Good, good, my friend!" Jor-Ahel exclaimed.

"That is wonderful!" Queen Nerilka smiled. "I am very happy my precious Senefreya will go with you. She has agreed to do this mission and she will help you, Captain Caine. I am happy you both are bonded together in love. That will greatly help with the mission."

"Hey, what about us?" Joanna piped up, Barto nodded vehemently beside. "Sir, what about us?"

"I'm not sure, Petty Officer Pettigrew." Gaston responded, his eyes reflecting his uncertainty of what to do with them. He looked at the Pharoah for an answer. "What do the galactic diplomats have in mind for my petty officer and her charge? I am at a loss what to do for them."

"It is up to them, whatever they choose, together or individually." Pharoah Ra-Azeris suggested. "What will you choose, my guests of honor?"

Joanna and Barto looked at each other, both of them nodding happily, already having made up their minds.

Joanna turned to face the Captain. "Sir, Barto and I, we are very fond of each other and would like to stay together for the rest of our lives, here in this beautiful land of Egypt. Ancient Egypt. Barto at least wants to. He tells me he is not happy back home, where the deaf are not valued. Here he feels the respect of the royal family and everybody else. I do want to stay with him. I have grown quite fond of him." She patted Barto's cheek. "He makes me laugh."

"I like her too!" Barto signed, grabbing Joanna's face and kissing her. "I'm going with her, wherever she goes, no way I'm leaving my interpreter, no way!"

After the laughter died down, Gaston smiled at Joanna. He placed a hand on her shoulder. "You are henceforth released from your duty as Petty Officer Third Class of the USS Arcanus. May you and Barto have a long, prosperous life in this land. I will certainly miss you both."

"Yes, me too." XO added. "We would not have come this far without yours and Barto's help. His knowledge is quite mind-boggling. I wish you both happiness, also. Perhaps we can visit each other. I am not that far at Duorakara Valley."

"Oh, we'd like that, sir!" Joanna declared happily, holding hands with Barto, who nodded as if he understood the conversation.

"Excellent, again!" Pharoah Ra-Azeris clapped his hands. "So…my Queen and myself, we wish you all and our precious Senefreya a long, prosperous life and love in your respective missions. All of us do."

"But is she happy with the mission? With me?" Gaston asked. "Senefreya, I mean."

A hand touched his shoulder. Gaston looked up. Senefreya stood beside him, her hand stroking his shoulder, her smile warm and loving. She kissed his cheek. "Oh, my darling, I am quite happy to go on this mission with you. Of course, I will help you with my abilities. We will rebuild a brave, new world, together. You will see."

"And your son, your child, will become the Great Leader of this new world." Queen Nerilka added with a touch of aplomb. "The galactic diplomats have foreseen this."

Stunned, Gaston stood up and placed his hand on her stomach. "Our son?"

"Hmmm, yes, our son." Senefreya laughed softly. "We are with child. And there is more…remember I was telling you and everyone else how much I wanted to go home…"

Gaston nodded, trying to absorb this wonderful news of a child on the way, but a piece of his mind worried about their safety in that other world he was supposed to go with Senefreya.

Still, it was nothing they could not handle. Senefreya appeared powerful like an Amazonian warrior. She was no longer lost and afraid.

"Yes, go on…" Gaston urged her. "You did mention several times that you wanted to go home?"

"Yes, and last night, in your arms, my darling Gaston." Senefreya whispered, touching his hand, still resting on her stomach. "I realized that I was finally home…home in your arms. So, you see, I am home with the love of my life I have been searching for all of my life and home is where you are, here, there, or elsewhere. I will go with you, my darling. You are my home."

"And my home is with you, also…Senefreya, my love…" Gaston whispered, enveloping his arms around the beautiful woman about to be his life partner, his wife, the both of them embarking in a long, difficulty journey to rebuild a new world at an alternate universe. Their lips met in a long, deep kiss, the both of them oblivious to their surroundings.

Epilogue

A bright flash of light burst out in an instant from that one source that managed to survive the horrors of death and destruction, along with several others scattered far and wide, all of them standing tall and strong among the floating mist of grey, dust and equally grey, dimly-lit skies. The sun was but a shadow of its former, blazing countenance, hidden behind the grey dust and radiation clouds floating aimlessly all around environs. That one source?

The General MacArthur…

A colossus among the giant redwoods, its surviving, massive height of 275 feet with a diameter of 36 feet stood out in abject loneliness among the surrounding, melancholic panorama of the dust and grime-infused air and gloomy, grey earthen ground.

"Oh, dear." Senefreya commented, as she exited the large, open cavern within the colossal trunk of the General MacArthur, with Gaston beside her, both of them dressed in heavy, military camouflage jumpsuits to better withstand the awful environment before them. They had been warned beforehand, but somehow, upon arrival out of the giant redwood, where the time portal resided, they were still utterly unprepared for the worst.

"My god." Gaston exclaimed, his eyes surveying the depressing, dismal environment below a dim overcast of irradiated clouds, the sun only a pinpoint of light behind these clouds. "It really happened here, this stand-off with Cuba that had failed, the other alternate reality. My god. It really happened."

"Yes, it happened, my love." Senefreya reached out for his hand. "It happened. All that energy from your reality in this awful conflict with Cuba had to go somewhere and it was sent here in this alternate universe. It is the way the universe works. Energy cannot be created or dissipated, but it can change…it can go somewhere else, into another pocket of overlapping universes allowing it to manifest its truth in a different direction. So, here it happened, your war with Cuba."

"You sound like Dr. Breslov, himself." Gaston chuckled, gripping Senefreya's hand with a passion. "I'm having a hard time wrapping my mind around you when you are like this, the science professor spouting practical and applied physics left and right."

"Very funny." Senefreya pushed him away. "Just you wait and see. I'm the best you could have in this world. Hell, anywhere in this universe. Just you wait and see."

"No problem." Gaston pulled Senefreya closer, kissing the top of her elongated, head amidst her thick dark hair. "Spout at me all you want forever and ever. I love you, my darling."

"I love you, too, my love. My true love. My wish come true." Senefreya laid her head against his strong, muscular chest. "Like I said before, I am home now. With you."

Gaston nodded, hugging her tightly. Looking around the desolate environment with the smell of death and destruction all around the few scattered redwood trees, the ground no longer the healthy, brown, black, and green colors of earth and grass and shrubs and leaves, the sounds of crickets and the hoots of owls silenced abruptly.

"This is going to be an enormous challenge, Senefreya. Our mission, I mean."

"Yes, I agree, my love." Senefreya whispered. "This world looks so empty, so sorrowful, as if begging for life to come back. All life. Back to where there were songs and beauty and lush overgrowth of fauna and flora and our beautiful golden sun shining its healing rays on us all. Just like back there from where we had come."

"Indeed. Just like back there." Gaston responded. "I already miss it." He took in a deep breath. "Do you suppose anyone survived this cataclysm. This nuclear blast?"

"Listen…" Senefreya lifted her head from his chest. "Do you hear it? A crackle of twigs or something like that? Can you hear it?"

Gaston nodded. "It's almost like whisper, a rustling, but yes, I'm hearing it. Someone or something is coming at our direction." He reached around for the weapon strapped at his shoulder, the AK-47 bayonet rifle. "Stand behind me, Senefreya."

"Most certainly not, my love." Senefreya retorted standing firmly in her spot. "I have my own powers. We will deal with them together."

"I do not want to lose you, my darling. I will not risk it. Just stand behind me. I will feel better."

"As you wish, my love. But just this once. I will still help you. That is my mission." Senefreya moved behind her partner, half of her body exposed in case she needed to use her powers. Gaston may not understand the extent of her powers, yet, but she after months of self-training and meditations, she knew the extent of her capabilities, having grown exponentially as her date of birth arrived and passed.

She was not afraid at all, but at this moment in time with potential danger approaching, it behooved to her best to do what he wanted. He needed to focus and she was in the way with her arguments.

"Halt!" Gaston demanded loudly, lifting the rifle to shooting range, barely able to discern any movements in the dusty, gloom of the radiation cloud and gravelly earth surrounding the surviving redwoods. "Who goes there! Identify yourselves! Immediately!"

"Wait! Don't shoot!" A familiar voice rang out, a voice from long ago, when all was well and life moved on serenely. A voice he knew.

"Marijana!"

"Yes, it's me, Gaston, my son! It's me. Please don't shoot. I am not alone."

"Come out, wherever you are, Marijana, it's okay, now. I know your voice. Bring out the people with you. It's only me and my wife. Come out. We are waiting here for you." Gaston strapped the AK-47 back on his shoulder.

Puzzled and curious, Senefreya moved up beside Gaston. "You know these people?"

"Yes, my love." Gaston smiled. "Marijana was my surrogate mother in my other world and I brought her here from Germany long before this nuclear mishap with the Soviets and Cuba. She wanted to live among the redwoods and so, I built a tavern for her in these woods.

"A tavern?"

"Yes. It was called The Ausbringen Tavern. It's gone now, I would think. Look, here they come."

A straggling, bedraggled group of nuclear survivors, mostly adults and a couple of families with children, their skins covered with ash and dirt, several of them hungry and thirsty, appeared from behind the surviving remnants of the redwood trees, cautiously approaching Gaston and Senefreya.

"Oh, they look terrible." Senefreya exclaimed sadly. "How in the world did they survive this disaster?"

"I think I know how." Gaston nodded knowingly. "What's more. I now know who built that bunker."

"What bunker?" Senefreya asked.

"That bunker I found a half-mile behind the tavern, now gone from the blast. I would think the bunker is still standing, made of stones firmly pressed together, no windows, only a door, all made of stone. Just like the pyramids."

"My people." Senefreya exclaimed softly. "It must be my people who built that bunker."

"Yes, your people, darling." Gaston smiled. "They came through that time portal inside the General MacArthur. They must have visited earth hundreds of years, like they said. This bunker was one of their outpost, I imagine."

"But, no windows?" Senefreya asked.

"The real standing abode in that bunker, my darling, is actually the underground rooms, well-protected from anything above. All the rooms have tables and chairs and beds and even a well of water. Expertly designed and built by your people. Obviously, the underground rooms saved these people from the bombs."

"Indeed." Senefreya nodded proudly. "And now we must help them, my love. That is our mission. It's why we were asked to be here. To rebuild a new world with your expert leadership and my abilities and powers. Everything we need is under the Sphinx." She put a hand on her stomach gently. "And our son…"

"True." Gaston hugged Senefreya. "All true. We will build a world just like Atlantis and ancient Egypt with all the grace, beauty, and peaceful community, with all the powers of their advanced technology. Hell, we could be better than my other homeworld, so much better."

"And no more wars." Senefreya added firmly.

"No more wars." Gaston agreed. "Come, let's go greet Marijana and the survivors. We have much to do."

Arm in arm, Gaston and Senefreya kissed briefly in a firm attestment of their love and commitment to each other and the daunting, gargantuan task ahead of them. Together, the couple slowly sauntered towards the tired group of survivors with a firm sense of confidence and courage in their calling to create a brave, new world…of the future.